'What does it mean to live with integrity in the United
St~

... new novel... The way that ...
these stories is masterful, and becomes a meditation on
storytelling itself'

Daily Telegraph

'A book of wintry landscapes, family secrets and alco-
holism, but it's also a paean to the art of listening well
that is especially welcome after the last twelve months
of stridency... *Ashland & Vine* is built on the trust that
evolves between talker and listener; the movement of a mind
trapped in its own uncertainties and a series of tableaux
which build to a strange and stirring kind of redemption'

Guardian

'*Ashland & Vine* is a great book... It proceeds with such
loping grandeur and is so tight-lipped about its themes that
it takes a while for the realization to dawn that it is nothing
short of an American epic. That, however, is what Burnside
has written: a drifty, dreamy, dramatic epic'

The Times

Le mal se fait sans effort, naturellement, par fatalité; le bien est toujours le produit d'un art.

Charles Baudelaire

Process as process is neither morally good nor morally bad. We may judge results but not process. The morally bad agent may perform the deed which is good. The morally good agent may perform the deed which is bad. Maybe a man has to sell his soul to get the power to do good.

Robert Penn Warren

Then said he unto me, Son of man, hast thou seen what the ancients of the house of Israel do in the dark, every man in the chambers of his imagery? for they say, The Lord seeth us not; the Lord hath forsaken the earth.

Ezekiel 8:12

But part of it is, yes, it's easy to get lost in America.

Bill Ayers

for Claudia Vidoni

1 3 5 7 9 10 8 6 4 2

Vintage
20 Vauxhall Bridge Road,
London SW1V 2SA

Vintage is part of the Penguin Random House group of companies
whose addresses can be found at global.penguinrandomhouse.com

Penguin
Random House
UK

Copyright © John Burnside, 2017

John Burnside has asserted his right to be identified as the
author of this Work in accordance with the Copyright,
Designs and Patents Act 1988

First published in Vintage in 2018
First published by Jonathan Cape in 2017

penguin.co.uk/vintage

A CIP catalogue record for this book is available
from the British Library

ISBN 9780099554936

Printed and bound by Clays Ltd, St Ives Plc

Penguin Random House is committed to a sustainable future
for our business, our readers and our planet. This book is
made from Forest Stewardship Council® certified paper.

MIX
Paper from
responsible sources
FSC® C018179

JOHN BURNSIDE

Ashland & Vine

VINTAGE

ALSO BY JOHN BURNSIDE

Fiction

The Dumb House

The Mercy Boys

Burning Elvis

The Locust Room

Living Nowhere

The Devil's Footprints

Glister

A Summer of Drowning

Something Like Happy

Poetry

The Hoop

Common Knowledge

Feast Days

The Myth of the Twin

Swimming in the Flood

A Normal Skin • The Asylum Dance

The Light Trap • The Good Neighbour

Selected Poems • Gift Songs

The Hunt in the Forest

Black Cat Bone

All One Breath

Still Life with Feeding Snake

Non-fiction

A Lie About My Father

Waking Up In Toytown • I Put a Spell on You

JOHN BURNSIDE

John Burnside is amongst the most acclaimed
writers of his generation. His novels, short
stories, poetry and memoirs have won numerous
awards, including the Geoffrey Faber Memorial
Prize, the Whitbread Poetry Award, the Encore
Award and the Saltire Scottish Book of the Year.
In 2011 he became only the second person to win
both the Forward and T. S. Eliot Prizes for poetry
for the same book, *Black Cat Bone*. In 2015 he
was a judge for the Man Booker Prize. He is a
Professor in the School of English at St Andrews
University.

BAKE PIES, CHOP LOGS

The day I met Jean Culver was also the day I stopped drinking.

For a long time, I tried to believe that this was mostly a coincidence. True, it was Jean Culver who proposed the experiment, but she only did it in passing and she didn't press the point. I could do what I wanted, that was always understood. There was no judgment, no expectation that I would stop forever, no demand that I should join some support group. I just had to choose to stay sober for a while, to show that I could do it. That was how she tricked me, in the beginning. She made me think that quitting was what I already wanted to do. Or if not wanted, then needed. The truth was, I needed a rest. I needed to create some distance between Laurits and me, to go back to something not quite defined, but secret and transformative, like the place you go back to in old pop songs. Most of all, I needed to stop blanking out each day's end with whatever makeshift oblivion I could achieve and live with whatever came – the memories, the second guesses, the repetitions of the same old questions. I needed to break out of the sheer tedium of my repetitive existence. Get drunk, sober up, get paranoid, get drunk again. Maybe, by then, that was worse than anything else. That tedium of the self. Not *my*self, but *the* self as random burden, imposed on a whim by some malevolent visitor from an old fairy tale. Some myth, say, from the forests of Estonia, where Laurits always said he truly belonged.

Nevertheless, I wasn't thinking about any of this on that first morning. In fact, I wasn't thinking at all; I was just going through the usual motions. When I opened the gate to her yard, I had no idea that Jean Culver even existed and what I wanted more than anything was to go home and lie down in my narrow, chalk-white bedroom, waiting for some kind of miracle to happen. I had been working for three hours by that time, if you can call what I was doing *work*, trailing around in the heat with the same eleven questions for anyone who answered their door and was prepared to give me a few minutes of their time. Mostly, the doors stayed shut, and the questions remained unanswered, but that wasn't unusual, even in a more pleasant, middle-class neighbourhood like this one. Still, after nursing my hangover up and down a dozen driveways to houses that were, or at least seemed to be, empty, I was close to giving up and taking the rest of the day off, and I don't know what impelled me to make one last call before I headed back to what passed for home. Maybe I was thinking about what Laurits would say if, as usual, I came up empty, and maybe it was simple curiosity: Jean Culver's house wasn't even on my list, which was odd, because Laurits was always painfully thorough about that kind of thing.

Laurits. He was the reason I was out there, hot and sticky and hung-over, with a mouth like sandpaper and cramps in my legs. Laurits – nothing else, no Christian name, just Laurits, which he said was Estonian. My boyfriend, housemate and, now, my supposed collaborator – though how this project was a collaboration I still failed to see, since I was the one wandering around in the heat, having doors closed in my face, an object of derision, pity or both. I didn't know what I was doing or why, but when I asked him to explain he said all I had to do was follow the instructions he had provided: pick an area of town, more or less suburban, where people might be home during the day – old people were always the best subjects – and ask them the eleven questions he had prepared. Questions like: What do you remember best from childhood? What was your happiest moment? If you were to be reborn in another form, what would you choose?

'So what then?' I said. 'I mean, if they even speak to me, do I have to get them to sign something, or can I just go ahead and record them?'

'No recordings,' he said. 'All we need are the stories.'

'So I write them down?'

'No. You just make notes. Not verbatim, nothing like that. Just enough so that, when you get back here, you can remember what they said, more or less.'

'More or less?'

'Yes.' He studied my face to see if I understood what was required. He had told me, more than once, that what he needed was always very precise in his own mind, it was just hard to explain it to other people. 'I want you to hear the story, and then come back and tell it to me in your own words. As well as you can remember it. It doesn't have to be perfect. Just what you remember – and maybe, hopefully, what you add of your own accord.'

'Add?'

'Yes.' He smiled. 'Little – embroideries.'

'And what? You film me telling somebody else's story?'

'Maybe.'

'But you pick the questions.'

3

'Definitely.' His smile widened. 'That's my part of the collaboration.'

This was all typical of him. He complained that he found it difficult to explain things, then made his explanations deliberately vague, with a touch of the absurd thrown in. That was Laurits, who was – well, what exactly? An artist? A film-maker? No – nobody bothered making films any more, not according to Laurits. Or not the way they used to do. Now, everybody was an anthropologist. Yet he did make films, or rather, he made collages of found movie stock mixed with scenes he shot himself and, even if they didn't have stories, even though most of what they contained were things he'd taken from somewhere else and spliced together out of context, they were still films. Laurits was attached to the Creative Arts department at Scarsville College; he got grants and research funding to develop his work; he had a PhD in Film Studies and taught undergraduate classes on Literature and Film. But he wasn't a film-maker, he said; he was an anthropologist. Film-makers tell stories, even if they try not to, but he wasn't interested in stories. For Laurits, a story was just the string on which the real pearls were threaded. What he wanted was atmosphere, texture, weather. When people tell stories, he would say, they lie about what happened, but they don't lie about those other things – or not deliberately, at least.

That was the gospel of narratology, according to Laurits. I was out in the June heat wandering from door to door as part of an anthropology study into all the ways people lie when they remember the past. At least, I thought that was why I was out there. On most projects, Laurits didn't do anything. He just handed a basic script to his so-called collaborators – he had several collaborators, all of them as confused and in need of verification as I was – and left them to figure out the

4

minutiae. The only difference between me and the others was that I lived with him. We shared an apartment. We got drunk together most nights. Sometimes we made love, though I'm not sure making love is the right term.

I met Laurits in Sidetracks, which was the closest Scarsville came to an arty student bar. By then, I was a few weeks into my second college career. I'd given up my first when Dad died; then, after waiting vainly for his ghost to find me, I applied for a place at Scarsville and, to my surprise, they accepted me. By then, the house at Stonybrook was gone, and I didn't have much money, so to save on rent, I moved into a cheap room in the least elegant part of town and ate nothing but rice and fruit. Dad had been dead for months, but I would still wake in a panic every morning, with the thought in my head that he had never actually existed. That I had dreamed him — or rather, that he had been someone quite different from the man I knew, and I had just imagined him the way I wanted him to be. In fact, if he could come back and look inside my head, he wouldn't even recognise himself. It was a different kind of dawn in that part of town, a slow, non-committal light coming in along the back alleys, finding small pools of former times here and there between the houses, smashed plant pots and broken fences and yards that used to have dogs in them, but didn't have anything now but stale earth and smashed glass. Not like home. At home it was so — crisp. Clean. Sun on the flagstones I had helped Dad lay out, watching him work with all the care of a man who knew that, as far as landscaping went, at least, he wasn't a master craftsman. Naturally, in my disturbed state of mind, it took me less than a week to fall in with what the old-time movies used to call *the wrong crowd*. Of course, I didn't think of it in those terms then; I didn't think of it in any terms, I just drifted from drunk to sober to bitter to maudlin nights by the radio, listening to the songs Dad used to like and, though all this outward drama seemed to be going on, I wasn't really feeling or thinking anything. It wasn't like I was even very attracted to Laurits that first night. If anything, I thought he was crazy, a bored man wasting his time with people he didn't much like. I mean, it's not as if we gazed at each other across a crowded room, or any other such nonsense. If anything, we met by accident, as people drifted off or moved from place to place to get beside the persons that *they* had been gazing at across a crowded room. So you could say that it all happened by default. But then, that was how everything happened during those years, for people like Laurits and me. We weren't the kind of people who were out there in the night looking for a *relationship*. For us, that word conjured up an emotional dishonesty that we had no choice but to refuse – and there really was no alternative. Everything we could ever feel or think or say in such a situation had already been scripted and televised. There was nothing left to say. All we had left was the quality of our refusals.

I was with a girl in my American Cinema class, a beautiful, dark-eyed Minnesotan called Ruth who was not only hugely intelligent but a real poet, as well. I mean, truly. I'd read a couple of things in student magazines after we first met and, no question, she was good. Trouble was, she was also beautiful and popular and she seemed to know everybody, which was how we ended up more or less attached to the group of slightly older people that Laurits was with, a mixed band of around ten later-twenties postgrad and free-theatre types sitting around two big tables, all of them halfway drunk, all listening to Laurits argue with some guy who was in the group, but not really with it – a fellow traveller, someone who was tolerated rather than accepted. The guy's name was Eric, which I quickly discovered, because Laurits was one of those people who called his antagonist by name all the time, laying it on all the way through the argument, completely unnecessarily. Eric had just said something in defence of a certain kind of wealth, the usual stuff about how the mega-rich were actually good for the economy, how they created employment, how they were always setting up foundations to dole out money to the deserving, not to mention the arts, and in particular theatre and film-makers, people like Laurits, in fact, and so, bearing all that in mind, surely it was better to learn from their successes and try to emulate them, than to run them down all the time like they were criminals or something. And wasn't what made the US so successful as a nation, and maybe also why *we* were so different from Estonia (at this a hint of a sneer came into Eric's voice, though at the time, I didn't know why), wasn't it that ability to work hard and grow and aspire that made America great?

Laurits listened politely. It was clear that Eric was irrelevant to him, that his argument wasn't even worth answering. But it was also clear that he wanted to play – and he liked having an audience. The fact is, Laurits was a natural performer, though he only performed because he was bored. I didn't know it then, but that was his reason for everything. He was bored, so he made films and wrote essays in obscure journals. He was bored, so he argued with his intellectual inferiors in bars and pizza restaurants. He was bored, so he drank. I tell myself, now, that the arrangement we had was different, that it meant something, but I can't be sure. On the other hand, I can't be sure what drew me to him, either. He was tall, good-looking, highly intelligent, imaginative; he was an artist, with a resumé to prove it and there was the added attraction of a dark side, which had gotten him into trouble on a couple of occasions. I thought those stories were exaggerated until the first time I saw him get into a fight. Those stories were not exaggerated. He had a dark side, and it wasn't pretty. Still, if I think about him now, I don't think of him as someone I loved. As I described it then, as I describe it now, we had an arrangement, mostly tacit, but an arrangement nevertheless. That word itself says all that needs to be said about my relationship with Laurits.

'Sure, Eric,' he said. 'You are absolutely right. It's much better to aspire to wealth than to actually have it. Because it's the journey, isn't it? It's climbing the ladder, working hard, being the best you can be and making use of your God-given talent, isn't it, Eric? Being there with all that money is such a drag, looking down at all the people you fucked over on the way up is a drag, Eric, and it's a drag to look at a TV and see all those starving kids in refugee camps, naked and abandoned, their families dispersed, their tribe going extinct – *extinct*, Eric – just so some asswipe in the so-called developed world can have a bigger yacht. Thousands of seabirds washed up on some far shore because your company cut a few corners. Better to be on the way up than to be that asswipe, because if it turns out that you *do* have one human bone in your body, if it turns out you're just not enough of a psychopath to believe the whole world is your own personal toy, then you are going to fail, and failure hurts, Eric. Failure hurts, even when it's honourable. Hollywood is always telling you that the good guy, the guy with a heart, is happier than the billionaire alone in his mansion with nobody to love him, but it's not true, Eric. It's not true. It ought to be true, but everybody knows that, in America, if you don't got money, you're nothing.

And that's the dilemma, isn't it, Eric? You want to say, leave it to the other guy, leave it to the psychopath, but in America, if you can't be that guy, you're a failure. And all the time you know that guy is an asswipe, because no matter how hard he works to prove that he's not, everybody knows he is, and then it's such a drag for him – almost as much of a drag as it is for you being a failure. It's such a drag to have to stop stock-piling yachts and Old Masters and Scottish castles and dedicate yourself to your foundation. It's a drag, Eric, but then it's always been a drag. Look at John D. Rockefeller. Look at Henry Clay Frick. They all had their foundations and their good causes but that was all a big smokescreen for what was really going on. I mean, you must have heard about the Matewan Massacre, Eric? Homestead? Or maybe Ludlow, Colorado, April 20th, 1914? That was another high point in the history of American philanthropy, Eric. You should look it up.'

Nobody said anything. Eric sat staring at Laurits, blinking behind his glasses, the half smile on his face extinguished now. Then everybody laughed and started drinking again. A guy in a faded black Huey Lewis T-shirt, sitting three away from Laurits with a very pretty, overdressed blonde, raised his glass. 'Christ, Laurits,' he said. 'Did you rehearse that? Come on. Tell me true. Did you just invent all that stuff?'

Laurits shook his head. 'Look it up,' he said. 'It's in the history books.' He feigned seriousness, and it was obvious that he was returning to a familiar theme, one that he knew would annoy Huey. 'Americans don't know their own history . . .'

That was a big part of his shtick, The Forgotten History Of America – and on the rare occasions that I thought there was some good reason why I was out walking streets where nobody ever walked, it was that Laurits believed somebody

9

out there remembered *something* about that America. It didn't matter what. Anything would do. I had been pursuing this for over a week, going from door to door, hung-over, tired, bathed in sweat, and I hadn't come up with a single story. I had been repulsed by all kinds of people, from snippy hausfrau types to a muscle-bound Korean guy with a pit bull collared in each fist; I had walked up to one perfectly pleasant-looking house, on a perfectly ordinary street and felt – what? Some strange sense of threat or incipient nightmare that prevented me from ringing the bell or knocking, no matter how hard I tried? Or had I just panicked, because I knew something was in there, behind the sunlight and the stillness, behind the closed screen, something terrible, waiting in the hallway? Two days earlier I had been trudging round a leafy suburb with Copland's *Quiet City* in my headphones – the Bernstein live 1990 performance, which I shouldn't have been playing, because it was one of Dad's favourites – and I just hit a wall in my mind and came to a stop, ridiculous, helpless, staring up into a willow tree and sobbing like a child, my face wet with tears and snot, my T-shirt sodden with sweat. I had stood there a long time, unable to go on, and it was only after several minutes that I came to myself, with the sensation of being watched, and looked around. Nobody was visible. There was nobody on the street, or in any of the front yards. Maybe somebody was observing me from a window somewhere, but if they were, I didn't see them. I pulled off my headphones and tried to dry my face, but it was useless. I was a mess.

Now, as I stood at the gate to a house that wasn't on the list, maybe I was thinking I had finally come to the right place. Only, it wasn't on the list, and I wasn't sure if I should check it out – not because I wasn't curious, but because I didn't know what Laurits would do, when he discovered that

I had found a house that wasn't on the list. Maybe, if I did find somebody here, their story would be invalid for some reason. Lack of provenance, insufficient documentation, that kind of thing. Maybe this house didn't exist and when I tried to come back for the follow-up, it wouldn't be there. Because it wasn't on the list and it wasn't on the map he had given me either and, in my present state, I was all too ready to believe in phantoms.

Not that it would be hard to miss, tucked away behind a stand of trees at the far end of Audubon Road and I might have walked straight past that narrow entrance gate, if I hadn't been drawn in by the sound of someone chopping wood, a sound I knew from a previous existence, when Dad was still alive. It was a sound I loved: a steady, dark, vigorous sound that brought back vivid and painful images of our old house at Stonybrook, my father in his faded blue shirt, the axe glinting in the sunlight as he worked, splitting each log with a single, clean blow then moving on, only stopping occasionally to listen to the quiet of the woods. As a child, I convinced myself that the woods around our house went back to a time before the settlers arrived; ancient Iroquois lands, full of blue jays and cardinals and families of tender, sweet-lipped deer. They were my private, haunted realm when I was a child, my small promise of heaven and, at the same time, proof of the history my father claimed as his own, for was he not at least part Native American and therefore entitled to look at those woods in a different way from his neighbours? Now, like the house, those woods are gone, and so is my father, killed by an illness he kept secret from me, but not from his lady friend, Louise, till it was too late even to say goodbye.

After the funeral, I kept thinking he would come back. Not alive, like Lazarus, but as a ghost, coming into the house at night from the darkness of the woods, where he had joined the many ghosts of his people. I had never been alone before, I had never existed in such a vacuum and I thought the least he would do – the one thing he would *know* to do – would be to come back and haunt me. My own, private haunting; my own secret ghost. I wouldn't need to see him. He wouldn't have to make himself visible, like the ghosts in old films. I wasn't looking for a misty shape coming up through the yard in the early morning; I didn't expect his likeness to be waiting for me in the kitchen when night fell. I just needed to feel that he was there. A presence and, now and then, a voice. Or maybe nothing more than a minor, even disputable irregularity in the natural fabric of things. The sense of someone moving in an upper room, while I was sitting in the kitchen, staring out at the snow. A cup or a glass mysteriously finding its way to the sink, when I was *convinced* I had left it in the hall. I wasn't asking much by way of evidence. I didn't need proof of life, just some glimmer of an afterward when he had turned around and looked back, just for a moment, before he proceeded into whatever was to come.

Dad used to say, in his usual, half-muddled, half-joking way, that the best house is the one you don't know is there unless you already know it's there. That was true of our old house and it was true of this one, which provided a first point of resemblance, but what also drew me to this stranger's home – or rather, to this stranger's yard, since I couldn't see the house itself at that point – what drew me *in*, like the child drawn, involuntarily, to the witch's house in a fairy tale, was the teasing memory it offered, a memory that said I really had been happy once and, based on that evidence, could be happy again. The trees were different – mostly cottonwoods here, where once there had been birches and pines – but everything else had the same air of natural disorder, a disorder I hadn't seen in the other houses on that suburban road, with their perfect lawns and picket fences with ornate, slightly ridiculous finials. Mailboxes in the shape of birdhouses and birdhouses that looked like mailboxes. Old Glory fluttering from a miniature flagpole above the porch. Alongside the surprisingly long driveway that ran up to the house itself, wild flowers grew in tangles under dogwoods and mock orange, and there was enough shade and cover for the other forms of life – the swift shadows that skitter across a night-time lawn, the trash eaters and whangdoodles and varmints – that the neighbour folks' yards were designed to scare away. This yard didn't belong to a gardener. There was no order, or nothing that came out of a book or a landscaper's blueprints. This was *wild*, or as near wild as it could be – and that reminded me of home too. Meanwhile, as I walked up the drive and turned the slight curve it made through the trees, I was drawn in by the sound of logs splitting, a steady rhythm characteristic of someone who knew what they were doing. Like my father. So maybe what I was expecting to see, as the house came into view, was a ghost with an axe, a palpable, everyday ghost, working in the afternoon heat in a faded blue work shirt.

The sight that greeted me wasn't a ghost, however. The faded work shirt was the same, more or less, but everything else was different. I suppose I had been expecting to find a man there, axe in hand, labouring in the wide, sunny clearing between the trees and the house, and I had probably anticipated someone younger. What I found, instead, was a woman who, at that stage, with her back to me, looked to be in her late fifties or early sixties. She was tall and slender; not stick-thin, by any means, but thin enough to suggest that this work ought to have been too heavy for someone of her age and build; an elderly woman in an old shirt, cream-coloured jeans and a pair of scuffed, ankle-high boots. As I stood watching, taking her in, she seemed totally absorbed in what she was doing and, because I thought she was unaware of my presence, a stranger in her yard, staring, I didn't know what to do next. A long moment passed; then, when I had decided to get out while I still could and head back to the road, she turned around, axe in hand still, as if she would strike me down with it if I made any attempt to deceive her.

'Well?' she said. She spoke brusquely, but she didn't seem hostile, only matter-of-fact. Or, it wasn't brusqueness so much as propriety. Her speech was formal, and she had a slight accent, though I couldn't have placed it. 'What is it, exactly, that brings you to my door? The US Mail hasn't had business here in some time and I do not encourage visitors.'

I didn't know what to say. The way she looked at me, the curiosity that showed through the outward formality, was unsettling and I found myself tongue-tied, idiotic, a foolish and unwarranted intruder, breaking into her perfectly regulated day with nothing to say for myself. Earlier, I had set out a basic script; now, faced with this axe-woman, I realised that it had never felt natural.

'I'm conducting a survey,' I said. It was exactly what Laurits had told me never to say. What I was offering these people wasn't a survey; it was an opportunity to tell a story. A chance to be heard, the secret tissue of truth and lies that everyone conceals in their heart, hinted at and, though only half revealed, exposed to the kindly light of another human being's attention. Not everything would, or could, be divulged, he said. What he was after were the hints, the clues, the points at which the private account of the world diverged from the

14

official position. The soul's narrative. But then, after that had been divulged, it was supposed to be left to chance as to how much of it was carried forward. Was it only now, face-to-face with Jean Culver, that I could see how insulting that would have been, had it even been possible?

'A survey?' The faintest trace of a smile, not unfriendly, but tinged with something close to contempt, passed across her face, though her look wasn't contemptuous of me, and there was something in her expression that, while I could not have said how, conveyed as much. 'What kind of a survey?'

I shook my head. 'Well,' I said, 'it's not *exactly* a survey. More a kind of . . .' I cast around for some acceptable description. 'It's more that . . . I'm collecting people's stories. Life stories. Oral . . . histories.'

'I see.' She wiped her forehead on the sleeve of her shirt. 'You're not very good at this, are you?'

'It's an academic study,' I said, suddenly feeling that it was important not to be sent away. I didn't know why but, all of a sudden, I felt desolate, alone in the world like a child lost at the fair and I thought, for that moment, that I would give in to tears. I tried again. 'It's different from the usual approach to oral history, where—'

'Does this have something to do with the millennium?'

That took me by surprise. It was only a few months away, but I never thought about the millennium. For me it was something that belonged to television and popular magazines. 'No,' I said. 'It's a narrative project that—'

She made a face at this and waved her hand – and though I couldn't have said what seemed different about her, I suddenly saw that she was considerably older than I had guessed. It wasn't her face, so much, that gave this away; it was how she moved. An economy she had developed over years that reduced all effort to a minimum, without seeming infirm. 'Forget all that,' she said. 'It's a hot day and I'm tired from chopping all this wood that I probably won't even use.' She smiled, as if she had just made a joke, then she looked back at me and gave an abrupt, though not unpleasant, laugh. 'Can't help it though,' she said. 'I have to chop a little wood every day. It's a way I have of driving off the spleen and regulating the circulation.' She looked at me to see if I recognised the reference, then she laughed again. 'Come into the house,' she said. 'I'll make you some herb tea.' She looked me up and down, then shook her head. 'I'd offer you something stronger but I can see that would be ill-advised.' She smiled again. 'Come on in,' she said, her voice kindly this time, though the kindness felt like some courtesy she had just remembered and didn't usually bother with.

I felt the sting of her remark, but I didn't know what to do. I had no desire to go into this strange woman's house – which was odd as, officially at least, to gain entry was the very reason I was out there in the cloying heat – but I couldn't summon the energy to do anything else. The woman turned and headed toward the side porch, where a door stood open to the quiet of the woods and to the gaze of whatever might be out there and it reminded me of how Dad would do the same thing, throwing the kitchen door open on a summer's morning and leaving it ajar all day, as if in welcome. Even in the winter, even when the snow was falling in the pale blue space between our house and the birch woods, he would sometimes just leave that door halfway open, and you would smell the cold, crisp air when you went through to fix a pot of coffee.

Jean Culver didn't look back to see if I was following her. I guess she didn't care one way or another. It was time for a break, she was tired, as she had said, and, if I wanted to come, I would come. I did follow her into the house, though, and maybe the reason I did was the sense I was beginning to form – an intuition, I guess, since I had nothing to base it on – that this woman was different from anybody else I had ever known. She was someone who had made peace with the world on her own terms, someone who had stopped caring about minor things in order to concentrate on what really mattered. Not that I had any idea of what might matter to an old woman who lived off by herself in the woods. For, as I came up the porch steps and encountered the pure stillness of the house, I was certain that she was vitally alone in the world, and that she liked it that way. The porch was neat and tidy, with small trees in ornate pots set around the edge of the space and a few chairs backed up against the wall; inside, a narrow hall led directly to the kitchen, where the woman was already filling an old-fashioned, non-electric kettle.

'I have camomile, cinnamon and apple, and peppermint,' she said, scanning the counter next to the stove. 'Let's see now. Rooibos. I've never quite taken to that. Sea buckthorn and Honeybush, somebody gave me this one, but I haven't tried it yet.' She looked to see if I was paying attention. 'Lapsang souchong. Orange pekoe. Darjeeling. Or maybe you would prefer a cup of coffee?' She waited patiently for me to answer, though she could probably see that I didn't know what I wanted. I just needed to sit, to be still. She was smiling, still. 'Let's try the buckthorn, then,' she said. 'I'm told it's very refreshing.'

I nodded. The kitchen was a wide, high space and, with all the windows open, it didn't seem to belong entirely with the house, as if its true allegiances were to the garden. In the middle of the room was a huge, square table made of what looked like pitch pine, so old that you could imagine it being put together from the salt-washed timbers of the *Pequod*, the grain open and long and dark with age. Houseplants dotted the table and the counters, a long row of geraniums and African violets lined the window shelf that ran from the sink in the corner to the door. Other than that, the room was uncluttered; functional, though not bare. It looked like nothing had changed there for fifty years, but it was clean and fresh and everything was in good order, which made me think of a poem by Marianne Moore, for some reason, something about fluted columns made modester by whitewash.

The kettle boiled and Jean Culver went about the business of making tea with no great haste. Though I was quite sure, by now, that she lived by herself in this house, she didn't seem like some lonely old lady grabbing the chance of some company when it happened along. On the contrary, it was clear to me that she was happy with her own company. There was no sign of a pet, no cats pacing around the space in the middle of the sunlit floor, tails high, studying me for signs of malice or weakness, no yappy little dog barking and scratching at a door somewhere in the interior of the house. Her conversation was considered, and not at all urgent; she seemed not so much curious as aware of a politesse that demands certain enquiries, questions about home, or place of origin at least, questions about family and career and suchlike things. I noticed that she did not enquire further about my supposed survey. When the tea was made, she set it all out on the table – cups and saucers, a plain white ceramic teapot, another, more ornate pot full of thick, dark-golden honey and a plate of home-made cookies. We sat down. There was a long silence, in which she was clearly waiting for me to say something. Remembering my manners, I asked about her family, which I immediately realised was not what she had expected, or wanted, from me.

'I was raised by relatives, after my parents died,' she said, her voice matter-of-fact, even a little hard. 'Also, until recently, I had a brother.' She looked straight into my face as if she was trying to work something out. 'He died last fall,' she said.

'I'm sorry for—'

'Don't be,' she said, her voice sharper now. 'He was old. Older than me, even. I can see from your face that you find that hard to believe.'

'Not at all.'

She smiled. 'Being old has its advantages,' she said. 'One of them is knowing that death isn't that far away. Your own death, other people's, it's all the same. So one day the phone rings. You are halfway through making fried apple pie, but you put the rolling pin down and go answer . . . Then you go back and make the best pie ever. It was his favourite, as it happens, but that wasn't why I was making it.' She smiled again, sadly it seemed, as if she had accidentally remembered something she usually kept at bay. Some old happiness that was too difficult to hold in her mind for any length of time. 'Later, there would be a season to pick out something black and book a flight to Virginia for the funeral, which turned out to be a pretty thin affair, just me and a couple of people he knew from work. *I* didn't know them, and they didn't talk much, afterward. A short passage from Ecclesiastes – neither of us was ever religious, but it seemed appropriate.' She lifted her head slightly as if she was about to recite those same verses, then had second thoughts. 'When you get to my age, most of your friends are dead people. But that's not how you think of them. You remember the lives, not the deaths. I've never been one for funerals, but you do your duty. Meanwhile, there are pies to bake and logs to chop. By now, that feels like a good enough life.' She poured me some tea; it smelled summery and green and a little bitter. 'I'm not talking about happiness. When I hear people talking about happiness, I have no idea what they mean, but then, it's not something you talk about, it's something you do. Bake pies, chop logs. At a certain point, the mere sense of living is joy enough.' She gave her abrupt, short laugh. 'Goodness, listen to me talk,' she said – and her accent, whatever it was, seemed more pronounced. Virginia, she had said, but I didn't know if that was it. 'It takes a lifetime, for some of us at least, to know that the best things in life are the boring, everyday things.' She helped herself to some honey. 'They're not really boring, of course. It's just that we lack the imagination, when we're young, to see those everyday chores and rituals for what they really are. And all the big adventures,' she twirled the spoon in her tea and smiled, to herself mostly, though I didn't feel excluded. 'Well, they're not so great while they're happening.' She looked at me closely. 'You don't know that yet,' she said. 'But there's still time. And then, I promise you, things get much clearer than you ever expected them to be.'

I had no idea what she was talking about, of course. In fact, I didn't understand much of what she said that afternoon. Yet I have to confess, she intrigued me. Not because what she said seemed very appropriate to my life – after all, what did she know about my life, other than that I had a hangover? No: it was how she was, how she moved, her strange economy, that sense of someone totally self-reliant that she projected without making any effort to project anything – that was what intrigued me. The tea was bitter and the cookies were a little dry, but that didn't matter. It didn't even matter that I found her conversation bewildering at times, especially when she talked about my life as if she knew all about it. What mattered was that I envied her. I envied that economy. I envied that self-reliance. I wanted to be like her, which was absurd, because, as the afternoon slipped by, I had every chance to study her face in closer detail – and it was clear that she was very old indeed. Too old to be chopping logs, for sure. Too old, even, to be living alone. I wanted to ask her when she was born, just to confirm my estimate of – what? I didn't know. I just thought of her in this house, alone, in the winter. How did that work? Did someone come in? Did she have a car? I would begin framing a question and making ready to ask it, but she kept skittering away like this was some kind of game, like she knew what I wanted to know and wasn't ready to let me ask it by roundabout means. She didn't want me to be polite about it. If I was going to ask, she wanted me to ask. Directly. Honestly.

Finally, I found a gap in the flow of conversation. She had been talking about food, about the recipe for fried apple pie that she had learned from her guardian. She promised she would make some for me sometime – and that gave me an in. 'So,' I said. 'Is that a Virginia thing? Fried apple pie?'

She smiled and permitted herself a slight nod. 'Not just apple,' she said. 'You can make it with peaches. Apricots. For apples, I would add a little more cinnamon.'

'So that's where you're from,' I said. 'I can hear an accent but I can't quite—'

'I'm not from anywhere you would know,' she said. 'But I've lived in several places, including Virginia.' Her eyes sparkled. Yes, that old cliché – but she really was brighter and more alive than most young people I knew. 'Is this part of the survey?'

'No.'

'I don't mind,' she said.

21

I shook my head but, suddenly, I wasn't sure. If my curiosity wasn't part of the survey, in a way, what else was it? 'I just thought,' I said. 'You mentioned earlier that your brother was in Virginia and I seem to remember—'

She gave her short laugh and nodded. 'Well,' she said, 'I have to go somewhere in a while, but I'll tell you my story, if you like. Not today, but soon. I think you might find it interesting.' She leaned forward and fixed me with her eyes. 'All you have to do is make me one promise.'

I was taken aback by that, of course. 'What promise?' I asked.

'You must promise to stop drinking for five days.'

And that was the moment, right there. It was a preposterous request, but that was the moment when my life changed. Not because of what she said, but because I didn't get offended and walk out of that kitchen and back to my daily round of booze and hazy sex with Laurits and wishing for a ghost that I knew would never come. I didn't even argue that whatever I did or didn't do was none of her business. I just felt an odd, airy sensation in the middle of my chest, a sensation that I can only compare to the wind blowing through an open window, billowing the curtains, then letting them fall back, empty. When I did speak, my voice was thin and far away and so uncertain that it might as well have been an admission of guilt. 'Excuse me?'

She shook her head and gave what might have been a sad smile, as if she was already beginning to regret what she was about to say. 'If you can stay sober till Tuesday next, come back then. Maybe I'll take you to Sacred Grounds. We'll call it an excursion. Do you know it?'

I nodded. Sacred Grounds was a local café. I had never been there, but I had heard of it. A year back, some big chain had come to town and set up five doors away from the local café

22

and hunkered in, waiting to take over. It was a standard tactic and it usually worked. In this case, however, people rallied round. They organised a boycott. They handed out flyers. If anything, Sacred Grounds did even more business than usual. The chain withdrew.

'It's a coffee shop, mind,' she said. 'They don't sell liquor.'

'I know that.'

She laughed. 'It's all right,' she said. 'I'm just teasing. You have to put up with that, when you consort with old people.'

And that was all. She didn't make me say anything, and I knew she had no way of telling whether I would stay sober for the next five days, but an agreement appeared to have been reached and now, with the tea finished and the unspoken contract there between us, she fell quiet and we sat like two old acquaintances with nothing much to say, in a kitchen that I sensed was once the heart of the house, an almost public place where people came and went freely, family and friends, say, maybe even a neighbour or two, before the neighbourhood had become a series of neat suburban streets in which a house like hers seemed so out of place. But then, it probably wasn't like that when she first arrived. Maybe, then, it had been cottonwoods and wild flowers all along the road, animals trailing through the gardens undeterred, owls calling in the night. I don't know why I thought that, but it seemed to me there were stories to tell, and, as she led me back out through the hallway – I caught a glimpse of a large room with rows of bookshelves through a half-open door and a scent that I couldn't identify – I felt that I was carrying away something more than the promise of a story.

GREGORY PECK

When I got back to the apartment, I found Laurits draped over a chair, watching TV, a row of bottles from his favourite microbrewery lined up on the floor beside him. On screen, Gregory Peck was staring inscrutably at some distant object, that classic Peck gaze, and I knew the movie, but I couldn't remember what it was. Not that it mattered. I wasn't in the mood for film talk and, even though I hadn't agreed to Jean Culver's strange sobriety deal, I didn't want to have a drink, not even a beer. I wanted to shower, then lie down in my own bed. Laurits rented the apartment from a friend, and technically I wasn't a tenant, I was just his live-in girlfriend, but we had our own rooms and, mostly, we slept alone in them. My room was small, narrow, very white, and almost perfect. The kind of room a nun would inhabit, not a Christian nun, maybe, but someone from another denomination. A Buddhist nun, say, if there are such people. They had Buddhist monks, so I guessed they would have Buddhist nuns too. Not that the denomination mattered. It was just, I didn't want a cross, or a Bible, or anything like that. Just the white walls and a comforting narrowness, like I was only taking up the exact amount of space I needed to sleep and wake up and get dressed in. Laurits had the one large room in the apartment, but it was darker and more elaborate, with old, maybe antique and certainly meaningfully provincial furniture, most of it from his friend's store, Blue Barn Antiques, all patina and local provenance and character. When we had sex, we did it in Laurits' room. It was a kind of unspoken agreement, which for me had something to do with keeping my little nun's cell intact, though I have no idea what it meant to Laurits. I think he thought the atmosphere was more appropriate. His room had *narrative*. That was one of his words, narrative – meaning, not that there was a story to something so much as that, whether it was a place, or a person, or a situation, it was something that lent itself to the possibility of a story. Of story itself, which was more than things just happening. Laurits had a whole heap of theories about narrative. One time, he explained at length to a group of SIU students we met at a pizza place in Scarsville how the real tragedy of American life, back in the 60s, hadn't been that the president was shot, but that he was shot in Dallas, Texas, a place that, for Laurits, had almost no narrative value whatsoever. If the assassination had happened in Washington, or New York – or even St Louis for that matter – everything would have been different. But *Dallas*? What was Dallas? A grassy knoll. A book depository. No history, no precedent, no – provenance. Laurits was obsessed with stuff like this. American narratives. American history, which was never quite history as real historians understood it, the way, say, European or Japanese history was history. That was why Americans confused history with the movies so easily, he said, because the history they had ended up with was so much less interesting than the stories any committee of scriptwriters could concoct during a single afternoon at the office. Laurits claimed to have met people who didn't know that the Kennedy assassination was a real event. They thought it was part of a movie. One guy he met had even asked him who had played JFK in the film, not the remake, but the original.

Of course, Laurits was a liar. Everything about him was a lie. He claimed to be Estonian – and it was true that he had an Estonian name, but he had only ever been to Estonia once, on a long weekend trip when he was travelling around Europe, and his family lived in New Jersey. Estonian was a nationality with narrative content, and he could use it pretty much how he liked because nobody in Scarsville had any idea where Estonia was. Oh, sure, some of the Political Studies types could point to it on a map and they could tell you it was a former Soviet satellite, but that was all and back then, in a world still without Wikipedia, our presumed knowledge was much more modest than it is now. Laurits knew everything, though; or at least, we thought he did, because there was no way to check the facts he would produce, with apparently breathtaking accuracy, about this place that he considered holy and drenched with significance, a land whose folk songs were unique and unparalleled in their beauty and tragic grace, and whose forests were still relatively intact, not turned over to any logging or mining corporation that had enough money to pay the necessary bribes. Yet even as he conveyed all this about his supposed homeland, freshly emerged from the Soviet yoke and yet, at the same time, one of the most ancient and complex cultures in Europe, it never sounded like he was criticising America. Or not the real America, which he assumed everybody understood in the same way he did – as *the people*, those working and those deprived of work, the poor who struggled to make ends meet and the good country folk who were fighting to hang on to the redwood forests and bluestem prairie grass.

I didn't know about any of this. Estonia, the Kennedy assassination, the Soviet yoke – it was all just words to me. What I liked about Laurits, when we got together – or no, what made me feel calm around him, was the fact that I knew he wasn't lying for a reason, he was just having fun, making it all up as he went along, the way Dad used to do when he talked about his Native American roots and his memories of the land he had known as a young man. Land that was vanishing fast, land that should have been native, not Christian. Land that, after five hundred years of white people, was little more, now, than smoke and ghosts. Which was strange because, in everything else, Laurits was nothing like my father. In fact, in most things, he was his polar opposite. Where Dad was gentle, humorous, always creating space around himself for others, Laurits was curious, mocking, in-your-face and, when he applied his rules about narrative rigorously, he could be thoughtless, even cruel. But I didn't care about that. I wasn't thinking about it then, and it doesn't really matter now, but the only reason I was living with Laurits was that he talked so much. That, and the white room. For which I paid a share of the rent, though not much and some weeks, when he knew I didn't have the money, he let it pass. It was the talk that mattered. With Laurits around, I didn't have to speak. I didn't have to *be* anybody. I didn't even have to listen. I could go anywhere and just drink and let the whole thing wash over me, all the talk and the outrage and the laughter and it didn't matter, for a while, that Dad wasn't there, because there were times, late on a Saturday night or halfway through one of Laurits' after-hours parties back at the apartment, when it sounded almost exactly the same as when he had been.

*   *   *

Dad didn't say very much about his childhood. It was as if his life only began when he left home, somewhere up in northern New England, and drifted down to Pennsylvania. Not far, but far enough. I don't know how long it was before he met my mother and, in his own words, got married too young. They must have been happy when they first met, but, again, I have no idea how long that happiness lasted. After my mother left – I was six years old – he used to say, with no obvious bitterness, that marriage was the only known antidote to youth. He said it against himself, though, not my mother, whose departure he had foreseen for some time and, after a few months of putting new systems in place for getting me to school and looked after while he was at work, he regarded the whole sorry tale of his own marriage with something close to bemused good humour. That was one side to him, a side he had developed quite deliberately to deal with the official world of work and social existence and institutions – he had developed an ability to see everything in terms of systems. I didn't know what it involved when he went to the office, where his title was senior designer, but I understood, growing up, that while his own nature tended toward wildness, toward the woods and the river and occasional disappearing acts where he would go off for a week at a time to the back of nowhere, he had decided that the only way to deal with that social, official world, was to see it all as a series of interlocking systems. That principle applied to everything, even his marriage; when my mother left, he simply saw her absence as a systems problem, which could be fixed easily enough by the application of common sense, money and preparedness. Outwardly, at least, that principle worked.

Still, he didn't really know what to do with himself until Louise showed up, eight years later. He hadn't had enough time to learn the pleasures of being alone, he would say. Now, with my mother gone, he had me to bring up on his own – and he was a good father, always there when I needed him, sitting by my bed and holding my hand when I couldn't sleep, talking me back to the pale gold light of my room when I woke from a nightmare. He would tell me fairy stories – I don't know where they came from, maybe he made them up himself – stories that always ended with some bad old king being kicked out of his palace, which was then transformed into a public pavilion where children could go to dance and sing, and the palace grounds were made into gardens where everyone, even the poorest in the kingdom, could come for picnics and circus shows. Those stories weren't like anything I ever read or heard elsewhere, never about a true king regaining his throne, or the seventh son of the seventh son winning the princess. They always ended in the victory of the common people. After a while, I began to understand what he was doing, but I never let on. It was the only education he could offer me. A sense of fairness. Equality and justice for all. A good system.

I never learned why Dad left home so young. He rarely spoke about his parents, never talked about school or friends from the old neighbourhood. He seemed to have grown up on his own, running wild in the woods. He didn't describe the landscape, but I imagined birches and aspens, deep buttery yellows in the fall, ice-hard and still in winter. One thing he did say about his origins was that he was part Abenaki on his mother's side – but that was all he ever told me about either of his parents, so I had nothing much to go on when I tried to imagine what had to have been a strange and possibly controversial romance. Whenever I asked him for more details, though, he'd just shake his head and say he couldn't remember much, just that they were two people from different backgrounds who met in a café one day and fell in love.

'Where?' I would ask him, impatient for more story.

'Where what?'

'Where did they meet?'

'I told you. In a café.'

'Where?'

'I don't know. Somewhere in Vermont.'

'You don't know where?'

He would shake his head and give an odd half-smile. 'They didn't talk,' he said.

'They didn't tell you anything?'

'Not much.'

'But telling stories is a big part of Abenaki life,' I'd say. 'I looked it up. Stories are central to their culture – they even think a story is, like, a living thing.'

'Well, nobody told *me* any stories.' He would shake his head, as if to say he wasn't hiding anything, that he would tell me more if there was more to tell, but there wasn't. 'They didn't really talk. Though, if I had to guess, I think, maybe, it would have been Franklin County. Where they met. My old man travelled around quite a lot, looking for work.'

And that was as much as I could get out of him. He had no photographs, no letters or documents, so I was free to imagine what I liked, and I made my grandmother a pretty, dark-haired girl turning around in the café light, a careful smile on her face, wanting to trust this white man she had just met – how? Was she alone? Unlikely. With friends, who sat quiet, maybe covering their mouths to hide their nervous laughter, maybe a little frightened for her, because they knew white men were not to be trusted? I didn't know.

That picture became more and more detailed and vivid in my mind's eye, even as I became more and more aware of how hypothetical it was. Yet it was real, too. I could see that girl in my father's face when I looked close: the darkness in his eyes, his crow-black hair, an odd, almost abstract quality in his expression when someone talked to him, as if he couldn't quite understand what they were saying. Or no: he understood, but he was wondering if that was all, if there might be something that he wasn't quite getting or, more likely, that wasn't being said. Because he didn't understand how that could be all. He didn't understand how they could live their lives so detached from the world around them, from the woods, from birdsong, from the scent of the river on a spring night. It bewildered him, that his neighbours existed in that way, and then, at the same time, he was plagued by questions about the other world, the world that his native side – his Indian other – was still, not so much in touch with as plugged into, plagued by a secret knowledge that wasn't quite complete. He knew things, he had a way of walking in the woods or out over the snow that carried him across the earth more lightly than others, but there was nothing to bind it all together. There was even some part of his mind that had inklings of a former language, a speech that was more rooted in the land and the blood, with specific words to describe how the woods brightened after a storm, or the sudden gravitational pull that flickered across your body when a flock of geese passed overhead in their thousands. Not that he talked about any of this directly. He talked a lot, he told stories and repeated memories of people he had met and things he had seen in passing, but he said very little about his own life. I had to work to imagine him as a child: free, maybe a little wild, a boy full of a black, glittering energy that he didn't fully understand and couldn't

31

do much with, in company at least. After my mother left, he would say that their getting married was the real mystery of his time on this good earth – but I knew he couldn't dismiss that part of his life so easily. For even if he was contented in his loneliness, there was also an edge of longing to his days that he couldn't hide. A restlessness that was usually good-hearted, but also puzzled and, occasionally, by his own admission, there had been moments of random cruelty, a curiosity about hurt that he couldn't altogether escape while he was growing up. He never gave details, but he told me once that the other children were afraid of him, because of some things he had done. Sudden outbursts of rage that had puzzled him as much as they had scared his victims, instances of blood and, once, a boy with a broken nose and wrist, beaten down for some reason Dad couldn't even recall afterward.

I didn't want to hear those stories, of course – but he told them for his own reasons, just as he told me his skewed fairy tales for a reason. He didn't want me to go into the world unprepared for what might be in my blood. He could show me what he knew, but he didn't want that to be exclusive, because what the world knew could make life easier, and less isolated, if you could come to terms with it. He knew this in his heart. It was the one sure thing he understood about the world. Systems thinking. What scared me, though, was the opposite fear. I didn't want to lose what he had – and I certainly didn't want to exchange it for what school and marriage and everyday work had to offer. I wanted to stand outside on a winter's night and listen, the way I could see him listening – and I wanted to hear what he heard. Only, I didn't. I heard nothing, or nothing unusual, at least. For him, the woods were magical, the river was at least partly an old spirit from another time, but for me, even if I found them beautiful, in the end they were just trees and water. As a child, I sometimes came close to believing. I would walk around in the dark, convinced I had some kind of sixth sense, that I could feel the gravity of any object in my path and navigate accordingly and if it didn't always work, I could convince myself that it was there and that, sooner or later, I could find it. After he died, though, that sense of the world just slipped away and all I knew for certain was what I *didn't* want – which was pretty much everything.

Dad's passing interrupted my studies. Or, no – not his passing so much as the several months that followed, when I couldn't come to terms with the fact that he wasn't there any more. That he no longer existed. He had been ill for some time, but he'd hidden it from me and I'd only found out when Louise called, one icy December morning, a week before the end of first semester. It had snowed just the day before; now the town was glittering white in the winter sun, people going up and down the street in their winter coats, happy and lit up with the wonder of it, like the impossibly kind grown-ups in old picture books. It was all so right, so like something from long ago that, to begin with, I didn't understand what Louise was saying. Something had happened. I had to come right away. That was all she said, at first, her voice soft and careful, as if she hoped what she was saying wouldn't scare me if she said it quietly enough.

It felt strange, hearing her talk like that, like listening to somebody rehearse a script. A story. What people said in books and movies, but not in real life – but then, Louise had always been like that with me. She was Dad's special friend, I knew that, but I didn't think they were having an affair, or not in the usual way, and I knew Dad would never

33

get married again. Still, Louise was always worried about what I thought regarding her role in Dad's life and she was always careful around me. Sometimes, I would come back from town and I'd see her car in the drive; then, for a minute, I'd stand outside and listen, Louise's bright, happy voice singing out through a window, and it would be strange, how suddenly she would be transformed into this shadow of herself the moment I walked in, all careful and unobtrusive, like those prospective second wives in movies, trying too hard not to look like they are taking the dead mother's place. Only my mother wasn't dead, she was just gone. Louise didn't know that, though, and she took her relationship with Dad and me so seriously, it was like something she was doing as a job. The problem was that the job she was doing was one of those ancient, tribal professions that nobody pursues any more. Sin eater, say. Or chaperone. I knew she was doing that movie shtick, being patient, not pushing, hoping she would win my trust by degrees. Only I didn't care enough to reject her, any more than I cared enough to play the game, or not to the point in the script where we came together and hugged and were united in our common love for Dad.

That day, however, calling on a bad line across a thousand miles of snow, she was different. Still careful, but less sure of the rules she had to follow. She knew how to be the respectful special friend, she knew how to be the discreet lover, if that was what she had been all those years, but she didn't know *this*. She did as well as anybody could have done under the circumstances, but I didn't properly register what she was saying. Not at first, anyhow – and when I did, it wasn't the words; it was something in her voice. A tone. Careful, yes, but not as soft as before. Like for the first time, she had to engage with me as herself, and not just as the special friend. That was how I knew.

'What is it?' I said. 'What's happened?' Which was a script too, something people didn't say outside books, unless they had learned it from books, and used it, because, as the knowledge dawns, there's nothing else to say. There was a long silence on the line. I'd only just gotten a cellphone – Dad had bought it for me so I never had to be out of touch, though he knew I didn't like them. I'd never know whether the other person had stopped talking or if they had been cut off. Not that I had many calls that first year of school.

It felt like a long time before Louise spoke again. When she did, it was as if something had broken inside her, something physical – and I realised that what I had taken for hardness in her voice was just her trying to contain her own feelings, so as not to make this about *her* – and I understood then, maybe for the first time, how much care she had put into not intruding. 'He's gone, honey,' she said. It was odd, her calling me honey like that. She had called Dad honey once, in my presence, then she'd gotten all embarrassed. She called people honey and darling and pet names all the time, but she had never called *me* honey before, and now it felt odd, like we were suddenly supposed to be united in grief, or something.

'Gone?' For a moment I wanted to go back, to convince myself it was all right, that Dad had run off somewhere like he used to do when I was a child. He'd get in the car and drive away, then come back a few days later, no explanation, just that far-off, quiet look in his eyes. My mother never asked him where he had been, or not in front of me, anyhow, but it was her I put my question to, not him, when I summoned enough courage to ask for an explanation.

'I don't know where he goes,' she said. 'He just needs to be by himself for a while.'

'But why?' I insisted. I was six years old and even at that age, I knew that, by asking her, I was voicing some kind of accusation.

'Well,' she said, 'I think he has to be alone. Maybe he's afraid of what he might do, if he couldn't get away for a while.'

That frightened me. That phrase, *what he might do*. I didn't know what it meant and, after she said it, I didn't want to know. But she didn't understand, she thought I was afraid for her, or maybe for myself, even though I couldn't have imagined my father being violent. She laughed – a laugh that was probably meant to be reassuring, though it didn't work that way. 'It's all right,' she said. 'He would never do anything to harm *you*. It's just . . .' She shook her head. 'I don't know,' she said quickly, almost dismissively. 'It's just how he is. He needs to be alone sometimes.'

I studied her face. I didn't know her. She had never been close to me, never read me stories or taken me places, like the mothers in books and movies. She was kind in an abstract way, and sometimes she gave me things, but she wasn't ever wholly there, in my world. 'Will he go away forever?' I said.

She seemed startled by the idea, as if she had never thought of it for herself. 'No,' she said. 'Of course not.' She forced a smile. 'He would never leave you.'

And that, at least, was true. After she left, a few months later, he didn't run away on his own any more. A distant look would come into his eyes sometimes, while he was working, or cooking a meal, but he stayed where he was. He had a kid to look after. Except, now that I was away, safely embarked on my own separate life, he had disappeared again, this time for good. It was as if he had just been waiting for the right moment. Louise said something else, but I didn't take it in – and then, startled by the echo of what my mother had said, over a decade earlier, I registered what it was she had told me. 'He's gone,' she had said. 'But you haven't lost him. He'll always be there, somehow.' She paused, listening to hear if *I* was listening. 'He loved you more than anything else in the world,' she said. 'And he'll always be there—'

That was all I heard that day. Before she could say any more, I turned off the phone, so she would think I had been cut off. Or maybe she would guess what I had done, but if she did, I knew she would forgive me for it. She knew about loss, it was as if she had been practising for it her whole life. Some people do that. It's a vocation, like sin eater, or chaperone. They know how to be when somebody goes away, or dies. That was how she had hooked up with my father in the first place. She had seen something in his eyes, she had understood that, even if he had known all along that he didn't want to be with my mother, he had also lost something and he didn't quite know what to do with himself. Later, when I got home, through the funeral and the days and weeks that followed, Louise was always there, comforting, forgiving, living alongside the emptiness I felt, respectful enough not to try to fill it, or to tell me what to do. I dropped out of school and I would probably have stayed dropped out – dropped out of everything – if I hadn't lost the house at Stonybrook too. For Louise, that was the real surprise; it seems Dad mortgaged the place for some reason, and by the time the money all got worked out, the house had to be repossessed and sold on for half of what it was worth. I don't know. I didn't pay attention to the details. Louise stepped in and looked after it all and, when I had nowhere to live, she offered to take me, just till

I found my feet again. That was when I decided to go back to school. I didn't dislike Louise, I think I even loved her a little, for how she had been with Dad, but I couldn't stand to be in her house, being looked after, being silently encouraged to find my feet. So I became a student again, but I couldn't go back to what I had been doing before, which was why I gave up Emily Dickinson and Marianne Moore, why I gave up all the wonderful suicides and the crazed drunks, Weldon Kees and Hart Crane and John Berryman, all those poets I had loved. To someone in my precarious mental state, the study of poetry was probably too dangerous anyway. Better something practical – and easy, too, in the sense of not being new. I didn't want anything new, so I took up film-making. I was already a movie nerd, so why not use that? Why not make things easy for a while, till I could work out what I really wanted? I had no great ambition to make art, or anything of that nature. Which was good because, if I had, that ambition would never have survived Laurits – and maybe that was another reason I moved in with him, just a month after I arrived in Scarsville. He was larger than anybody else I knew. He was expansive. Whenever a dark gap opened up in my life, he simply filled it. For a while, I was truly grateful to him, for that, at least.

Maybe it was Louise, with all her talk of Dad still being there that made me dream up the idea of a haunting. Maybe it was that last trace of the lyrical, making mischief in my sorry heart. I don't know. All I know is that, for a while, I felt sure he would come back, partly because I was asking so little of this prospective ghost. He didn't have to say anything; he just had to be there. A hint, a trace – that was all I needed. And then, when nothing came, I told myself that was okay, too. It was more than okay, in fact, because Dad – or the Abenaki in him – believed, or at least said he believed, that the dead who have lived a good life go straight to the next existence. They get reborn in the form they most loved, or most resembled while they were alive and then they are gone from this world as the people they were, even though they are here, still, as something else. They don't come back to haunt us because they can't, they are too caught up in that new life and, anyhow, they probably remember nothing of what they were before. The only ghosts who come back to haunt their old world are the damaged and the malevolent. It sounded like a mix of Buddhism and some old pagan idea of metempsychosis mixed in with a hearty dose of pop karma, but that was what he believed and, when he talked about it, he could be persuasive. Louise once said to me that he wasn't sure he was half-Abenaki, he just liked the idea of it. Maybe he was, maybe he was just an eighth, or a sixteenth, but that didn't matter, because it freed his imagination to construct a liveable world. I was angry with her, when she said that; but on reflection, I didn't doubt that she was at least partly correct in her assumption. Being Abenaki allowed him to create a moral and spiritual system that was lacking in the world he dealt with day to day. It allowed him to say that some people got to be reborn as deer, or fish, while others have to stay on as ghosts, pinned to their old lives because they had been hurt in a way they couldn't heal. So, according to his system of thinking, I ought to be glad he didn't come back and in some ways I am, but then I remember the old stories he would tell, about uncles and grandmothers returning for a night to talk to the living, to give them advice and reassure them and I wonder why he couldn't do that for me. Or maybe it was just that I missed him so much that a ghost – any ghost – would have been better than nothing. On a good day, I can imagine him being reborn as an eagle or a hawk; or maybe as a tree by a lake, filling with birds, or snow, with the changing seasons. That would have appealed to him. Though, in the end, I like to think of him as a bird. Something migratory, one of those terns that fly from pole to pole, following the sun's light over glittering waters, its eyes scanning the shallows for the glint of a fish. That would be good. To come back as a bird with a memory of the man sealed inside its hollow bones, a microgram of additional soul that would guide him to the life beyond, and the life beyond that, till the time came when we met, not as the selves we had been, but still recognisable at some subtle, almost gravitational level. Had I spoken about any of this to Laurits, though, he would have said that it's when you have thoughts like these that you know you are really in trouble – and though I was never foolish enough to tell him my ghost fantasy, I was gratefully aware of how thoroughly he would have mocked me, if I had.

PATRICIA NEAL

The next five days were difficult. Not Ray Milland *Lost Weekend* difficult, not John Lennon screaming in his cold-turkey hotel room difficult, but difficult, nevertheless. I had come off alcohol once before, but not after so many months of solid drinking; I knew about the night sweats, the dry retching and the sudden, terrifying cramps where you think your calf muscles are going to tear themselves apart; but what I hadn't counted on, this time around, was the beauty of the nightmares. Mostly, my nightmares were expressions of ordinary fear, ordinary shame: public nakedness, claw-fingered harpies coming out of the dark, their nails tearing at my face, long, slow drownings in my own bed, during which I would be awake, aware, trying desperately to raise myself, like some abandoned Lazarus, from a mattress that was sinking slowly into dark, befouled water, and not being able to move, or even cry out. Those DT horror clichés. On the second night I woke thinking I had been screaming so hard that the whole neighbourhood would be out, the cops breaking in the door to see who was being murdered. Then, when I finally regained the power in my arms and pushed myself up into a sitting position, the room was still, silent, normal. No echoes dying away, no flashing blue lights, no detectives. What was different during those next five days, when I told myself I wasn't quitting because Jean Culver had told me to, what was new was the landscape inside my head, a landscape that was unutterably beautiful one moment, then quietly, perversely frightening the next.

I say unutterably beautiful, because I couldn't find words to describe those dreams when I woke – and I needed to describe them, not to someone else, but to, or rather, *for* myself. Those dreams were like astonishing, surreal movies, genuine works of art. If I'd had a camera and a budget I would have wanted to find some way of transferring them on to video, to make them visible and, so, fix them in time. The dream I had that first night of – it seems weird now, using words like *sobriety*, like some fully paid-up member of AA, but that was what it was. Sobriety. What those AA leaflets don't tell you is how strange the first days of sobriety are. The dreams, the hallucinations, the nightmares even – they don't say how beautiful they are. That first night, I found myself on a wide shore – really, impossibly wide, stretching for miles in all directions, flat, very fine silty sand, grey mostly, but silver or even fox-coloured in places, a wide flat space where a thick fog had settled. That was where I was, inside that fog – but it was also me. I mean I was inside it and it was me, we were interchangeable, so everything I saw was me, as far as the eye could see, which wasn't much, most of the time, but now and then there were flashes of damp light and the fog cleared slightly, just enough to see a flock of wading birds rise up off the sands and flicker away, almost silently, just a murmur of wings, then fog again and silence. It was unbearably beautiful. I didn't want to come out of that fog, not ever, and I would have stayed – what would that be like: to stay inside a dream? To select that space and remain there for the rest of a lifetime? *The Soul selects her own Society – Then – shuts*

42

the Door . . . How would that be? Would it take madness to make that happen?

I didn't want to come out of the fog, but I couldn't stop myself walking and, at first, it seemed fine to be moving onward, no direction, no compass, no chart – but then, subtly, things began to change. The fog began to clear and I found myself at the edge of a spill of massive rocks at the foot of a cliff. No one was there, but I had a sensation of being watched and, before I had time to register it, the fog was gone. Or not just gone, but obliterated, as if it had never been. Now I was standing at the foot of the cliff, and there were rocks all around me, rocks that had recently fallen and rocks that had been there forever. I looked around. Nobody was there, but I felt alone and exposed on that rocky shore and I wanted to be somewhere else, somewhere sheltered, back in the fog, anywhere but here. I kept looking around, and I knew there was a way out, I knew it, and I knew I could find it if I only looked hard enough – and then I saw it, a path into a cleft in the rock face that led up toward the light, away from the beach, but before I could take it, a gang of men and boys came running toward me, screaming, howling, naked men and boys with terrible injuries, as if they had come through a labyrinth of steel blades. As if they had run a gauntlet of steel blades that sliced into and through their limbs and their flesh, cutting their arms and legs, cutting their faces, slicing into the skin again and again as they ran, so that now, as they emerged from whatever that machinery had been, they were too damaged and slashed to know they had come through, too blinded by their own blood to know that, too late, they were safe. I stood still, as they came screaming and howling around me, brushing against my body, men and boys without faces, men and boys I didn't know, bearing down upon me so fast that, any moment now, I would be borne down and drowned in a wave of cut and bleeding flesh. That was the moment I woke up, when the weight of their onrush finally knocked me to the ground and, before I was submerged altogether, I woke in my own bed, in the half-light, almost saved, except that I couldn't move, and the weight of the bodies kept pressing down on me, while I struggled just to breathe.

The good thing about Laurits was that, when I retired into my tiny, white cell – yes, Emily Dickinson came to mind, her voice at the back of my head like the solitary, all-knowing chorus in a Greek drama – when I withdrew from the world and sat alone with my books, or just gazing silently out at the patch of neighbouring yard that was visible from my window, he never disturbed me. If I was anywhere else, he would draw me in to whatever he was doing, or wanted to do, or talk about, and that usually involved booze and whatever drugs he had recently obtained. When I closed the door to my cell, however, he left me alone. Yes, he was mostly a companionable drunk, for all the usual reasons, and yes, he encouraged me to drink more than I should but, usually, that didn't matter. Of course I had thought about giving up, getting clean, running in the first cool of day, doing yoga, doing t'ai chi, whatever the latest fantasy was, but the fact that it didn't last had nothing to do with Laurits. It was my choice, and while it was true that I could usually be counted on to come down on the wrong side, it was also true that he didn't push me. If I wasn't there, he was more than happy to drink on his own. Which he did – only, when he drank alone, he never got properly drunk. He just drank and drank and thought himself into corners – new projects, new theories, new quests for some shred of wisdom that, as brilliant as it seemed for the first hour or so, usually came to nothing. Nothing at all – until, in the aftermath, inspired, not by alcohol and amphetamines, or whatever his source had been over the previous several days, but by exhaustion and futility, he would come up with something interesting. He had won prizes and grants for putting himself through that purgatory. He used to say, if the funders had only known where he got his ideas, the money would soon dry up. My sense, though, was that the exact opposite was true. The funders – Laurits' generic term for anyone and everyone who might give him money – were probably quite aware of his methods. They just needed people with enough edge to make credibly risk-taking work. Enough edge, but not too much; risk-taking, but not revolutionary – which made Laurits their perfect client, an artist-anthropologist-provocateur who asked all the right questions about the air-conditioned nightmare, but didn't have the conviction to come up with any answers. His work some called it art, some called it documentary – was fierce and confrontational at times, but it was also safe, because, in the final analysis, it had no real moral content. Laurits was happy to throw up his hands and say how ridiculous, or disgusting, or venal the world was, but he didn't want to change it. He didn't want to cure, or heal, or confront – and that made him safe. Had he prospered a little longer, I do believe his work would have won him real attention, maybe a kind of alternate art-scene stardom, but he wouldn't have enjoyed the attention. In fact he would have hated it – and then he would have made a film about how disgusting he was, selling out his non-existent principles for a tawdry fifteen minutes of fame.

*   *   *

I emerged from my room, oddly cold, but with an ugly fever, on Sunday morning, after two days of nothing but water and fruit. I knew Laurits would be working because, out of perversity or maybe for good reasons, he always said that he worked best on Sundays, while the rest of Scarsville was observing some kind of latter-day Sabbath, reading the newspapers and waiting for lunch to appear. I knew he would be working, and I lingered long over my bathroom ritual, so that I emerged whole again, like a normal person. Then I brewed some coffee, fixed myself a basic, post-fast breakfast – granola, apple slices, half-milk, a slice of toast spread thinly with peanut butter – and carried it through to the dining room, where Laurits was working. I never did understand how his films got made – he shot some of the material himself, I knew that, but most of the time he used existing footage, manipulating it to expose, not so much its own basic flaws, as the conditioned responses his viewers might have to the content – porn scenes, travelogues, sports footage, it didn't matter, whatever he borrowed from the public realm he transformed, so it always left questions hanging in the air. His films were well regarded in some quarters, but he said they were all bullshit in the end. The original idea hadn't been bullshit, he said, but the finished piece never lived up to that original thought. He always insisted that there were no stories in these home movies – his term, not mine – because he despised plot, hated suspense, the lie of it, the clumsiness of the artifice, but I don't think the audience saw it that way. I think, if there is no obvious story, then the viewer infers one. Laurits said his life wasn't about events, or the continuous sense of a self as story that the socialisation process tries to sell us on. He said he wasn't interested in relationships of any complexity, he was just looking for those elusive textures and degrees of light and shade, the nuances, the climate. It was about the fabric of the world – or, no: it was about those moments and places where the fabric of the world was frayed or torn.

Now, he had just started a new project: working title *Corrida*. The dining room, which we rarely used, had been temporarily set up as a kind of studio, with several TVs, a couple of VCRs, a brand-new DVD player, various recording devices and cameras, all the equipment he needed for his work scattered about in no real semblance of order, though Laurits always knew where to find what he needed. That Sunday morning, while the good people of Scarsville were at church or preparing lunches for family and friends, he was sitting at the table, with a screen on his right side playing a bad porn film, while the screen to his left ran footage of what looked like a bullfight.

It was clear that he had selected the films he was working from for their drabness. The colour was bad in the porn movie, the bullfight footage looked amateurish and the picture kept spiking. Laurits had a thing for animals. For what we do to them. Here, the bull was being goaded by a horseman with a lance, the horse's belly circled with thick gold padding, the sharp point of the lance just holding the animal at bay as it tried to gore the horse, while four or five other men moved in and out of the bull's line of vision, fluttering purple and gold capes, trying to draw it away. When it turned and charged madly at the first of the men, another would distract it, then another man moved in and performed a few confident passes with his cape, getting the bull so bewildered that, at one point, it came down into the sand horns first and went head over heels, landing on its back for a moment before getting up and angrily charging on. Only now, the capes were gone, the men had withdrawn to various spots on the far edges of the arena, leaving the bull bewildered, unsure where to charge next – and that, strangely, was the most poignant moment. The bull's bewilderment. Its confusion. It stood there, working things out, or so it seemed, about to give up this pointless pursuit – then one of the capes moved closer and fluttered a little harder, and it was off again, charging wildly at something that it did not understand.

On the other screen, four men stood together, naked except for their socks, looking at a woman. Clearly, they were the ones who had tied her to the bed, though not as tightly as might be expected, for there was obvious give in the ropes (soon it became clear that this was deliberate, as they moved her body into different positions for the various ways they wanted to use it), but what troubled me most, to begin with, was the fact that the woman was wearing glasses. Why was that? Why would the men not remove her glasses, when they removed and carried away her clothes, her shoes, her purse? That seemed sinister to me, but I didn't know why. The other thing of note was that the woman appeared to be dazed and groggy. Not drunk, but possibly drugged. All the while the men were using her, she didn't cry out or struggle even though it was very clear that what was happening was in no way a pleasure for her. She seemed – what? Not defeated, exactly, and not exactly resigned to her fate. She was just far away, groggy, dazed – though, on second thoughts, perhaps not from drugs so much as from shock. Yes; that was what was happening. I saw it now. The woman was shocked that she had somehow come to be in this position. That she had allowed herself to end up in this place, powerless and alone. Maybe she had trusted one of the men, thinking that what was about to happen was an intimate rite that would unite them in their curiosity, or their – what? What was it they might have shared? I found myself considering this question seriously for a long moment before I saw the connection between the two films. The connection that had made Laurits choose them, which was the way the bewilderment of the bull was matched by the woman's confusion, how neither of them were able to comprehend what was being done to them, because what was being done had no meaning. It was pointless – or it was for the bull and the woman, at least. On the other hand, for the men in the bullfight film, in their fancy gold brocade and hats, as for the porn-movie men in their absurd ankle socks, the meaning was obvious. That was the tragedy, or was it the bathos? The meaning was so obvious to the perpetrators – who acted like priests in some banal ritual – and so horribly absent for the victims. This was why Laurits has chosen these films. I stood a while, glancing back and forth between the screens, then I moved away, feeling slightly tainted, as if I had somehow agreed to something that I ought to have refused.

I don't know why Laurits wanted me to move in with him. Maybe it was just laziness: he liked having me around, but he had guessed that he probably wouldn't make the effort to come find me, if I wasn't close by. To begin with, we had reasonably good sex, or it felt good enough when sex still mattered to me. I'm not saying this right, I guess: sex matters to me still, but I can't imagine loving someone now, and I'd have to be able to do that to get back into anything physical. And that's not even right, because I can imagine loving someone, but that someone is abstract, a character in my own mind, and I know I created him so no real person could find a way in. That imaginary lover is too – fine. Incomparable. He helps me keep my body pure. Back when I was with

Laurits, I was too open, too exposed. I thought, then, that I couldn't love anybody, so it didn't matter who I loved, or had sex with, or wasted my days on. But that was the very opposite of true. I was so hurt by the absence of my own private haunting that it didn't matter what else happened; it didn't matter who I loved, who I had sex with, who I talked to and called my friend. And I think Laurits was in a similar place. He was bored; I was grieving. Sometimes it amounted to the same thing.

It's hard to believe, considering how much we drank and how many drugs we took, but the sex was good. For a while it was, anyhow. We liked to watch movies together, not porn, or not the usual thing. It was more vintage erotica, I suppose. Classic French movies, say, like *Story of O*. That was a favourite of his. He'd found this old VHS copy, dubbed into Russian for some reason, all the words coming out wrong so it just made you more aware of the sound effects, the moans and the whipping. It was laughable, really, or it would have been if it had ended there, but it never ended there. We would sit drinking, watching O as she was delivered to the castle, or wherever it was they had taken her, and we would get more and more drunk as the humiliations got more and more intimate and shameful, and then – well, I won't say we acted out what we had just watched, but that was part of it, certainly. That was the goal. Sometimes, he would get carried away, and he would hurt me a little. I mean – really hurt me, so it left marks on my skin. He would hold me down and cover my face, I'd be tied up, and I liked it, most of the time. But I was scared, too, because I knew how that film ended, how they all ended, and I wanted to believe that he wasn't thinking about that too. I wanted to believe he wasn't thinking about it – and

I couldn't, because I knew that some end was there, no matter how much he made it seem like a game, or a ritual. A ceremony – that's what he called it once. I knew that, beyond the game, beyond the ceremony, there was an image, not of death itself, but of something like it, and I was afraid and ashamed, not just because I thought Laurits was using me to find that image, but because I was collaborating with him. Or maybe not collaborating, exactly – but I didn't make any effort to draw a line. I didn't define anything that allowed for safety. I'm not saying I wanted him to kill me, or hurt me badly, but I knew, somewhere in the pit of my stomach, that I wouldn't be able to stop him if he did.

The soul selects her own society, says Emily. Yes, but there is no end to the perversity of the soul. How else to explain how I came to be living in that apartment? How else to explain how Laurits came to be with me? Sometimes I would try to analyse it, to figure out what had driven us together. I considered all the options: guilt, self-hatred, genuine perversion, though it was probably something a bit less dramatic. Boredom, say. Or mental illness.

'Maybe I'm a bit bipolar,' I said one day, out of the blue, not quite sure I'd actually said it aloud until it was too late. We were lying in his bed, smoking some amazing weed, two bottles of muscat into a Saturday afternoon. It was springtime and the window was open. Bob van Asperen's recording of Girolamo Frescobaldi's *Cento partite sopra passacagli* was playing quietly in the background.

Laurits grunted. 'Crap.'

I laughed. For a man who liked seventeenth-century harpsichord music, he was wonderfully insensitive. 'Excuse me?'

'You can't be *a bit* bipolar,' he said. 'It's a clinical condition. Like depression. If it's not clinical, it's not depression—'

51

'Fuck, Laurits,' I said. 'Why do you have to be so . . . ?' I searched for the word, but I was too stoned.

He held back for a moment, so I could see that he had something serious he wanted to say. Because he cared, in his abstract way. He cared enough to correct a misunderstanding, at least. It was like life was just a convoluted extension of the school debating club: all you had to do to fix everything was present a cogent argument. 'What people usually call depression is natural,' he said. 'It's a perfectly normal response to the world we have to live in. Sometimes you can tolerate it, sometimes you can't. But that's sorrow, or maybe grief.'

'Grief?'

'Yes. Grief.'

'What do you know about grief?'

He stared at me, as if my words had hurt him. As if I had failed to recognise some special area of expertise. 'I know *everything* about grief,' he said. 'I almost made a film about it once. A real, Jiminy Cricket, honest-to-goodness American movie.'

'That'll be the day,' I said.

He ignored me. 'It was based on a true story about this old woman – no, I'm going to call her an old lady. This old lady, let's say her name was Frances. I like Frances; it's a good name. Like Frances Farmer.'

'There was nothing special about Frances Farmer,' I said. 'Just because she was a rebel.'

'I'm not going to debate you,' he said. 'Let's just say this old lady is called Frances. She lives in Pennsylvania, in a little house on the edge of town – well, let's not call it a house. I went to see it one time and it's nothing more than a cabin. Frances had lived out there all her married life, and she had loved her husband – shall we call him Sam—'

'Why Sam?' I said.

'In honour of Sam Shepard, American genius,' he said, and I remembered that Sam Shepard had been in the biopic they made about Frances Farmer, he and Jessica Lange, drawn in, presumably, by the politics of some original script that ended up, as most original scripts end up, butchered on a studio floor.

'Okay.'

'So the trouble starts when Sam dies. He and Frances were always close, and of course, they had lived their whole lives out there in the little cabin in the woods, close to nature, living with the seasons, alone in their joy. They have kids – not sure how many, but one of them is a daughter who moves to the nearby town and forgets about the cabin in the woods and all that joy and starts auditioning for Little Miss Normal.'

'Now, now,' I said. 'She can't be all bad.'

'Who says she's bad?'

'I sense a villain coming on.'

He laughed. We were now halfway through another bottle of muscat. Bob van Asperen had fallen silent. 'There are no villains,' he said. 'Just cabins and woods and, well, there would have to be snow. And death, of course.'

'Of course.'

'So Frances lives on in the little cabin in the woods and, who knows, maybe she catches sight of Sam in the shadows every now and then, maybe she catches glimpses of him when she goes out in the snow to fetch logs, but that's fine, she's not crazy, she's just an old lady with decades of love behind her. And she's happy, in her way. She's grieving, that's true, but then, this is what the authorities don't understand about grief. Which is why they send in the cops, when the daughter tells them—'

'Wait,' I said.

'Wait what?'

'The daughter,' I said. 'You didn't give her a name.'

'You're right. But it's not important—'

'No,' I said. 'I feel a villain coming on. She has to have a name.'

He shook his head. 'All right,' he said. 'Roll another and I'll tell you her name.'

'You roll another.'

'I can't, I'm telling the story.'

'Fine.' I gathered up the makings. 'So – what is her name?'

'Patricia,' he said.

'As in Patricia Neal,' I said.

'Absolutely. So, anyway, the daughter—'

'Patricia,' I said. 'And I don't think Patricia Neal has to be the villain just because she was in that awful Ayn Rand movie.'

Laurits scowled. Patricia Neal had been great in *Hud*, but Laurits couldn't quite bring himself to forgive her for *The Fountainhead*. 'So *Patricia* is concerned that her mother is becoming depressed. It's all right to mourn but this is taking things too far. She doesn't come into town any more, she doesn't come to see little Frankie and Johnny and make a fuss of them and buy them hot dogs and Bassetts' Ice Cream, she just sits out there in her cabin, alone on Saturday nights, and that can't be healthy, can it, so she must be—'

'Bipolar?'

'Depressed. So Pattie goes to the Social Bureau and they all go out there and Frances says, no, she's fine, she just wants to be left alone to enjoy the woods and grieve for Sam, as nature intended. Only Patricia isn't happy about this, so she keeps pushing and then, after another couple of weeks or so, she has nagged the authorities into getting very official on this nice old lady and, before long, they have a court order to bring her into town, for her own good you understand, for a psych-eval. And she's tried explaining to them that, no really, she's fine, all she wants is to stay out in her familiar place, birds at the window, snow on the logs, raccoons clattering across the roof at night. What she can't say, of course, is that she is involved in a larger project – because grief is always a much larger project than anybody ever imagines – and she is waiting for it to come to its full – fruition. Maybe that's not the word, but whatever the word is, she can't say it because, all her life, she's relied upon the grace of the unspoken, the graciousness of others when events are larger than they are.'

'Is there a story here, somewhere?'

'Yes.' He poured himself the last of this bottle of muscat, but I knew there was more. There was always more. 'Yes, yes, yes. It's a real story, not some   It's real. A story about an old lady who is about to be taken by force from her home and, because she doesn't know what else to do, she takes her husband's old shotgun and fires it off – not *at* anybody, you understand, just as one last, exasperated message. One last plea to be left alone. At which point, the cops circle round. It's a siege. You know how cops love a siege. Especially rural cops. All that overtime, and talking to the press. Or not talking to the press. That thrill of walking past the reporters and cameras and saying *No comment*, like you do that kind of thing all the time. And they do it all by the book, they isolate this dangerous criminal, they establish a *zone*, and when that's done, they set up the speaker truck and they bring in the Barry Manilow.'

'Beg pardon?'

'Barry Manilow. Scientifically proven in the classic siege or hostage situation. A few days of Barry and law and order is soon re-established.'

'You're kidding.'

'Well, maybe not a few days. In this case, Frances lasted forty-seven days. At which point she handed herself in.'

'Wow.'

'That's right.'

'So what happened?'

'What?'

'What happened?'

'How the fuck would I know?'

'Well, isn't that the story?'

'No, no, no.' Laurits put on an annoyed face, but I knew it was an act. 'The story is the siege. The story is Frances in her cabin, making the coffee last, finding ways to commune with the woods and all, with Barry Manilow in her head day and night. That's the story.'

'But you can't end it there,' I said. 'I want to know what happened to her.'

'I told you. She left the cabin. That's all that matters.'

'No,' I said. 'That's wrong. There's an afterward.'

He frowned but, again, I knew he was putting it on. 'Okay,' he said. 'She left the cabin. Her daughter wanted to take her home, but she refused. So she ended up living in a care home. Which her daughter pays for to this day.'

'Is that true?'

'Sure it is. But it's still not relevant. All that matters is that she left the cabin. Which was inevitable, what with the Barry Manilow and all. In fact, her true life was over after the first three bars of "Copacabana".'

'Who are you to say that? You don't know what her life was like, after.'

'No,' he said. 'I told you. There is no *after*. They stole her true life. She was there to grieve. That was her task.'

'Her *task*?'

'Her task was to grieve,' he said. 'To be alone. To commune with nature. That was the task and that was her story. And that's a movie I would watch,' he said. 'No story, no suspense, no closure. Just a woman and the textures of her grief. Can you imagine anything more honest than that?'

I didn't say anything. Was it my task also, to grieve? Was that why I was there, in his apartment? Was I a case study? I handed him my glass for a refill. 'You're right,' I said. 'It's an American Classic. I can see it now. Dianne Wiest as Frances. Laura Linney as Patricia. Barry Manilow as Himself.'

He snorted, but he was amused, I think. You never knew for sure with Laurits. He reached down to the side of the bed for another bottle of muscat. It was never quite clear to me where he got the money for all this. The wine. The drugs. All this *lifestyle* that he wasn't hypocritical enough to give up. 'My ass it is,' he said.

SACRED GROUNDS

I couldn't pretend it was part of any deliberate plan, but five days after our first meeting, almost to the hour, I turned up at Jean Culver's house stone-cold sober. True to my word, I hadn't had a drink since we'd talked, and though I still wasn't quite the girl I used to be, I was surprised at how much difference those five days had made. I hadn't realised, till then, how long it was since I'd not been either blind drunk or hung-over or, in the ever-briefer gaps between the two, pleasantly half-cut – an expression I had from Dad, who would explain that he never got drunk because he always fell asleep by the time he was half-cut. Now, I felt something close to good. Whole. Intact. Oddly compact, if that's the word. In possession of my faculties and then more, as if those faculties were now rearranged in a more elegant, economical way. At times, as I walked down Audubon Road, I felt elated, my body trim, lightened, almost capable of flight – but I was glad when those moments passed. They felt too dangerous. Excessive. I preferred the time in between: the calm, the gravity, the sense of self-containment.

I didn't notice the girl at first. She must have been standing amongst the trees when I arrived and then, when she saw me, she stepped warily out into the light, like a deer, not sure what kind of threat I might present. She was in her early teens, I guessed, very white, with straw-coloured hair and light, almost powder-blue eyes that seemed illumined by some inner flame. Or some inner fever, maybe, some permanent excitability that she couldn't extinguish. Something about her reminded me of a face I had seen in a painting by Paul Klee – the same pale colours, the light shining through – though I couldn't remember if that face had been a girl or an angel.

There was a brief pause, as the girl stared at me, sizing me up, deciding something. It seemed, for a moment, that she was about to speak, her lips moving slightly, but no words coming out, so I wondered, for the briefest second, if she was mute. Then her mouth formed a perfect closed o shape, her lips – a little too red against that white face – pursed obscenely, and slowly, perfectly, an egg emerged. How she held it still at the end of this extraordinarily controlled process seemed close to miraculous, but just as soon as the roundish, perfectly white object had fully emerged, it was drawn back into the girl's mouth in the same slow, careful mechanism. When it had vanished entirely, she stood watching to see how I would react – and I knew that it wasn't that she was performing a trick, or expecting applause, it was that she had just tried to tell me something, as if she had wanted, not to impress or surprise me, but to communicate. Only, by the time that realisation formed in my mind, and I understood that I wanted to offer her something in return, some word or gesture, she had turned and run away, out of the sunlight and back into the thin shade of the trees, so light on her feet and so slender and white as to seem almost translucent. It took seconds for her to disappear amongst the leaves – and I realised that what I hadn't seen before, on my last visit, was just how deep the woods were on that side of Jean Culver's house. Did she own them all? Or was there some invisible fence line, long grown-over with weeds and vines that divided her plot from some other, equally hidden domain?

My first knock at Jean Culver's door went unanswered, so I knocked again, then pushed the door open and stepped into the hallway. The house was silent. I was aware of the girl, somewhere outside, watching from her special place amidst the leaves, and I wondered if Jean Culver knew she was there, if maybe I should have been more discreet and not allowed the girl to see that the door was unlocked. What if she was a thief, or worse? She could be harmless; she could be a danger to others. What if she saw her chance and, having waited until I was gone, crept into Jean Culver's home with malicious intent? I wasn't sure what to do. Should I call out? Turn and retreat some distance, maybe keeping an eye out to see what the girl would do next? Several possibilities crossed my mind – and then I saw Jean Culver, in a plaid shirt and black jeans, an axe in one hand, a cup in the other. She had come from the kitchen, I supposed; though, if she had, she had done so without making the tiniest sound. Had she been watching the business with the egg through the kitchen window? Why was she carrying the axe?

Her face registered no surprise at seeing me. If anything, she looked pleased I was there. 'So you came,' she said. 'I wasn't sure you were going to show.

'Oh,' I said. 'I'm sorry, I should have—'

She waved her free hand and set the axe down against the wall. 'No, no,' she said. 'I'm glad you came. Come into the kitchen and I'll get ready.' She started for the back of the house, toward the deep warm shadowy interior that seemed to me so strange and, at the same time, so reminiscent of Stonybrook. Behind me, the door was still open.

'Ready?' I said.

She turned around and smiled happily, like a child looking forward to an outing. 'We were going to Sacred Grounds,' she said. 'My treat.'

'Ah.' I glanced back toward the open door.

'Are you all right? You seem – preoccupied.'

'There's a girl in your yard,' I said.

'What girl?'

'A strange . . . girl . . . She has – a very pale girl . . .'

'Ah!' Jean looked pleased. 'That's Christina. She likes the trees.'

'Christina?'

'Christina Vogel,' Jean said. 'Her people live – oh, I don't know. Off that way somewhere.' She waved vaguely back toward the polite end of Audubon Road, with its lawns and fences and basketball hoops, and it was clear from the gesture that she didn't think much of the tidy street, or of Christina Vogel's people. 'She comes for the trees. And the birds.' She turned and walked into the kitchen, and I followed, still aware of the open door. 'Sometimes she sits out there all night, listening to the owls.'

'Owls?'

'Yes.' Jean had gathered up a big canvas bag and was filling it with things she seemed to think she would need for our excursion. A wallet. A camera. A notepad and pencil. 'Barred Owls. They like it here.'

'Is she – all right?'

Jean laughed. 'Mad as a bag of snakes,' she said.

I couldn't tell if she was serious. 'Why is she in your yard?' I asked; then thinking that sounded confrontational, I modified my tone. 'I mean, do her people know where she is?'

Jean turned to look at me. 'I don't think they care much,' she said. 'I don't mind having her around here. She's no trouble.'

'But shouldn't she be in school?'

'That's school's problem, not mine.' She thought for a moment. 'I guess I like having her around because she is so childlike. She's a kind of innocent. A natural.' She looked around to see if she had missed packing anything. It was like watching someone prepare for a day-long hike, rather than a trip to the local coffee shop. 'We do well to remember ourselves as children,' she said – and before I could prevent it, the thought crossed my mind that herself as a child had happened a very long time ago. Jean nodded, as if approving something. 'I'm not talking about the ones who made nice and sang along with the rest of the class,' she said. 'I'm talking about the child you were in private . . . The curious one. The little girl you were when nobody was looking.' She was still smiling but her eyes were serious and, though I couldn't tell what she was thinking, I detected a hint of anxiety in those eyes. 'Do you remember her?' she asked.

I nodded, but I didn't say anything.

'Really?' she said, her eyes fixed on mine, as if she thought she would catch me out in a lie.

'I remember some things,' I said. 'I spent a lot of time by myself.'

'When nobody was looking?'

'Yes.'

'Not even from inside your own head?' she said.

I didn't know what to say. I understood what she meant, but I couldn't answer the question. I thought I had been pretty independent as a kid, but now, all grown up and far from home, I still felt like somebody was watching me. My mother, say, peering over the rim of a coffee cup, as if wondering how I had come to be living in her house. Jean was still watching me, waiting for my reply. 'I don't know,' I said, and I really didn't.

She gave a slight nod. 'Never mind,' she said. 'It takes a long time to get all those bastards out of your head.' She smiled when I reacted to her unexpected choice of words. 'I'm only just getting there myself. You just have to keep at it.' Her smile widened. 'All right, now. Let's go get us some coffee.'

It was another hot day, but I felt easy with it, slow and strangely graceful in a way that I hadn't felt since I was a child. Back then, I would go out into the woods in the summertime. I'd stay there all day, through long afternoons, the heat stifling, time slowing almost to a halt. Sometimes I would follow a trail that led deep into the woods, so you thought it would never end, that it would go on forever, nothing but trees and sun and sky. Of course, I was just a child and what seemed immense to me then was an ordinary stretch of woodland at the edge of town, and even then, I knew there had to be an end to it. So every time I went out, I walked a little farther, and then farther still. It probably wasn't very far. I can't say for sure, because they cut down all those trees and now there's nothing but housing – executive homes, with streets named after what used to be there – but it couldn't have been far. I wasn't a brave child. Still, I was curious. One day, I found a single apple tree, so deep into the birch and aspen woods it seemed an apparition. I should have guessed that it was a sign of something, but I didn't find the far edge till a few days later, when I went beyond the apple tree and came to a road – a narrow, country road, but paved, winding away in both directions to who knew where. And that was where I found the house that became part of my mind, a piece of my imagination, the place where, in stoned reveries and deep, frightening dreams, I sometimes find myself going from room to room, listening for something. For someone. In reality, I never saw the inside of that house, though I conjured it up in my imagination: a grandfather clock ticking in the hall, but everything quiet otherwise, nothing to hear and nobody there and, at the same time, the sense that somebody was waiting, listening or maybe looking down at me, from somewhere above.

'You know, I ought to be used to it now,' Jean said suddenly, interrupting my reverie. 'But I still can't believe how much this town has changed.' She glanced at me, remembered I was a newcomer, some random student, just passing through, and she shook her head. 'What surprises me is how people let things happen,' she said. 'The money people, you don't expect shit from them, but the folks who live here, the ones who have to put up with it all, you'd expect them to fight more. Get angry. Tear something down.'

I nodded. It was one of those things old people say. Everything's different, it was better in the old days, and probably it was true, mostly. Dad would say it, whenever they cut down some more of the woods, and I imagined myself saying it in some future life, thinking back to this time, now, and telling myself it was perfect. Writing Laurits out of the story, or condensing him down to the handful of good days, back when we first met.

Jean laughed, as if she'd read my thoughts. 'You're right,' she said. 'I'm being . . .' She shook her head. 'Still,' she said, 'this old main street was something way back when. Walking home from the movie theatre on a summer's night, that smell of candy and blossom on the air, the soft light all along the street and music coming out from somewhere, some new love song on the radio . . .' She looked at me. 'I'm not talking about rock music, you understand.'

I smiled. 'What's wrong with rock music?' I said.

She grimaced. 'What's wrong with it? Well – where do I start?'

I laughed. 'Your mother probably hated those new love songs you're talking about,' I said. 'It happens every generation.' Her face changed. Not a big change, she didn't frown or look aggrieved, nothing like that, it was just a slight dulling of that amused brightness in her eyes, and, again, I realised that this gruff exterior, this friendly combativeness that I was getting used to was really just a cover for something she didn't want out in the open.

She shook her head and began walking again, but she didn't say anything for a moment. Then, after ten or twelve steps, she stopped and looked at me. 'Listen,' she said. 'What do you hear?' I cocked my head slightly, to show I was listening, but she ignored me. 'What do you smell? What does this feel like to you, walking on a summer's day through your own home town? Does it feel like home? Does it feel like something you'll never forget?' She examined my face as if the questions she was asking were more than rhetorical – and for a moment I thought she really was expecting an answer. But she wasn't. 'Once upon a time, everybody walked. We would walk into town to meet friends. We would walk around the neighbourhood and stop to chew the fat with people sitting out on their porches. I'm not talking about hiking here, I'm talking about the lost art of walking and the good that came of it. When did it first happen that, if you saw somebody walking in your neighbourhood, you called the police?'

I shook my head. I couldn't imagine myself calling the police about a suspicious pedestrian. The truth was, I couldn't imagine myself calling the police about anything.

Jean Culver grinned. 'So you really did stay off the sauce,' she said. It wasn't a question; she knew the answer, but I couldn't tell if she was genuinely surprised.

'Yes,' I said.

'Why?'

'I don't know,' I said – and I didn't know, or not altogether. I knew it had something to do with her, but I didn't want to say that in so many words, partly because I didn't want to admit it. Yet another part of me felt, somewhere at the back of my mind, that I shouldn't make this an issue for her. A burden. I didn't want her feeling she had achieved something by telling me to get off *the sauce* as she put it, and then feel let down when I started drinking again. Which I most certainly would. 'It was time for a change,' I said.

She grunted. 'Long overdue, I'd say,' she said.

'Well, I wouldn't go that far.'

She stopped walking. We were just a few yards from the entrance to the café. 'I'm not judging you,' she said. 'I don't know you and it's not my place to mind one way or the other what you do with your life, or to your body. I am making an observation, nothing more.' She studied my face and, for the first time, I began to wonder what this all meant to her. She had almost driven me away, yet here she was, waiting – anxiously, I thought – to see if she had offended me. But why? Why did she even care if this conversation continued? Was she just some lonely old woman, grateful for some company, or some kind of distraction, but too proud to admit it? I looked away. We were standing in front of a second-hand bookshop, the window a display of children's adventure books and illustrated classics. *The Last of the Mohicans. The Wizard of Oz.* Several books by Laura Ingalls Wilder that I remembered from my own girlhood and, suddenly, it felt strange, not being that girl any more. I had lived so surely in her world, in her skin, and now that her world was gone, it seemed there was nothing to take its place. It was as if I'd started out on a long bus trip, but somewhere along the way I had missed a connection.

For a long moment, Jean Culver had been waiting for me to speak, to make some response, to walk away, to laugh out loud, something. Now, she was moving on – and there was a hint of relief in her voice, I think, that I hadn't left her there and walked off to find the nearest bar. Or did I imagine that? I didn't know then, though I think I do now. I couldn't be sure. Being sure is something I've learned to be careful of. 'All right,' she said. 'We can't stand here all day.'

After hearing Jean describe it so enthusiastically, Sacred Grounds was, on the surface, something of a disappointment. There was a counter at the far end of one big room, and behind that a sense of depth and clutter, a real kitchen, not like the backroom areas you see in franchise places. The room was dotted with tables and chairs, where a few people were sitting, singly or in pairs, talking over coffee, doing crossword puzzles, or just staring into space. At one table, a girl around my age was poised over a sketchbook, drawing pencil in hand, her eyes on nothing in particular, presumably waiting to be inspired. On the walls, which were old brick painted over in a kind of apple-blossom pink wash, a series of framed photographs were arranged as in a gallery, each with its own descriptive label. A few were marked with red dots. Mostly, they were snow scenes. Some looked to have been taken in Scarsville, others could have been anywhere. The image nearest to me was of an old-style Illinois farmhouse in deep snow, taken from across a field – or maybe from the highway. It looked timeless, obdurate and, at the same time, oddly fragile, like it could blow away, or become totally immersed in the blizzard, at any moment.

Jean led the way to a table by the window. Outside, a man in a winter coat was standing in the middle of the sidewalk, talking to himself and gazing away to something only he could see. Recently, it seemed, there had been more people on the street like that. Or was it so recent? Maybe I was just noticing them more. Jean Culver sat down with her back to the window, apparently unaware of the crazy guy on the other side of the glass. 'So tell me about yourself,' she said. 'Not everything. Just the salient facts.'

'I'd rather hear about you,' I said.

'Fine,' she said. 'But I'd like to know a little about who I'm talking to.'

'I'm just a student,' I said. 'Making movies. Collecting stories.'

'Why?'

'For a project I'm doing with my . . .' I thought for a moment. I didn't know how to describe Laurits. My boyfriend? He wasn't that. My collaborator? Hardly.

'Yes?'

I shook my head, but I didn't answer. I had the feeling she already knew the lay of the land, as if she could read me like a book, but I didn't mind that. In fact, I didn't mind it at all. It was easier than trying to say what Laurits was to me, because then I would have to think about that and, for a long time, I had gone to great lengths to avoid this prospect.

She did the thing she did with her mouth. To say she pursed her lips wasn't quite right. In reality, she clamped them together, as if she was about to make some immense physical or mental effort. 'I know you're grieving,' she said. 'And no harm in that.'

I looked at her. 'My God,' I said. 'Where did that come from?'

She didn't answer. She was still looking at me closely, as if she was trying to figure out a riddle or solve a puzzle of some kind, which should have made me uncomfortable, but for some reason, and in spite of the sudden turn in the conversation, it didn't. Her eyes lingered on my face a moment longer and I looked back, waiting for what she would say next. I was beginning to see that there was no predicting what Miss Jean Culver would say next, but I was also beginning to see that I liked that. She was real. Now that Dad was gone, the only other person I knew who was real was Laurits, but he fell into a quite separate category of real than most people. We sat like that for a moment, enjoying the sense of stalemate, then she looked around, taking in the room. 'I never had much time for church,' she said. 'But a place like this, where people take care about what they are doing, that's good enough.'

'It's just a café,' I said. 'They sell coffee and . . . cookies.'

Jean laughed and shook her head. 'No,' she said. 'It's a café all right, but it's not *just* a café. The owner of this establishment knows everything there is to know about coffee. I don't mean in some preppie smart-alec way. She loves good coffee, and she's the one who makes most of the delicacies too. Not

69

just cookies, but flapjacks. Banana bread. Vegetarian breakfasts.'

'You're a vegetarian?'

'I have been for thirty years,' she said. 'Not because of the killing, you understand. We kill all the time. We kill to make electricity. Every road we build is a trail of death. I can't do anything about that, but I don't need to collaborate with the industrial agriculture complex. I learned that from . . .' She broke off. 'Pretty girl, too,' she said after a moment, then laughed at my puzzlement. 'The girl who runs this place,' she said, with the hint of a twinkle in her eye. 'Not much more than a girl, and pretty as a picture.'

I looked away involuntarily, off toward the counter. Nobody was there, but out back somewhere, somebody was talking. It was a man, a young man, and it sounded like he was talking to himself, or maybe doing some kind of inventory. 'Blue Mountain. Caturra. Harar . . .' His voice tailed off, then somebody else spoke. It was a woman's voice, but I couldn't hear what she was saying. I looked back to Jean. 'Do they come to the table?' I said. I was thirsty. Not as thirsty as I had been at the beginning, maybe, but I needed something. A coffee, a glass of water, it didn't matter. When it's only a substitute, nothing matters. Thirst is thirst and when it's nothing more, anything quenches it. When it isn't, nothing does. An image of the jug of water by my bed flashed through my mind. The condensation pearling on the glass; the tiny, perfect air bubbles forming on the inside surface.

Jean got to her feet. 'No,' she said. 'We go up. But I can do that. You sit, gather your strength, and I'll go give Damian our order.' She gave me a cartoonish, wiseacre grin and I smiled. It felt odd. I hadn't smiled in a long time. 'What would you like?' she said.

70

I shook my head. 'Surprise me,' I said.

'There really are advantages to being old,' she said, after the coffee had been duly delivered, along with two slices of what looked like carrot cake. 'One of them is that nobody sees old people. As long as you're clean and not too eccentric, you're invisible. Which is fine by me.'

I didn't say anything. I assumed she was joking, but she looked serious. Thoughtful. The odd thing was that, though she talked about herself as an old person, she didn't seem so. She chopped logs in the heat of a summer's morning and, apparently, she walked everywhere. She lived alone in that big, old house, and she looked after herself just fine. She didn't smell of any of the usual things old people smelled of. Today, because I'd interrupted her wood-chopping plans, her plaid shirt was crisp and newly laundered. If you stripped away outward appearances, she would probably come out younger than me on any test anybody cared to devise – and, for me, this particular day was a good day. A very good day. I wasn't bathed in sweat, I didn't have a headache. I felt alert, aware. In fact, I felt more alive than I had felt in weeks. Months, even.

'On the other hand,' she said, 'it's good to be seen from time to time. That's why I come here. Just to make sure I haven't disappeared altogether.' She looked at me, to see if I was taking any of this seriously, or even listening.

'I don't know that there's anything so bad about disappearing,' I said, surprising myself. I hadn't intended to say that. I hadn't intended to say anything. Though now that I had said it, I didn't think of it as a negative comment. I just liked the idea of vanishing, the lightness of it, the sheer lightness of the space I might leave behind.

'That's not healthy talk for a girl your age,' she said. 'I'm the one most likely to disappear in the short to mid-term.' She allowed herself an indulgent smile. 'The grand exit is my show, young lady, and don't you forget it. You have a long way to go.' She kept her eyes fixed on my face a moment longer, so I would know that, in spite of the smile, she was deadly serious now. Then her face relaxed. 'All right,' she said. 'Time for the first story. Are you ready?'

I began fishing in my bag for my notebook, but she laid her hand firmly on mine and shook her head. 'No notes,' she said. 'Just listen.'

'But I have to ask you—'

She shook her head. 'No questions, no notes, no interruptions,' she said. 'I'm an old woman and my memory isn't what it was. If you interrupt, I'll lose my thread. You don't want me to lose my thread, do you?'

'No,' I said. 'But the project is—'

'This isn't the project,' she said. 'It's just a story.' She smiled, as if forgiving in me some weakness of which I was sadly unaware. Then she began.

'I was born and raised, for a while at least, in Alabama,' she said. 'It was one of those towns where everyone knows everyone else's business, I'm sure you know the kind of place. It doesn't matter what it's called now. Fact is, it's not really there any more. Maybe it never was. Maybe it was a fiction all along—'

'Why do you say that?'

She dismissed the interruption with a wave of her hand, but she didn't rebuke me. The wave was enough. I sat back and, as if relieved of a burden I hadn't known I was carrying till then, I forgot about Laurits' questionnaire.

'Some people say we don't remember being babies, or even small children,' she said. 'It's just that we absorb what the grown-up folks remember about us from that time, things they talk about around a kitchen table over dinner, all those embroidered memories of how little Jessica wandered off into the woods and wasn't discovered until nightfall, or how baby James fell into the horse trough and just floated there, calm as you like, staring up at the sky, till somebody came and scooped him out. Years later, grown-up Jessica is hanging out the sheets, or cooking fish for dinner, and she sees, in her mind's eye, the sudden dark creeping through the dogwoods, the flashlights dancing as the boy from the feed store comes stumbling into the clearing where she sits, quiet as a stone, waiting to be rescued. Or James, who calls himself Jimmy now, finds himself in a bar at closing time, talking to the waitress, a girl he's taken a shine to, though she's young enough to be his daughter, and he tells her, in great detail, picturing it all as he speaks, about how he lay in the cool, steady water, gazing up through the heat haze at a blue that is still so vivid, he says, that it could have been yesterday. Some people say that's what happens, that it's all stories and phantom impressions, and some say that we remember every single moment, from the dim murmur of the womb to the first gasp of breath and on, moment by moment, year after year, storing it all away in some vast congressional library of the self, to be recovered if it should ever be needed, but for the sake of everyday convenience, lodged for decades in the unconscious.

'I don't know who is right, all I know is that, now, after seven decades, I remember being born, and nobody told me about it, because the occasion of my birth was also the occasion of my mother's death. No one ever held me to account

73

for that but, by the same token, nobody ever entertained the company at dinner with amusing anecdotes about my infancy. And the fact was that, all the time I was growing up, I didn't know that my mother had died while giving birth to me – my father said she had died when I was two years old, and I didn't think to doubt him, even though I had no image of her in my mind, no memory at all, and whenever I asked my brother about her, he would get upset, and wouldn't want to talk about it. Later, that bothered me, because I did believe that I ought to have *some* recollection, however vague, but I didn't even try to figure it out until I was older. Old enough to notice that, when people talked about their earliest recollections, those memories always revolved around their mothers. Strange, how we do that. When I was in the hospital, after I had my own brush with the Reaper, I only thought about places. Places, and flowers. I thought about Pink Lady's Slipper poking up through heaps of dried bark in the woods, and Cherokee Rose rambling twenty feet and more along some old broken-down fence in the farmlands just south of town. I'd close my eyes and see clumps of Spider Lily clogging up the shallows of the river, and acres of Spring Beauty sprinkled across the lawns like tiny wet stars in the first days of March. I saw the street where we lived, the gardens and the trees and I remembered how everything smelled of Magnolia, heavy and rich and sweet, all up and down the avenues and around the courthouse. I didn't think about my father, or my brother, and I didn't have even the shred of a memory of the woman who bore me – and that suddenly seemed strange to me. If I had been two years old when she died, surely I would have remembered *something* about her. A look, a smile, a stray lock of hair falling over her eyes as she leaned in to gather me out of the cradle. The sound of her voice, the smell of her perfume. Soft laughter in the next room, a silhouette at a bedroom door, somebody calling her by name. *Something*.

'But there was nothing. A space, a gap, an empty shelf in the library of voices and eyes and private colours at the back of my mind. I had time enough to search, lying in my hospital bed, but I didn't come up with a thing and, after a while, I began to put the pieces together, making a story I didn't want to believe, but couldn't dismiss, from hints and things unspoken, gaps in the family story that nobody had ever needed to explain, because we had taken such pains, all three of us, to pretend they didn't exist. Later, I called my brother and asked him the question that had been hanging in my mind for weeks, while I struggled through the surgery and the rehabilitation, forcing myself to walk again, recalling the dusty heat on my bare legs and the drowse of bees when I went walking through the goldenrod at the back of the Haverford place. I hadn't spoken to him for a time; he'd been travelling again, and he never could say what he was doing on those trips of his, or how long he would be away, so I didn't ask and months would go by, sometimes, when we didn't speak. That day, I asked him how he was and what he had been doing and he evaded the question, so I figured that I wouldn't beat about the bush. I just asked him, straight out.

'He didn't say anything for a while. I even thought, for a minute, that he'd put the phone down and gone off somewhere, to talk to someone – I could hear noises in the background, so I knew he had people there – but after a moment he spoke. "Why are you asking about that now?" he said. "You ought to be concentrating on getting well."

'"I am," I said. "I am getting well. But it's slow, which means that there's been plenty of time to think. And I've thought about this for—"

' "She died the day you were born," he said. "I don't remember much, but I know it was that day. She hung on for several hours, I think, but she had some kind of complications – I don't think anybody ever really knew what – and there was nothing they could do for her." He listened for a moment, trying to figure out how I was taking the news, I suppose, then he carried on talking. His voice was flat, like he wanted to hide something from me – and he did, of course. I knew that right away. He'd been hiding it for years and, that day, all he could do was be as matter-of-fact as he could, in the hopes that I wouldn't figure out how angry he had been. Angry with our mother, angry with whoever it was who couldn't do anything – Dr Reynolds, I guess – but, most of all, angry with *me*. It wasn't a man's anger, I knew that; it was the anger of a four-year-old boy whose mother has been taken away from him, leaving a squalling scrawl of a baby sister who had to be lied to, for her own protection, all the time we were growing up. I knew that, and I also knew, just then, while he was talking, and as if I had known it all my life, that *that* was why we had been so close as children. Keeping that secret had made him the perfect older brother, the one I could always rely on when things were hard – and keeping that secret had been the beginning of a long process that had forged him into the man he would become, a man that many people thought of as a hero, just as fire and pressure forges a sword or a horseshoe out of cold iron. "It's a long time ago," he said. "There's no point in going over it all again."

'I didn't say anything, because it was obvious to both of us, as soon as he said it, that it wasn't *again* for me. It wasn't going over some old story that was better left untold, it was finally learning the truth. "That must have been hard," I said, after a moment.

' "Hard?"

' "Keeping that secret."

' "It was," he said. "For a while. But I got good at it. Besides – you were my kid sister. It was my job to protect you from stuff like that."

'I laughed at that, in spite of myself. I couldn't help it – but it wasn't meant. Or not to be cruel, anyhow – though, when he didn't speak again, I immediately wondered if he'd taken it that way. "You did a good job," I said. "I always loved you for that."

' "I loved you too," he said, his voice softening a little. Then someone spoke in the background, quite close to the phone. And I wanted to say something else, but he got distracted by this person talking – asking him a question, I think – and I didn't say what I wanted to say. I'm not sure I had the right words, anyway. We had been through so many strange days together, strange days and that vicious, ugly summer, when he had stood in the street and watched as our father was shot down in broad daylight, and he hadn't been able to protect me from *that* because he was too taken up with saving himself. Becoming a man. Someone I used to know told me that becoming a man – by which, I think, he meant becoming a good man, or a decent one, at least – was a victory of sorts, though it was always a pyrrhic victory. I don't know. I loved my brother, but something happened to him, as he went through that process of becoming a man. He lost something. Or maybe he found something hard – something *unyielding* – in himself that he hadn't known was there. I used to think that came of watching our father die, but it had been there all along. I had seen it, I just didn't see how powerful it was in him.

'We were very close, growing up. Well, that's one way of saying it. We were close because I was his responsibility, even before our father died. With our mother gone, and our father so busy, it fell to Jeremy to keep an eye on me – and he did, though he didn't always enjoy having me around. What big brother would? He had his own friends. He had things he wanted to do that shouldn't have involved me. Still, he was pretty gracious about it, most of the time. I didn't know, back then, that he was carrying this big secret about how our mother died, but if I had, it would never have occurred to me that he thought I was to blame. It wasn't my fault; he knew that. Still, he was just a boy, after all, and there must have been times when he wanted to get away.

'Don't get me wrong. Jeremy was a good boy, a kind boy. But he also had a temper. Most of the time, you wouldn't know it, but if somebody wronged him, there was going to be hell to pay. I remember, once, a boy in our neighbourhood came up behind him and pushed him off a wall. We were all down by the creek at the time, Jeremy and his friend James. Always James, never Jim or Jimmy; mother's orders. And me, of course, tagging along as usual, not really wanted, but always happiest when I was with the big boys. Jeremy was sitting on a stretch of old broken-down wall, kind of an embankment or retaining wall by the roadside, watching James walk out into the creek in his bare feet, his pants rolled up to the knees, his hands dangling in the water, him saying how, if you were real patient and kept real still, you could catch a fish that way, and Jeremy was laughing at him, so he didn't hear when Billy Hardy came down the track with two of his cousins. Those Hardys had cousins all over the county, each one meaner and uglier than the next. It was like an infestation, like one of those plagues out of the Bible. I saw them coming and I knew right away what Billy was intending, but before I could sing out a warning, he had come up on Jeremy and given him a hard shove. Any other time, it might not have worked, but Jeremy was off balance, looking out at James and laughing, and he went straight off the wall and hit the ground. Hard. For a long time, he lay dead still, so I thought Billy had hurt him bad or maybe killed him, but Billy and the cousins didn't care, they just stood there, peering down at him and laughing fit to bust.

'It took Jeremy a while to recover his breath. As I said, he just lay there for the longest time, no expression on his face, so I thought he was unconscious. Billy and the cousins were laughing, then turning to look at James and me, like they were daring us to do something, but we didn't do a thing. James stood in the creek, the fish sliding past uncaught, and I stood at the edge of the wall, staring down, thinking my brother was dead and we were both in real trouble now. Him for dying, and me for not stopping him. Only, he wasn't dead; though what he did next was almost as bad. Billy Hardy wasn't scared of anybody, so he didn't have the good sense to get the hell out of there while the getting was good, and the cousins were the kind of boys who are brave by association, too dumb to be scared on their own account. Not that they were in any danger. It was Billy who had done the pushing, and it was Billy whose laughter rang out loudest as Jeremy got to his feet, slowly at first, then a little faster, a confused look on his face, like he was still only half there, so I guess nobody saw it coming, what happened next. I know I didn't. James had started wading in from the creek, but he was in no hurry. But then, Jeremy didn't need him. Jeremy didn't need anybody.

With his first blow, he sent Billy reeling. He didn't use his fists, he hammered down on that boy with the full weight of his forearm, like he wanted to kill him – and maybe he did. He was that intent on the business that, afterward, I couldn't look at him, there had been such hate in his face, and such a coldness to how he went about beating on Billy, raining down blows with his arms, then his fists, till the boy was on the ground. Then he lashed out with his feet, kicking the soft meat of Billy's ribs and belly before he could cover up and protect himself, the cousins edging away before one of them turned and ran, and then the others ran too, noiselessly, desperate to be gone from there, to be away from this. I don't know. I'd never seen real violence before, and I don't imagine they had. Nothing like this, anyhow. A fist fight, maybe. But nothing so cold. Nothing so – enraged. James had come up the rise, his clothes dripping, a stunned look on his face – and I could see that he was scared too, now. And still Jeremy did not stop. It seemed to go on forever – then I heard a sound, a high desperate cry that I didn't know I was making, but it *was* me, and that was what stopped him. Maybe it was the only thing that could have done. For a moment, he stood looking at the bloodied child at his feet, then he turned and gazed at me as if he was confused about something. As if he didn't know why I had screamed, or why I thought anything was wrong. I will never forget that look. Later, when he refused to talk about what he had done in France, or Korea, or any of the other places where he saw action – as the old euphemism goes – I remembered that look, and I wondered what he had done and what he had seen and whether some part of him had enjoyed it.'

All of a sudden, just as she finished speaking, I sensed something happening behind me, and I turned, startled, even a little frightened – as if her story had come to life, and her violent brother had returned from the grave, intent on doing some kind of harm – and I saw the man who had been talking to himself on the sidewalk. He looked more scared than dangerous; tall, wide-eyed, absurdly out of place in his winter coat, he closed the door behind him and glanced around the café, his expression not unlike that look you sometimes see in animals, creatures solidly inside their own bodies, gazing outward, a little curious, but also wary of the other bodies around them. This was a man who knew, as animals know, that human beings can be surprising in any number of ways and he had the air of someone who had long ago decided that it would be wrong – discourteous, even – not to be prepared for anything. Now, he was undecided and he might have stood there for a long time, if the young man behind the counter – the young man Jean had referred to as Damian – hadn't come out and, with a grace and gentleness that seemed almost unearthly, pointed to an empty seat, a few tables away from us.

'Here's your table, Arnold,' he said. 'I've been saving it for you.' The man nodded and advanced slowly, carefully, to the appointed chair. When he got there, Damian nodded, and Arnold sat down. '*Café au lait?*' Damian said. If it was a question, that was only from exaggerated courtesy, a refusal to presume. Arnold nodded, and Damian gave him an odd, congratulatory smile, as if to suggest that Arnold had made a wise choice. 'Coming up,' he said.

After he'd served Arnold, Damian went back to the counter; a moment later, though, he was heading in our direction, a coffee pot in his hand. 'Either of you ladies care for a refill?' he said. I noticed that he was rather handsome, with a thin, aquiline nose and very dark blue eyes set rather closely together, which, I remembered, was supposedly the sign of a neurasthenic personality type.

Jean nodded. 'You on your own, Damian?' she asked.

Damian shook his head and refilled her cup. 'Griffin is doing something in back,' he said. 'Something electrical.' There was just the smallest hint of a drawl in his voice.

'Annette's not here?'

Damian frowned – and I could see why someone like Arnold could trust him so easily. Everything he felt was written in his face. He was, or at least he seemed, incapable of deception. 'Her sister had an accident,' he said. 'She's gone down to Carbondale to help out.'

'What kind of accident?'

'You know, she told me, and I can't remember now,' Damian said, with an embarrassed smile. 'I think she broke her leg. Or maybe her arm. I don't know.' His smile shifted into a grin. 'I'm hopeless with details,' he said, backing away gently, his attention drawn to a tall, bearded man in a red plaid shirt – Griffin, I supposed – who had just appeared behind the counter, clutching some kind of machine part. 'Let me know if you need anything else,' he said.

Jean nodded; then, as Damian made his way back to the counter, pausing to check on Arnold as he went, she turned to me. 'Well,' she said, 'you don't get to meet Annette today. That's a pity.' She was passing it off as no big thing, but I could see that she was disappointed. 'And here I am going on for the last hour about my brother. As if it was his story we were here to tell.'

'I don't mind—'

'No,' Jean said. 'His turn comes later. I have to tell this story in the right order, or it won't make any sense. Not that

82

anything needs to make sense, I guess. But it's a comforting illusion, don't you think?'

She waited a moment for a reply, but I had nothing to say. I wasn't sure anything had ever made any sense to me. Things just happened, like scenes in a movie. Some scenes were beautiful, some were tragic, or something like it. Some just went wrong, like when somebody gets a boom in the shot, or a car flashes by, drowning out the dialogue. The scenes didn't connect, though. It was just one thing, then another.

Jean gave me a quizzical look, as if she had just read my thoughts, then she went on. 'This part of the story is about my father,' she said. 'No, it's not about him, it's about how he died. He doesn't really come into it; he's just the victim. The victim's never really part of the story, is he? It doesn't matter what he was like in life, what he ate for breakfast or how he laughed at the funny papers or why he went on mourning his first, lost, beautiful love for years, not because he didn't know there were plenty of other fish in the sea, but out of some kind of dumb perversity, or pride, or whatever it is that makes us do the really stupid things in life.' She laughed. 'Listen to me, now,' she said. 'Is there no end to all this foolishness?' She looked at her coffee cup as if she'd only just noticed it was there. 'Well, now,' she said. 'Where were we?' She thought for a moment. 'My father,' she said. 'A good man, in many ways. An honest man, up to a point, which is the best any man can do, unless he locks himself away and lets the world go to hell on its own account.' She nodded slightly, as if she were taking stock of something, testing to see if there was anything she had missed.

'We didn't call him Dad,' she said. 'We didn't call him Father. We just called him by his name, which was Thomas. I didn't wonder about that at the time, though I did later. At the funeral, I wondered when it had started, but it was just what we had always done. We called him by his name, and I always thought of him that way, like a friend, though he wasn't a friend, he was a father. As good a father as his circumstances allowed, bringing us up alone and all. He was funny, in a quiet way. When I was small, he would read to me from the funny papers. He was kind, for the most part, even when we didn't recognise the kindness, but he could be strict, too, when the occasion demanded. He was pretty hard on Jeremy, at times. Not me, though. Or not so much. I didn't know it then, but I think he let things slide because of what had happened when I was born. Because I had killed my mother. His wife. He was careful with me, maybe because he couldn't afford to take any risks. He didn't want me to know what had happened, and he was afraid, maybe, if he got angry with me about something, that it would bring back memories. I don't know. When I think about him now, I think of him as fair, serious, and, I have to admit, a little remote at times. He had things on his mind. Business. Politics. There were things he was involved in that we didn't know about. I imagine he thought that was for the best.

'As a man, he was well liked by most of the town, and hated by more than a few. He had no illusions about that, but it didn't bother him. If he had made enemies by doing what he thought was the right thing, that wasn't a matter for concern, but it wasn't a matter for pride either. He wasn't some hard-nosed moralist – he was ready to compromise if it would help a situation. He wouldn't sacrifice his sense of what was right, though. That was what got him killed, I guess. If you're known as someone who never bends, then people find ways of working around you. They despise you for making things difficult, but they accept that this is how you are made and they stop thinking of you as a person and just treat you as an unfortunate obstacle. But if you're one of those people who usually knows how to compromise, and then, for some reason that they cannot understand, you suddenly get stubborn and refuse to budge over something that matters – by which I mean, something that matters to the people with real money – then anything can happen. That's something you can't afford to forget, especially not in the South. When the world is small, the big fish can do pretty much what they please. If anybody has to pay, it won't be those people.'

She broke off suddenly, and a look of annoyance crossed her face. 'I'm not telling this right,' she said. 'I should have started at the beginning.' She closed her eyes and took a breath. 'All right,' she said. 'From the beginning.

'My father, Thomas Culver, was a lawyer, and he cared about the law. Not so much as to be totally rigid about it, but he lived by its spirit. There were things you could overlook, and principles you had to defend. I never did know all the details, but when I was almost twelve years old, and Jeremy was fifteen, he became involved in a land-purchase deal that went wrong, and that cost some important people a not insignificant sum of money. The money wasn't the worst of it, though. As I say, Thomas Culver wasn't beyond compromise, and I know, now, that he occasionally turned a blind eye to what he would have called irregularities, but he wasn't the kind of person who would stand by and see people swindled – and it seems that was what this deal amounted to. I really don't know the details and, at the time, Jeremy and I were totally, blissfully unaware of what was happening. Nothing in my father's demeanour suggested he was worried or unhappy about anything and, if he stayed late at the office a little more often than usual, or if he seemed preoccupied at times, it wasn't our business. We were children. I think I would have been happy to remain that way forever.

'So all I remember clearly now is a moment. It was a warm day in the early summer and I was ill with something serious enough to keep me from school. I had a temperature, as I recall, but it couldn't have been very serious because Dr Reynolds hadn't been called and my father was always careful, at the first sign of anything serious, to get us checked out. Of course, that could have been a sign of what was going on with him, that he didn't call the doctor. That is possible. I don't think so, though. Before he left the house that morning, he came into my room to say goodbye and that is my last vision of him – the man I had always known, standing there in the light, in his necktie and glasses, a man who almost certainly knew that trouble was coming, though I can't imagine he had any idea of the form it would take. He wasn't going to burden us with those worries, though. He was smiling and joking, testing me to see how ill I really was and he must have been satisfied that, for the moment, it didn't seem to be too serious. That was the last time I saw him, and I can still see him now. I see him in my mind's eye and I hear him saying my name as he straightens the sheets and kisses me goodbye. And I had no reason to believe that anything bad was going to happen, but I remember thinking how much I loved him that day, and I'm glad now that I had that thought, because it showed in my face, when I said goodbye – it showed in my face and Thomas knew it. I didn't say anything, but he knew.

'I didn't see what happened later. Unlike my brother, who should not have been there. I wasn't a witness – and nobody told me anything more than the bare facts afterward. So I don't know how I can picture it all so clearly. The shooting,

86

I mean. I see the shooting, which is impossible. Sometimes I think I made it up from a book, or a movie. I created a scenario, I made up a story and, now, I see it all, just as it must have happened. Only I didn't see it. Jeremy saw it. He shouldn't have done – it was one of those chance events that, usually, wouldn't matter very much. He would have been in trouble for skipping school, but that would have been all. Nobody knows why he changed his plans that day, because nobody ever thought to ask. He should have been in school, but he walked into town instead and when he saw our father leave his office and head off down Vine Street on foot, he must have taken it into his head to follow him. Jeremy always had something of the spy about him and he would have been curious, seeing our father out on the street without his briefcase in the middle of the morning – that wasn't usual, though there had to be a reasonable explanation. My brother, having nothing better to do, decided to play detective.

'It wasn't till much later that he told me everything he witnessed that day. How our father left his office, like he was just out for a stroll, and headed south, away from any place he would have been expected to have business, to a house on the corner of Ashland and Vine. That wasn't a bad neighbourhood, as such, but it wasn't a place where people had much to do with fancy lawyers and Jeremy was surprised when the door of that particular house opened – our father didn't even have to knock, it was like whoever was inside had been watching for him – and he stepped quickly inside. Jeremy didn't see who it was that let him in, but something about the house, the setting, the time of day – *something* – held him there and he waited, and watched, till our father came out. At first, he just stood on the corner, where anybody passing by could have seen him – though nobody passed by that he knew. Then, when it became clear that he was in for a long wait, he crossed to the other side of the road and took up a position in the shade of a French oak, where he wouldn't be so conspicuous.

'And maybe that was a mistake. Maybe, if he had been more conspicuous, the man who shot our father would have seen him, and maybe, if he had, he wouldn't have parked his truck a few yards from the junction, just as the courthouse clock struck two, then got out and walked quickly toward that house on the corner of Ashland and Vine, as if he knew exactly when my father would leave. That man's name was Arthur Brigstock. He was the dumbest person in town, but nobody ever suspected he was anything worse than mean. That's Arthur Brigstock, people would say. He talks a lot, but that's all it is. Talk. Nobody suspected he was dangerous. Nobody even began to imagine him capable of shooting a man twice at point-blank range, of looking into his face and watching him die. Not until he did exactly that, on a bright summer's day, on the corner of Ashland and Vine. Ashland and Vine, Ashland and Vine, Ashland and Vine. The words sing in my head, constantly. Like a curse.

'Of course, everybody guessed that someone had put him up to it, but nobody said anything. The men who ran that town put him up to it, and he was so happy to have been chosen by them that he didn't even begin to see any larger plan. He was too dumb. Thomas knew who he was, and what kind of man he was, and I imagine, in the split second he recognised that it was Brigstock blocking his way, even before he saw the gun, he would have known that he was lost. He used to say that talking could make all the difference – if you can get a man talking, then he'd be less likely to do something stupid, but Brigstock wasn't someone you could talk to. He must have thought he had some pretty important friends that day, and he must have felt pretty big himself, doing their bidding. He got close, do you see? A man like that, it's all he ever wants his whole life, to get close to the power. To have the masters look kindly upon him, even if it's only for a moment. Later, when he'd played the part allotted to him, those powerful friends hung him out to dry.

'It all happened very quickly, so quickly, Jeremy said, that he didn't really believe it. It was as if there had been some mistake, as if the world had tilted slightly, but just for a moment and, once it got righted again, everything would be reversed, and go back to how it should have been all along. Of course, Jeremy saw it all from where he was standing: Brigstock walking from his truck with his hands by his side in an odd, awkward manner, our father leaving the house at exactly that moment – Jeremy was still wondering what he was doing there, and he wondered if Brigstock was something to do with it. Only that didn't seem possible because there was no reason for our father to have anything to do with such a person. The woman was the real mystery, though. A tall, dark-haired woman, standing just inside the doorway to the house, watching our father go, and it seemed strange, the way she was standing, the way she was looking at him. It seemed odd. Not – businesslike, was the word Jeremy used, but what he meant, maybe, was that it didn't seem appropriate, because our father didn't have any reason to be there, in the middle of a working day, and he certainly didn't have any business being there with a woman. That was in Jeremy's head when he heard Brigstock speak – or maybe he didn't speak, not words at least, but he made a sound, so that our father turned toward him, and Jeremy thought he was smiling, though he wouldn't have been smiling at this man. Because he really did know everybody in that town. Thomas Culver knew who they were and where they came from, what their failings were, who they owed money to, who they had cheated out of property or land, and he must have thought he knew all there was to know about Arthur Brigstock. Besides, at that exact moment, when Brigstock spoke or made a sound, he raised his left hand and our father would have seen the gun. But then, it all happened in a blur. What should have been a series of moments, each with its own logic, became one long moment where it was impossible to separate one thing from another – the smile on our father's face as he turned away from the woman, the recognition in his eyes when he saw what Brigstock was doing, the gun going off, the silence and then a voice – no, more than one voice, but my brother couldn't have separated out what his voice did then and what the woman's voice did. Brigstock didn't say anything. He was working quickly now, and I guess even he was smart enough to know that he had to do what he had been told to do with what all the old books used to call *despatch*. That cruel word. After he fired – two shots, quickly but deliberately and at point-blank range, the first into our father's chest and the other, a few seconds later, into his head – after he'd done what he had to do, that stupid, worthless man turned and walked back to his truck and drove away. The gun was never found, but that didn't matter. There had been two witnesses and even though they were just a woman and a boy, they were enough. Naturally, we didn't know until later who the woman was. So we didn't know about the scandal for a long time. I didn't know for months, and I might never have known, if Jeremy hadn't given in to my nagging at him and told me the whole truth, but it seems that *the scandal* was all that mattered to the good people of our little town. A cold-blooded murder had been committed, and all anybody talked about was Ashland and Vine. What was a man like Thomas Culver doing in that part of town? He didn't have any business there. But then he did have business there, they would mutter wherever they gathered together. Oh, yes, he had business there, all right. In fact, he had some very delicate business with a certain Miss Catherine Bassett.'

Jean broke off and looked out across the room. I thought she was about to break down, to show some emotion, but her face remained still, touched with nothing more than the thoughtfulness that comes when, after giving some kind of factual account, or statement of evidence, someone looks back over what they have said, to be sure they have left out nothing of real significance. Finally, she spoke. 'Cliché number one. Not everything is as it seems. First we thought our father could do no wrong. Then people were calling him a philandering hypocrite – and that was just the polite folks. But he wasn't either of those things. He was just a man. Which is also a cliché, because there's no such thing. If there was, then Brigstock was just a man too, and the men who sent him there that day were just men.'

'What happened after that?' I said. I wasn't sure what I was asking, though, or about whom.

She looked at me and shook her head. 'What happened?'

'To you. To—'

'We went away. They sold our house, all my father's assets, it was all put in trust and we moved to Virginia.' She thought for a moment. 'Jeremy had to go back and give evidence, and Brigstock had to go to prison for a while, but they had bought him a decent lawyer who used *the scandal* to portray him as a good deal better than he was. Seems he was related to Miss Bassett in some way, and that he'd shot Thomas to protect her good name. Something of that nature. Nobody else was involved, he said, it had been his idea. As for Miss Bassett, she locked herself away in that house on Ashland and Vine and wasn't much seen again. When somebody tossed a brick through her window, she'd have the window repaired.' She looked at me directly for the first time since she had concluded her story. 'After that,' she said. 'I wasn't a girl any more. Not because they killed my father, but because of what they said. How they lied about what he was doing on Ashland and Vine that day. I do understand that it wasn't the usual kind of lie, but it was a lie, nevertheless. Yes, he was there to see Miss Bassett. But it wasn't like the story they were telling – and I know now that it was this lie that finally ended my childhood, a few months later, when Jeremy got tired of me nagging at him to tell, and gave me the full story, from the shooting to all the things people said in court, and he did tell me the whole story, every detail, because he had been hurt and angry for so long and because I was . . .'

She looked at me, but there was no expression in her eyes that I could interpret as hurt, or anger, or betrayal. Still, I knew what she had been about to say. Jeremy had told her everything because he couldn't carry it by himself any more and, now that they were far from home and alone together in a strange house, she was the only one he could hurt with this story sufficiently to make it real. He would have given details – and he would have explained all the ugly, harsh facts of what his little sister didn't understand, not because he wanted to, but because he could not have done otherwise. He had no choice. 'I'm sorry,' I said, knowing how empty that was and, at the same time, knowing she could read what I would have said, had there been any way of saying it.

She nodded. 'I guess that's why I like having Christina around,' she said. 'She reminds me of something. Not a younger version of me – I wasn't like her at all – but . . . The condition. Being a child. Being a girl. There are whole rooms of girlhood that I never got to see. I don't know what they are like. All I know is that I missed them.' She reached out and touched the back of my hand, very gently. Her own hand was cold, in spite of the warm day. 'We all have to mourn,' she said. 'The real trick is not to throw everything else away.' She let go of my hand and got to her feet slowly. 'Will you walk back with me a way?' she said. 'I could do with the company.' I stood up. Arnold had gone and Damian was in the back somewhere, talking to someone. Jean nodded. 'Cliché number two,' she said, then she thought again and smiled. 'Well,' she said, 'let's leave cliché number two for next time.'

FIRST AND SECOND LOVES

When I got back to the apartment, I found a note on the dining table. It was the usual Laurits scrawl, barely legible, but I could make out enough to know that he'd be away for several days. Naturally, he didn't say where he was going, or why, but that didn't bother me. By then I'd gotten used to his sudden disappearances, and anyhow, his absences gave me space to think my own thoughts – or rather, to remember that I had ideas and projects of my own, things I wanted to pursue and never did, not because Laurits applied any pressure or persuasion to work with him instead, but because I was too scared of failing even to begin work on them. I suspected, even then, that the story project that had so fortuitously connected me with Jean Culver was not much more than one of his games – and later I had those suspicions confirmed, though not in the way I would have expected. I guess that, when I had time to think about it, I was grateful to him for having sent me walking from door to door in the suburbs, though I also knew that I couldn't be sure of his motives. Maybe he'd just wanted to give me something to do. Maybe he'd wanted me to have to listen to someone else, and not just the voice in my own head, stupidly going over an old story that I was supposed to be done with. Maybe he had just been using me as one of his subjects.

When I was alone, though, I did think about my own ideas. The stories I wanted to tell. The films I wanted to make. I wasn't so naïve that I didn't realise that part of the reason I was living with Laurits was that he was doing what I wanted to do, or something like it, and I guess I thought, or imagined at least, that something of his energy – something of his mystery – would be transferred to me, through some kind of osmosis. I had no wish to imitate him, and I wasn't his protégée – he wouldn't have taken on the role of teacher any more than I was willing to be his, or anybody's, pupil. But then, maybe that was the problem. I didn't want to be anybody's student. I just wanted something to happen. Of course, I did assignments and got reasonable results, but those assignments were just a kind of work. They tested what we had learned, technically, in the abstract. The programme I was on was considered to be quite innovative, even unique in its way, but I was, apparently, missing all that. I wanted to make real films, not assignments. In my own mind, no matter what the grades indicated, I wasn't learning anything very useful.

I remember Laurits' first film. At the time, I didn't tell him I'd seen it. Because it was just after we met, I thought he would suspect me of studying up on him, which would look like prying. That first piece of work was a simple proposition, but then, most of what Laurits did seemed simple, on the surface at least. What he had done was to make six short films of things in motion – a landscape seen from a passing train, a horse running, two girls in perfect whites playing tennis on a dirt court, a flock of birds wheeling around an old pier, a young woman climbing an ornate spiral staircase in some old European city, a train, possibly the same train as in the first sequence, moving through what seemed to be the same landscape, which he then alternated with six films of five people – and one dog – sleeping in various places. Telling it like this makes it sounds even simpler than it was – and it certainly doesn't sound moving, or inspiring, or even interesting. But it was what he had done with each of the sequences that moved me. Because it *was* moving. I can't explain why, all I can say is what he did – and maybe that is why I can't learn from him. When I look at his films, I am only an audience, but what he wanted, from me, from anyone, was a possible collaborator. Or maybe a co-conspirator. I can say that there was something about the way he shot each film that heightened its effect, though that isn't saying very much. I could say, for example, that the landscape seen from the train is only glimpsed through the gaps in a damaged fence or barrier, so the eye is constantly working to make things out and whoever is watching is constantly aware of losing things, of having objects flash by unheeded while trying to identify something else. Or I could say that the film in which the girl who had been climbing the spiral staircase and is now asleep in a chair is at once touching and erotic, but I can't say why the technique he uses in each example should have made any difference. All I knew was that I wouldn't have thought to do any of the things he had done. I would have made it more elaborate. I would have tried too hard. The short films I had made for assignments, like the three independent pieces of work I had started and abandoned, all had the same quality, which was the exact opposite of what happened in Laurits' short films. I was asking the audience to look, I was trying to win something. Laurits commanded attention by not caring about it. He was making these films for some other reason than getting people to look at them. Maybe it was just that he was so bored with the world outside his own imagination that he had to do something to occupy himself.

It was still warm but, by the time I met Jean Culver at the door of Sacred Grounds to hear about Cliché Number Two, the clouds had rolled in and the rain was coming down hard and quick and surprising, the scent of it sweet and grassy after the long dry days. Jean was dressed in a thin raincoat over the usual work clothes, and I felt a little foolish to have come out in just a shirt and jeans.

As I hurried inside, my hair spotted with raindrops, my sleeves rimmed with damp, I noticed that the art display had changed. Now, where the snowy urban landscapes had been, a series of brightly coloured photo-abstracts lined the walls, creating a kind of carnival atmosphere in this space that, a week ago, had seemed so cool and classical, like a tiny island of winter in the summer heat. As Jean headed for what was obviously her usual table by the window, I stopped to look at a picture that caught my eye, an extreme close-up of a piece of graffiti, bold sprays of paint in powder blue suggesting a face, but where the eyes should have been, two black holes from which a pair of sad cartoon eyes gazed out, as if something, or someone, was trapped inside the wall, something live and capable of suffering, sealed into the concrete forever. I looked at the next picture. On the surface, the mood was completely different, all soft, fuzzed peach and terracotta tones where the first had been blues and greys, but the theme was, if not exactly the same, at least similar. The image was of another wall, but this time it had been taken from farther away, possibly through a zoom lens. The wall was old, grainy and dotted, here and there, with deep, rust-coloured holes. At the exact centre of the image was a high narrow window with an ornate wrought-iron balcony, behind which the word BEAUTÉ had been sign-painted in crisp black lettering on an ivory-white surface. It was a fairly crude piece of work and maybe a little obvious – Laurits would have found its earnestness amusing – but there was something touching about it, the word reduced to mere typography in its iron cage, the very idea of beauty called into question.

Jean was watching me, waiting. I took the seat opposite her, the same as last time, but there was nobody on the street. 'What do you think?' she said.

'Hm?'

'The exhibition,' she said. 'What do you think?'

'It's – interesting,' I said.

'Ah. Interesting.'

'I didn't see it all,' I said, annoyed at myself for going on the defensive. 'I mean . . . I like the ones I saw. They're a little naïve, but there's something . . . eerie about them.' I saw that she was watching me closely, that she really was interested in what I thought. But why? What did it matter? I glanced up at the picture nearest us, a riot of reds and greens, more graffiti strafed across a whitewashed wall, but I couldn't make out the details. 'Why do you ask?' I said.

She didn't speak for a moment and I wondered if something I said had offended her in some way. Finally, she looked up at the red and green image. 'Annette made these,' she said, simply.

'Annette?'

'I told you about her,' she said. 'The woman who owns this place.'

'Ah.' I turned and looked back at the powder-blue face. 'I have to look at them properly,' I said. 'I do like that one.' I pointed.

Jean nodded. 'Have a look around,' she said. 'I'll order the coffee.'

I spent the next fifteen minutes looking at the exhibition. There were eighteen photographs in all, each of a wall, or some detail of a wall – a piece of graffiti, the blank stare of a window in an abandoned house, even a simple crack, running from the top to the bottom of the photograph, at once ominous and strangely beautiful, with its suggestion of ruin. Technically, none of these pictures was much more than competent, and yet, for reasons I couldn't have explained, they made me ask questions. They proposed something; they interrogated. Why are ruins beautiful? What do we mean when we talk about beauty? Is a wall a shelter or a prison? Maybe that sounds pretentious – Laurits would have thought so – but this was what I was thinking as I walked around the room, slightly self-conscious, aware of the other customers, and of Jean, who was talking to a woman at the counter, ordering our drinks and some kind of cake. One image I recognised right away: it was a wall at the old slaughterhouse, where Laurits was shooting part of his new film. In Annette's picture, the focus was on a simple, ferrous-coloured stain on a pale-green surface, a stain that suggested blood, but could just as easily have been rust. That was what I had thought at the slaughterhouse, too. Unless you were aware of the history, anything could be anything, but when you knew, you interpreted, you jumped to conclusions, some of them true, maybe, some false. There was no way of knowing. But then, was that what Annette had been after, when she took this photograph? Or was I simply overlaying Laurits' view of the world on to her work? How could I know? I couldn't ask her, it was my job to make sense of all this. She wasn't supposed to explain it to me.

When Jean resumed her seat, I went back to the table and sat down. A moment later, the woman she had been talking to appeared. She didn't say anything as she set out the coffees and two identical slices of rich dark cake. Jean let her finish her task before she spoke. 'Annette, this is Kate,' she said. She sounded absurdly formal. 'She's been admiring your pictures.'

Annette smiled and I realised that, when Jean had described her as pretty, she hadn't been doing her justice. This woman was beautiful. There are types of beauty, and there are grey areas between beautiful and attractive, or pretty, or sexy, but in this case, there could be no doubt. Annette reminded me a little of the young Ava Gardner, the Ava Gardner of *The Hucksters*, say, before the studio system, not knowing what it had, decided to bury her natural beauty in mere glamour. She was medium height, with thick dark hair pulled back into a loose ponytail and rather pale skin. She wasn't wearing make-up. Her blouse had a dark stain on the cuff, her black jeans were faded and slightly dusty with what I assumed was flour. She was one of those women who have no idea of how beautiful they are – and I suspected that nobody had ever seriously pointed it out to her. Maybe some drunk at a party, blind with abstract longing and Dutch courage, someone easy to ignore, but for anybody else, her beauty would have been intimidating, something it would have seemed improper even to mention, like a scar, or a birthmark. 'I just started with a camera,' she said. 'Before this, I was painting.'

'Kate's an artist too,' Jean said, her eyes twinkling. She was enjoying herself, which seemed both unfair, because in one way we hardly knew one another and, at the same time, flattering because, after the story of her father's murder, I felt somehow included in her world.

'Oh, really?' Annette stopped being polite and looked at me with interest.

I shook my head. 'I'm not, really,' I said. 'I'm studying at the college, working toward making my own films. You know how it is.' It wasn't lost on me, any more than it was on Jean, and probably Annette, how inane I sounded.

'Wow, films,' Annette said – which redeemed the situation somewhat. Maybe we could have a competition to see who could come out with the dumbest item of small talk. 'I've been thinking about getting into that.' She smiled and dipped her head. Even on a first acquaintance, I knew this was one of her fallback gestures. It wasn't conscious or artful, so it was perfectly charming. 'Well,' she said, 'I'll let you enjoy your cake.' She turned to Jean. 'I altered the recipe slightly.' She was assured now, back on safe, practical ground. 'See what you think.' She glanced back to me. 'Pleasure to meet you, Kate,' she said.

'You too,' I said.

We took our time, savouring the coffee, enjoying the quiet and the sound of the rain at the window. Now I understood why she always sat here, in the window. It wasn't the street that interested her, it was the weather. Finally, she broke the silence. 'I was going to tell you about Cliché Number Two today,' she said. She gave me an enquiring look, and I nodded to show that I remembered. It seemed to me she was treading carefully, not wanting to recall too much of her last story. 'It's about love,' she said. 'I know, I know. There are so many clichés about love, it's hard to know which to choose, but this one's a little subtler than some of the others.' She smiled, happily it seemed, like someone relishing the chance to play a favourite game. 'Would you like to take a guess at what it is?'

I shook my head. 'Um . . . Well, I suppose *love makes the world go round* is too obvious.'

'That would be gravity,' she said.

'How about *love is never having to say you're sorry.*'

'Nonsense.'

I thought for a moment. I wanted to find something good, something that might surprise her. 'All right,' I said. 'What about this: *Perhaps everything that frightens us is, in its deepest essence, something helpless that wants our love.*'

'Goodness,' she said. 'Who said that?'

'Rainer Maria Rilke.'

'Well, well, well,' she said, appreciatively. 'It's a good one, and I'm going to have to think about it. But it's not Cliché Number Two. In fact it may not be a cliché at all.'

'So what is Cliché Number Two.'

'It's slightly different, but here goes.' She took a moment to consider. 'A French writer once said: *Ce n'est pas le premier amour qui compte, ni le second, ni le dernier. C'est celui qui a mêlé deux destinées dans la vie commune.*' She smiled. 'In some ways, it might not be a real cliché, but if you're someone like me, well . . .'

'I don't understand French,' I said. I had just consumed a sliver of Annette's home-baked cake. It was very good. Now I was wondering what element of the recipe she had altered. I still felt I ought to seem annoyed with Jean for setting me up, though I knew she hadn't done it to embarrass me, but to see Annette blush when I praised her work. Which I hadn't actually done. Though praise had been implied. And she had, in fact, blushed, just a little. Did Ava Gardner ever blush? Maybe early on. Not later, though. *Femmes fatales* don't blush.

Jean feigned surprise. 'Well, apart from Rilke, it would seem that they don't teach you anything at that college of yours, do they?' she said.

'Not much,' I said.

'Still, Rilke makes up for a good deal.' She was quiet for a moment, finding the right translation in her head. 'It's not the first love that counts, nor the second, nor the last. It's the one that has mixed two destinies in – how shall we translate *la vie commune*? We can't just say shared life, or everyday life, or—'

'The common life?' I said, already thinking that this was just too easy.

She nodded. 'Yes,' she said. 'You could say the common life. The part of life we share with others, as opposed to—'

'The chambers of our imagery,' I said.

She regarded me with some surprise. 'So,' she said. 'Rilke *and* Ezekiel.'

I didn't tell her it was Laurits who had supplied the Bible quotation, but then I never talked to her about Laurits at all. They were different worlds.

'The chambers of our imagery,' she said, approvingly. 'And – *la vie commune*. They always seem to be out of balance, don't they?'

'Well, yes,' I said. I didn't need any persuading on that point. 'But what does all that have to do with love?'

'Well, I'm the wrong person to ask that question,' she said. 'There was never any place for my kind in *la vie commune*, not when it still mattered.' She smiled, but there was no sadness in her face and I decided, with shameful presumption, that all of that was history to her now. 'But I've been thinking about how fervently I used to believe in the idea of a first love. How nothing else could ever replace that. And it can't, but then it's not a question of replacing something, is it?' She looked at me. I shrugged. I could honestly have said, then, that I had no idea what she was talking about. 'I used to be such a purist,' she said. 'Love once, love forever. Otherwise, how could it have been true the first time?' She laughed, and it was clear that she was laughing at herself. I wondered if, maybe, she was talking to herself too. 'Now, I know it doesn't matter how many times you fall in love, because you're always falling in love with the same person. The first, the second, the last, they are all different, and all the same.' She looked at me, as if to say, had I understood her yet. 'We should go on falling in love, again and again, right to the end, no matter how hopeless it seems. No matter, at my age, how hopeless it *is*. But then, at my age, nothing needs to be requited. It's just the fact of feeling it at all that shows – what do they call it in hostage situations?'

'Hostage situations?'

'Yes,' she said. 'In hostage situations, when the kidnappers have to show that the person is still—'

'Proof of life?'

'Exactly. Proof of life.' She nodded, apparently satisfied, though whether it was about finding the right phrase, or something else entirely, I couldn't have said. I used my fork to break off another tiny slice of Annette's cake. For a moment, Jean Culver seemed far away, and I remembered again that she was an old woman.

'She's very beautiful, wouldn't you say?' she said suddenly.

'Excuse me?'

'Annette,' she said. 'She's very – beautiful.'

I forced down the morsel of cake I was eating. I couldn't believe how stupid I had been right up until that very moment. 'I can't say that I noticed.'

Jean knew I was pretending, but she didn't care. 'I come here for the excellent coffee. But most of all, I come here to see her.' She took a sip of her coffee and sat back. 'I would say she reminds me of someone, but it's not really like that . . .'

I nodded. I thought I understood. First and second loves. Last, hopeless loves. It was all love, in the end. 'Who does she remind you of?' I said.

She came back to me from somewhere. She had been gone, just for a moment. 'I think it's time for the next instalment of the story,' she said. 'But first, let's order some more of this delicious cake.'

She was at the counter a long time, talking to Annette and a very tall, sandy-haired boy who had just come in out of the rain. The boy, who was maybe seventeen or eighteen, had the look of a high-school basketball player, long-limbed and slender, but not gangly, not awkward the way tall men can be at that age. There was, in fact, a surprising grace in the way he held himself, his body poised and very still, as if anchored to the ground, his hands in constant unselfconscious motion when he spoke. I could see that he knew Jean, but he couldn't hide the fact that, whatever he was saying – it was clearly amusing – was mainly addressed to Annette. Of course. Like Jean, he had a crush on her, and he was here, damp from the rain but completely oblivious, because he couldn't keep away. It was quite touching, watching them together, the old woman and the college athlete – if he was even college age – brought together by their common infatuation with a woman who seemed to have no idea of what was going on. Or did she? I studied Annette's face, but I couldn't see anything there, other than the usual interest a person shows for people she knows in passing and likes, but who mean no more to her than that.

When Jean finally returned to our table, she was smiling. 'That's Alan Swann,' she said. 'He's something of a local legend.'

'Basketball.'

She nodded. 'Yes,' she said. 'You know him?'

I laughed. 'No,' I said. 'It's just . . . Well, it's obvious.'

She looked back to where Alan Swann stood waiting for his coffee – to go, it seemed. 'I suppose you are right,' she said. 'Though he could have been a brilliant young Classics scholar. Or a poet, maybe. You shouldn't always go by looks.'

I laughed. 'I don't think so,' I said. 'Besides, you don't get to be a local legend for that kind of thing. It has to be sports, or something that makes money.'

That last remark had come out more cynical, or maybe more bitter, than I had intended, and we sat for a moment in silence. A young man, not Damian, brought our second helping of cake – Annette was still talking to the local legend – and Jean used her fork to break off a large piece, placed it carefully in her mouth and considered the new recipe's effectiveness. I was waiting for the story, but she showed no sign of wanting to begin. It was possible, of course, that she had forgotten about it altogether while she was talking. But I didn't think so. What was becoming clear to me was that Jean Culver lived by a different clock than the one that ran my life. Hers was slower, less impatient, more forgiving. I wondered what she was thinking, as she sat there, occasionally breaking off morsels of Annette's cake with her fingers. 'You've read a lot,' I said.

She shot me a quizzical look, as if she wondered why I would be so foolish as to break such a perfect silence, then she gave what could have been a genuinely rueful smile. 'I've been alive for a long time,' she said.

'Well, maybe, but—'

'I was lucky,' she said. 'I learned early that you do what you can with the things you are given. In my case, a very unusual public library and an acre of greenhouses.'

'Greenhouses?'

She seemed to remember what we were here for then. The story. The explanation of her second cliché. She drew herself up, took a sip of coffee, made a face. Then she began.

'After my father was killed, we went to stay with Aunt Charlotte and her husband, Avery,' she said. 'Avery's family had been growing apples and pears and stone fruits for three generations, before Avery expanded into the flower business.' Her face lit up. 'Frangipane,' she said.

'Excuse me?'

'The new ingredient,' she said. 'Frangipane. Just a hint.' She watched as I took another sliver and tried it. I couldn't detect anything out of the ordinary, but then I wasn't sure what frangipane tasted of. Frangipane, I supposed. To keep her going, though, I nodded, and she continued. 'Later, Jeremy told me it never happened, but I still have a memory of being alone in our house for days after the funeral. Jeremy says Aunt Charlotte came and stayed with us for a week before we moved to Virginia to live with her and Uncle Avery, but I remember us alone, cooking our own food, lying awake in bed at night, not even trying to sleep, listening to the owls hunting along the river. I remember the quiet of those nights and I remember the sad bewilderment of the days, when we would stay clear of each other for hours, not wanting to be in the same room because – well, I didn't know about Jeremy, but when I was alone, if I was alone for long enough, I forgot

Thomas was dead. I would stand in the hallway or at the top of the stairs, listening for him coming home at the usual time, his voice calling my name through the still, echoey rooms. I would lie on my bed, staring up at the ceiling, and it felt as if time was just about to stop, as if, at any moment, nothing would ever happen again. I remember this, even now, but Jeremy says it never happened. Aunt Charlotte came and moved into my mother's old room for a week. Then, after the funeral, she took us away from that place forever.

'She wasn't our real aunt. She was a cousin of my father's, someone I didn't even know existed when she turned up at our door, summoned by my father's partner at law, Joel Crane. Apparently, there had been an instruction in Thomas' will that said, in the event of anything happening to him before we were old enough to look after ourselves, we should go to Aunt Charlotte. I remember how strange it felt, thinking that I had a guardian, like some character in an old novel. In fact, my father had dealt with several such cases – they were not so uncommon – but it had never seemed to be something that could happen in my world. To have a guardian. To have everything I would one day own held in trust by people I didn't even know. I'd never imagined any of that – and I guess Aunt Charlotte and Uncle Avery, not to mention their four children, had never thought about it very seriously either.

'So I'm not blaming them, now, and I didn't blame them then, when I say that they weren't really family to us. They were good people, it was just that they weren't my people. And we weren't theirs, either. By happenstance, we had fallen into their world and they were in no way prepared for that. Somebody once said that home is the place where, if you have to go there, they have to take you in. It's not a very appealing notion, is it? Giving somebody a home shouldn't have to be an obligation.' The smallest flicker of an apologetic expression crossed her face. She had decided to assume that I knew that the quote about home was from Robert Frost, but she wasn't sure. Ezekiel could have been a fluke. 'But what choice did we have,' she said. 'What choice did any of us have? Charlotte had to take us in, and we had to make the best of it. Everyone did and we all did our best. We had Christmas, birthdays, Thanksgiving, just like any family. We had things we didn't discuss, like most families. Of course we never spoke about what had happened that fine summer's day on Ashland and Vine and, in time, we almost succeeded in locking it away at the back of our heads – even Jeremy, who had suddenly turned into someone I didn't recognise, a quiet, very gentle, rather bookish young man, somewhat remote with others, but always very kind and careful with me. The big surprise, though, was how studious he had become. He spent his whole life in books, he kept up with all the latest developments in science – he had a particular interest in physics – and he taught himself, first French, then German. He was quite the scholar.

'As for me – well, I read a good deal too, but I was never systematic about it. Some things I did, to start with, because Jeremy was doing them. Not so much the science, but I did learn French and I got to practise with one of the women who worked for Avery and Charlotte. But I was more practically minded, and – well, I have to be grateful to my guardians, who had to take me in, for they were the ones who introduced me to my trade. Or at least, they got me started on the right path, anyhow. I had never had the least notion of what I wanted to do with myself, before I moved to Virginia. I had no reason to think about it, really, but there's nothing like being an orphan to focus the mind.

'Well, I might have been a tomboy back then, but I had always loved flowers. Now I saw a way of making a living with something I knew I would never tire of, and I set about learning everything I could about the floristry business, not just from Aunt Charlotte, but also from the staff who worked in the greenhouses. There were three regular women who came in, but my favourite was Eliza, who seemed to know everything there was to know about nursery practices and floristry. She was a big woman, heavy and slow on her feet, and I guess she had something wrong with her – a heart condition, or something to do with her lungs, maybe – because there were days when it was difficult for her just to breathe. Sometimes, she would disappear and Charlotte would explain that Eliza was too ill to come to work, but she didn't even think of letting her go. Eliza taught me all the tricks of the trade, how to pep up a flagging bouquet, how to make a buttonhole last that little bit longer, all the little dos and don'ts, as she called them, and she would sit with me for hours, telling me what each flower stood for. Every flower, every colour, every combination has a meaning, and even though most people don't know them, it's good to be able to tell a customer some piece of information when they are planning a party, or a wedding. It's a story, or you make it into a story, and then you connect. Every flower has its own meaning, every state has its own flower – Virginia's is the dogwood, which is very interesting to work with – even the months of the year have flowers, the way the zodiac signs have birthstones. Eliza knew every association, every lucky and unlucky combination. For instance, I still wince when I see someone taking a white-and-scarlet bouquet to a hospital because, in England, they call that arrangement "blood and bandages", and as far as I know the nurses still turn away visitors who come to their wards bearing red-and-white bouquets. Eliza told me about that superstition just a month before her final illness. A few weeks later I was visiting her in hospital, with my few stems of achillea – for health and healing – and I like to think she saw them in my hand, though she made no sign of recognising me and she died that same night. That was the end of the first real friendship I ever had, and I missed her badly for a long time. A few months later, I turned twenty-one and took control of my money and, with it, my own life. I cut myself a huge bunch of sweet peas, said goodbye to Charlotte and Avery – by then, Jeremy was in the army – and set out to make my way in the world. I didn't think of myself as a businesswoman, though, and I knew I would need help. I had to find someone who could do all the financial and administrative side of things, while I got on with the practical side – and, indirectly, that was how I met Lee.' She thought for a moment, then she took a man's wallet from her canvas bag and opened it to a small, rather grainy photograph that I could barely make out under the worn plastic covering. 'Lee was the most beautiful person I ever knew – and, outside family, she's the only person I have ever really loved.'

I looked closely at the picture. It showed a woman in a plaid shirt and a heavy coat with a border fork in her right hand. She bore no resemblance whatsoever to Ava Gardner – or to Annette, for that matter – but it was clear that Jean was drawn to a certain type. Dark hair. Dark eyes. A certain ambiguousness about the mouth. I couldn't tell from the picture how tall Lee was, but she looked slender and rather elegant, in spite of her work clothes. Yet I would not have called her beautiful, in any conventional way – not on the basis of this image. It reminded me of how the descriptions of so many great beauties of the past jar so often with their photographs, of a feeling I always had, looking at those images, that something was missing. A trace of vitality, a miraculous *élan vital* that commentators were always remarking upon, that simply didn't show up in the photographs. The June who drove Henry Miller and possibly Anaïs Nin to distraction was, in the various portraits I had seen of her, just another woman, while almost nothing of Zelda Fitzgerald's supposed beauty comes through in the many images that were made during her heyday. I handed the wallet back to Jean. 'She's very beautiful,' I said.

Jean put the picture away quickly. 'Oh, this doesn't really show her at her best,' she said. 'But photographs never do, do they?' She gave me an odd searching look and I had the impression again that she could read my thoughts. 'Apparently, they don't really capture the soul after all. Anyhow, this one is a bit misleading, but it's the only picture that survived. In reality, she had very little to do with the garden side of the business, though it couldn't have prospered without her. She was the one who built up our client base. That side of things was a mystery to me, but she seemed capable of anything. For example, in 1945, before she joined me, I had just one delivery car, and it wasn't even a proper van, it was just the back seat of my 62 Coupe. Three years later we had four vans on the road, delivering not just flowers and plants, but all kinds of other things. It was her idea to build up the American Garden side of the business. That was what we called it, then. The American Garden. We would do instant transformations of any plot of land, no matter how bare, no matter how unpromising. We created two-day oases of green for garden parties and instant dream gardens for people who had just moved into new homes in the suburbs. Anybody can do that now, but it was new then. And very soon, we were what everybody wanted to be – a success story. Yet we were just a company of hard-working women acting out the script we had been given. Lee and I paid our employees higher than average and we made a point of employing women only, though we didn't advertise the fact. Women drivers had fewer accidents. Women nursery workers and gardeners worked harder because they had gotten it into their heads that they had to be better than the men if they wanted to succeed.

Everything was going according to script, and I didn't doubt that this was the way to live a good life. The war had taken its toll on everybody, but it had provided business opportunities and a pool of skilled female workers, and when it was over, there was a new mood of prosperity and home improvement that we cashed in on. We had a broad client base. I can't say I really understood what any of this meant, mind you, but Lee did. Even if I hadn't fallen in love with her, she would have been the one defining person in my life, the business partner who gave me the confidence to prosper.

'Well, as I said before, I was always considered a tomboy. Which is fine when you're ten, but not when you are twenty and no boyfriend in sight. Not that I ever thought of myself as different, growing up, it was just a name people used. I didn't think anything of it. Or not until I realised that I had acquired a euphemism.' She smiled sadly. 'Which I did, of course, quite early on, though to begin with I didn't understand what people meant by it. And when I did – well, I resented that word pretty badly. Tomboy – even now, I wonder about the etymology. But back then, the real question, for me, was what it all meant. Had I been shaped by how people saw me, by what they called me? Or had they sensed some quality that was always there, but hadn't yet come to the surface? Because to tell the truth, until I met Lee I had no idea that I was so very different. I wasn't attracted to men, but then I didn't know any men who were so horribly attractive, and I assumed that was that. Maybe, one day, I'd chance upon the right fellow and fulfil all the expectations other people seemed to have of me. Which was a little rich, considering I had no expectations of other people. I just wanted to get on with my life and be left alone to work it all out for myself. And after I met Lee, I worked things out very quickly. The trouble was, she didn't. She didn't work it out until things had become very complicated and, even then, it wasn't as straightforward for her. She did find men attractive, and she wanted the usual things – a family, mostly – so when John Cameron happened along, straight out of the army and full of pep and vinegar, as the politer folks used to say, she thought she had found a passable version of Mr Right. My, that man had a high opinion of himself. Unfortunately so did everybody else.

'He met Lee at a client's party – she was the one who did most of the socialising, of course, and some of our clients were quite well off, which was seductive, in its own way, if you were susceptible to such things. I wasn't. By then, we were doing very well, but I still drove the same old car, and I dressed the way I had always dressed, the way I still dress now, more or less and, to be frank, there wasn't much that money could show me. All I wanted was to be left alone to get on with building up the business. And my reading. Books had always been my escape from the world, though I liked to think they were more than just an escape. It all went together – books, the gardens, walks on the lake shore. There was a place Lee and I used to go sometimes, a little inlet that nobody else knew about – well, not for a while, anyhow – and we would drive out with a picnic and spend whole days there. Evening would fall over the water, and we would sit listening to the tide, watching the seabirds fly home. That was when I was happiest, when it was just us, two friends sitting quietly, listening to the world. As far as I was concerned, we had everything we needed. Then John Cameron showed up and everything was different.

'I have to admit, I didn't take him seriously at first. He seemed so full of himself, I thought Lee would see right through him. He was a businessperson of some kind, I never really understood what he did, but it had to do with transportation, some company he had inherited from his father. Like us, he had done well after the war ended, but he was very different from us, socially. He had some kind of style, I have to give him that. He had taste. He started taking Lee to society events and she liked being in those circles. I don't know about the sex, or if there even was sex. By the time Cameron appeared on the scene, she was twenty-eight, very beautiful – and mysteriously unmarried. She had her own business, but that seemed to amuse him more than anything else. He thought she was clever for working it all out, was puzzled by my existence and pretended to think I was just one of the gardeners, but I don't think he ever suspected we were – well, what were we? I guess I've held off on that, but that's not for any big dramatic reason. The fact is, I wish there was more to tell. Before Cameron, we had been occasional – and I mean very occasional – lovers for a few months, but the truth was, we were both quite awkward and maybe a little shy, too. Which would have been good, if we could have gone on and taken things slowly, finding out who we were and what we wanted. The real problem, though, was that she was afraid of a future that didn't hold all of the things it was supposed to hold. And she wanted children. She didn't want to be somebody's aunt. She wanted to be a mother.

'This, for some reason, was a complete mystery to me. At the time, I don't think I had a maternal bone in my body. That might have changed later – or would it? I loved Jeremy's children. On at least one occasion, I even risked prison for Jennifer, but does love like that always have to be seen as maternal? Can't it just be love? Simon and Jennifer were my blood, after all, just as Jeremy was my blood. Ah, but I'm getting ahead of myself.' She looked at me. I have no idea what the expression on my face looked like to her, but suddenly she laughed. 'It's all right,' she said. 'Don't look so tragic. We're nowhere near the tragic part yet.'

I wasn't sure what to do then. She seemed different, almost desperate to conceal whatever her real feelings might be, behind that veil of amusement. 'Is there a tragic part?' I said.

She smiled. 'We're talking about love,' she said. 'There's always a tragic part.' Then, all of a sudden, she stood up. She looked worried, or maybe she had thought of something she didn't want to remember. I couldn't read her. 'I need some air,' she said. 'Do you mind if we go for a walk?'

'All right. But – just one thing,' I said. I didn't know, then, why it mattered but I wanted to hear her tell that common life quote again. No – I wanted to know who had said it. I wanted to know so I could look it up because it had got something moving in my head and I didn't know what it was. 'That French writer,' I said. 'What was his name?'

'Ah,' she said. 'He's not so well known. Not any more. His name was – Frangipane!'

I was confused for a moment. Then I saw Annette, who must have come back to our table while we were talking, maybe to find out what Jean thought of her altered recipe, but possibly for another reason entirely. Now, she was smiling happily at Jean, pleased by the obvious success of the cake. 'You're right,' she said. 'Well done. But – how much?'

Jean grinned and shrugged on her raincoat. 'I'm not sure,' she said. 'Give me a hint.' She gave me a conspiratorial sideways glance, as if I was in some way part of the exchange and, for a moment, I thought maybe I was. 'I'm going to try it out at home.'

'No hints,' Annette said. They were like children playing a game that delighted them, even though they knew it was silly. 'You'll have to work it out by yourself.'

Jean nodded. 'All right,' she said. 'Done.'

By the time we got outside, the rain had stopped. After the conversation with Annette, which had seemed so pleasant, Jean was suddenly restless, wanting to be away, to be on the move and, as she strode off ahead of me toward the old courthouse, I was struck again by her improbable energy. She didn't seem unhappy, only preoccupied, as if the past had welled up too quickly or too hard in her mind and she needed to break the spell, to be out and walking in the damp, sweet air, to clear her head and forget whatever the tragic part of her story was for a while. I didn't know what that tragic part was, but it seemed clear to me that, now she was halfway through the telling, she had hit a place she couldn't get past, or not easily, not for now. She was walking quickly, not looking back, as if she had forgotten me, and I hesitated a moment, wondering if she needed to be left to herself for a while, before I made up my mind and followed her along the bright, empty street, past the old county court buildings, before she swerved off to the right and headed down Ridgeview, past empty lots and anonymous commercial

117

buildings, heading for Shelleyville, the workers' cooperative village built by a nineteenth-century industrialist and social visionary back in the 1890s. Finally, she stopped at a crossways and stood at the kerb, looking out toward what once would have been the edge of town and was now all sprawl.

'People come here to get married,' she said. 'They like to recreate the old days, as if the ceremony could take them back to some better time and hold them there, untouched by all this. I suppose, since they are indulging in fantasy, they think they might as well go for broke – to have and to hold, in sickness and in health, happy ever after, some notion of the good old ways. I don't know why they persist in deceiving themselves, but then I'm not in a position to judge, am I? I've been to three weddings in my life and I can't help thinking that marriage is an absurd attempt at mutual – no, communal – deception. To me, it's like a vaudeville horse: two people joined together at an awkward angle, trying to pretend they are one and everyone else pretending the illusion is a total success. That's what *la vie commune* means to me – a great big game of Let's Pretend, where everybody gets to play their part. Everybody but me. There wasn't anywhere in that *vie commune* for my kind of tomboy when I experienced my first halting and awkward love and I can't pretend it wasn't so, especially after what happened to Lee. I've heard folks claim that married people can be happy, that they can live for fifty years together and be fulfilled by the experience, but the only marriages I have seen at first hand were dim, secret chambers of misery from which, now and then, the prisoners emerged to put on brave faces and act as if everything was fine. My brother, with his pretty wisp of a wife who turned into a cold ghost within months of the extravagant, fairy-tale ceremony that everybody thought so beautiful. So perfect. Well, that might have been his first love, I don't know, but I know it wasn't his last – only, what chance did those affairs have, when he couldn't escape from the haunted house. No – he could have escaped. He just refused to, out of bad faith and misplaced loyalty.'

She was standing at the kerb still, staring at a house on the far side of the crossways. It was a medium-sized, rather ornate two-storey building with steep tiled roofs and high windows, prettier and more elaborate than the neighbouring homes, though whether this had been so when it was built or was the result of more recent improvements, it was hard to tell. The porch had neat, white and grey painted railings and two simple, yet oddly imposing white columns, the lawn was damp and a little unkempt, with dark, low shrubs, once neatly trimmed but now rather shaggy, as if the owner had gone away for a while, or maybe had fallen ill and couldn't maintain the plot to its usual standards. I waited. I felt awkward, standing there in the middle of the street, but Jean seemed not to care. She was old and she probably thought that made her invisible – and maybe it did, but I felt, for a long moment, like we were being watched and I glanced around, looking for prying eyes. It appeared, though, that the street was empty. Everybody here would be at work, or school, or the mall.

Jean took one last look at the house, then started away, turning left so we were winding back on ourselves along a wide, empty road where all the houses looked the same. It was something of an effort to catch up with her, and then to keep pace as she walked, and we carried on in silence, she immersed in her thoughts, while I pondered her sudden rambling outburst on love and marriage. I wanted to stop, to ask about Lee – I already knew, rather than suspected, that the tragic part to which she had so lightly referred earlier had something to do with her and, even though she and John

Cameron were nothing more than names to me, I had begun to feel a growing apprehension. But why? Whatever had happened was far in the past, and it couldn't be undone now, no matter how involved in Jean's story I allowed myself to become. Yet wasn't that part of how stories work? Wouldn't it be different if what she was telling me now was *happening* now, so I could entertain the illusion that I, or someone, could do something to change the course of events? It crossed my mind, then, that I had been living with Laurits for too long, and I had a sudden image of him, in my mind's eye, standing in the road ahead, his camera trained on us as we walked on, the rain beginning again, first as slow, dark drops, then as a steady downpour. A moment later that image vanished and all I could see was Jean's face. She was laughing. 'What the hell are we doing?' she said. 'We're getting soaked.' Then, she wasn't laughing any more, but her eyes were bright and, even though her face and hair was wet now with the rain, the old vivacity had returned. 'Let's go home and get dry,' she said. 'Next time I'll tell you all I know about wedlock.'

THE GOOD WAR

Laurits got home late that night. He woke me coming in and I looked to see what time it was. Two o'clock. I had gone to bed early, purged and relaxed by the hot bath I had taken after the rain; then, feeling cosy in the white pyjamas I rarely wore, I lay for a while drinking herb tea and reading a collection of James Agee's film writings. I must have fallen asleep around ten o'clock, but I didn't remember exactly. From the way he was moving about the apartment, it was clear that Laurits was trying not to disturb me, but he had never been good at sneaking around – and that had surprised me, because I had assumed he would be. That was foolish, I know, but I had imagined that, because he was so evasive, he would be light on his feet – yet nothing could have been further from the truth. The more he tried to be quiet, the noisier he was. And that was strange, too, because under normal circumstances – when he was working, say, or just sitting by the window, lifting his head every now and then to glance out at the street below – he was almost completely silent.

I thought about getting up and having a coffee with him, but I decided not. I knew I wouldn't be able to sleep again, now that I was awake, but I didn't mind the prospect of lying there in my white bed, my head empty, the sound of Laurits moving around in the apartment combining with the occasional noise from outside – far away, in some place I hadn't even bothered to identify, freight trains came through in the night still, their horns calling in the dark, one of the few sounds I knew that could be called genuinely plaintive. I liked plaintive, it was better than the muteness of whatever else I was enduring then, something that both Laurits and Jean, in spite of their obvious differences, insisted on calling grief. Only I didn't think it was that, I thought it was something smaller, something that would go away eventually, of its own accord, the way sadness or a guilt-stricken hangover does – and I have to admit, the great pleasure of that time, after the first adjustments were done with, was the lack of a hangover and, with it, surprisingly, the absence of a certain kind of sadness. The absence of the usual paranoia, too – that customary horror of waking and not knowing what you have done over the last five, or ten, or twenty-four hours. The sense of having been totally naked. Totally visible, right down to the shameful, bleeding spine of your – what? Mourning? Self-abasement? Maybe it was grief, after all, that drove all that together, and the reason I wouldn't admit as much was because I wouldn't have been able to see an end to it if I had. I didn't see that an end was already a beginning. By then, because I was feeling better, I thought all I had to do was stop drinking. Stay hidden for a while, then go back out into a world that wasn't just a story told by an old woman whose motives for sharing those stories – and for sharing them with me, of all people – I was no closer to understanding than I had ever been. If she really was trying to cure me, I couldn't see why. Who was I to her? Who was I to anyone? Or was that the whole point? I was nobody, and so a perfect choice. Jean Culver could tell her stories and not feel like she was just talking to herself. On the other hand, even if I know now that I was wrong, or at least not entirely right, I did believe at the time that she had set out to cure me because she had to give me something in exchange for listening to her stories. Like Scheherazade who doesn't just defer the moment of her death but at the same time humanises the king with her narratives. That was an acceptable idea and, even though it made me sad, it created an acceptable sadness to replace the sadness I had nursed through the months of hard drinking.

The next day, I probably would have slept late, but Laurits was awake again, crashing around in the apartment, getting his equipment together and packing it up in various bags and rucksacks. Laurits refused to own any kind of vehicle. Not a car, not a truck. Not even a motorcycle. If he could walk or take a bus to where he needed to go, he would do that. If not, he would get a rental car. Today, it sounded like he was preparing for a shoot, which meant he'd rented a car and it was waiting outside at the kerb, all new and shiny – something that still gave me a little thrill of embarrassed pleasure. I liked new cars, they reminded me of Dad, who wasn't usually materialistic, but from some old habit he bought a new car every couple of years.

For a while, I tried to go back to sleep. Laurits wouldn't be long, I thought, and then I would be alone again. But it was hopeless. I checked the clock. It was six thirty. He couldn't have slept more than a couple of hours. I got up, pulled on my bathrobe, and walked through to the dining room, curious to know where he was going, in spite of myself. 'Good morning,' I said. I tried to keep my voice as even as I could. I didn't want him to detect any hint of veiled criticism: the one time I had mentioned how noisy he was when he couldn't sleep, he had been crestfallen. Not angry, not defensive, not even hurt, exactly – but crestfallen. Like a child who has tried very hard to perform a very simple task, and failed.

'I didn't wake you, did I?' he said.

I shook my head. 'I was thinking,' I said.

He crammed one last item into the biggest of his many bags, then zipped up. 'Well,' he said, 'it's good that you're awake anyway. You might like to come with.'

'Come with where?'

'To the slaughterhouse.' There was a hint of a question there, to show that he remembered how unsettled I had been – his word, of course, not mine – on our last trip to the old Scarsville abattoir. He was making part of his new film there; though, because he was so secretive, I didn't know what the film was about, or what role the slaughterhouse played in it. One part of me didn't want to go, of course. The abattoir was abandoned now, but it was still hung, from room to room, with the paraphernalia of processing and killing, and that was something I found, not just unsettling, but distressing. Yet there was another part of my mind that wanted to know what Laurits was doing in those damp, cold buildings and maybe just being there while he worked would reveal some elusive insight into his methods that might help me in my own work. It wasn't likely, of course, and a slaughterhouse had struck me, on that first visit, as something of a cliché. But if anyone could redeem a cliché, it was Laurits. That was what he did – only I couldn't figure out how and I wanted, more than I knew, to understand that trick. 'All right,' I said.

'Great,' he said. 'But don't be long, okay?' He gathered up a pair of large bags. 'I don't want to waste the light.'

*   *   *

I have no good reason to believe in ghosts, but I knew from our first afternoon there that the old Scarsville slaughterhouse was haunted. By what, I couldn't say, but I felt it again when Laurits unlocked the side door – where he got the key, I had no notion – and we walked into the first of the many large rooms I had tried to put out of my mind.

It was terrible – the years of blood and panic that had soaked into the walls, the cold phantoms conjured up from the stains on the floor – though, deep and old as they were, they could have been oil or some kind of chemical for all I knew. Still, I saw what he meant about the light right away. It was sunny again, but there was a freshness and transparency to the air and, even when we were inside, the light that streamed in through the windows looked pure, miraculous, in stark contrast to the disused machinery and the dead spaces of the killing rooms. Laurits was entirely unaffected by the surroundings, of course, but I was already giving way to a growing sense of dread that felt like a test, or a rite of passage. It was a strange thing: at times it seemed that something was there, not behind us so much as all around us, a mass of bodies just out of sight, but when I turned to look there was nothing, just that empty space, a space so desolate, in spite of the occasional flicker of sunlight high in the broken roof, it seemed more vapour than substance. I felt it right then as a place of mourning – not human, but animal mourning, a desolate grief for others of their kind, but also themselves, after the scent of fear and blood brought home to them what was happening a few yards ahead on the killing floor. To lighten the weight of that spell – which, for some reason, I didn't want to break entirely, or not yet at least – I wandered from room to room, reading signage that must once have meant something, peering into side rooms that seemed at once sinister and innocent, places where bloody death and dismemberment might have happened, though they could also have been nothing more than storerooms. Hooks hung from the ceilings, chains dangled from the walls. In tiny spaces, behind thick slats of plastic, pieces of old hosepipe or electric casing littered the floor, the concrete beneath streaked with lines of deep, rust-red that ran down to sunken drains. In one room, a row of battered metal hoppers, each with its own label – CATEGORY 2 NOT FOR HUMAN CONSUMPTION – had been pushed into a corner and left to rust. It was dismal, and lonely and, at the same time, purely ascetic – or at least, it could be, as seen by someone as detached as Laurits.

It was while I was thinking this about him that I noticed he was gone. He had been setting up equipment in the largest space, a room so long that, if you stood at one end, the other would be dark, no matter how bright the day outside. For a moment, I felt a kind of panic – not at being left alone out there, but at the idea that he had gone into hiding, made himself invisible, and was now watching me, observing, maybe with a handheld camera at the ready, to capture the scene if I did something that interested him. He would do that sometimes – it was his old girlfriend he had filmed sleeping in his earliest film and he had told me, once, that she was upset that he had done it without her permission. Told me, in fact, as if I would share his surprise at her reluctance to become a character in one of his movies. He had never done that to me – maybe I wasn't glamorous enough – but that didn't matter.

I stood still and listened. At first I heard nothing – I had noticed this last time we were there, how there weren't even birds singing in the broken roof, or in the straggling shrubs that had colonised the empty parking lot. That had made immediate sense. I remembered reading in a history book how the killing places of the old Scottish clans were still silent, no birds singing, no animals in the near vicinity, over a hundred years after the murders and summary executions had ended. One writer told of seeing a hare running across a field in a straight line, then suddenly veering away at the sharpest of angles from the pit where the Campbells used to behead their enemies at Finlarig. That, I guess, would be a haunting – all the dead souls residual in the soil and the air, startling the senses of whatever living thing came near. Such phenomena didn't need a Scottish castle to exist, they could just as easily happen in an old abattoir, where the collective grief and fear of millions of animals had gathered. I remembered that Jean Culver was a vegetarian and I wondered why she had made that decision – she had said it wasn't about killing, because we have to kill to live, but if not that, then why?

I had been listening for a long time – maybe thirty or forty seconds before I heard the voices. They were not close enough for me to make out what was being said, but they were close enough that I could track them, as I walked along the inside of the building to the narrow space at the back where the door that Laurits had opened earlier was still standing open. My first impulse was to go outside and see who was there; then, because I was closer, and could make out the tone – not angry, but touched with annoyance – of the person who was speaking to Laurits, I stopped dead and moved to one side, so that if either of them came close to the door, I would still be invisible. I came as near as I could to the open door, my back to the wall, and listened. I still couldn't make out the words, but I noted that the tone of the other speaker, whom I still had not seen, was gradually settling into something calmer, not amicable, yet, but less hostile, less annoyed. Now, he seemed to be reasoning with Laurits, or possibly setting out some kind of terms, his voice softer, grudging, ready to slip back into anger if he encountered resistance. When Laurits spoke, he assumed the same tone, or almost the same. Conciliatory, but also slightly grudging, as if his trust or his trustworthiness had been questioned. The other man's voice came back at him, and I heard the words 'you better be right' and something that sounded like 'shadow with the money', though that couldn't have been right. A moment later, the other man was walking away – I could hear his footsteps on the grit – and Laurits was alone, presumably watching him go, because he did not come directly inside.

I walked quickly back the way I had come and looked out at the first window. Just a glance from the side that allowed me to see the vehicle the man was driving, though not the man himself. It was a red Silverado, and it looked new. Whoever this man was, he had money. I ducked away from the window and walked toward the back of the building again. Laurits was just coming through the door, an odd look on his face, as if he had just won a bet.

'Who was that guy in the truck?' I said, trying to seem no more than curious.

Laurits glanced at me then walked over to where he'd left one of his bags on the floor. 'What guy?' he said.

'That guy,' I said. 'The one in the red truck.'

'Oh.' He didn't look at me. 'He's a friend.'

'Really?' I paused a beat, so he could pick up on my tone, but he wasn't buying. 'I've never seen him before,' I said.

'He's nobody. Just a friend.'

'He didn't sound like a friend.'

'What – were you eavesdropping?'

I saw that I was supposed to back off, now that he was asking the questions. But I wanted to see it through, some way or another. 'I heard some things,' I said. 'Tone of voice, mostly.' I was staring at him now, but he didn't break off from what he was doing. 'And he didn't sound like a friend.'

He allowed himself a moment's very minor irritation. 'So what's the big deal?' he said.

'The big deal is, I don't think he's a friend and . . .' I searched for something decisive to say, but I *was* backing off now, and it came out badly. 'I didn't like him.'

'You didn't *like* him?' Now he was amused.

'No,' I said. 'I didn't like him.'

Laurits looked up now and smiled, with just a hint of sarcasm in his face. 'Well, now,' he said. 'We can't like everybody, can we? Or where would be the fun?'

Something had happened in grade school. I don't remember what it was, and I don't suppose it matters now. It would have been one of those events that are automatically tragic and unbearable when you are nine and somebody you thought was kind turned out mean, or maybe you lost something – a pen, a diary with its own gold lock and key, something that could be replaced any time, only it couldn't because it was special. I don't know if I had been sent home early. Maybe somebody had brought me back in the middle of the day, thinking I was ill, because for some reason the teachers in that school always thought you were sick when you were really unhappy, or hurt in your heart, or your soul, or wherever the hurt a child feels that flutters in her chest like a bird and will not be consoled. I don't know. All I remember was how my father brought me out of the house to the edge of the woods – it had been raining, I recall, and everything was still wet, with the late-afternoon sun coming through the branches – and my father lifted me up, right up over his head and said: 'Listen!'

I didn't want to listen at first, and then I did, but I didn't know what I was listening for. There was nothing special there, no sound that you couldn't hear any time out on the edge of the woods, after a quick, summer rain. I could hear water dripping from the leaves and twigs, birds singing, a dog barking in the middle distance, but I didn't know what I was supposed to be hearing, until I did. What he wanted me to listen to was exactly the world I could hear any time, the world I could hear but never attended to, the background, the sound of time passing, the difference between one commonplace sound and another that seemed just like it until I tuned in and noticed all the tiny differences, all the music of the world continuing while I was feeling sorry for myself. I wouldn't have been able to say that in so many words then, but it worked, and that night we had my favourite food – fried eggs over easy and honey pancakes – and I forgot what it was that I had lost, forgot it to this day, when it seems that nothing could really be lost, or nothing but him, in his blue shirt and striped tie, home early from work so I wouldn't be alone in my grief over nothing.

Now, I know that you only really lose one or two things in a lifetime, and maybe just one, of which the rest are echoes. Now, when I have the compulsion to walk out the door, to give away everything I possess and start again, I don't do it, and I don't pretend order is real, or even possible, just because I've paid all my bills and torn up my notes for school the way I did that first time, when I quit college and sat staring out the window at Stonybrook until they came and told me that even that was being taken away.

I know the difference, now, between order and nothing and it makes no difference because knowing is not enough. Knowing something like that is like knowing a fact, like the population of Estonia, or how long the Great Wall of China is. Now, there is nothing left to consider but the supernatural – which Emily Dickinson said is only the natural disclosed. I could go out a thousand times after the rain has fallen and stand by a tree and I would hear nothing, because I am listening, now, for what isn't there any more. Now, when the phone is ringing somewhere in the house, too far away to answer, or when I open the back door and new snow halts the light, till everything stands in its own penumbra, something easy in me fails, and I see a man I knew for just a fraction of his life coming home from the Christmas Market with a tree wrapped in sacking and a bouquet of holly. Sometimes, when I go out to listen to the night, I know that somewhere beyond the rain and the sound of traffic, somewhere at the far edge of my world, even though, from his perspective, *he* is in the midst of it all, a man is standing in his yard, or under a street lamp, watching the bats circle some pale, bronze light. He's not my father, I know that. He is somebody else, somebody I don't know, but he's a man who knows all he can possibly know about bats – and he is out in his winter coat, in the rain, just so he can watch one solitary creature flying in what look like random loops around a lamp, knowing they aren't random loops at all, but a complex and ever-changing map of intelligence and desire. He is out there, somewhere, with his instruments and his notebooks, in rain, in snow, in the greenish gloaming of a warm summer night. I could go looking for him any time. I could find him whenever I wanted. He would be a good person to know and maybe

131

he would tell me something, something about bats, that I have never heard before, but he wouldn't be the person I am listening for, and no matter how badly it hurts – no more or less, maybe, than that lost pen or diary from third grade – I don't want anything that could be mistaken for a replacement.

I walked to Jean's house early the next morning. When we'd parted, she hadn't told me when to come next and I didn't have a telephone number for her, so I walked over to her house, thinking to find her in the yard, chopping wood, or tending her wild garden. I felt stupidly proud of how well I felt, proud of the fact that my body was that little bit lighter, that I didn't break into a sweat halfway over. I remembered how, when I was nine or ten, I would go out and walk about all day, in the woods, or along Teale Road, watching the people go by in their cars and when I saw the faces of the bored children staring out at me, I felt lucky and free, like a vagabond, or a Mohican from my storybooks. I didn't know how I had lost that girl; she seemed to have strayed into some other world, or another medium, like the black and white of old movies, where all the lost and perfect things seem to go. I'd always loved those old films. *The Magnificent Ambersons, Shadow of a Doubt, Rebecca.* As a teenager, I thought my first real love affair would happen in black and white, and that meant some part of it would last forever. The movie theatre and late-night TV were the only church I ever had: when an old film came on TV, I would study all the varieties of monochrome: snow on a road from the 1920s; cat's-paws of light in a Viennese sewer; the various incandescent deaths of Jimmy Cagney. I would have given anything to spend an hour in that place.

Jean wasn't in the yard and, when I found the side door locked, I suddenly felt worried about her. She had seemed so strange when we'd been walking in the rain, strange like the old person she should have been and wasn't. It made me think that something in her had broken and she couldn't maintain the illusion of detachment that she had adopted. I knocked at the door, but nobody answered. I looked up to the second-floor window. I didn't know which room was hers, of course, because I had never seen beyond the hallway and the kitchen. Then I knocked again. Still no answer. I was on the point of giving up and walking away – to where, I didn't know, but I certainly had no desire to go back to the apartment – when the door opened and Jean appeared. Surprisingly, she was wearing a dress – an old, slightly faded blue cotton dress, but a dress nevertheless. I looked down at her feet, half expecting to find them clad in the usual work boots; instead, she had looked out a pair of slightly scuffed powder-blue leather shoes with a half-inch of heel that she obviously hadn't worn for years, the kind that would have been fashionable in the 1950s. Clearly, she hadn't heard me knock; when she saw me, she gave a mock scowl, as if she had been caught out in a lie, or a bad magic trick.

'Good morning,' she said. 'I didn't know I was expecting you.'

'I thought I'd drop by,' I said. 'See how you were.'

She nodded. 'I am perfectly well,' she said. 'And how are *you*?'

'Good,' I said. 'I'm good.'

'Excellent. Then you can come with me,' she said. 'If I make any significant purchases, you can help carry them.'

'Purchases?'

Her face softened and she looked at me directly for the first time. 'We're going to a yard sale,' she said. 'Somebody I used to know. She lives near the old fire station on Lafarge. A pleasant walk, at the very least.'

It took no more than twenty minutes to walk over to the house on Lafarge – where, as Jean had said, what looked like the entire contents of her old friend's house was set in rows and untidy piles in the front yard – but that was all it took for everything to darken a little, the sun vanishing behind a cloud, a sudden coolness on the air. When I'd set out, it had been warm; now it was shifting gradually into one of those days when it seems the summer is about to end far too soon, a foretaste of autumn in the smoke-bush by the fence, a damp light clinging to the porcelain dolls and glassware set out neatly on trestle tables, an odd, silvery glaze on the bone handles of old cutlery, one set of knives still in the box it must have come in, carried home from a bygone department store, or delivered in the mail on a day like this, that new, clean smell and the glint of the steel against the velvet becoming a moment in the old lady's life that was still remembered, along with the occasions of everything else on those tables: commemorative plates, polished copperware and jewellery boxes that, in this light, could be thought of as antique.

Jean paused at the gate and looked around. 'There's nothing I wouldn't buy from someone who drags her life into the yard and sets it out for everyone to see,' she said. 'Even if she wasn't a friend.' Her eye came to rest on a middle-aged woman at a smaller table near the door to the house. She was talking to another woman, around her own age; on the table, next to a large, battered cash box, a book lay face down where she had broken off from her reading to converse. Nobody else was in the yard. 'That's Kathleen,' Jean said. 'Mary's oldest daughter.' She sighed. 'I'd best go say hello.' She laid her hand on my arm. 'No need for you to come too,' she said. 'Last time I saw Kathleen, she was pretty hard going.' She pointed to the nearest of the tables, piled high with books. 'See if you can find something interesting,' she said. 'I'll not be long.'

True to her word, Jean did not linger. More people arrived, women of around Kathleen's age, mostly, so it was easy for her to pay her respects and move on without the visit seeming too brisk, and she bought several items – things she clearly did not need – before she found me out amongst what was now becoming a small crowd of friends and curious passers-by. I had been looking at the books, many of them old zoology textbooks, mixed in with out-of-date atlases and maps, a few classic novels and a miscellany of the kind almost any household might acquire over the years. Collections of folk tales for children. Cookery books. Books on stamps and travel and European art. A few slim volumes of poetry, including some contemporary work, which had come as a surprise. I had picked out three by the time Jean got back to me.

'Well?' she said.

'I was thinking of buying these,' I said.

Jean glanced at the books. 'All right,' she said. She handed me a heavy winter coat to hold while she fished out her wallet. 'Call them a gift,' she said. She took a ten-dollar bill from the wallet and handed it to me. 'Do you mind paying?' she said. 'I don't think I can take another encounter with Kathleen.'

'Where's your friend?'

She smiled sadly. 'Mary's not here,' she said. 'She had to go to the hospital. The yard sale is to help raise money for her to go back to Mexico before she dies – but I'm not sure she's going to make it.'

I was puzzled. 'She's Mexican? Her daughter—'

'No, no, she's not Mexican,' Jean said. 'She *was* an ornithologist, specialising in Troglodytidae. Which, as I am sure you know, are—'

'Wrens,' I said. I had done a project on wrens in school and it felt good, for once, to know as much about a topic as she did.

She smiled, happy again suddenly. 'That's right,' she said. 'Or to be strict, the true wrens. Mary was an expert on the true wrens, especially *Pheugopedius felix*, which is also known as—'

'The happy wren,' I said. It had struck me, working on that school project, what a beautiful, absurd scientific name this was and I had gone in search of other creatures whose name suggested they were permanently happy, or fortunate. There were cats, of course. There was a butterfly, the Arabian Wall Brown. There was a species of caddis fly. The funniest was the stinker sponge, *Ircinia felix*.

'That's right,' she said. 'There are eighty or more species of true wren. Mary spent her entire career studying them, but her favourite was the happy one. That's why she wants to go back to Mexico, one last time, because that was where she was happiest.'

By the time we got back to the house, I was exhausted. The heavy coat had seemed easily manageable at first, but as the day had warmed, and as I had worked to keep up with Jean – whose burden of assorted glassware and various household items seemed not to bother her in the least – I had begun to struggle. Jean noticed this, of course, but she didn't say anything and she didn't slow down. Still, when we finally reached her kitchen, and she deposited her several purchases on the table, I thought even she had begun to feel a slight ache in her bones. She seemed glad to be able to set her goods aside and, after she had made tea and set a plate of assorted pastries and cookies on the table before me, she sat down with an expression of satisfaction tinged with unmistakable relief.

'Well,' she said, 'it's good to be home again. Though it's a pity I missed Mary.' She poured me a cup of the tea, a pale, faintly green brew that I tried not to think about too hard. 'I shall have to call and see how she is tomorrow.' She passed me the cup. 'Honey?' she said.

I nodded, though I wasn't sure if honey was what I wanted. The tea was exactly the colour of the frog I once had to dissect in high school.

Jean fetched me the honey pot. 'We didn't finish our story last time, as I recall,' she said. 'So if you're ready, we can take up where we left off.'

I helped myself to a cookie and nodded.

'Maybe we can save time, though, by telling two stories at once. Two stories about wedlock, you might say. They're both puzzles to me now, though I guess that's always going to happen. We're always puzzled by damage and loss. And yet, when you look back, months, or years, or decades later, it isn't hard to see that the whole story was bound to end badly.

'I try to imagine, sometimes, what happened when Jeremy and Gloria met. What it might have been that made him fall in love with someone like her. But I don't know anything outside the barest facts. They met, and something happened to them. They married and whatever that something was, it faded faster than the bride's bouquet. As for me . . .' She considered for a long moment. 'When I told you about Lee, last time, I was talking about something that feels like a dream now. I remember details – I remember them vividly, but I can't put them together. I mean, I can't make those details into a story. All I can really say for sure is how it began. It's odd, isn't it, how easy it is to remember the early days. Maybe it's because they were the happiest. Maybe because they seemed so innocent, like any two people falling in love. I guess, looking back, we had fallen in love earlier and just hadn't thought to mention it. But I didn't know that, then. I didn't know much at all, in fact. There were times, when we were alone together, when I half guessed, from something in her eyes, the way she looked at me, but I didn't know for certain and, besides, something like that would have been too lucky to be true. Or that was how I saw it then. I had the idea that good things don't just happen. Only they do – and that's when you're in trouble.

'How it began was just a day, like any other. I had been working in the floristry and I'd got lily pollen on the sleeve of my shirt. I always wore an apron, but I was careless and, anyhow, clothes didn't matter to me. Or no – it was more than that. I was deliberately careless of my appearance. I didn't want anybody to think I cared. Especially Lee. Being a grown-up tomboy with dirt-stains on my jeans was a kind of defence and, at the same time, it was a signal to anybody who chose to wonder about it that I wasn't looking for some man to ride in on a white horse and gather me up in his arms. I knew very little about what I did want, but I knew it wasn't that. Maybe I didn't *want* anything. I certainly didn't believe that I had any right to ask anything from Lee. That struck me as a kind of impossible dream, like a scene in a movie, and maybe I liked it that way.

'Lily pollen isn't hard to get out. It's impossible. If you touch it, that's pretty much the end. I might have had a chance of getting rid of most of it if I'd taken the shirt off and given it a good shake, but, when I pulled off my apron and walked

138

into the office, Lee was there, a pile of paperwork on the desk. The very idea of working in an office makes me shudder, still. I mean, I can do it, it's not that difficult. It's just so dreary. I would never have been able to build the American Garden up to the level we got it to, if I'd been obliged to do paperwork every day. I would have run off to Idaho and got a job on a potato farm. I'm not sure what that would have entailed, but it would have to be better than bookkeeping.

'I'm not sure Lee didn't feel the same way, but from the moment we got together, she made it her task to cover pretty much all of the administrative work. I did the ordering, when we had a landscaping job to do, but that was about it. I'm sorry, now, that I never stopped to think about it, but I should have seen that she was more like me than she pretended. She probably found all those invoices and bills as boring as I did, but I never thought to ask. That day, she had been in there all morning, and maybe the pollen stains were just a way of justifying a break, because she ought to have known that I didn't much care. Nevertheless, she got up and started fussing as soon as I walked in, fetching out some Scotch tape and wrapping it around her fingers, talking all the while about how I'd got pollen on my prettiest shirt and how I had to get it out or it would stain forever. I knew the Scotch-tape trick, of course – I also knew it didn't really work – so I stood quiet for her while she carefully applied the first band of tape, then discarded it to start another.

'I was a little surprised. She knew I didn't care about the shirt. Though I remembered later that she had complimented me on it once, saying how she liked the colour – it was plain blue as I recall – but I'd not thought anything of it, then. She knew I didn't care about my clothes, and she also knew that the Scotch-tape trick didn't make much of a difference. Once you get lily pollen on your clothes, you've got permanent stains. So I just assumed all the fuss was her taking a break from the sheer boredom of office work and I stood there, letting her work, a dumb smile on my face, no doubt. Happy. Awkward. Waiting for all the fuss to be over and wishing it would never end. And that was when she looked up and – well, I really don't know how it happened, but she reached up and touched my cheek, not with the Scotch-taped hand, I feel obliged to say. Then she kissed me. Or I kissed her. I don't know. I think it was her, but I can't be sure.'

She looked at me, to see what effect this story was having. I think she believed it made me awkward when she talked about the women she found attractive, and she clearly got some pleasure out of this, but the truth was, I didn't feel awkward at all. It was at times like those, when she searched my face for a reaction from two generations earlier, that I felt sorry for her. She had lived in her big house amongst the cottonwoods a long time. Even though she went out into it whenever she could, some part of the world had moved away from her.

'I have to believe that Jeremy and Gloria experienced such a moment. The same pull, the same hesitation and then – the same certainty. Because that's what I felt, then. Certainty. It didn't matter about anything else. The one indisputable fact was that Lee and I belonged together . . .'

She rose from her seat and refilled the teapot, though she didn't need to. It was just business. She needed a pause, a moment's silence. When she brought the pot back to the table, she seemed studied, distant, not telling this story to me so much as rehearsing it, to test it for something. But for what? Accuracy? Incompleteness? Was there one tiny flaw in the fabric of the narrative that might be discovered, one loose thread for her to tug at and so unravel the whole thing?

'Jeremy must have felt that certainty, because he lost no time in courting Gloria – or rather, courting her family and friends – and then marrying her as soon as circumstances allowed. I can't recall how long it all took, but I know it was quick, because the first I heard of it was when he called from Virginia to tell me about the forthcoming wedding. A formal invitation would be coming soon, he said, but he wanted to be sure I kept the date free – as if I would even consider missing it. But then, we'd been apart for a long time. We hadn't seen each other for almost two years. I didn't know how much he had changed, but something in him must have recognised that, if he had changed, I might have done too.'

'You said before that he had changed,' I said. 'But I didn't understand how.'

'Well, it goes without saying that he had witnessed terrible things. After all, not many men carry around the memory of seeing their own father being shot down in the street. That, in itself, marked him for the rest of his life. But it was something that happened in France that really changed him.' She hesitated, and it seemed to me that she didn't want to tell the story, but after a moment, she began speaking. 'You know already that Jeremy didn't talk much about the war,' she said. 'He didn't talk much about anything. Later, when he was doing whatever he ended up doing, he didn't talk at all. He just disappeared mysteriously, then returned, just as mysteriously. Nobody even knew where he was. So you can imagine that he didn't tell me how he came to be in France, in 1944, behind enemy lines. Maybe he was captured and escaped, maybe he was there as a spy – it seems likely that, with his knowledge of French and German, he might have been used in that

141

kind of role. Whatever brought him there, though, it led to a complete mental and moral crisis from which I don't think he ever really recovered, in spite of the "philosophy of life" he adopted later.'

I was intrigued. I knew I shouldn't interrupt, but I couldn't help it. 'Philosophy of life?'

'Maybe you've heard of it?' she said. 'It's called "As If". *Als Ob* in German. It was formulated by a man called Hans Vaihinger, and it was quite popular for a while. It starts from the basic assumption that, because life is hopelessly irrational and unpredictable, because there are no explanations for what happens, because the world is random, we have to construct our own ideas of order – Vaihinger calls them *fictions* – in order to live peacefully amidst the chaos. We accept that these fictional ideas of order and meaning are not true as such, but if we are able to will ourselves to live "as if" they were, then we can obtain some semblance of a meaningful life.'

'Like – fake it to make it,' I said.

She raised her eyebrows at that, but did not respond. 'Rationally, we may be quite certain that there is no God, and that our morality – based on the culture within which we were educated – has little relation to the world itself, which is a maze of contradictions, illusions and random noise, but if we choose, if we *will* an ordered world, even if it is a fiction, it is better than the chaos we would have to endure otherwise. Everybody does this, anyhow, to some extent. Vaihinger simply extended the fiction to include everything. So we behave "as if" there was a God, and "as if" America was the land of the free and the home of the brave, *always*. We take it for granted that, even when they seem irrational, the orders the general sends down the line, or the policy decisions the government makes, are *always* for the greater good, even if they seem incomprehensible to ordinary citizens. We have to believe this, because the alternative is to question everything and if we do that, we end up powerless to act at all, in what appears to be a constant state of uncertainty and chaos.' She picked up one of the poetry volumes I had set down on the table when we came in and studied the cover. 'A philosophy like that must feel like a gift to the people in power, but it's also very appealing to someone who is desperate to find meaning in life. And nobody needed to find meaning more than Jeremy did. He'd seen his father murdered, he'd seen the system fail to identify the real assassins, though it would have taken very little investigative effort to do so. Then, one day in France, sometime in the summer of 1944, he was taken by a group of Resistance fighters to the site of a massacre, in which around three hundred people had been killed. The victims were women and children, mostly, and it was clear that they had been slaughtered and tortured with the utmost brutality. His French friends wanted him to see what had been done, apparently by a Waffen SS group; they said they needed him to be an independent witness. He told me later that the massacre must have taken place the day before these fighters reached the village. Nothing had been touched, the bodies still lay where they fell. Half-naked women, their bellies slit open. School-aged boys lying face down in their own blood. Somebody had even tried to crucify a young child. He had seen terrible things in that war, he said, but nothing like this and it seems clear to me that, whatever shred of native hope had sustained him till then, it finally withered that day. Later, when he was eventually returned to his unit, he submitted an official report, but he didn't tell anybody else what he had seen. He didn't talk to me about it until he couldn't bear it any longer. If I had known about that at the time, I might have understood a whole lot of things a whole lot better. Like why he married Gloria. Why he changed so completely. Why he became what he became. He wanted to make sense of things, things that nobody could have made sense of. So he chose the fiction.

'Still, even if I had known what he had seen, I would still have wondered why he chose Gloria to sit at the centre of his chosen fiction. Because, the instant I saw her, I knew he was making a mistake. He had told me in the letter that she was beautiful, and she *was*, in her way. Though maybe I would have called her attractive. That's what everybody used to say, when I was younger. *Attractive*. Do they still say that? They do, I imagine, but not in the same tone of voice as back then. Attractive was something special, in those days, though I was never entirely sure what it meant. Was it different from beautiful, the way "pretty" was? Was it a kind of show? A performance? Gloria may have been attractive, but then she had been trained all her life to attract. Nothing else, you understand. She was a machine to attract men's eyes, a machine to win their attention, to win it and hold it. Even her name was attractive. It was as if it had all been decided by some good fairy the day she was born. Gloria would be attractive. Gloria would be popular. Gloria would get any man she wanted. So why was it that, to me, she was a grotesque, like some creature of a different species altogether, elegant, contained and – what? I suppose I thought she wasn't quite real. In fact, when I first saw her, it was like the time I first saw an artificial Christmas tree – you know, those old brush-bristle trees they used to have? Which is ridiculous, but what can I say? She was just like that, as if she had only been brought into being for some temporary function. All she had to do was attract. There was so little of her. She was made for Prom Night and military balls. That's where they met, of all places, at a military ball.

'As I said, it was a whirlwind romance. I was far away. The first I heard about it was when he called to say they were engaged and by then the ink was already dry on the wedding invitations. And I thought, this is a mistake. It wasn't Gloria's fault, she was right for *someone*, I don't doubt, but my brother didn't have the resources to be married to a person like her. That idle life of playing a part, of thinking up new compliments and courtesies, that wasn't him. He didn't have the ability to take nothing seriously and that was de rigueur in those circles. He was an old-style romantic, or he had been, growing up. In that way, he was like me – best suited to loving from a distance. I travelled down to Virginia, to meet a future sister-in-law and all I saw was sugar and spice and all things nice, ready to crumble under the sheer weight of her own attractiveness. It just wasn't right and I was shocked that he couldn't see that. Not that I said anything. How could I? He had just come through a war. He thought he had found happiness. Not just a wife, but a family, a circle of friends, everything he had lost when our father was killed. How could I pull him aside and ask why was he marrying this – creature?

'So the whole affair lumbered onward, and for reasons that I cannot for the life of me understand, I personally organised the flowers for two weddings that year. One for my brother and one for the woman who, now that she was drifting away from me, was suddenly my "best friend" – her words, whenever she introduced me to John Cameron's family and business associates. Every time she said it, I felt sick. Two weddings in less than a month: that was a lot of work, on top of the usual day-to-day business. In both cases, I performed my task with a good deal of reluctance, and in both cases, I outdid myself. Still, it seems odd, how things coincided: less than a year after that moment in the office, when I knew, for certain, that Lee and I belonged together, Lee met John Cameron and a few months after that, in June 1947, she married him. Two weeks later, I travelled down to Virginia for my brother's somewhat more elaborate nuptials. All credit to them, the Barnes family knew how to put on a wedding. Mother Barnes was not in the least happy about my role in the preparations, and she hounded me all the time with suggestions and questions and downright professional insults, so it was all I could do to keep my temper, especially when I had just watched the love of my life drive off in a fancy sports car with a man she didn't really love. Of course, the tomboy sister of the groom didn't get to argue with the Mother of the Bride over floral arrangements, and what did or did not go with the bridesmaids' dresses.'

There was a long pause and, for a moment, I thought she was on the point of tears. Then she looked at me directly and smiled. '*As if*,' she said. 'My poor brother.'

I shook my head. 'Maybe it did help him make sense of things,' I said.

'Things don't make sense,' she said. 'Or not on our terms, anyhow. That's something we just have to accept.'

'Maybe some people find it too difficult.'

'It's the easiest thing in the world,' she said. 'All you have to do is take a look around.'

'So what else is there?' I said. I felt angry, suddenly.

'There's a world,' she said. 'And it *is* orderly. It doesn't often do what we want it to do, and it hurts us badly, sometimes. It's also beautiful in any number of ways.'

I had no response to that. It sounded too easy, as if everybody could just turn around and be as stoical as she was. But was she really so self-reliant? Was she as strong as she seemed?

For the first time, I felt suspicious. For the first time, I experienced just a hint of doubt. 'So,' I said. 'What happened next? You said you were going to tell me two stories.'

'I have,' she said.

'You didn't finish one. You didn't say what happened to Lee.'

'No,' she said. 'I didn't.'

'So what happened next?'

'She left.'

'On her honeymoon?'

'Yes.'

'So what happened after that?'

Jean was studying my face now. She had become aware, or at least half aware, of my sudden judgment and it seemed she was both interested and amused. 'I didn't see her after that,' she said.

'What?'

'She was gone.'

'That must have been a long honeymoon.'

She laughed. 'I can't imagine the *honeymoon* lasted very long,' she said. 'But I didn't see Lee again.'

'That's it?'

She smiled sadly, but there was an unbearable calm about her. 'That house we walked to in the rain,' she said. 'I bought that house for us. Naïve as I was, I thought she and I could make it work, that we could – pretend. As If. But she married John Cameron and that was that.' She rose from the table and went out into the hall. For half a second, I thought that she had finally given way to her emotions, but she returned right away, holding a piece of paper. 'John Cameron sent me a letter,' she said. 'I still have it. He said that Lee had decided to leave her position as co-director of the American Garden to pursue other interests. He said it had been a difficult decision for her, and that she didn't want to discuss it further. He hoped I would understand and informed me that his lawyer would be in contact, with a view to making some sort of settlement. He added that he and Lee had agreed to instruct the lawyer to settle on terms that I would find favourable.' She looked at the letter, as if checking to see if she had forgotten anything. She hadn't, of course. She knew that letter by heart, word for word. 'That was how I made my fortune,' she said. 'I bought Lee out at less than a quarter of what her share in the American Garden was worth. And I never saw her again.'

'I'm sorry,' I said.

'Oh, don't be,' she said. 'It was a long time ago.'

'Don't say that.'

'But it was.' She smiled. 'Do you know what I remember best? It was after the ceremonies were all done with, and she and John Cameron got up to dance. Lee was a beautiful bride and, I have to admit, John Cameron looked good in his wedding suit. Somebody was talking to me, saying something about the flowers, but I wasn't listening. I was thinking, what if I just walked over and cut in, just like that? Just walked over and tapped him on the shoulder. What would have happened?'

She gave me a questioning look, as if it mattered what I thought. 'Well,' I said, 'maybe you should have done.'

'I should have,' she said. 'But I didn't. We never danced, Lee and I. A few hours later, she came to me and said goodbye. John Cameron was right at her side, very obviously and solidly at her side. All that day, she had avoided me. But then she wasn't herself. She was a wife now. She took my hand for a moment, said goodbye, and gave me a brave smile. I thought there were tears in her eyes, but I can't be sure. She took my hand and said goodbye, and then she left. John Cameron thanked me for the beautiful flower arrangements. Then they drove away and I never saw Lee after that. She didn't even write, which is awful when you consider it, but at the time all I could think was that we had never danced, and how I would have given anything to have danced with her, just once, before she left.'

DREAMING KOREA

When I woke next morning, I heard voices. Possibly, it was the voices that had wakened me, but I didn't think so. I had been dreaming that I went back to my home town, only nobody I knew was there. Dad was gone. Louise's house was empty and a little run-down, one window boarded up, with a For Sale sign out front. In the dream, it was winter, but the people in the streets were dressed in summer clothes, men in T-shirts and jeans, women in thin cotton dresses. The clothes were old-fashioned and a little worn, like they had been purchased from a thrift store, or a yard sale. Everybody was poor. I glanced at the clock. It was nine thirty-seven.

I listened to the voices all the time I was getting showered and dressed. I could hear Laurits – he was doing most of the talking, but I couldn't make out what he was saying – and there were at least two others, both women. They sounded young. One had a European accent, maybe Dutch or German, and it was obvious, from the tone of their voices, and the way they laughed more or less in unison, that these women were friends. I got a sense that Laurits didn't know them well. Maybe he had just met them. How long had they been here? I knew that, when I'd fallen asleep the night before, Laurits had been out and I hadn't heard him come in, but surely it would have woken me up then, if he'd brought these women to the apartment and they had stayed all night. I looked out of my Buddhist nun's window at the tiny patch of sky I could just see, if I tilted my head to the side. It looked cloudy, but not entirely dull, a day that might brighten, or give way to rain. I pulled on some jeans and a green turtleneck sweater and went through to the dining room. When I had left her, the day before, Jean had suggested we meet at eleven o'clock and go to see the great earth mounds at Cahokia. She would get her car out of the garage, she said, and we could drive over – it wasn't far. Seeing that I didn't know what Cahokia was, she had explained a little, and I had been intrigued. Now, I was looking forward to getting out of the apartment as soon as possible.

The first surprise was that Laurits and his new friends were sitting at the dining table, eating breakfast. That was something we never did. We didn't have regular mealtimes and there was, or I'd thought there was, a tacit agreement between us that we wouldn't use the table for anything but work, and we ate out, mostly, or in front of the TV or a computer screen. Sometimes, stoned, we ate in Laurits' bed. My normal breakfast routine was a bowl of Grape-Nuts, saturated in milk and maple syrup if there was any, with sliced apple or a handful of dried fruit, which I ate in my room or, if I was in a hurry, at the tiny counter in the kitchen. I had never seen Laurits consume anything like a proper breakfast – so this was a surprise, an elaborate spread with bread products and grape jelly and butter in a proper butter dish that I'd found in the cupboard, but never used. Coffee, milk, cream, peanut butter. They even had croissants.

Laurits gave me an amused look when I came through the door. 'Hey!' he said. 'You're awake.'

The look the two women gave me was more appraising. They were the kind of people who judged others and decided quickly, based on appearances, what they would think of them forever after. I never knew what to look for, so all I registered was that, in what appeared to be matching midnight-blue ballgowns, they were rather overdressed for breakfast – in this apartment at least. That, and the fact that they were both pretty in the more predictable ways, the taller one dark, with deep brown eyes and a face that was slightly too regular to be considered beautiful, the other pale-skinned and fine, her thick, reddish-brown hair threaded with ribbons, like some theme-park princess. They were both around twenty-five, I guessed, and it was clear that being here, in our apartment, was some kind of novelty for them. When they had first met Laurits, he would have told them he was a film-maker, and they would have been intrigued, thinking he meant the same thing that they would have understood by that term. By now, though, they were just slumming.

Laurits stood up, pulling out a chair for me. I looked closely at his face and wondered what kind of high he was on. 'This is Lauren,' he said, pointing vaguely at the beribboned redhead. '*Und hier ist Barbara, aus Stuttgart,*' he added, bowing slightly, and only partly in jest, at the dark-haired woman.

Barbara looked at him, then turned to Lauren and faux-smiled. Then she turned, almost ceremoniously, to me. 'I hope we did not wake you,' she said. Her speech was very even, the way people speaking a foreign language sometimes sound.

'I'm fine,' I said. 'I'm just going to grab some coffee and . . .' It was my turn to force a smile. 'I'm going on an outing today,' I said. 'With an old friend.'

Laurits looked up. He had been tearing the last of the croissants into straggling, buttery shreds. 'Really?' he said. He looked surprised. 'Where are you going?'

'To Cahokia,' I said.

'What's that?'

'It's an old Indian site,' I said. 'The people who lived there built huge earth mounds, sometimes a hundred feet high.' I sounded like a bad guidebook. 'The whole of Southern Illinois was covered in these earth mounds but most are gone now.' The women were staring at me now. They probably thought I was insane. 'My friend is an expert on lost Indian tribes,' I said.

Laurits was grinning. 'Get the hell out of here,' he said, with no attempt to disguise his scepticism. Maybe he thought this was the start of some kind of game. He considered for a few seconds, then glanced at Barbara. 'Maybe we should come too,' he said. 'I'm sure Barbara would be interested in learning more about our native peoples.' He grinned. 'What do you say, Barbara?'

Barbara didn't answer. Instead, Lauren spoke, her eyes fixed on me in order to avoid looking at Laurits. There had probably been some joking about the similarity of their names the night before, wherever it was they had met, and Laurits would have played his Estonian card. Maybe they would have flirted. Now, however, with all the attention clearly directed toward Barbara, Lauren was getting just a touch prickly. 'Please don't be offended, Kate,' she said. 'But I'd rather climb the Gateway Arch in a high wind dressed in ballet shoes and a tutu.'

That made me laugh. I couldn't help it. 'Well,' I said, 'I don't think you'd make it. But I'm sure you'd look great trying.'

*　　*　　*

When I got to Jean's house, I found her in the kitchen in a raincoat and boots. She had changed her mind about taking the car, she said, but she still wanted to go out. In fact, she seemed eager to be up and about in the open air – so I didn't understand why we couldn't go to Cahokia as planned. However, she had decided. We could go to Cahokia another time. On a warm, sunny day. 'But for now,' she said, 'let's just go for a good long walk.'

I didn't know what to say. She had made it clear how important she thought the Cahokia site was, how much a part of our history, even if we knew very little about the people who lived there. We needed mystery in our national backstory too, she had said. We need the unknown, a near-blank screen on which to sketch out our myths and legends. Now, she seemed to have forgotten this altogether. 'Well, I'm not sure about a *long* walk,' I said. 'I think rain is on its way.'

'It's summer rain,' she said. 'It doesn't matter if we get wet.' She thought for a moment. 'But then, maybe you're right,' she said. 'Maybe we should just stay at home and keep dry.' She took off her waterproof coat. 'Tell you what,' she said. 'We can sit here in the dry and *both* tell stories. How would that be?'

I felt a trap forming around me. Had she set up this entire piece of theatre for a reason? ''What stories?' I said.

'Well,' she said, 'you could tell me something about your mother.'

'Nothing to tell,' I said.

'Nothing?'

'She left when I was six,' I said.

'So you must have some memories of her.'

'No,' I said. 'My dad brought me up by himself.'

'So,' she said. She studied my face. 'Tell me about him.'

'There's not much to tell. He told me stories, I guess.'

'What kind of stories?'

'Made-up stories. I mean – he made them up.'

'Uh-huh.'

'He was kind of an artist,' I said. 'He worked as a designer.' I tried to think of some specific thing my father had designed but I couldn't. 'He designed – textiles . . . Things like that.'

'When did he die?'

I blinked hard. 'Eighteen months ago,' I said. I didn't know what she was doing, or why, and for a moment I suspected her of some kind of intentional cruelty. The kind of game that Laurits might play.

'That's hard,' she said. 'Both parents gone.'

'Yes,' I said. 'I miss him.'

'I suspect you miss them both,' she said.

I shook my head. 'Maybe once,' I said.

She smiled and set about the concoction of one of her exotic teas. Her earlier restlessness was gone; now she seemed, if not relaxed, then settled, at least. 'Maybe,' she said.

She didn't resume her story from the day before until the tea was ready. It was a thin, red liquid that smelled slightly of flowers. 'I told you not long ago that I'd only ever loved one person,' she said. 'And that is true, the way a story can be true, or not. But it's also true that, for a long time, I would lie awake wishing that someone – *anyone* – was there with me. A body, a voice, a mind that I reflected and answered to, a body and a mind that answered to me. It might sound like a contradiction if I say that I have always been happy living alone, but it's true. I prefer solitude to all the available options, but this didn't stop me from wanting things that *weren't* available. It didn't stop me wanting the impossible.

'I remember, it was a Sunday in March when Lee told me she was going to marry John Cameron. She had suggested we drive out to the lake that Sabbath morning – we liked going out on Sundays, when the rest of the world was singing hymns and offering up prayers to whatever God they worshipped. It was too early, of course. The wind off the water gusted cold and sharp. The sun kept emerging tantalisingly through the clouds, then vanishing again. Nothing was in bloom yet, almost nothing was in leaf. I believe I knew what she was going to say before she even spoke and for the first time I realised that it had been inevitable, one way or another. She had always wanted that other life. She had always wanted a child. I understood that. I just didn't understand why it had to be John Cameron's child. Lee, of all people, could have chosen whomever she wanted, or so I thought – though part of me knew that this wasn't true either. She was beautiful, yes, and she was a successful person in her own right, but she was getting older and she was too hard-headed and independent for most of the men who had seen the war and now just wanted to come home and be looked after and feel in control of their lives again. It took a man with John Cameron's arrogance to think that he could have that kind of life with Lee. Other men had been attracted to her, but they had moved on. There was too much of her and most men saw that.

'So she told me, as we stood in that cold wind, staring out over the lake – and I wasn't really surprised. Still, there are questions you have to ask, even though there is no way you can ask them and also seem reasonable. Not the right word, of course, and I don't know, now, why I went through the pretence, ever, of being – reasonable. Because I had no rights? Because it wasn't for me to hold on to her, when I knew what she wanted most was the one thing she couldn't have with me? "Do you love him?" I said.

'She smiled, but she didn't look at me. She just stared out at the water. Then, still smiling, she shook her head. "He's interesting," she said. "I know you don't see it, but there's something more there, something behind the – appearances." That last word gave her pause, I could see that, and I could also see that she was afraid. She was taking a gamble, and she knew it.

'"Appearances?" It was all I could do, to echo that hint of doubt, that wisp of fear in her. Though I knew that, had I been more neutral, had I not so obviously despised John Cameron from the first, I would have been in a stronger position.

'She laughed. I thought, at that moment, that I was the only person who could see through that laugh. That only I knew when she was hiding a sadness that, for all I know, she never really put away. I still believe that – or I want to, at least. Because it's most of what I have left. "You've never liked him," she said. "But how could I expect that?" She turned to me and took my hand. "But try to see," she said. "Try to be happy for me, so that I can be happy."

'I could have been more generous then. I could have steeled myself. I could have been a friend to her. But the thing was, I knew she was making a terrible mistake. Not just for her, but for both of us.'

Jean looked at me expectantly. Maybe she was waiting for a judgment. I still didn't know why she was telling me this part of the story – or any of the story for that matter. Was it really just to keep me sober?

'Anyhow,' she said. 'You know the rest. But what I really wanted to say was that, even if you only ever love one person, even if you can't imagine anybody else ever taking their place, there are other feelings that cannot be excised. There are other – needs. Nobody should be ashamed of what is needful. A father. A mother. A lover. A touch, a word, a body. And for a long time, I did lie awake, wishing there was somebody next to me. Somebody to touch. If I learned anything, after Lee went away, it was how important it is to have someone you can touch. Someone who touches you. What I didn't know was that, halfway across the country, in a swanky house in Virginia that he lived in less and less as time went by, my brother was learning the same thing.'

I had nothing to say. It had suddenly come to me that my mother could be anywhere, and I wouldn't know. She could be dead. Maybe there was somebody out there in the world who would have written to say that she had passed away, that she had suffered no pain – the things people write, the things people say. Was this the first time that idea had come to me? I looked out at the garden – and at that exact moment large inky drops of rain began to fall. I wondered where Christina Vogel was.

I could feel Jean's eyes on me, but she didn't follow up on her insinuation about needing a mother. 'I do believe Jeremy loved Gloria, at least to begin with. On the other hand, I believe the main reason he married her was because, like Lee, he wanted to have children. If he hadn't met Gloria, he would have found somebody else. I'm sure it wasn't as conscious, or as cynical, as I am making it sound, but I do know that he chose to believe, according to his supposed philosophy, that Gloria was what she seemed, that he was meant to have children with this particular woman and live, if not happily ever after, then comfortably, at least. They would make a family and that family would live by certain values. Values he had come to see as intrinsic to the best that our society – American society – was supposed to stand for. He had seen barbarism in Europe on an almost unbearable scale, and he knew that if America had a function in the world, it was to oppose that barbarism. But how could we do that, when we lived in a society that could let a man like our father die on a street corner and not punish the real culprits? That must have been a constant test of his philosophy. The trouble is, he didn't have anything else.

'The real test of his "As If" philosophy must have come as a surprise, though. Because, "As If" or not, he genuinely loved Gloria. To begin with, in fact, I think he even adored her a little – and for a long time, their family and neighbours and even complete strangers passing in the street must have thought that they were the perfect couple. Nobody seemed to mind when his life gradually became a complete secret. Nobody minded that he never talked about his work. At some point he mysteriously left the army and started working for some agency connected to the military, though what his role was after the war, nobody seemed to know. All any of us knew was that it had something to do with the government, which was considered to be a good thing in those days. Patriotic. Possibly brave. Nobody asked questions about that, ever. All anybody knew for sure was that he had to travel a great deal and they admired Gloria for how well she dealt with him being away so much. They didn't know what was happening behind the facade, because those two people – the possible spy and the belle of the ball – were, in their different ways, experts at keeping secrets. Only I guessed that something wasn't right between them – though I didn't know what it was until much later. Long after the wedding. Long after the children were born. Even then, I wouldn't have known anything if Jeremy hadn't come to visit me, then stayed over a few days. He came unannounced, quite out of the blue: I opened the door one day and there he was, standing in the yard with his suitcase. That first day, and all the next, he seemed vague, oddly distracted, and I knew he had something on his mind that he wanted to tell, but wasn't ready to say out loud. The next night, I made him a fancy dinner, got in several bottles of good wine, then sat and watched as he drank glass after glass, until he was almost, but not quite, drunk. I'd never seen that side of him, and he wasn't actually drunk – well, I don't think he ever did get drunk, as such. It would have been too much of a loss of control. The wine certainly relaxed him, though, and that evening, in the space of two hours, he told me what had been going on at home, told me all about the embarrassing and humiliating burden he'd had to carry for years, pretending to all the world that everything was just fine. Of course, I wasn't the best person to tell his secret to, but he didn't have anybody else.'

I nodded, as if I understood what she was talking about. I was waiting for her to resume what I thought was the real story. When she didn't, I asked the question I thought she had been waiting for. Or had she expected me to know without being told? 'So,' I said. 'What was his secret?'

She let out a soft, pained laugh. 'Well, it was a complicated tale he told me that night, and it wasn't made any less so by the fact that, drunk or not, he was in something of a confused state. The short answer to your question, however, is one of the oldest and saddest facts there is. It's the ruination of many a marriage that husband and wife are rarely equals. In this case . . . Well, let's say that Gloria was never a very warm person and I don't think they ever had much of a sex life.' She gave me an odd, mock-schoolmarm smile. 'I'm not embarrassing you, am I?'

I smiled back. 'You're not embarrassing me,' I said.

'Good,' she said, a little too brightly; but her smile faded as she went on with her story. 'Well, my brother, romantic that he was, stayed true to his philosophy and decided that, if he continued to pretend everything was fine, things would get better. Of course, part of him wondered if he had done something wrong, and he put himself through all kinds of self-examination to try to work out how he could be a better husband. He loved his wife and, when the children came – I find it painful imagining how that came about – he loved them more than anything in the world. He didn't care, he said, what he might have to do, but he would do anything, if it could only be like it was at the beginning. That surprised me, but there was, apparently, a beginning when things seemed fine. It didn't quite outlast the honeymoon, but it had happened, or it had happened in his mind and that was all that mattered. At one point, she had loved him, so if he did the right thing, she could love him again. Because he was sure there wasn't anybody else, and I think, if there had been, he would have found out. After all, he was a spy. Though when he did learn the truth, it happened altogether by chance.'

'By chance?'

'Pure luck,' she said. 'That's what he told me. Though he must have felt like a fool when he discovered the letters.'

'Ah,' I said. 'Letters.'

'Yes,' she said. 'Though it's not what you think. It was the letters that led him, indirectly, to the truth, but he hadn't been looking for them. He simply came across them by accident one day, while looking for something else, and – well,

I don't know why he was so surprised that there had been someone else before him. Another attractive young man. Perhaps it was unfortunate that, all through that whirlwind romance of theirs, Gloria had said nothing about the summer-long romance that she had been caught up in the previous year, while Jeremy was fighting behind enemy lines. But why would she, after all? Good girls didn't talk about that kind of thing and, anyhow, it would seem that *romance* wasn't quite the right word for whatever had gone on that summer. The boy's name was Matthew, as I recall, though I don't know how I know that. Perhaps Jeremy mentioned it in passing at some stage, as he blundered through his account of how his attractive wife suddenly froze and became – what? I don't know, to be frank. There's no word for it now, is there? Back then, the euphemism would have been Ice Maiden, but even that wasn't altogether accurate, no matter what problems she and Jeremy had in the bedroom. Because, whatever else she was, Gloria was no Ice Maiden. She was, in reality, a fairly sweet person, an affectionate mother to her children, and solicitous – oh, painfully solicitous – about anything affecting Jeremy's physical health. And that was what people saw. Not the secret bewilderment, or the unanswered questions. A happy couple, two beautiful children, a fine home, loyal friends, a wife who would do anything to ensure her husband's happiness. Nobody knew that it was all a performance, nobody knew that, except for the begetting – I am using the biblical term for a good reason here – except for and other than the begetting of the children, Gloria was . . . Well, Jeremy didn't know what to call it. Cool. Physically cool. Emotionally distant. It wasn't just the sex; after a while, he couldn't even touch her. When he did, something in her closed up, the way a sea anemone closes in on itself when

162

you brush its tentacles. That's how he described it, anyhow, and I have no reason to doubt him.

'Of course, he tried to talk to her about it, but she just shrugged it off. She told him everything was normal, and that made him wonder if he was mistaken, because – well, as he said, he didn't have anything to compare his life to. Maybe that was how a normal marriage went. I must say, I had to smile when he said that. I asked him if he'd tried to find help, if maybe he could have raised the problem discreetly with some kind of medical person, but the very idea horrified him, I think. It shamed him to seem so – repellent – and, not surprisingly, he started to think that it was all his fault. He must have done something, he must have been – well, he'd known other women before Gloria, women that, as they used to say back then, weren't the marrying kind, and he probably suspected he had been too . . .' She laughed. 'It's hard to believe, in this day and age, isn't it? I believe he thought he had shown some side of himself that she found repellent.

'Then, one day, he found the letters. That, in fact, was what had driven him to visit me so unexpectedly. Finding those letters. I can see him now, looking for something when Gloria was out, going through old papers and accounts. Old certificates, deeds, the letters he himself had sent her while he was away – and instead he came across Matthew's pathetic, hurt letters, most of them not much more than notes. Poor Matthew. He had been young and very much in love and he was confused by Gloria's behaviour, how she was so warm one minute, then cold the next. How she seemed to care for him but then . . . I imagine you get the picture. In one way, those letters vindicated Jeremy, to himself at least, but at the same time, they damned him to a lifetime of doubt. Had Gloria *ever* loved him? How could he know? Had she just been pretending, those first few months, as a means to the only end she had ever been taught to pursue? When she had kissed him, had it been real? When they had made love . . .

'I don't know what happened after he left here, two days later. He never spoke about it again, and I didn't ask because it was obvious that nothing had changed. I believe that, for a long time, he still loved her, or he wanted to, at least, even after the affairs started. And though there was always a cover story, I'm sure Gloria knew about the other women. Yet it appears she never said anything about it. Not a word. Soon the happy-ever-after illusion was paper-thin. Theirs was a house of unspoken hurts and fears, and that's what the children grew up with. No out-and-out lies, no fights, no arguments, it was all very civilised, but those children knew something was wrong. I was so angry with Jeremy and his stupid philosophy, that he didn't see that. He just thought they could keep up a polite facade and everything would be fine. But children *know*. Maybe they can't put what they know into words, but you can't hide anything from them and all Jeremy and Gloria did was to deny them an explanation – and all the time, it felt like some terrible sin was just about to be exposed, or worse, confessed. That was how it felt to me, anyway. I can't say what the children felt. All I know is that they withdrew into their own private and arcane worlds.' She shook her head. 'I remember, once, I went over there and I found Jennifer in the garden with a dead bird she'd found under a tree, a baby that must have fallen out of its nest. She'd put it in a box and she was talking to it, singing it songs and telling it stories – I watched her for a long time and she didn't even notice I was there.'

Jean was far away now. It wasn't even her story, but she was far away in it, and I wanted to bring her back. 'So what else did he say?' I said.

She looked at me. For a time, she had forgotten I was there; now she was back and I realised with something of a shock that it was this quality of attention – an attention that fixed on me like a flashlight picking out some lost thing in the dark – that had drawn me to her in the first place. For that look, I had forced myself to stay sober. For that look, I had lain awake in my bed, while the night revolved around me, the sweat drying on my skin, my muscles contracting till I thought something in my legs would snap. 'He talked about the war,' she said. 'There's no need to go over that now, we've all seen what was done, they made an industry of it, in the end, as they do with everything. What bothered him most, though, what he kept coming back to, was how senseless it was. He had gone to war thinking that, no matter what cruelty or violence he might witness, he could make sense of it all. Because it was a just war, nobody even thought to doubt it. Through his philosophy, he'd even made sense of our father's death, it seemed. That was the only time he ever talked about what happened on Ashland and Vine, and I was hurt, I think, by the fact that he had suffered through that without me. Not seeing it happen, but working it out afterward, making it rational. Our father had enemies, after all, so it made sense, in some odd way, that someone might seek to harm him. But the massacred women and children he had been forced to look at – he didn't understand that. The village had been in ruins when he went in, but in spite of the horror, he could see right away that what had been done there had been delib- erate. Inhuman, yet logical. Utterly brutal, and utterly efficient. This wasn't some crazy with a gun trying to impress his betters and it wasn't men at war doing things that they would desper- ately blank out later, any way they could. He had witnessed terrible acts of cruelty, things that happened in the heat of battle, but this was a cool and extended act of torture and murder, carried out in the plain light of day, and he didn't understand.' She gave an odd, hurt little smile, as if she was the one who had borne witness to those unimaginable scenes. 'No philosophy could help him with that,' she said.

Jean looked at me, but I had nothing to say. I was the last person to talk about the effectiveness of life philosophies. 'Still, one thing should have been obvious,' she continued. 'It should have been obvious to everyone that my brother and his attractive wife were afraid to disagree. That's always a bad sign, don't you think? They didn't argue, they didn't fight, because they couldn't control what the outcome would be. Because, in the end, they were both tired. I'm sure Jeremy wanted to leave, maybe Gloria did too. But then, he couldn't leave, because that would mean leaving the children. So he stayed – and I can imagine that, with his philosophy to keep him going, he just tried to keep sight of that beautiful girl at the military ball, smiling at him across the room. The affairs wouldn't have meant anything, other than having someone to touch. He probably chose his partners carefully – women whose circumstances were not unlike his own, women who didn't want more from him than he had to offer. Warmth, touch, an evening's kindness.'

She fell silent, then. It was an easy silence, touched with sadness, perhaps, but not uncomfortable. Outside, the rain was blurring the windows, splashing through the leaves of the trees. The door to the garden was still wide open at the end of the hall. 'So tell me,' I said, after we had observed the quiet for what felt like a sufficient time. 'What were the children like? When they were very young?'

She smiled. 'They were wonderful,' she said, glad to move on now. 'Simon was such a serious child. He was very well behaved, he never complained. He adored his father, but he got very upset whenever Jeremy had to go away somewhere. And, of course, by the time Simon was seven or eight, Jeremy was away often.'

'That must have been hard for both of them.'

Jean nodded, but she didn't speak. She was looking at something in her mind's eye, examining it, maybe wondering if it was something she still believed, or had begun to doubt.

'So what did he do?' I said. 'How did he cope with his father being away so much?'

Jean shook her head slightly, but I didn't know if she was expressing her disappointment in my question, or some memory that she didn't want to think about. 'I remember, once, I went down there for a visit, when Jeremy was in Korea,' she said. 'Gloria looked happy, very much at ease – I didn't visit often when Jeremy was away, after all he was my brother and, officially, he was the one I was there to see. When I did, though, Gloria always seemed more – relaxed. I used to wonder how their friends didn't notice that difference, but maybe she just tried harder with them. She seemed to feel she didn't need to try that hard with me. Maybe she knew that I had seen through their act. I don't know. Anyhow, we were sitting in the garden room one day – yes, they had a garden room. And a library. As far as appearances went, they had a very good life indeed. Gloria loved her garden and she picked my brains for new trends and ideas whenever I went down. That was what she was doing then, when Simon came in and sat down in a chair by the window. The sun was on his face, and he had his eyes closed. And it was odd, how still he was, sitting in that chair with the sun on his face. So, just for fun, when there was a break in the conversation, I asked him what he was thinking.

'For a moment, he stayed exactly as he was, then he opened his eyes very wide and looked at me. "I'm dreaming Korea," he said.

'I looked at Gloria, but she turned away. Then, after what I can only call a decent pause, she stood up and forced a smile. "Well," she said. Simon was watching her, the way a cat watches when it wants something from someone. "I'd better see what's going on in the kitchen. Would you like some iced tea, Jean?"

'I tore my eyes away from Simon, who was still staring at his mother. "That would be lovely," I said.

'Gloria nodded. "Would you like something to drink, young man?"

'Simon didn't say anything – it was clear he wanted her to know that he was ignoring her – then he stood up very deliberately, just as she had, and went out into the garden without a word.'

Jean shook her head in what I took to be sad wonderment. 'I guess we should leave it there,' she said. 'But we can continue tomorrow, if you like.' She gave a mischievous smile. 'Maybe you'll have a story for me, by then?'

I didn't know what to say. It seemed to me that she didn't want just any story – she wanted something specific. Only I didn't know what that was. 'Maybe,' I said.

She laughed. 'I have an appointment in the morning,' she said. 'But if you come in the afternoon around three, I'll tell you about Jennifer. I think you'll be surprised.'

JOHN BANISTER

When I got in, Laurits was watching a movie with the sound off. No evidence of the morning's extravagant breakfast remained. Even the dishes had been washed and put away. He looked up. 'Hey,' he said. 'Wanna beer?'

I flopped down on the couch and studied the movie. 'Later,' I said.

Laurits flashed me a curious, possibly concerned look. 'You hungry?' he said.

'Not yet.'

'Okay.' He looked back to the screen. A woman was kissing a man, tears rolling down her cheeks, in an American hotel room. 'How was Cahokia?'

'Didn't go,' I said. 'Too wet.'

'Ah.' He watched the lovers struggling in silence for a long moment. Then, when the leading man broke away from the woman – I didn't know who he was, but there was no doubting he was the lead – he smiled happily. 'Isn't it strange,' he said. 'All those leading men, back in the day. Isn't it strange how sexless they all were. How – safe.' He glanced at me, seeking confirmation, but I wasn't interested. Not that he cared. Right now, he was talking to himself as much as to me. 'Gregory Peck. John Wayne. Charlton Heston.' He paused, thinking of the next candidate for the list.

'Cary Grant,' I said.

He smiled and shook his head. 'Poor old Cary,' he said. 'He had his moments, I guess. *Suspicion*, maybe. But the ending's all messed up.'

'Which one's *Suspicion*?'

'Joan Fontaine marries Cary, then it turns out he may be some kind of sleaze who wants to kill her for the insurance, only he's not . . .' It always seemed odd to me, that he remembered movies by their plots, because that wasn't how he watched them. To him, a film wasn't about love, or betrayal, or murder; it was a sequence of individual scenes about snow, or hotel rooms, or desert landscapes. He knew every actor, every director, every writer, but all he cared about was the background and the cinematography. The mood. The texture. The atmosphere. 'You know. She got an Oscar for it.'

'Who did?'

'Joan Fontaine. Are you okay? You don't look too good.'

'I'm fine,' I said, but something had changed on-screen, some shift of mood, and he wasn't really listening. 'So who is *this* guy?' I said.

He snorted. 'You don't know?'

'No,' I said. 'That's why I asked.'

'Franchot Tone,' he said.

'Are you sure? He looks too old.'

'I'm sure.'

'What's the movie?'

'*Jigsaw*.'

'What year?'

'1949.'

'Director?'

'Fletcher Markle.'

'Fletcher who?' I said. 'I never heard of him.'

'Canadian.'

'Oh.' I didn't want to play this game, because it always ended up at the same place. The question, whatever it might be, was irrelevant. What mattered was the last word. No – what mattered was that the most ridiculous, the most untenable position should win out. That was how we were, when we weren't fucking or drinking. We took refuge in the untenable. We sought comfort in the trivial. It would have been remiss of us, not to push the conversation to its farthest level of absurdity. At any given time, I didn't want to play this game – and then I played it. Under the circumstances, there was nothing else to do. 'I may be out on a limb here,' I said. 'But I'm going to say Clark Gable.'

He smiled, weighing up the odds. 'Gable?' He gave it a long moment's thought. 'Actually, that sort of works,' he said. 'I suppose the real test is: some nice girl like Anne Baxter brings the guy home to meet her mother, and if Mom thinks he's not good enough to marry her nice daughter, then he's probably quite interesting.'

'Nobody was *ever* good enough for Anne Baxter,' I said. I was waiting for him to say something about the morning's events, but I knew he wouldn't. 'So, where are your friends?' I said.

'Gone,' he said.

'That's good to know.'

He looked up. 'You're damp,' he said.

'It's raining,' I said.

'Really?'

'I'm just about to have a long hot shower. Probably have an early night.'

'You want a drink?'

'Nope.'

'Are you annoyed?'

'About what?'

'Barbara and . . .' He had already forgotten the name of the red-haired woman.

'Lauren,' I said. 'And no, I'm not annoyed. Well, I am a little.'

'It was an idea I had,' he said. 'It's not what you think. I just had an idea.'

'An idea for what?'

'A movie,' he said. 'A full-length feature. Totally mainstream.'

'All right.'

'I'd worked out the basis of the story.'

'Do tell.'

He winced. 'Twins,' he said.

'What? Those two? Twins?'

'Yes.'

I laughed. 'They look nothing like twins. A striking Germanic brunette and – well, Princess Lauren from La La Land with ribbons in her hair.' I laughed again, but I believed him. I'd never imagined something was going on with the two women. I'd been annoyed, I realised, because they had used the table for breakfast. 'Why do you want to make a feature film?'

'I need money.'

'Why?' I didn't understand. He always seemed to have plenty of money.

'It's a long story.'

'Tell it,' I said.

'Anyway,' he said, 'I'd given up on the movie by early afternoon.'

'It shouldn't even have lasted that long,' I said. 'So why do you need money?'

'Never mind,' he said. 'It was a stupid idea, twins who don't look alike.'

'It was a stupid idea,' I said. 'So – why do you need money?'

'I told you. It's a long story.'

He glanced at the screen, then sat a moment in silence. When he finally spoke, he had leapt to a different subject entirely. 'Let me ask you a question,' he said. 'Let me ask this. What would you do if you only had two hours to live? It would have to be watch *Chimes at Midnight*, right?'

'Fuck you,' I said. 'I'm going to have a shower.' I started for the bathroom.

'That was a test,' he said, suddenly. 'And you passed with flying colours.'

'I don't do tests.'

'Anybody else would have—'

'I don't do tests,' I said – then I stopped, turned back. 'What would you do with the extra five minutes?' I said.

'Excuse me?'

'*Chimes at Midnight* runs for one hundred and fifteen minutes,' I said. 'So what would you do with the last five minutes?'

He gazed at me with awe and wonder, but he didn't say anything. Barbara would never have known the exact running time of any classic movie. Least of all *Chimes at Midnight*. I wasn't sure why I did, in fact.

'You sit there a while,' I said. 'Maybe you can come up with something interesting.'

'You've probably guessed already that Jennifer was rather a strange child.'

Jean had been in the midst of setting out a small feast of cakes and cookies when I arrived at exactly three o'clock. I searched my head for memories of something that might have led me to guess anything about Jennifer at all.

'She wasn't any of the things girls are supposed to be in the world she grew up in. She wasn't attractive. She didn't want to relate to other people much. She had a series of school friends, carefully chosen, and quickly discarded when she discovered their secret flaw—'

'Secret flaw?'

Jean smiled. 'They weren't perfect.'

'Somebody should have taken her to see *Some Like It Hot*,' I said.

Jean laughed. 'She would have missed the joke,' she said. She lifted the lid off the teapot and sniffed. 'It smells – intriguing,' she said.

'What is it?' I had been meaning to ask her about her collection of strange teas. I assumed it had something to do with Annette.

'Aniseed, lime flowers and ginger,' she said. It sounded terrible. 'You have to let it stand for a while.'

'Maybe we should let it stand forever,' I said.

She frowned. 'It's good for the throat,' she said.

'My throat's fine.'

'Excellent,' she said. 'This will make it perfect.'

In the end, the tea was very good, though that might have been due to the addition, in my case, of the two large spoonfuls of honey. Then, as soon as everything was ready, she plunged straight into her story. 'When she was a little girl, Jennifer used to sit in her room and sing to herself for hours,' she said. 'When anybody asked her what she was doing, she would say she was thinking. Even later, it was always as if whatever the grown-ups demanded of her was just an irritating distraction from the real world, the world that *she* had populated. She was a rebel right from the start. She would get angry about things she shouldn't even have been aware of, stories she heard on the radio, the terrible atrocities of history. For a while, when she was around seven, she made a series of powerful, very free drawings of elemental figures – or not even figures exactly. She wasn't interested in representing people or everyday objects. The shapes in her drawings were more like abstracts. Elementals. Gloria used to ask where all this was coming from, as if she couldn't have guessed that Jennifer was angry. It was painful, to see so much anger in a little girl – but the problem was, everything she got angry about was real. What she heard on the news. The things she read in books. The racism all around her, every day, which every other white person seemed to take for granted. She loved Jeremy, but she was angry at him all the time for being away so much. She didn't understand why he wasn't there.

'In most things, Simon was very like his father. Early on, I think, he more or less adopted the same approach to life, the belief in order and home and apple pie, only he didn't have the philosophy behind it to know that it was a necessary fiction. He just absorbed it. Jennifer, on the other hand – well, she examined everything, and when she found it wanting, she called it out. She argued with her teachers. She was just twelve when she started refusing to go to church. I don't think Gloria was a believer and, by that time, I knew Jeremy only went because it was a part of his chosen fiction, but they were adamant that she should accompany them to services on Sunday morning. Everybody went to church in those days. It was a family occasion. But Jennifer fought them every inch of the away – and eventually, she won.

'Yet even though they seemed very different from one another, the strange thing was that the lives they lived, the decisions they made, the way they talked about things even, *everything* about those two children was formed in response to their father. In their different ways, they were trying to win him back from something. For years, when they were too young to understand, they felt him slipping away from them, and they didn't know why. He would have said he was just doing his duty. He would have said that he was trying to make the world a safer place for them to grow up in. But they *knew* he had choices. He could have chosen to stay home more. He could have asked for a desk job, or changed his employment altogether. So the obvious conclusion was that he *wanted* to be someplace else, and not at home. To begin with, they thought that was because he had stopped loving Gloria. As I said, children know when things aren't right. Later, I think, they thought he'd stopped loving them.

'Perhaps the story that best sums up Jennifer's character is the one about John Banister.' Jean threw me a questioning look, but I had no idea who John Banister was. She smiled. 'It's all right,' she said, 'I'd never heard of him either. Nobody had.' She poured us both some more tea. 'Jennifer was a straight-A student, and those teachers she hadn't alienated with her fiery political arguments thought she would go far. Even the ones who didn't like her much had to admit that she was brilliant. So we were all very interested to know what she would do when she graduated high school. Politics or law were the most likely directions. But she was also a first-rate scientist, way ahead of her cohort in biology and chemistry. Now, it seemed, *everyone* was waiting to know what she would choose to do. What she did choose says everything about the kind of teenager she was.

'"I'm only interested in lost causes," she told me, when I went down to Virginia that summer.

'"I see," I said. "So what does that mean?"

'"They don't want me to do history of science," she said. "Mother wants me to do law."

'"And what does your father want?"

'She pulled a face. "Oh, well," she said. "You know him. Whatever she says, he says. The echo."

'I had to smile at that. "So what do you plan to do?"

'"History, to begin with," she said. "Then I'll specialise in history of science."

'Well, I didn't doubt that she would do what she had planned. I remember, when she was – I don't know, maybe fifteen – she read a magazine article about Bunny Girls. Do you know what that particular social phenomenon was? For people like us, it was just a silly idea, a story in the newspapers, but Jennifer took it up and made it into her latest cause. She wrote an essay about it for school, and she told everyone why it was wrong. Feminism hadn't come to Gloria's circle – I don't imagine it ever did – so everyone was mystified by the strength of her feelings. People would say, it's just a bit of innocent fun and, well, the girls probably enjoy dressing up. Jennifer said, if they wanted the girls to dress up as animals, they should let them choose which animals to be. Then she made a whole series of animal masks, as examples.'

'Animal masks?'

'They were beautiful,' she said. 'Jennifer loved to make masks. But this time it meant something, because in her alternative to the Bunny Club, the women wore masks according to what animal they wanted to be that night. Only,

177

there were no bunnies. No cute little furry creatures – and no demeaning clothes. The women in her club would just wear plain, dark suits, but they could be lionesses, or jaguars, she-bears, vixens, hyenas. You get the idea.

'Eventually, it emerged that the reason she wanted to study history of science was John Banister, an obscure seventeenth-century English clergyman who was shot in a hunting accident before he could complete the first ever flora of Virginia. Banister had very little money, so he acted as a guide for hunting parties to obtain funds, and contrived somehow to combine that work with his vocation. It should have been altogether straightforward – he led the hunters into the back-woods where the game was plentiful, and while they hunted, he would botanise, finding specimens, collecting seeds, building up his herbarium collection. Not much of his work remains, but it is clear that he was an excellent scientist. A botanist, principally, but he also worked on insects. The trouble was, not all of the hunters he led on those excursions were as skilled in their art as Banister was in his – and one day, some fool shot him.

'After he died, his herbarium and other specimens were sent to London, where the collection was split up and sent out to a number of English botanists. Very little survived as identifi-ably the work of John Banister – and only a very few of those who received his field notes and specimens gave him any credit at all for his work. What Jennifer wanted to do was go through the records, in Virginia and in England, and somehow sift out what had been stolen from Banister. She would then use this to recreate the flora of Virginia that Banister had intended to write. She knew, of course, that this would be like finding a needle in not one, but several haystacks, a totally lost cause, but then, that was what attracted her to the project in the first place. Later, she gave up on the Banister project – but not because it would have been too difficult, or because Gloria wanted her to do law. No. Her new plan was hatched after she had a conversation about Seneca with one of her professors. After that one fleeting conversation on something she wasn't even officially studying, she switched to philosophy. She wanted to know what constituted a good life. Not a passive, play-by-the-rules life, where you simply obey the current laws because – well, if you did that, you accepted segregation, for a start. You accepted war. You accepted sexism. She had a phrase from Seneca she had memorised: *Quam angusta innocentia est, ad legem bonum esse.* See – I still remember it, after all these years.'

I shook my head in a show of incomprehension that was only partly for her benefit. 'What does it mean?'

She laughed. 'You don't know?' she said. 'I thought you were a scholar.' She stood up suddenly and walked over to the bookshelf by the window. 'I have it here, somewhere,' she said. 'Jennifer gave it to me to read.' She reached up to the top shelf, picked out the book she wanted right away and opened it at the exact page she was looking for. 'This is a book about anger,' she said. 'Anger and duty. It's about doing the right thing, in the right frame of mind. No anger, no inappropriate emotion. Jennifer always said there was too much emotion back then, which was understandable, for anybody who really knew what was going on. But that was the test, she said. You had to see what was going on, then you had to act for the greatest good – and that kind of action should be done with a clear head. Seneca says each of us has a duty to defend those who are threatened, and to avenge those who have been wronged – but this must be done calmly, without anger.

'But how do you know what the greatest good is? The law doesn't tell you – laws are made for the rich, to protect property and uphold The System. That was the word back then – you don't hear people saying that so much now, but in those days it stood for everything. The rich. The government. The military. The law. But the law isn't about doing good.' She walked back to the table, sat down and started to read. Or maybe she wasn't reading, maybe she was just going through the motions. Looking back now, I can't help wondering if she didn't know the whole thing by heart. 'What man is there who can claim that in the eyes of every law he is innocent? But assuming that this may be, how limited is the innocence whose standard of virtue is the law! How much more comprehensive is the principle of duty than that of law! How many are the demands laid upon us by the sense of duty, humanity, generosity, justice, integrity – all of which lie outside the statute books!' She looked up at me, then clapped the book shut. 'That was the big question for her. She wanted to live according to that sense of duty. To do good. Active good. To defend and avenge. Most of us would be more than happy with just being more or less innocent. Especially now. Words like duty and virtue are quite out of fashion and have been for a long time, wouldn't you agree?'

I shook my head to indicate that I didn't know *what* to say. It seemed to me, then, and it seems to me now that, no matter how good you are, you can't *do* good on your own. It was pointless even to try – but I didn't say that. I just shook my head and met her stare as well as I could, and I couldn't help thinking that, on some level, she was judging me, just as her niece might have done.

'In this world, under The System, Jennifer said, you can be as moral as you want to be, just so long as you don't interfere with the rich folks' business. But this is exactly the problem for the ordinary person. We can be good according to the law, we can even do more than that. We can be good friends and neighbours, visit the sick, give money to charity, all those good things that people do. Beyond that, though, there's the old dilemma: how do we *actively* do good – which, sooner or later, means how do we oppose evil? When that question arises, most good people move from the question of what is right to the problem of what is best for them under the circumstances. Jennifer understood this. She also understood that good people naturally hesitate when action is demanded. But she couldn't accept the proposition that the best lack all conviction, while the worst are full of passionate intensity. She believed that a time always came when the best were obliged to act . . .'

She smiled. 'I'm not telling this as precisely as she would have liked,' she said. 'For one thing, she didn't think in terms of best and worst. She was interested in the choices people make. She didn't condemn people for not "doing something". She didn't judge other people and find them lacking because they were afraid for their children, or their jobs, or their own safety, for that matter. On the other hand, she judged herself. I was seeing a good deal more of her at that time, because when she switched to philosophy, she moved to Chicago and she would come here for visits now and again. As I recall, she was interested in knowing more about the Committee on Social Thought – Hannah Arendt had been a member, though she left a year before Jennifer arrived. Her interests quickly shifted, however. In those days, Chicago was also the centre of the Students for a Democratic Society movement – I imagine you've heard of them?'

I nodded, though I could only recall the haziest facts about that time. Anti-war. Civil rights. The 60s. Woodstock. That was about it.

Jean sensed my uncertainty. 'SDS is an important part of our history. SDS, the Black Panthers, the Young Lords, they are our history and it's important that we remember them as they were, and not as the entertainment industry would like us to. If we forget those people, then we lose something that should have been dear to us. If you watch television, you'd think that generation was all about taking drugs and avoiding the draft. Black Panthers terrorising the streets – when the opposite was true. It was a shock, when the police murdered Fred Hampton in his bed and most of us didn't want to believe it. But Jennifer and her friends shamed us, or some of us, into paying attention. Now, decades later, you have all the evidence you need to know the truth. Thing is, the truth about what's happening right now will only become available in another five decades, by which time it will be too late to do anything. That's why you have to study history. Has the system changed in any significant way? No. Then you can assume that it will continue to behave now as it did half a century ago. You have to use that evidence. You don't give them the benefit of the doubt, you question everything.

'*Vietnam.* When I was young, nobody had ever heard of Vietnam. Nobody could have found the place on the map and nobody would have bothered trying, until the government started sending people over there. Even then, most of us thought it was a good thing. We believed America was there to protect its friends against the Spectre of Communism – and why not? Why would anyone think otherwise? Our generation had seen how half of Europe vanished into a kind of shadow world after 1945. Our generation knew how evil Stalin was – which meant that communism must be evil, too. That was simple logic. My own brother thought we'd made a big mistake, not pushing on into Russia after the war. He and his fellow soldiers had gone through hell to prevent Hitler taking over half of Europe, only to stand by and watch while the Russians did exactly that. We all remember, now, how millions of people were killed in the Nazi death camps, but we forgot, even as it was happening, how many millions were spirited away to Russian gulags. So later on, when Jeremy heard his daughter and her friends talking about The System he was mystified. Well, at first he was. Then he got angry. Quietly, of course, all internalised and sclerotic, but no less corrosive for that. He hated their ingratitude to the one country that had dared to found itself on an impossible ideal, rather than a system. He didn't see that America controls its own people just as assiduously as it bullies others abroad, and back then he wasn't alone. But his children saw – and they couldn't understand why he didn't see what black people had to suffer – we called them Negroes then, and now we call them African Americans, but I still like the word black, which shocked me a little when I first heard Jennifer use it, because – well, you weren't supposed to say that. You were supposed to say Negro. That was polite. So why was it that you could say white?

'I didn't worry about Jennifer when she joined SDS, but when Jeremy found out, he was – crushed. He didn't say so, but it broke his heart. He'd wanted his children to have happy, rewarding lives, untouched by any outside force and he'd sacrificed a great deal to that end. Not that he wanted anybody to acknowledge that sacrifice. He once said that no decent father would want his children to know what he had given up for them. You just want them to know they are loved. But it's that kind of helpless love that leads to superstition. That kind of love begets fear. He was so afraid of loving them too much, of letting them see that all he cared about was that they were safe, that he ended up looking like he didn't love them at all. His love turned to superstition because there was nowhere else for it to go, nobody to share it with. Gloria loved the children too, but it was the love a normal parent feels for her child, with room enough for a life of her own, such as it was. But Jeremy – he wanted their world to be perfect. So perfect that they should have no say in it because, after all, children make the wrong choices all the time. They wander. They dare. They have no idea how vicious this world is. It was my brother's job to keep them safe.

'But then, safe only goes so far. You can't foresee everything, no matter how vigilant you are. Even what you can foresee, you can't forestall. Most of all, you can't prevent children from doing things – usually the one thing you most wish they wouldn't do. It was hard enough for Jeremy, knowing that Simon was in Vietnam – but it got a whole lot harder when his brilliant daughter's angry face flashed across the screen on a news report about the riots outside the Democratic Convention in 1968. He was – crushed.' She pressed her hand to the teapot to see if it was still warm. 'He wanted to save them from the world he knew,' she said. 'The world that shoots your father down in the street right in front of your eyes. The world of massacres and torture and all the things he had seen and couldn't talk about. And some part of him knew that he couldn't protect them – and that was the hardest thing of all for him. He knew in his heart that casualties are inevitable, but he just couldn't stop trying.' She sat back and let out a deep sigh. 'I'm sorry,' she said. 'I'm going to have to take a break. I'm getting tired, and we need more refreshments, don't you think?'

*　　*　　*

Mercifully, the refreshments consisted of coffee and a range of home-baked delicacies, including two fried apple pies. I had assumed, when Jean broke off so suddenly, that storytelling was done for a while, but as soon as the coffee was poured, Jean began again. She was pretty fired up, now. 'I'm sure you've seen documentaries about the 1968 Democratic Convention. That was the one where Mayor Daley prevented the news media from broadcasting clear acts of police brutality against anti-war protesters in Lincoln Park, while at the same time trying to prevent actual Democratic Party members who supported McCarthy from entering the hall. The one where the kids ended up shouting, as the police beat them with billy clubs and nightsticks, *The whole world is watching, the whole world is watching*, over and over again. I was paying particular attention to the convention because I knew Jennifer was part of the protests, but I wasn't worried to begin with, because she had told me she would only be involved in peaceful demonstrations and, naïvely, I thought that would keep her safe. Of course, everybody knew that Chicago under Richard Daley was one of the most corrupt, most racist, most violent cities in the developed world, but I didn't think they would attack the unarmed pacifists who had gathered with David Dellinger in Grant Park, or not the white ones, at least.

'But that was exactly what they did. After the first police attack on the park that day, many of the protesters had broken away, slipping off in small groups to reassemble on the Loop. Those were mostly the more radical people, and the police should have known that the ones who stayed with Dellinger were totally committed to non-violence. At that time, Jennifer still thought of herself as a pacifist and, though she was tempted to go the other way, she decided to stay in the park. Like the rest of the crowd, she watched anxiously as Dellinger, who wanted to hold a peaceful march to the International Amphitheatre, tried to negotiate with the police, but it soon became clear that, not only were the authorities refusing to permit them to march, they also had no intention of letting them leave the park peaceably. They wanted a fight. It was all very confusing, and Jennifer didn't know what to do – earlier that day the police had singled out Rennie Davis, one of the main leaders of the demonstration, while he was trying to organise stewards to maintain order near the bandstand, and they had deliberately and systematically beaten him unconscious. Now, it seemed, the same thing was going to happen again.

'Jennifer told me how inevitable it all felt, how the police seemed to have decided to beat people down, no matter who they were, before anybody did a thing. They were scared, she said. There had been a whole heap of inflammatory rhetoric from the Yippies and some of the other radical groups going into the convention, and the police were afraid of not being able to handle the protests. The stupid thing was, they then proceeded to attack the most peaceful group of demonstrators in front of a whole array of cameras, in broad daylight, as the people who had stayed with Dellinger tried to leave the park via Michigan Avenue. All through the days of the convention, the police had used tear gas and billy clubs to attack people, but this had mostly happened at night and, besides, none of it could be shown live, because while it was going on, Daley wouldn't let the news networks have access to electrical power. So they had to film whatever was happening, then run it on the late-night news, or even the next day. But that day – it was Wednesday, August 28, 1968 – the networks were forced to decide whether armoured policemen beating unarmed civilians, mostly kids, on the streets of Chicago was more newsworthy than what was happening inside the convention. Eventually, after an even more violent attack on the intersection outside the Conrad Hilton, they decided to highlight the police.

'Jennifer told me she didn't really understand what had happened until much later. She got through mostly unharmed, but many of her friends didn't. She saw the injuries. She heard the stories. She had been determined to remain non-violent, but that determination began to crumble as soon as the convention was over. Meanwhile, the police war on the Black Panthers continued. By the time it culminated with the murder of Fred Hampton, in December 1969, Jennifer had decided. Her inner Seneca counselled direct action. For that, she realised, she had to go underground.

'And that was that. One day she was there, the next she was gone. She could have been anywhere. She could have been dead. None of us would know. She didn't tell me what had happened until several months later, when she appeared suddenly, in the early hours of the morning, asking for money and a place to stay for a day or two. By that time, Simon was gone – though I didn't tell her about that – and her parents had been worried sick since she disappeared, but when I tried to get her to call them she refused and warned me if I told them I'd seen her, she would never trust me again. It hurt to hear her talk like that, and it hurt to have to keep that secret, but I knew that she meant it and I wanted her to know she had at least one place she could come to for help and maybe, when things got better, to work things out and get back to her old life. I didn't know, then, that her old life wasn't possible any more. If I *had* known, maybe I would have turned her in that very afternoon. It grieved me to know that Jeremy and Gloria didn't know where she was – and when she left, I wouldn't know either. Nobody would. The days passed and we did what we did: Jeremy went to work, Gloria played golf on the good days, and got drunk slowly through the long, humid afternoons – and all the time they were waiting for the telephone to ring. For a knock at the door. Some official letter. When nothing came they were glad – until they started to wonder what that meant. No news isn't good news. It's just silence. Then, early one morning, that silence was broken and I was offered a passing glimpse of what her life was like. Life on the road. Life as a fugitive. Poverty. Grime. It wasn't the least bit glamorous. In fact, it was ugly. Paranoia is ugly. Suspicion makes people ugly. The reason Jennifer gave me for not calling her parents was chilling – she thought Jeremy would turn her in – but I had to accept it or I would have been cut out of her life too.

'I didn't know what she was doing. What group she belonged to, what she had done, who might have suffered because of her actions. I believed that she wouldn't deliberately hurt anyone, but I had no grounds for this belief. She had changed. We sat for a long time, talking, and I tried to get her to tell me what was happening, but she gave nothing away. Not then, not ever. So the story I am telling you now is full of missing details, hypotheticals, possibilities, unconfirmed sightings. Pointless questions. Evasive answers. "When was the last time you saw your parents?" I said, when she was settled with a hot drink and some food.

'"I don't remember."

'"Have you written to them? Called them?"

'"It's too dangerous," she said. "Besides, I think I know what Dad would do if he knew where I was."

' "What do you mean?" There was something in her voice that scared me. Like she had cut herself off forever, mentally burned all her bridges. "Don't you think that he'd want to help?"

' "His idea of help would be to turn me in," she said. "We both know this. It's too dangerous to go within a hundred miles of him. In fact, I'm taking a big risk being here."

'I suddenly felt angry – and suspicious. It was contagious. The thought passed through my head that she had only come to me for money, that if she'd had somewhere else to go, or some other source of funds, she would have gone there instead. "So why did you come?" I said.

' "What? Aren't you pleased to see me?"

' "Of course I am," I said. "But I'm worried, too. I'm scared. We all are."

' "I understand," she said. "But I had no choice. Something more had to be done and the only question was, who would do it? Because peace wasn't happening. Civil rights wasn't happening. If anything, it was all getting worse. That was why we decided to disappear, so we could be more effective."

' "We?"

'She didn't respond.

' "Doing what?"

'She gave me a hard look. "I cannot and never will discuss anything related to the group." It sounded like a prepared statement. "Please don't ask me to do that. If you trust me, if you believe our cause is just, help me. If not, tell me now, and I will leave."

' "I trust you, Jennifer," I said. "But I'd feel better if I knew something."

' "I can't talk about it."

189

' "Is it these people I've been reading about in the papers? The Weather people. Are you one of the ones making bombs?"

' "I will say one thing, then you have to stop asking these questions," she said. "Do you understand?"

'I nodded. I felt that, if I tried to speak, I might break into tears – because even though she was there, even though I knew that she trusted me enough to be there, I also knew that I had lost some part of her already.

' "I am not a member of the group you just named," she said. "My aims are similar to theirs, however, and I respect what they are doing. That's all I can say."

'I nodded again. "All right," I said. "What do you want to do now? Have you had enough to eat?"

'She studied my face for a long moment, then she gave an odd smile, like she had run out of hope that anybody would ever understand what she was doing. Or that was how it seemed to me. Ever since she first disappeared, I've read books about that time, and they all suggest the kids were angry with their parents, dead set on violence, in it for the excitement. That just wasn't true – but I think she already knew how the story was going to be told. "I've had enough," she said. "Thank you." She got to her feet – a little unsteadily, it seemed. "If you don't mind, I have to sleep."

'And that was that. I showed her to her room, put out some towels and left her to sleep. It felt as if we had just signed some kind of contract. I don't know – a treaty, of sorts. I knew she was in a bad place, or she wouldn't have come asking for help, but I also knew that, when she lay down in that bed and let herself drift off to sleep, she was placing more trust in me than she had allowed herself with anyone for a long time. I could have picked up the phone and turned her in – part of me thought that was the better decision – but I didn't.

I loved her and she was a grown woman now. I had to believe she knew what she was doing.

'After that, she would call from a payphone somewhere, just to say she was fine, but she wouldn't tell me where she was, or what she was doing. Once, she turned up at the house with a man. It was midnight, but I heard the car pull into the drive and I got up to let her in. To begin with, we talked in the yard – which seemed silly to me, if she was so bent on secrecy. The man was older and, from his voice, he seemed like a kind-hearted person, but she wouldn't tell me anything about him, other than that he was a friend. He kept out of the light, stood back in the shadows, and he only spoke twice – I noticed he had a strong Boston accent – but I knew that he was the one behind the visit. Jennifer came inside for a while, but he stayed out in the yard by the car. She looked thin, but she said she was fine. She talked for a while, then she told me that she and her friend needed money for gas and food. I didn't have much cash in the house but I gave her that. She wouldn't take a cheque, so we agreed that she would come back the next day after I'd had a chance to go to the bank. I invited them to stay, but she said it was too risky. They'd be fine, she said.

'I had decided, by then, that I would never argue with her. I would take whatever she said and did on trust. It had been painful, keeping her secrets, but, as painful as it was, it was also a privilege. Any secret is a privilege. And if it's a good secret – if it's a matter of life or death – you can't help but keep it to yourself. Even if you wanted to tell it, you couldn't, because there's nobody in the world who really knows how this secret works. Nobody else really appreciates the great beauty that would go out of the world, if your secret were to be told. Does that sound fanciful?'

'I don't know,' I said. 'I've never had a secret to tell.'

Jean nodded. 'You have to treat it as a gift,' she said. 'Or it becomes a curse. I never told Jennifer's secret, but I lost her all the same. Maybe I was bound to lose her anyway. The best I can say is, I respected the choice she made, even though I didn't agree with it.'

'So when did you see her last?'

She shook her head. 'Oh, long ago,' she said. 'She came through a couple of times in the early 70s, always in the small hours, and I gave her whatever I could. Whatever she needed, really. Not that she asked for very much. I had money, after all – and she knew that. She could have asked for more. I would have given her anything and I'm not ashamed to say it. I had no way of knowing what she would do with the money I gave her, but I still believed she wouldn't hurt anybody. I read in the papers about the bombings. The town house. The bombing of the Pentagon in 1972. The attacks on police stations, the State Department. Gulf Oil. ITT. Those were all attributed to the Weather group, and she had said she wasn't with them, but I didn't believe her. Besides, every time a bomb went off, Weather Underground got the blame. What impressed me, though, was that nobody got hurt. Those bombings were symbolic – they were acts of retaliation against injustice. Did the money I gave her go toward those actions? Maybe. I'd rather think she spent it all on coffee and gasoline, but then, that's part of the action too, isn't it? Everything she did was directed toward the same end.

'The last time I saw her was in June 1974. Later that month, a bomb went off at Gulf Oil's office in Pittsburgh, though of course I have no way of knowing if she was involved in that. A couple of months after that, I got a postcard from a small town in Washington State. It wasn't signed, but I recognised her writing. She said she was starting a new life with a boy from Clarksville, Illinois. I haven't seen or heard from her since.'

'Who was the boy?'

She laughed. 'Ah,' she said. 'I should have explained.' She thought for a moment, trying to remember something. 'No, I can't recall the tune now,' she said. 'It was a song she used to listen to. "Last Train to Clarksville". By the Monkees. Before your time, I'm afraid.'

I shook my head. I had seen the Monkees on TV. I even remembered the song – 'Last Train to Clarksville' – it had been a big hit, but all I could recall of the lyrics was a single line that went something like *I'll meet you at the station*, or *You can meet me at the station*. Something like that. But the truth was that, apart from the Monkees and a few movies, I really didn't know anything about that era at all. Nixon. Watergate. The Weathermen. To me, it was mostly background to great films like *Medium Cool* and *The Parallax View*, or wonderfully bad ones, like *Zabriskie Point*. Jean told it all from memory, at times with an almost documentary attention to detail, as if it were engraved somewhere at the back of her mind – and it probably was, from months and years of waiting and worrying – but it was all stuff that had happened before I was born and it wasn't the kind of history they taught at my high school. What I knew about these events, when I knew anything at all, I knew from television and movies, or worse, from trivia games – and that was why this town-house bombing story seemed vaguely familiar. I wouldn't have dared to tell Jean this, but I knew about it because I'd read an article about how the building next to Dustin Hoffman's Greenwich Village apartment had blown up, and how Hoffman had personally rescued a number of paintings from the ensuing fire, while the two surviving bombers fled from the wreckage. It turned out that they, and three others, had been building a bomb in the house when it went off accidentally. Nobody knew what they had been doing, of course; one of the neighbours let them shower in his apartment and lent them clothes to wear, though I couldn't remember if that was Hoffman or somebody else. The one thing I did remember very clearly was that somebody – and this was definitely not Dustin Hoffman – had gone back inside the building after being warned to stay out because his completed tax return was in there. Meanwhile, the two young women who had survived the explosion were able to vanish into the night without a word of explanation, in spite of the number of police who attended the scene.

So, because of Dustin Hoffman, I was aware of all this, and maybe more, but it wasn't history for me. It had never been history. It was trivia. If a film star hadn't been involved, however tangentially, I would have known nothing about the town-house bombing of March 6, 1970. Just as I knew nothing, or next to nothing, about all these events Jean was telling me about. The bombing of the Capitol building in March 1971. Or the bombing of the Pentagon in May 1972. Or the attacks on ITT and Gulf Oil and the Kennecott Corporation. It was all just facts. Just – trivia.

'There was a line in the chorus,' Jean said. 'Jennifer would sing it all the time. *And I don't know if I'm ever coming home.* She liked that, long before it meant anything more to her than a line in a song. Or maybe it had always meant something special – maybe she had always . . .' Jean studied my face. 'We communicate in all kinds of ways. To ourselves, too. Sometimes I go around with some old song in my head, no idea why and then, suddenly, in the middle of the afternoon,

I remember the words. And it was a message from – what? My subconscious mind? I'm not sure I believe in that. Back of the mind, maybe, but . . . Anyhow, that was her message. She was telling me she wouldn't be coming home again. And she never did.'

'So you haven't seen her since 1974?'

'No.'

'And you didn't look for her?'

She smiled sadly. 'I let it go to begin with. It was her choice, after all. But then, after a long time, I began to wonder where she was. What she was doing. Years had passed, most of the Weather activists had come out of hiding and almost nobody had gone to jail. Some of the leaders even had jobs at universities and law schools. So why should she stay in hiding when there was no need . . .' She shook her head. 'I never did understand how it all worked. How things seemed to end, and a new era would begin, when nothing had really changed that much. But then, Jennifer had always said that her generation wasn't unique. They were just part of a longer struggle that started long before they came on the scene and – well, I guess it's still going on now, somewhere. Anyhow, I thought about it for a while, then I decided it would do me good if I went on a road trip. Which I did.'

'You went looking for her?'

'Not exactly,' she said. 'I just went on a road trip, that just so happened to take me to the place where she posted that card. I wasn't seriously looking for her. I knew she must be living under a false name, and I didn't really have any expectations. But then, one spring day, on the Oregon coast, I stopped at a little arts and crafts gallery that doubled as the only decent coffee house in that town. I wasn't looking for clues, nothing like that, I just wanted a coffee and a good angle to try and figure out who or what was following me—'

'Wait a minute—'

'Yes, I know,' she said. 'It sounds paranoid, but I could feel it in my bones. Somebody was following me and I wanted to know who it was. So I was just acting casual, stopping off for a cup of joe and a slice of pie, when I saw something – and this is strange, because I wasn't looking for anything particular but I recognised immediately that several items, several artworks that were for sale in that gallery, were all made by the same person and that person was Jennifer. Which meant she was close.'

'How did you know she was the one who made them?'

'I just knew,' she said. 'They just reminded me of the work she used to do when she was a teenager, all the drawings and—'

'But that could have been—'

'No,' she said. 'It was *her*. Like I said, there were several items for sale, so I bought one, not making any big fuss over it. Then, while the woman who ran the place was wrapping it for me, I asked her if the artist was local. She didn't answer right away – I don't think she wanted to talk about it – but I must have seemed all right to her and she told me a name, a false name, of course, and said that she didn't know where the woman lived, that she came by once a month or so to drop off more pieces and pick up any payments. She thought she lived somewhere up the coast, but that was all she knew, she said, and I didn't want to seem too curious, so I let it go. Then, when I went outside, there was a man standing by my car, a man in a dark suit, who obviously wasn't a local.' She paused for effect. She had never told this story before and it thrilled her, I think, in some dark part of her mind, just telling the details. A man in a dark suit. Not a local. How did she know that? Maybe she had even imagined it all – she had already gotten the notion that she was being followed into her head and she would have been inclined to see dangers that weren't really there.

'So what did he want?' I said.

'I don't know,' she said. 'Maybe it was nothing. I walked over to the car and he turned for a moment and looked at me. His face was blank, but I could tell that he knew who I was. So I made some polite remark and he just shook his head and smiled. Everything else was neutral, and if he hadn't smiled, I would have forgotten all about it, but he *did* smile and there was something behind that smile, something . . . Superior. Like he was trying to say, it's just a matter of time. I'm here, and I won't be going away, or if I do, somebody else will take my place and eventually you will make a mistake and . . .' She broke off and looked at me expectantly, but I didn't know what to say. I knew she wasn't lying, but I wasn't sure I believed her entirely. It had been a coincidence, surely. Nothing more.

Jean laughed. 'God knows,' she said. 'It might all have been in my head. It was just . . . It was the way he smiled. Like he didn't care what happened, because he was enjoying himself.'

'So you didn't find the artist? The woman who lived up the coast?'

She shook her head.

'So it could have been anybody?'

She shook her head again. 'No,' she said. 'It was Jennifer. I was that close – but so was this man. Who could have been anybody. FBI. Police. A reporter. A phantom. I didn't know. All I knew was, I'd be putting her at risk, if I went any further.'

'So what did you do?'

'The only thing I could do,' she said. 'I went home.'

She was getting tired. I sensed that, but I also sensed that, if I didn't leave, she would keep going till some part the story that hadn't yet formed at the back of her mind, or in her subconscious, finally got told. Because this story was incomplete, even more so than the others, and some part of her believed that, if she could just go over it one more time, some new clue, some new understanding, would emerge.

'I don't know,' she said. 'I didn't want to turn around and just go back. And I've thought about it often since then. It was just – I couldn't take that risk.'

'No,' I said. 'I can see that.'

She smiled. 'Yes,' she said. 'But there was something else. Something I didn't know then, though I realised later that it was at the back of my mind all along.'

'What do you mean?'

'I didn't want to give Jennifer away,' she said. 'But at the same time, even while I was driving west, I didn't know for sure if I'd be welcome.'

'What does that mean?' I said. 'Of course you would have been—'

'She was hiding. When somebody is hiding, the last thing they want is to be found. By anyone.'

Her eyes were dark now. All of a sudden, she had the look of someone who hasn't slept in weeks. 'It's getting late,' I said. 'Maybe we should call it a day.'

She smiled – and it occurred to me again, as it had done several times before, that she always smiled when she was unhappy. It also occurred to me that I didn't know who that smile was for. At that moment, though, it just felt like some exaggerated form of courtesy. 'Maybe we should,' she said.

NIGHTS AT THE MORGUE

I found Laurits in his room, watching *Chimes at Midnight*. 'You look like a man who only has two hours to live,' I said.

He froze the screen and grinned. 'Maybe I have,' he said.

'Well,' I said, 'don't forget those five minutes.'

'Uh-huh . . . Listen, are you all right?'

'Sure,' I said. 'Why do you ask?'

'Just asking.'

'Ah.' I glanced at the screen. Falstaff and his accomplices in white friars' robes were chasing the hapless pilgrims away through tall slender trees in spring leaf, frozen now, timeless. 'I'm going to get some sleep,' I said. 'I've not been sleeping lately.'

He looked puzzled for a moment and I realised, suddenly, that since I'd met Jean, I had become something of a mystery to him. It felt good. 'I have to go away for a day or two,' he said. 'I'll be back on Friday. Maybe we could do something, Saturday?'

I nodded. 'Maybe,' I said.

He smiled. 'You don't sound very enthusiastic,' he said.

I didn't know what to say. We had been drifting away from one another for a while by then, I guess, but I didn't see that until later. I looked at him. Something had changed since we'd first met. He seemed more impatient, less sure of himself. 'I'll see you Saturday,' I said. 'Maybe we could watch a movie.'

'What movie?'

'How about *Accattone*? We haven't watched that in – decades.'

He grinned, but I knew his heart wasn't in it. 'All right,' he said. 'It's a date.'

It felt like autumn on the air, as I walked over the next day to Audubon Road. I had slept well, though, and I was enjoying the cool air and the ordinary pleasure of walking, my body light, supple – or suppler, at least, than it had been. By the gate to Jean's garden, Christina Vogel was keeping watch, like a sentry on duty, her face hidden by a beekeeper's veil and a wide-brimmed hat.

'Hi there,' I said. 'Is Miss Culver at home?'

The girl nodded, then shook her head. 'You have to say the password,' she said. 'Or you can't go in.'

I nodded. 'I knew that,' I said. I could barely make out her face under the thick black veil. 'Thing is, Miss Culver told me the password. But I forgot it.'

With some effort, she pulled the veil up and peered out at me. 'Is that true?' she said.

'Brownie's honour,' I said.

'Are you a Brownie?'

'I was.'

'Say the promise.'

'Okay.' I thought for a moment. It had been a long time since Dad had driven me back and forth to Brownie meetings at the old community hall on Teale Road. 'On my honour, I will try,' I recited perfectly from what seemed like another world, and maybe even another language, 'to serve God and my country, to help people at all times, and to live by the Girl Scout Law.'

Christina nodded gravely. 'Pass,' she said.

I found Jean in the kitchen, cooking stew. All around her were piles of diced vegetables and freshly chopped herbs from the garden – as far as I could tell, those herbs were the only things she deliberately cultivated, though she might have scattered wild-flower seeds around the edges of her patch of woodland, and maybe, long ago, she had planted some of those trees. The Chinese dogwood that was just visible from the kitchen window, say. The stand of shadbush beyond the lawn, where I couldn't tell how far the property went on. I had seen trilliums and clumps of lilies out there, so I guessed she had planted those.

'Oh, good,' she said. 'You're here.' She waved her knife hand vaguely. 'We need fresh tea. And there are blueberry scones in that tin over there.'

I didn't say anything. It amused me, how happy she was to order me about. It amused me, too, how she set so much store by fresh tea and home baking. It all amused me – and I was happy. Why was that? Why was I so happy, whenever it was just us, sitting for hours in her kitchen, eating cakes, like two old women whose lives were behind them? 'I almost didn't make it,' I said, as I brewed some tea, substituting lapsang souchong for whatever herbal mix she had been drinking.

'Ah,' she said. 'Did you forget the password?'

'I didn't know it,' I said. 'Nobody told me.'

She laughed. By now, the stew was set to go, the vegetables and chickpeas and herbs covered in a thick, yellowish stock on the hob. Jean sat down, and helped herself to tea. As usual, she dispensed with small talk. Apart from her curiosity about my parents, she had never asked me about my own life, about Laurits, or what I was doing at college. We were there for the story, and that was that. She took a scone from the baker's tin and spread it with some gooseberry jam. The scones were sweet and crumbly, with just a hint of moisture at the centre. 'I was telling you about Jennifer,' she said. 'About the secrets she made me keep. I suppose I felt privileged, being party to those secrets, but I felt guilty too, not being able to tell Jeremy and Gloria what I knew. Not that I knew that much. Still, I could have told them she was alive, at least. That she wasn't dead or in prison, or shacked up in some Haight-Ashbury drug den. I don't know – there were stories going round that must have scared them, stories about kids going mad on LSD, kids hooked on heroin. I hoped they would know that Jennifer wasn't like that. She was too serious. She'd told me once that, as far as she was concerned, the drugs on the street were put there by the government to keep black people down. Hard drugs, anyway. Heroin was an FBI conspiracy, she said. So I knew, at least, that she wasn't going to end up a junkie, like the scare stories in the papers. She was political. She was serious. She had to be careful all the time, living underground – and I knew how careful she was being, only I couldn't tell anybody that I knew, or I would never see her again.' She smiled grimly. 'So it was sheer bad luck that I was in Virginia when the FBI called Gloria to say they had found Jennifer's body.'

'Wait—'

She held a finger to her lips. 'Shh,' she said. She gave me a questioning look, then she resumed the story. 'I don't know what the occasion was, but I had gone down to visit Gloria, something I did all too rarely, even though I knew she was lonely and even my company was better than nothing. Jeremy was gone pretty much all of the time by then. I don't think she missed him, but she didn't like being alone either, and her old crowd, such as they had been, had melted away. People like that are superstitious. They have to be. In their world, only the lucky are tolerated and, after Jennifer disappeared, Gloria didn't seem lucky any more.

'Still, I have to say that I was shocked, that time, when I saw her. I'd driven down expecting to find a slightly older version of the woman I'd seen a few months earlier, and it really was a shock when I saw how worn down she was. We were all ageing, I knew that, and heaven knows she had gone through something like hell with both of her children, but this wasn't just the usual wear and tear. This was something else. It was frightening.'

'Frightening how?'

'Oh, don't get me wrong. She still had that same peach-blossomy look she'd always had, but it was too soft now. Too soft and too – dark. Something had dimmed in her.'

'Dimmed?'

'Yes. Like someone had left the room and switched off most of the lights. Not all, but most of them. Of course, I knew by then that her marriage was a facade. But that wasn't really what ailed her. I mean, marriage ages a woman, I'd seen that before, often enough, but this was a dimming of *everything* – her face, her eyes, her skin . . . You see, what had been attractive in her before was the light in her face, a brightness, a sense of expectation. Like she'd been promised all her life that the future would be beautiful, all she had to do was show up . . . It was all defined for her – marriage, motherhood, Christmas Eve, candlelit dinners, attractive, clever children . . . All she had to do was be her attractive, peach-blossom self.

Now, though, she had lost any sense of promise. All she had was a surface – keeping up appearances, pretending it was all one big merry-go-round. And it was, much of the time – a giant merry-go-round fuelled by gin and maraschino cherries. For someone who isn't really the social type, those visits could be pretty gruelling. Also, I was always nervous when I was away from home, in case Jennifer tried to call and couldn't reach me. What if it was urgent? What if she was in trouble and I was the only one who could help? She had told me once that I could go to prison for aiding a fugitive, and I had just stared at her, till she began to laugh. "What is it?" she said. "What did I say?"

'But I couldn't tell her. She didn't see that I would go to prison forever, if it meant she could be free to go back to her old life and start again. We all would – but she couldn't see that. Still, I didn't like being away and I was glad it was my last evening in Virginia – and it was all set to be a quiet evening, just Gloria and me, none of the so-called friends she could still summon up from time to time. It was a beautiful evening, early autumn, as I recall. The garden was full of asters and Japanese anemones. The sweet gums by the lake had just begun to turn, but I could still smell the last of the roses that I'd helped Gloria train around the balcony. When the phone rang, I didn't pay it any mind. Gloria went off to answer it and I sat dreaming in my chair by the French windows. I don't know if I could have lived like that all the time, but it was good for a few days now and then. Out over the lake a single bird headed home to roost. It was all a little too good to be true. Then Gloria came back in, her face white, her mouth trembling. "What is it?" I said. "What's wrong?"

'"That was the FBI Field Office in Richmond," she said. "They say we have to go right away."

' "What?"

' "We have to go," she said. "They think . . ." She thought for a moment. She'd had three drinks already. "I can't drive."

' "It's all right," I said. "I can drive. Just tell me—"

'Her face crumpled and she gave an odd, broken sound. The kind of noise a small animal might make – a lapdog, or a kitten, maybe – if you hurt it deliberately. "They found a body," she said. "They think it might be Jennifer."

'It wasn't Jennifer. I knew that before we even got in the car. It wasn't Jennifer because she wouldn't have gone anywhere within a hundred miles of Eastern Virginia. She had told me as much – so it had to be a mistake. But of course I couldn't tell Gloria that. Later, I heard that we weren't the only people they – the authorities, the FBI – had subjected to this particular form of torture. It seems some genius in the higher echelons had come up with this trick to put pressure on family members they thought might be sheltering people who had gone underground. They called in the late evening, when people were just about to go to bed. Or when they had settled down with that third Tom Collins, and they said they had found a body. They didn't say anything else. They didn't say how this body had come to be in their care, or how the deceased had died. Sometimes, they didn't even bother to find a body that looked very much like their suspect. Always, they were polite and courteous, formal, not invasive, but it was never in any doubt that what they were doing was a parody of what you would do in a genuine situation where the body of a loved one had to be identified. They didn't just want to provoke fear, they also wanted their contempt to be just visible behind the mask. I didn't know all that till later, though. At the time, all I had was what Jennifer had told me, the sad conviction that she had to be safe, because she had assured me, in so many words, that her father would betray her if she went anywhere near him.

'Still, as I drove Gloria's Lincoln Continental over to Richmond, I was already beginning to mourn. After all, at that time, I had no personal reason to mistrust the FBI. Jennifer had told me stories about their actions against the Black Panthers and other minority groups, but I had put it all down to the exaggerations of the street and, at the time, we all assumed they would draw the line at these well-meaning white kids who were our sons and daughters and nieces and sisters and brothers. But things had changed, it wasn't the 60s any more, it wasn't just kids with long hair and slogans, it was bombs in public buildings and hardened activists talking revolution. Now, things had turned ugly – or so it seemed to us, who hadn't ever seen how ugly it had been before, or maybe had caught glimpses of the ugliness and chosen to turn a blind eye to it. Now Nixon was in the White House on a law-and-order ticket and, now, as the sweet Virginia night slid by, I found myself mourning without knowing who or what it was, exactly, that I was grieving for.

'But I'd been right. The body they showed us wasn't her. It was a woman, maybe thirty-five, maybe a little younger, but any resemblance between her and Jennifer was purely academic. And I guessed as soon as we got there. As soon as the agent we'd been assigned met us at the door – I remember, he was shorter than I had expected, a crumpled-looking man with sandy-coloured hair and very cold green eyes – as soon this unprepossessing, rather bored-looking man showed us to the room where the body was laid out, dirty, the hair crusted with some kind of chemical or residue, the face dark and sunken, I knew that this was a cruel game they were playing.

That woman looked like she had starved before she died, her body was so thin and – small . . . She was – diminished in a way that was unlike anything I had seen outside those newsreels of war zones and famines. Had they chosen her for that reason? Had they chosen her for the suffering that was still inscribed on her face? I knew it wasn't Jennifer right away, because I had seen her a few weeks earlier – but then, Gloria hadn't seen her for years and, though it should have been obvious that this wasn't her little girl, she wasn't sure at first. They had said there was a body. They had called her house. She had sat in her ridiculous, expensive car, preparing herself for the worst, and how could it not be Jennifer, after all they had done? But it wasn't Jennifer. She stared for a long time at this pathetic skeleton, this parody of a beloved child who, even if she wasn't her child, would have been *somebody*'s daughter. Somebody, somewhere, was waiting, dreading this moment, dreading the call that had been delayed, or maybe suspended altogether, so the Federal Bureau of Investigation could have its ugly little game with us. Had they known Jeremy wasn't at home? Had they cross-checked his movements and waited till he was far away so they could bring in a frightened, half-drunk woman on her own and make her stand over the body of a stranger, frightened and desperate and then guilty for feeling glad that it wasn't the child she had lost? Because it didn't matter, it didn't matter at all, whether the body looked like that child – it still served as a reminder that, one day, any day now, Jennifer would be there, on a table in a cold room, possibly unidentified, maybe even unidentifiable. Or maybe she was already there. Maybe she was sealed away somewhere, a Jane Doe in some morgue in Ohio, or Wisconsin, and nobody would ever know who she was.

'The worst thing, though, was Gloria's laugh. She stared a long time at the body, and then, suddenly, she laughed and turned to the agent. "This isn't my daughter," she said – and she laughed again, the kind of tight, surprised laugh that you can't hold back when somebody does something so despicable, you can't quite believe it. "This isn't my daughter," she said again – and for a moment, I thought she was about to slap him. Maybe he did too, but his face didn't change. He looked just as bored as before, just as indifferent. I wondered, then, if this was something he did, if maybe he was some kind of specialist? And if Gloria *had* slapped him, would he have just smiled and asked her to sign some kind of release form? I stepped forward and took Gloria's arm. "Come on," I said. "Let's go home."

'Gloria looked into the man's face for a long moment, then she turned away. She wasn't crying. She was angry, though I knew that wouldn't last. I would drive her home and we would fix another drink. Then another. The anger would fade and all that would remain would be disgust. I had to get her home, before that disgust set in.'

She stopped talking suddenly, and looked away, off to the left. Christina Vogel was standing at the kitchen window, in her black beekeeper's veil. The window was open. 'What is it, Christina?' Jean said, her voice mild, barely even curious.

Christina seemed uncertain of the information she was about to offer. 'I saw an owl,' she said.

'Really?' Jean smiled reassuringly. 'Well, they come out in the daytime, now and then.'

Christina nodded, but she didn't say anything else.

'Where is it now?' Jean said.

Christina shook her head, and the black veil swayed around her eyes. 'Gone away,' she said.

208

'Well,' Jean said, 'that's what they do. They go away. They can't really see well in the daylight.' She took a scone and went over to the window. 'Here,' she said. 'Have a scone.'

Christina took the scone, shot a glance at me, then looked back to Jean. 'Can I have another?' she asked. 'For the birds?'

ZBIGNIEW CYBULSKI

Was it coincidence that we had been playing the Famous Death game at Sidetracks the night before Jean told me about Simon's disappearance? I imagine not. We'd played that game often in recent weeks, there was a sense of death in the air, or not death, but the beauty attendant on death, always a matter of fascination, not just to Laurits, but also to more than a few of the others. The game was simple. One player would choose a famous person from history and the others had to guess cause of death. The game didn't really have a name – in my own mind, it was called Famous Death, but nobody else called it that – and for once it didn't originate with Laurits. Nevertheless, he was the best player in the group. Because there were people at Sidetracks from a wide range of backgrounds and individual tastes, the subjects of the game could vary wildly – French kings, country singers, sports legends, explorers, movie stars, writers, painters. But we were most beguiled by the car wrecks and suicides, the bodies never found and those recovered from the cold debris days afterward, the frozen, the starved, the slow descents into madness, surrounded by bewildered or avaricious minions, the great mansion falling silent, then dark, like something out of those Orson Welles movies that, even though he never actually made them, we still viewed on a regular basis in what Laurits so liked to call the chambers of our imagery.

The chambers of our imagery – well, after all, that was the point of all our games. To bring out whatever we found at the back of our minds and show it in the common light, to share it with *someone*, and so have it be seen, because that was the best of us, that inward zone of fantasy and invention, and we felt lonely if we couldn't make it visible. It was just another variety of show and tell, a way of ratifying our visions slightly, pretending that they were nothing more than a variation on Trivial Pursuit. It wasn't the facts that mattered, it was the story. Laurits loved this game, though he always protested when it started up. It was too easy, he would say, too simple. It needed to be harder, or more complicated – and he would propose all kinds of alternate rules, new ways of playing that added more detail, a finer texture, more depth to the account. Not only that, it might shift the emphasis away from all the die-young-leave-a-good-looking-corpse-better-to-burn-out-than-to-fade-away stories that people were always pulling out.

'We all love a glamorous death,' he would say. 'People who die before their time in car wrecks and gun battles, or just walking away into the heat of a Mexican summer, high on whatever. The trouble is, history is written by the survivors. History is written by old people. People who didn't get to where they are by being glamorously dead. They get to where they are by courting power and then, when they have gained a little bit of power themselves, they tell the stories that accompany power. The official versions. Textbook versions. Lies.' He was always saying this kind of thing – or some variation on it – as if he took it for granted that it was obvious to all of us. But it wasn't – and he must have known that. It was just that he had decided, at some point in his life, that he would assume a consensus that ought to have been there, even if it wasn't. The way the people he was talking about – the rich, the powerful, their various operatives and minions – assumed *their* consensus. 'To get your wish and die beautifully on the lonesome highway at twenty-five,' he would say, 'you have to give up your part in the telling of the story. You are part of the story, but it's somebody else telling it – and you can bet they will tell it in all the ways that suit them. That's the price you have to pay.'

In spite of his criticism, though, Laurits usually chose someone from the history of cinema, almost always someone who died young. Of course, his favourite death – partly because it was tragic, but also for its sheer perversity – was Zbigniew Cybulski's. He hated it that some people thought that Cybulski had committed suicide; yes, he had been killed when he fell under the wheels of a speeding train, but it had been his custom to hop on and off moving trains all his life, something that seemed to have become a preoccupation for Andrzej Wajda, who foreshadows Maciek's death in *Ashes and Diamonds* with a scene where a passing goods train crosses a viaduct in the middle distance, directly behind Cybulski's head, just minutes before he is shot. Laurits would say that scene was inspired by André Kertész's photograph of a Meudon street scene, where a train crosses a viaduct at the far end of a road while a man in a wide-brimmed hat and a heavy overcoat walks toward us, carrying a large, flat object wrapped in old newspapers, an object that might be a painting, but is most likely a mirror. I wasn't so sure. I wasn't convinced that things were always so deliberate, even though Laurits could make an argument that would connect almost anything to pretty much anything else. Still, nobody could deny the significance of trains in Cybulski's art, as well as his life: our first sight of him in Jerzy Kawalerowicz's 1959 film, *Pociag*, for example, shows him hopping on to a moving train, then hanging out the window to wave to someone he has left behind. On the day he died, he had just spent several days in Wroclaw with his lover, Marlene Dietrich (who said of him later that 'he was the kindest, the most beautiful man in the whole world. He was so beautiful that every time I see his photograph I cry'). Marlene had decided to go to Warsaw and, though Cybulski was supposed to be filming in Wroclaw, he decided to accompany her and they bought couchette tickets on the midnight train to the capital. On reflection, however, they agreed that he should stay on for a few days to finish the film, then join her later – rumours persisted for years that they were planning to work together – but then, impulsive as ever, Cybulski changed his mind and ran after the accelerating train. As he attempted his trademark leap, he slipped beneath the wheels and was killed instantly. Dietrich was not informed of what had happened until the next morning. One of Laurits' prize fantasies – the movie he played most often in the chambers of his imagery – was of the film Cybulski and Dietrich might have made together. Naturally, in its ideal form, this film could only have been directed by Wajda. It would have been a masterpiece, of course, one of those impossible projects that history refuses to realise, because it only needs to suggest them, like Welles' abortive version of *Heart of Darkness*, or Robert Bresson's *Genesis*. Though it could not have ended with the scene that Laurits – in a fit of what I supposed was black humour – had once roughed out for my consideration, a scene in which, all of a sudden, the night train to Warsaw screeches to an emergency stop, just fifty yards from the platform where the central character, a legendary actress in her mid-sixties, has just parted from her much younger lover. When the actress asks what is causing the delay, the railroad staff shrug it off, but a kindly attendant, who knows nothing of her relations with the body that is presently being extracted from the train's wheels, brings her an extra blanket and a hot drink (laced, perhaps, with the best Polish vodka). 'Sleep,' he tells her. 'We will soon be on our way.'

That death was still there, at the back of my head, when I arrived at Jean Culver's house the next day. It was warm, but not too hot, sunny, the gardens along Audubon Road empty and silent. I listened for the sound of an axe as I passed through the grove of trees in front of the house, but it was just as quiet here as on the road – and there was no sign of Jean in the yard. The side door that led to the kitchen was open, her axe set against the porch wall, the hallway still, the entire house like a held breath in the summer sun. I called out her name as I passed through the hall and went into the kitchen and it felt, not only that she wasn't there, but that she, or whoever lived here, had just walked away, a few minutes before I arrived, leaving everything behind. I went to the foot of the stairs.

'Hello?'

My voice sounded small and alien in the stairwell. I had never seen the upper floors of that house and, for a long moment, I thought about going up and checking them, room by room, in case she was sick, or maybe injured, and couldn't respond to my calls. Maybe she had fallen down. Maybe she was lying upstairs, unconscious, maybe bleeding from a wound where she had hit her head on the edge of a table, film-noir style. It was easy to forget how old she was, but she *was* very old, and old people had accidents, no matter how fit they were. Their bones were more brittle, for one thing. I knew all this, and I know I had every reason to go and look – and yet, at the same time, I couldn't quite bring myself to climb that flight of stairs. It seemed too much of an intrusion.

All of a sudden I sensed something behind me and I turned. Christina Vogel was standing in the doorway, almost a silhouette, staring at me. I walked back down the hall to talk to her, hoping she wouldn't feel threatened and run – and, as I came, she did back away, but only for a few steps, out on to the porch. When the light fell on her, I saw that she was wearing a white chiffon dress with a scalloped lace appliqué neckline. It looked like a First Communion dress.

'Miss Culver has gone to see the doctor,' she said. She didn't seem frightened, but I didn't think it would take much to set her off, back to the safety of the trees.

I nodded. 'I love your dress,' I said.

Christina stood up on her tiptoes, and took a breath. 'First Holy Communion,' she said.

'I know. It's very beautiful. When did Miss Culver leave?'

'Today.'

I nodded. 'That's great,' I said. 'Did she leave a message for me?'

Christina nodded back, but she didn't say anything.

'Okay,' I said. 'What did she say?'

The girl smiled happily. 'She said she was going to see the doctor.'

Jean got back around an hour later. I had decided to wait, not because I thought Christina Vogel was capable of any deliberate malice, but I couldn't be sure that she might not accidentally do some harm. I had a notion that the girl watched Jean when she was chopping wood and maybe she spied through the window when Jean was baking, or making tea.

She might have tried to copy her, with grave consequences. Still, it had seemed that she was reluctant to come into the house when she first appeared. She had come to the door, but she hadn't come very far.

When Jean arrived, she didn't see me at first. She came through the hall and into the kitchen, and in the split second before she noticed me, her face looked dark. Grave. The moment she saw me, however, she brightened. 'Sorry,' she said. 'I had to go out for a while.'

'I know,' I said. 'Christina Vogel gave me the message.'

'Ah. I didn't think she would remember.'

'Is something wrong?'

'Wrong?'

'You had to go see the doctor suddenly,' I said. 'I just wondered—'

'Oh no,' she said. She filled the kettle. 'Everything's fine. I just needed to refill a prescription. I forgot to get a new supply of my little orange pills.' She set the kettle down on the cooker. 'You should have made yourself some tea,' she said.

For once, the tea was not in the least exotic. Ceylon tea, very dark, with milk and a small plate of cookies. 'I'm running low,' she said. 'I'll have to have a big baking day.' She smiled. 'So. Where to begin.' She studied my face, as if I would know the answer. 'I guess I haven't talked much about Simon,' she said. 'And that seems odd to me, now, because he was the one everybody noticed when the children were growing up. First, because he was so good-looking – if that marriage had one good outcome, it was my nephew's beautiful face. At first sight, when he was younger, you would say he looked like his father, but there was an extra quality, a fineness of feature and a kind of – I'm not sure how best to say it – a kind of depth that you could get lost in. Then, as he grew older, that quality got more pronounced, so by the time he was fifteen, everyone just fell in love with him at first sight. Jennifer never had that – she wouldn't have wished for it, either – and for her Simon was just kin, but she increasingly found herself with new friends, girls who latched on to her as a way of getting access to her brother. None of those girls lasted very long, though. Neither of the children had any strong friendships, they were too busy with other things. In Jennifer's case, her studies. Politics, even at any early age. Her artwork, of course. Those strange masks she made. Simon's interests were not at all academic. He loved animals, horses in particular. I have heard tell that Gloria was something of a horsewoman before she married, though I never saw that side of her. Simon, on the other hand, went out whenever he could get away. As a teenager, he would disappear for whole days at a time. Nobody ever knew where he was, but when they asked he would just say he'd been out riding. He was something of an artist, too, though his work was more obvious than Jennifer's – illustrative of things he had seen, rather than drawn for its own sake. His room was full of sketchbooks, drawings of snakes and birds and deer, sketches of trees, always things from nature. Though never horses, for some reason. I asked him about that and he told me couldn't draw people.

'"But what about horses?" I said.

'"Oh, that's easy," he said. "As far as I'm concerned, horses are people." I thought he would go on and say more, but he left it at that. For him, horses were people, and that was that. In fact, they were more than people, in the usual sense. They were kin. More kin, to him, than his parents. I don't mean to say he was anything less than a good son. He was, most decidedly, a good son. A dutiful son, in fact. But that was the problem, right there – he was dutiful. As I said, he loved Jeremy with a kind of fierceness when he was little, but as he grew up, and his father was away from home more and more often, he built his own, separate, detached world and, most of the time, he stayed there. Alone. He was fond of Jennifer, but she was younger and bookish and they had so little in common that there was a kind of abstract quality to his affection. What was more disturbing, though – sometimes I found it chilling – was his attitude to his mother. Again, he was polite, always, but it couldn't have been clearer that this woman did not interest him in the least. If she wasn't being a nuisance, with her neuroses and what he called her *fluttering*, she was plain dull. By the time he was twelve, his basic attitude was to humour her. It was like when a child decides that God and religion and the whole heaven business is a just a heap of nonsense, but keeps on going to church for his family's sake. That was how Simon finally was about everything, or everything to do with other people, at least. You looked at him and it was as if he was slowly disappearing. He got average grades in school, had no friends to speak of and, in spite of his film-star looks – and by his mid-teens he was that handsome – there were no girlfriends that anybody knew about. Then two things happened. One led to the other, I think, but whatever the truth of that was, he finally got his wish. He finally got to vanish completely from all our lives. Maybe I'll tell you that story sometime.' She put her hand on my arm, and gave me what could have been a grandmotherly smile. 'But now, I am going to have to rest for a while. It's been a busy day.'

'Wait,' I said. 'That's not fair. You said he got to vanish—'

'Completely,' she said.

'What does that even mean?'

'He was gone, Kate,' she said. 'That's what it means. Maybe I'll tell you another time, but now, I really have to rest.'

I nodded. 'Fine,' I said. 'Sorry. I just want to ask, seriously. Are you really all right?'

She patted my arm softly. 'I'm an old woman,' she said. 'I do my best to ignore that, but sometimes you just have to listen to your body. And my body says right now that I need to rest.'

'That's all?'

She smiled. 'That's all,' she said. 'Come back in the morning and I'll tell you about the man who gave the secret of the bomb to the Russians.'

'What about Simon?'

'His story can wait. You're not telling me you don't want to hear one of the strangest stories in twentieth-century espionage, are you?'

I smiled and shook my head. 'I can't wait,' I said.

THE GOOD TRAITOR

Jean was in the yard when I got to her house the next day. She had just finished chopping some wood – and though it was clear that she hadn't cut as much as usual, she looked her usual self. 'I'm just about to wash up and make some tea,' she said. 'Or would you prefer coffee?'

'I'd love a coffee,' I said.

'Well,' she said, 'let's go to Sacred Grounds.'

The coffee house was busy. Our usual place by the window was taken, so we found a table near the counter, where we could see Annette and another woman in the back room, busy wrapping cakes and cookies up in greaseproof paper. Then, when it was all wrapped, they laid the items out on a large baker's tray. 'Kids' party,' Annette called. Jean nodded. A tall girl with very long blonde hair came out to take our order.

Jean was eager to tell her next story. She seemed to have forgotten that she hadn't finished telling about Simon, but then, maybe that had been deliberate. 'Gloria passed away in the summer of 1984,' she said, as soon as we sat down. 'I don't usually use that term to talk about death, but it's the most appropriate in this case, because it seemed like she had been more or less absent for years so it was hardly a big surprise when she finally disappeared altogether. That was

220

how it seemed to me, anyhow. Maybe Jeremy saw things differently, but I don't think they had much of a life together at all, those last several years. Their children were gone, Gloria spent most of the time in bed, Jeremy was still travelling, though I'm not sure what he was doing by then. I know he didn't like the government he was working for now, but that had nothing to do with Jennifer's politics, or the fact that he had lost her because she thought – and this was strange, because he never seemed to understand – she thought they were on opposite sides in what, for her, was a war, pure and simple. But he never accepted that. He thought they had – what? Differences of opinion, maybe. I have to say, I was in awe of his ability to deceive himself about that – but then, he hadn't spoken to Jennifer for years and he'd never really understood what she was fighting for anyway. Like everybody else he'd always thought it was only about Vietnam – and now that war was over, surely she could give up and come back to the fold. It was *history*. How my brother, neither stupid nor naïve on most counts, could allow himself to succumb to the notion that, because something was *officially* over, it was really *over*, is beyond me. We were born in Alabama, we were raised in Virginia. Who better than us to know that nothing is ever *over*. You remember that book, the one they made all the fuss about, what – *The End of History*? Some Reagan guy wrote it, after the Berlin Wall came down, and it was all, look, we won, our system is better, blah, blah, blah, and everybody loved that idea. That it was all over, that we could just get on with exploiting everybody because we have the best system and as soon as they understand that, then they can work hard and join us and get their share, which won't be much, but it will be more than they have now.'

She broke off suddenly and gave me a sheepish look. 'Listen to me, now,' she said. 'I sound like her. Like Jennifer . . . Jennifer used to say, the real trouble with these people was that they thought everybody wanted to be rich like them. They couldn't understand that some people genuinely wanted other things, like peace, or justice. Real equality. Clean water everywhere, not just in the penthouse suite. She said she wanted to scream at them: I don't want your wealth. Your wealth is pathological. It's just another sign that you have no—' She grinned. 'No heart,' she said. 'But here I am again. Digressing. Where was I?'

'You were talking about—'

'That's right,' she said. 'My brother. Who really *believed*. Way past the point when any reasonable person could go on believing, he kept the faith. And everything I've been saying is relevant, here, because my brother really wasn't stupid, it was just that his loyalty was so strong, it took more than ordinary intelligence to break it. Why he was so very loyal is another question. He'd seen our father killed in the street and he had watched as the men who were responsible got away with murder. I don't mean the fool with the gun, but the men who gave him permission to be out there that day. The men he served. When Jeremy saw those men walk away with smiles on their faces, he should have learned a lesson, but he went completely the other way. He thought the system was broken and needed fixing. He didn't even allow himself to think that the system worked pretty much the way it was designed to work, in the interests of the men who had our father killed and other men just like them. He needed to be loyal to something. If Jeremy's is story about anything, it's about misplaced loyalty.'

'To whom, exactly?'

'Do you know what they called the bombs we dropped on Hiroshima and Nagasaki?'

I knew that, or I should have done, but nothing came into my head.

Jean shook her head and sighed. 'They were called Fat Man and Little Boy,' she said.

'Yes,' I said. I remembered it now.

'Fat Man and Little Boy.' She repeated the words with obvious contempt. '*That* was where his misplaced loyalty went. To *that*.'

'I don't understand.'

She patted my arm and continued telling her story. 'I remember when it happened. Nagasaki, I mean. Everyone was so – happy. As if something wonderful had been achieved. Then the telephone rang. It was Jeremy, calling to wish me happy birthday. With all that was going on, I'd forgotten . . . I asked him what he thought. He didn't want to talk about it, he just muttered something to the effect that, if people really understood what that bombs had done, maybe they wouldn't be celebrating. You see, even though he was a soldier, Jeremy believed we should never have used the bomb. He thought it put America in an untenable position with regard to the rest of the world. With this weapon, we possessed immense power – and he was afraid that power would taint us. On the other hand, he knew it was only a matter of time before somebody else, probably the Soviet Union, built their own bomb. Maybe something even more powerful. What would happen then? Jeremy saw that we would be drawn into a situation that was inherently beneath us, a game of cat and mouse that nobody could ever win. Nobody could ever win, but at the same time, all our energy would have to be given over to that game, and all the good things we could have done, if we hadn't been so engaged in something so ignoble, would never happen. As far as Jeremy was concerned, we could have achieved great things after the war. A new order. Worldwide cooperation to solve problems before they became serious, even before they arose. Instead, we got the United Nations, with its inner circle of privileged, veto-wielding states. Jeremy believed our strength lay in working with emerging nations, forging alliances, making friends. He didn't want the rest of the world to become a chessboard for two or three superpowers, but when the Russians and then the Chinese got the bomb, there was no going back. Now we had to act as if the non-nuclear countries were irrelevant – which, in a way, they had become. He hated the bomb. He hated that we had it, but he hated one thing more even more.

'Sometime in the late 1940s, it seems, he heard about a man who had worked at Los Alamos. He didn't know the man's name, or anything about him, all he knew was that he was the person who gave the secret of the device, the last piece in a highly intricate jigsaw puzzle, to the Soviets. He wanted to work on that, and he made the request several times, but he was always told he was needed elsewhere. So he started investigating the case secretly, on his own dime – and eventually, decades later, he found this man, though by the time he got there, he said, it was too late.'

Our order arrived. We had asked for coffees, nothing else, but when the tall blonde girl set her tray down on our table, there was an extra plate, with two slices of a moist, brown sponge cake filled with cream and raspberries that I hadn't seen before. 'Annette says try these,' the girl said. 'She says they're on the house.'

'Well, thank you, Julie.'

The girl smiled. 'You're welcome, Miss Culver,' she said.

'And thank you to Annette,' Jean said.

Julie set our cups and the plate on the table. 'Absolutely,' she said. 'Enjoy.'

Several minutes passed before Jean resumed her story. The cake was delicious, but it wasn't the usual kind of sponge cake. 'What is it?' I said.

Jean smiled. 'It's *Griestorte*,' she said. 'You make it with semolina and finely ground almonds.'

'Ah. No flour.'

'No flour.' She broke off another piece with her fork and tasted. 'Clever girl.'

I smiled. Then I realised she was talking about Annette.

Jean smiled back, and continued her story. 'Jeremy wasted years following any number of dead ends in his search for the Los Alamos spy, and he knew some of them had been put there just to misdirect him, or somebody like him. He just didn't know why. But by the time he figured it out, the whole story was irrelevant anyhow, just a footnote to history, nothing more. You see, he got his first real break a few months before the Berlin Wall came down. I don't know what his official work was by that time, but then, I never knew how official *anything* he worked on was. But the investigation that led him, finally, to Yonas Sax had never been official. Still, I guess he thought that it would redeem *something*. Nobody else cared by then, but he did. Give him his due, his misplaced loyalty wasn't to an institution, or to a person or a group of people, it was to an idea. He had learned not to trust institutions. As for people, he didn't know who to trust any more. But the idea. The idea was everything.'

'The idea?'

She looked at me, a touch of surprise in her face. Maybe she had forgotten I was there. 'Why, I told you. The idea of

America – As If version,' she said. 'The way we used to say it. *I pledge allegiance to the flag of the United States of America, and to the republic for which it stands; one nation indivisible with liberty and justice for all.'*

'You forgot God,' I said.

She shook her head. 'No,' she said. 'The God part came later. Sometime in the 1950s, as I recall. I guess As If needed a little bit of extra support, after Hiroshima and Nagasaki.' She smiled. 'I don't know the whole story of how he found Yonas Sax, or even how he could be so sure that this was his supposed traitor. All I know is, he flew to London on his own dollar, it must have been in July 1989. As I said, this wasn't an official case. He was doing this for himself. He wanted to look the man who gave away the secret of the A-bomb in the eye – and, according to his sources, this man really had *given* that secret away. No money had changed hands. No favours. Sax hadn't been "turned" in some elaborate sting, the KGB didn't have anything on him, he hadn't been caught in a hotel room with some honeypot and a stash of illegal drugs. Maybe if that had been the story, my brother could have understood him better. I imagine he blackmailed a few people in his time, and I'm sure he ran a few sting operations, or whatever they call them – the terminology eludes me, I'm afraid. So, yes, of course, he could understand human weakness. He understood girls, gambling, homosexuality. He understood the desire to hold on to an illusion of honour, even after it was hopelessly lost, but he couldn't understand a man like Yonas Sax. A man who knew, better than anyone, what the A-bomb could do. How could an intelligent, apparently decent man give away a secret like that? Now, Sax was living in Cambridge, England, where he had built a new life for himself. A new career, too – something to do with medical

226

research. According to the file, he was married, with two grown-up children. That was just one of the ironies that struck Jeremy as he worked through the file: like Jeremy, Sax had been born in 1925, in the same month in fact. They had married in the same year, their children were the same age. They both loved music. In another world, they would have been friends. And now, here he was, walking from his hotel, on a warm Sunday afternoon, to finally confront the traitor he had been trying to track down for over forty years. Only, when he got to Sax's house, a comfortable, though far from ostentatious town house about a half-mile from the centre, some kind of social event was in progress. The front door was wide open, there were people in the garden, a buzz of conversation from inside the house, kids running about the place, weaving in and out of the adults, a couple of teenagers sitting on the wall at the front of the property. A pretty, light-haired woman in an elaborate sari – though she wasn't Indian, Jeremy noticed – was walking in from a car parked at the kerb, carrying two great bowls of food. When she saw Jeremy she smiled and said, "Good afternoon," and he nodded, then carried on walking until he came to a broad dirt path through a patch of lush woodland, where he stepped off into the shadows. By this time, something was nagging at the back of his mind as he wandered through the woodland, but he couldn't figure out what it was. When he reached the riverbank, the path forked in two directions: one, he knew, led back to the city, so he took the other and decided he might as well stay in character. He would walk for an hour, then head back the way he'd come for another quick look at Sax's house, but only in passing. He hadn't planned on confronting Sax today anyhow. He would wait till the next morning, when everyone else was at work.

'Sax had retired early, according to his file, though he was still active in his field, attending conferences, even travelling to the US from time to time – which must have been strange. Jeremy wondered what he made of the changes that had taken place since he'd left. Apparently, Sax had once been a fanatical Giants fan – he'd grown up in Washington Heights, almost in the shadow of the Polo Grounds – and he'd retained an interest in sports, baseball primarily, but also boxing and track and field. Jeremy wondered if Sax still rooted for the US at the Olympics. He still had an American passport. How did it feel, when he was handing over key information to some KGB operative? Did he think about Mel Ott's decisive home run in Game Five of the '33 World Series? Sax would have been eight years old. How did *that* kid grow up to be a traitor?

'Jeremy was annoyed with himself, of course. He was aware of how foolish he was being, but I guess it all hit him at once. What *had* he been defending all his life? Liberty and justice for all – it sounds hollow now, but there had been a time when it felt real, something to work toward a step at a time and in spite of the predictable setbacks. For a while, some of us believed that the goodwill of good people might bring that system as close to perfection as the vagaries of human nature allowed – not perfect, of course, never perfect; we were never so naïve – and it was painful to watch as our generation settled for so much less. Even when it became clear that things had gone badly wrong, some of the most principled, the truest believers, hung on blindly for a long time. My brother was the truest of true believers – and it had cost him everything. He had lost both his children to America. He had lost his wife. He had allowed himself to be misled by the cruellest of deceptions – that old, misplaced loyalty upon which all empires are built.'

She broke off for a moment. It struck me that, in all this time telling other people's stories, she'd never said anything about what she felt or thought. *Her* politics. *Her* morality. *Her* notions of good and bad. If I could have done, I would have asked her that, there and then, but I didn't have the words and, by the time it had even occurred to me to ask, she had resumed the story.

'The day after the party, Jeremy returned to Sax's street and stood watching for a while. People emerged from various houses along the street and drove or walked away, a man passed, walking a pair of flat-coated retrievers, two very blond children cycled by in the direction of the river. Finally, a tall, thin woman whom he recognised from the file as Sax's wife emerged from the house and got into a grey car.

'Jeremy waited a few minutes, then he crossed the street and rang Sax's doorbell, slipping into character as a freelance journalist whose lifelong obsession with The Bomb had led him on a long and convoluted journey to Sax's door – and I am sure that, by the time the door opened, he believed this. After all, it wasn't so far from the truth. A good lie, like good theatre, contains more truth than deceit. If it's all invention, no matter how well constructed, we don't believe. Jeremy knew that, just as he knew that, when the door opened, it would be Sax who answered. The file had told him that the man and his wife lived alone now, their children grown up and moved away. It was possible that one or more of the guests from the previous day might have stayed over, but it didn't seem likely.

'He was right. When the door opened, it was Sax who greeted him, his face shifting from a welcoming expression – he was obviously expecting someone – to the vague puzzlement of someone who had made it his life's policy not to have strangers show up on his doorstep. "Hello," he said, assuming a neutral, uncurious expression. "Can I help you?"

'Jeremy studied the man's face. Sax looked young for his age, in spite of his grey hair and receding hairline. He had clear brown eyes, a firm mouth, and a boyish dimple in his chin that seemed, to Jeremy, somehow inapt. "Yonas Sax?"

'The man nodded, then waited a moment for Jeremy to speak again, before he realised who this visitor was. Or rather, what he knew. He stepped back, out of the doorway, and moved slightly to one side. "You had better come in," he said.'

'The script Jeremy had prepared was simple. As they made their way to the kitchen, which was right at the back of the house, along a surprisingly long hallway, he told Sax his cover story. The one thing he didn't give was his name – which Sax must have noticed, of course. Still, he listened politely and then, when the preliminaries were over, he offered Jeremy some English breakfast tea. "Or coffee, if you prefer," he said, a trace of mock, or possibly real, dejection in his voice. "I'm not allowed coffee any more," he said. "Doctor's orders."

'"Tea is fine," Jeremy said, as he took the opportunity to look around. The kitchen was tidy, clean, almost minimal. On the back wall, above the sink area, a wide picture window looked out on to a long narrow garden of climbing roses and iris beds and, at the far end, by a rusticated brick wall, a luxuriant apple tree, covered in darkly red ripening apples. It was like something out of Samuel Palmer, Jeremy told me – and I was surprised, because he had never admitted to an interest in art. He liked music, yes, but I didn't know, until he told me the story of that day, that he had spent long hours in art museums all over the world. He particularly loved

English painting – Samuel Palmer, Turner, John Linnell, William Hodges. He was quite the art historian.

'Sax put the kettle on. "I'm sure you have an idea of what you want to write," he said. "What I would ask is that you listen to what I have to say and, afterward, you don't misquote anything. I will tell you everything to the best of my ability, I won't deliberately conceal or overlook anything of what I remember, though it's been a long time and I don't remember everything exactly." He filled the teapot and carried it to the table. "Do you take sugar?" he asked, with a slight British intonation to his voice, though Jeremy couldn't tell if he was putting it on, or if it was just the effect of having lived in England for close to three decades.

'Sax didn't begin his story until everything was ready and they were sitting at the kitchen table, facing one another. When he did speak, he said what he had to say in cool, factual terms, with no special pleading and no visible emotion. Jeremy listened carefully, hoping for a note of remorse, or some kind of justification after the fact, but all Sax had to offer was a stark, simple account of what he had done, and then, as an afterthought, how he lived now, in Cambridge, trying – and, it seemed, mostly succeeding – not to think about the day when somebody turned up on his doorstep to take him away for questioning.

'"I have lived in fear of that knock for decades now," Sax said. "Not for my sake so much as my family's . . ." He looked at Jeremy, his face alert again, watchful and curious, like a chess master trying to read his opponent. "At the time, I really did think that knock would come at any time. Every day . . . Well, there was a level of apprehension that was difficult to deal with, in the context of a wife and children. I hadn't told anybody what I had done, not because I was ashamed or afraid of how they would respond, but because I didn't want to give them the burden of that knowledge."

' "You didn't tell anybody?"

' "No."

' "But your wife knew," Jeremy said. "She must have done."

'Sax shook his head. "It was harder on her than anyone," he said. "She knew most of the story, but not all, and I wished I could have kept more of it from her. Or at least I did at first. During the first year we were here. After that, something changed . . ."

' "What?"

'Sax smiled sadly. "We were happy," he said. "Not all of the time, of course. There were nights when I didn't sleep, nights when I feared the worst, but gradually, day by day, we learned to make the most of what we had for as long as we had it. As the years passed and it all seemed so distant, so far in the past, we began to breathe again. We had children, and now, as of last month, we have a grandchild. Life went on. We had routines, friends, memories that couldn't be taken away. I missed some things, like baseball and . . . the food . . . Little things. But the cost was . . . surprisingly low . . ."

' "And you never wondered if you had done the right thing—"

'Sax looked surprised. As if this was a question he hadn't expected. As if it was a question that was almost stupidly naïve. "I have weighed up the situation over the years," he said. "And I stand by the decision I made. But that isn't what matters – what matters is to have acted according to the best knowledge available at the time. You will understand, I know, that I cannot afford to entertain regrets."

'Jeremy nodded. He was, he said, a little amused by the assumptions Sax had made about his question. He looked directly into Sax's eyes. "I'm not here to ask why," he said.

"I didn't agree with your logic then, and I don't now, but I see how it works." He paused, as if to allow space for an apology, or at least some sign that Sax had understood how insulting his assumption had been. He let the moment linger before he spoke again. "What I want to know," he said, "is *when*."

'"When?"

'"When did you decide? Was it after Hiroshima?"

'"No."

'"I see. You thought, if they had only stopped there, the Japanese would have—"

'"No." Sax looked unhappy, though Jeremy didn't know why. "That's not it."

'"No?"

'"No," Sax said. "I decided before Nagasaki. Before Hiroshima. Before . . ."

'"Before?"

'"Around the time of the first test." Sax turned away and stared out at the sunlit garden. "I decided when I knew we had worked it out. Because I knew we would use it."

'"Which we did," Jeremy said. "And we saved tens, maybe hundreds of thousands of American lives."

'"I doubt that," Sax said. He sounded weary, all of a sudden. "But whether it's true or not, that wasn't the reason why we did it." Now, his tone implied that Jeremy really was being hopelessly naïve. "We all knew that, then, even if we don't acknowledge it now. We dropped the bomb to show the Russians what we had. It was the first major play of the Cold War." Sax studied Jeremy's face. By then, it was clear that he wasn't talking to a journalist. He shook his head. "You still haven't understood the main point," he said. "I gave away just one piece of the jigsaw – something that I had figured out – because I had come to see that the men I was working for were no better, morally, than those who, at that time, we thought of as the enemy."

' "No better than Hitler?"

'Sax leaned forward and rested his elbows on the table, so his face was no more than a foot away. "Hitler was finished by that time," he said. "So were the Japanese, for that matter." He paused, waiting for a reaction; then, when Jeremy didn't argue, he continued. "You're not a journalist," he said. "So who are you, Mr . . . ?"

'Jeremy shook his head. "I'm not a journalist," he said. "I'm just a citizen."

'Sax smiled. "Are you a military man?"

' "I was."

' "Where were you?"

' "When?"

' "You tell me."

' "Europe, mostly."

' "And then?"

' "The Pacific."

' "And then?"

' "Korea."

' "Tell me," Sax said. "Why didn't we drop the bomb on Pyongyang?"

' "It wasn't that kind of war."

' "It was exactly that kind of war," Sax said. "As was Vietnam. Why didn't we drop the bomb on North Vietnam? There were those who wanted to."

' "You know why," Jeremy said.

'Sax shook his head. He leaned back and closed his eyes, the weariness in his face more obvious, now, than it had been before. There was a long silence; then he opened his eyes and looked at Jeremy as if he had suddenly realised something good about him. Something honest. "Do you know how much a nightingale weighs?"

'Jeremy didn't say anything.

' "It's twenty-one grams," Sax said. "That's around three-quarters of an ounce."

' "I guess it is."

' "Which, it works out, is exactly the weight of the human soul," Sax said. "Well, according to the Greeks, it is."

' "I don't see how this—"

'Sax ignored him. "Of course, we can never know how rigorous they were in their measurements," he said. "Though I wouldn't be surprised if they were pretty thorough. What do you think – would you be more careful, trying to find the soul, than we were at Los Alamos?"

' "You can't compare the two. This is just—"

' "Why not? The ancient Greeks believed that, if you measured a man's body the instant before it died, then measured it again, one moment after—"

' "A *man's* body?"

' "I'm sorry?"

' "You said a man's body. What if it was a woman? Or a child?"

'Sax smiled. It was a sad smile, Jeremy thought, the smile of someone who had tried and failed for years to explain something he had discovered. "A child," he said. "A woman. It's all the same. The difference was always three-quarters of an ounce." Sax fixed him with his gaze. "Why? Did you think it would be different?"

' "That's not what I meant."

' "You should have asked what it would mean if it was a Korean. Or a Vietnamese. Didn't General Cumberland say that the Vietnamese didn't put the same high price on life as we do? How did that go, now? *We value life and human dignity. They don't care about life and human dignity*. I think those were his words, more or less. So – what do you think? With all that life and dignity, I'd have to assume that our souls are a little heavier than theirs."

'Jeremy sighed. "I don't have much time for the soul, as it happens. I'm more concerned with what actually exists. What actually happened."

'Sax laughed softly and shook his head. "Do you think that's a factual matter?" he said.

'There was a long silence, then. Jeremy could hear birds singing outside in the apple tree, a far whisper of noise in the distance that might have been traffic, a child calling from somewhere in the direction of the river. He wondered if he looked as exhausted as he felt. Sax gave him a wry smile. "I believe your superiors know who I am," he said. "In fact, they have known for a long time. They left me here to see what would happen. Maybe I would lure somebody out of cover and they could complete the larger puzzle. If that is so, I find it surprising that they didn't share their knowledge with you."

'Jeremy made no attempt to reply. From his point of view, the conversation was over.

'Sax nodded. "So why did you come here, Mr . . . ?"

'Jeremy shook his head. "I'm just trying to get to the truth," he said.

'"The truth?" Sax seemed faintly amused, but he wasn't mocking. If anything, he appeared sympathetic. "Can I ask how you're doing with that?"

'Later, as he was seeing Jeremy out, Sax tried one last time to find out whom he'd been talking to. "What did you say your name was? My memory isn't as good as it was."

'Jeremy told me later that, at that moment, the thought crossed his mind that, in another world, he might have called this man a friend. "I know how that feels," he said.

'Sax smiled. "Everything goes, in the end," he said. "But there are compensations."

' "Compensations?"

' "Nature gives, nature takes away. What we don't always see is that Nature also has a sense of humour. And – all those years when we felt obliged to exchange the days of our lives for – stuff. Money. Success. Social standing. All those years we didn't see that the only thing worth having, the only possession that's worth anything, is time. To own whatever time you have left – to own it, so it cannot be lost to distraction, or taken away by others, or filled up with trivial business – that's as close to happiness as I've ever needed to come. I am dying now, and for the first time, I understand that, far too often, I gave away the only thing of real value that I ever had." Sax stopped and smiled at himself. "It was interesting to meet you," he said. He led the way back through the hallway to the inner door with its stained-glass window and out into the front garden. The air had that smell that comes before or after a storm, a mix of greenery and ozone, Jeremy said, that reminded him of the forests where he'd hidden out with some partisans in 1944.

'Sax looked at him curiously. "For half my life," he said "I've been waiting for somebody to knock at this door. And now that knock has come. Only, it wasn't what I expected."

'Jeremy didn't know what to say to that. Or rather, he was already gone from that pleasant, sad town house. He had no space for Sax in his head any more, he told me. He was done with all that. When he got back to Virginia, three days later, he sat down at his desk and wrote his letter of resignation. It didn't seem to come as a surprise to anyone. A month later, he went to Vietnam, bought a house on the beach – a simple place, no more than a hut, as I understand – and became a civilian for the first time in his adult life. I don't know what he did during that period, but when he came home, a couple of years ago, he was empty and thin, almost transparent, like a piece of rice paper. But then, I think that was what he had wanted. To become transparent, so the light just shone through, without obstruction.' She smiled sadly. 'No more As If,' she said. 'Just the here and the now. Come what may. I guess he'd earned that much.'

ASHES AND DIAMONDS

It was a typical Saturday afternoon. That morning, I'd found a near-perfect copy of John Sayles' *Thinking in Pictures* in the second-hand bookstore next to Sacred Grounds – I went there on my own now, to be alone and drink good coffee and study Annette, who really was very beautiful, even if you weren't into girls – and now I was curled up with my lucky find, a jug of iced tea on the weird sub-chesterfield of a sofa that Laurits had bought in a thrift store and brought home, planning to give it a makeover, and he was perched stiffly on a straight backed dining chair checking his blood pressure with a home BP kit. This room was pretty basic when we moved in and became more so after we got organised and dumped some of the crap we'd inherited. Now all that was left was Laurits' unmade-over sofa, a wall covered in classic movie posters, and the chairs that only ever got used when one or other of us was working on some task that needed a table and on Saturday afternoons, when Laurits went through his exhaustive regimen of health tests. These were not only repetitive – he would take his BP several times, always getting a slightly different result, which frustrated the hell out of him – but also rigorous. He recorded those results he was satisfied with in a black ledger book, and pored over them periodically, looking for trends and indications, certain that some pattern was hidden in these random measurements, and that all he had to do was figure it out.

Considering how careless he was about every other aspect of his well-being, it would probably seem odd to one of the guys down at Sidetracks to know that he was so obsessed with his health – but that was where they didn't know Laurits. He wasn't doing this to try to prevent himself getting ill. I really don't think he was afraid of anything, least of all dying; it was just that, if some unknown disease was going to pick him off, he wanted to get some of the credit for the write-up. If the illness was just some obscure malady that usually only affected Mexican corn farmers or post-menopausal women from rural Canada, there would be some interest in recoding his experiences as a service to medical science – Laurits was strangely in awe of medical science – but if it turned out to be something completely unknown, then he would be able to claim it for himself, maybe even get it named after him, if he was quick and observant enough to carry out and, at the same time, *be* the subject of the first ever case study. 'Not everybody gets to have a disease named after him,' he'd say, as he studied his book of numbers. Sometimes, a mood of high excitement would overtake him, as he noticed some new detail in his daily habits, some irregularity that, if it only lasted a couple of days, probably meant nothing, but if it persisted, might be the first symptom of some larger ailment that, for the moment, was completely unknown to humankind. Almost anything could set him off. A craving for walnuts. A bout of vertigo that, according to Laurits, had nothing to do with the fact that he had stayed in bed for five days drinking endless bottles of muscat and eating nothing but canned fish and pickles. The time when his urine turned blue. It always cleared up just about the time he decided that he was on to something, but he never learned. 'Laurits' Syndrome, here we come,' he would say, with genuine glee at the idea of his own slow and painful decline.

Now, taking what could have been the twentieth BP reading of the afternoon, he was getting restless. It was a typical Saturday afternoon, which was fine in itself but, at the end of a typical Saturday afternoon, there was usually a typical Saturday night. I'd been surprised over the last three weeks – three weeks: I hadn't had a drop of liquor or touched any kind of drug other than Advil for *three weeks* – when Laurits had let me skip the customary Saturday routine, though I shouldn't have been. If I'd only thought about it a bit longer, I would have seen that he found this new game entertaining. Not to mention the fact that he didn't know why I was doing all this. Still water with a slice of lemon. Herb teas. I was becoming, if not a monster, then some kind of monstrous chrysalis, a creature in the throes of some frightening muta-tion, and he was curious to see what would eventually emerge from the cocoon.

On that particular Saturday afternoon, however, I could tell something was going on in his head. He was restless, jumpy. I don't think he was scared, or worried about anything – though he should have been. It was just that things weren't neutral, something was happening somewhere in the back-ground that was beyond his control, something that I didn't know about then, but he couldn't hide everything from me. Now, as he gave up in disgust and packed away his BP kit, he was barely even trying. He was acting like it was just another Saturday, but I knew something was in his head, just sitting there in his lower brain, like a cherry bomb waiting to go off. After he had stowed away his instruments – he always treated them with the utmost care – he went into the kitchen and fixed himself a drink. Not muscat. Jack D. He looked at me.

'You still on the wagon?'

I nodded.

'What's wrong? Are you sick?'

I shook my head.

'You'd tell me, right,' he said. He seemed anxious, but I knew it wasn't about my health. 'I mean, you'd tell me if you were sick?'

'Why? So you could film me dying?'

I gave him my best just-kidding look. He grinned. 'Why not?' he said. 'I mean, you couldn't just do it straight. There would have to be—'

I gave him a different look. 'Stop it,' I said.

He stopped. He always did, if I asked. The only trouble was having to ask. 'Why don't you do something?' I said.

He looked miserable. 'Because I need to go out,' he said. 'I need to *be* someplace.'

I looked around. Above my head, in stark green and black, Anthony Perkins stared down at me from the bilingual Belgian cinema poster for *The Trial*, Laurits' third favourite movie. 'What's wrong with here?' I said.

'I have to get out.' He stood, glass in hand, staring at the window. There was nothing to see there, other than the back wall of a hardware store, but his face brightened. 'I know,' he said. 'Let's go to Henrys.' He looked at me, a hint of appeal in his eyes. He knew I hated Henrys. 'We haven't been there for a while,' he said.

I didn't even dignify that suggestion with a response. I just went back to my book. The truth was, I didn't want to go out at all, and I certainly didn't want to go to Henrys. I might get by on soda at Sidetracks, but I didn't think I could get through a night at Henrys without getting high on *something*, and I really didn't want to put myself in that position. I wanted to stay sober. I liked the clean feel my body had, the lightness, the improved sleep, all the things they say will happen if you give up booze and drugs, things you never believe, until they happen to you. Besides, there had been what Laurits would have called a misunderstanding on our last visit – though I knew it would be foolish of me to remind him of that.

'Whaddaya say?' he continued, when I didn't answer. He knew I would give in, and not even eventually.

I knew it too, but I put up what passed for a fight. Not much of one, because he needed me to go with him and I always did what he needed, but it was the principle of the thing. 'Oh, come on, Laurits,' I said. 'There's nobody there but a bunch of old bikers. Everybody we know will be at Sidetracks.'

He shook his head. 'I don't want to be with those people tonight,' he said, quieter now. He came over to the sofa, took the book out of my hands, looked at the cover, then snapped it shut. 'Come on,' he said. 'It'll be just me and you. We can make it a celebration.'

'Oh, yeah?'

'Why not?'

'At Henrys?'

'Sure.' He grinned, and I was annoyed, because he knew that he was winning me over.

'What are we celebrating?'

'Us.' He glanced around as if looking for something. 'It must be some kind of anniversary by now. These things are important, you know.'

I laughed. There was no point insisting on Sidetracks. When Laurits didn't want to be around people, I knew it was a mistake to try and change his mind. How he felt around other people had always been a problem and how he got along with them depended on too many variables to take any risks. Even on a good night, he could start an argument in an empty room, but when he was in one of his Greta Garbo moods, he was impossible. At Sidetracks, there was an inner circle of almost-friends for whom he could do no wrong, no matter what, then there was a wider group of acquaintances who came and went, joining in on nights when it looked like something out of the ordinary might happen, but just as inclined to drift off to wherever there might be a possibility of interesting drugs, or rumours of a party. The main trouble was when a newcomer arrived. People would enter the circle by chance. A new boyfriend, say, or an old high-school friend on a visit would suddenly appear and there was never any knowing how Laurits would treat them. The first time they met him, many of these people would be beguiled, at the very least. I don't say they liked him, necessarily, but he captured their attention, he drew them in. There was such an air of expectancy in his vicinity, especially when he was in a good frame of mind. Something about the way he saw the world, the details he picked up on, the sudden twists and turns in the logic of a night, something about the games he played, and the games he made space for others to play, made him irresistible – at least to begin with. Maybe for some, there was a sense of danger. They were excited, and maybe a little frightened by the suspicion that, if they followed Laurits on his merry way through a long, toxic evening, they might end up doing something they wouldn't have dared do of their own volition. They felt brave, then, but I know that they also used him as an excuse, afterward, at the post-mortem. We all did. Sometimes the newcomers fell in love with him a little.

It wasn't sexual. It was – love, or if not love exactly, then confidence. Laurits was a magnet to people who lacked confidence, people like me, people who didn't usually feel included in the game. He included them in the game – and it wasn't just his game, it was everybody's. It wasn't just that they were audience, they were participants.

After a while, though, things changed. The new people began to realise that he wasn't really interested in them, he just wanted to see how they played their games – and he wasn't really present for them, as they had first thought. He was slightly removed, wilfully remote – and they couldn't get a handle on him. They couldn't be sure when he was joking and when he was serious, even though it should have been clear that Laurits couldn't really distinguish between the two. He could be generous, but it was a kind of formal generosity he practised, a matter of honour, like some tribal chief giving away everything he had at a potlatch, but his generosity eventually came to be just one more piece of evidence that, in truth, he wasn't really with them at all, he was just there. The newcomer would soon come to believe that, because Laurits didn't need anything, he didn't care about anything either – and that divided them into two groups, the ones who felt betrayed, and the ones who only liked him more. Some of them liked it, that they didn't matter to him any more than the wind, or a flock of geese passing overhead; others were shocked to realise that, to him, they had been nothing more than phenomena all along. That was a favourite word of his: phenomena. Everything to him, himself included, was some kind of more or less interesting phenomenon and he was puzzled that other people didn't see the world in those terms. When somebody who felt let down by him drifted away, he was always slightly bemused by it and disappointed, too – though only with them. Sometimes, it just exhausted him. The show. The game. Sometimes he had to get away, to be alone, or with me – which, he said, was much the same thing. One of the most endearing things about him was that he could say this openly, trusting me to know that he meant it as a compliment.

Henrys was as inconvenient a place to go drinking as it was possible to be, for two people who had no private transport of any kind. Most of the clientele arrived on two-wheeled vehicles, Henrys being mainly a biker bar. Strictly speaking, Henrys was the Two Henrys, the joint proprietors being a pair of near-identical ex-Angel types, huge, mostly gentle until, when occasion demanded, they needed to be lethal. They were both in their mid-forties, but when they were at rest you could still see the child in their faces, sweet-natured, good-humoured boys behind the beards and, in Big Henry's case, the scar that ran right across his face, so straight it looked like somebody had drawn it with a ruler. Big Henry – the name was both descriptive and ironic for, although Big Henry was *big*, his partner, whose moniker, inevitably, was L'il Henry, was so very much bigger. So, for me at least, it was a relief to see Big Henry behind the bar when we walked in. On our last visit to the Two Henrys, Laurits had got into an argument with a pair of blow-ins, and L'il Henry had been obliged to break things up a little more forcibly than usual.

The blow-ins had been in the wrong, as everybody in the bar that night could testify – and they probably did, after we were gone, though we couldn't be sure, yet, that we weren't *non grata* in L'il Henry's eyes. Big Henry's too, for that matter. Still, we had that going for us. The blow-ins, a short, nervy guy with a bad goatee, and a tall, skinny man of around thirty with thick, black, too-careful hair, had come in around nine, presumably spotted Laurits for the college type – though how, I don't know, because he didn't dress any differently from anybody else at Henrys, if you took away the leathers – and moved in gleefully for some fun. Naturally they picked on me to get to him.

'Hey, pretty girl,' the tall guy said. 'Why don't you come around over here and sit with a real man.'

Laurits couldn't help it. I know that. If he had waited a minute or so more and put up with just a little more of this crap, L'il Henry would have stepped in and sorted it all out. No noise, no violence. Just fear. I know he wanted to hold his tongue, but he couldn't help it. He laughed. Why wouldn't he? 'Oh, my, Mr He-Man,' he said. 'Did you think of that line all by yourself?'

The tall guy looked at him. He wasn't angry yet, but he was willing to be. The other guy looked nervous, though. Maybe he'd spotted L'il Henry, who had been playing pool with one of his cousins – everybody in that place was a cousin of his. Even some of the hippies, who looked like they'd faded to black around 1975, were cousins. I assumed that this was an honorary term. The tall guy tilted his head slightly. 'Was I talking to you, faggot?' he said quietly, the way tough guys say things quietly in old movies. He clearly didn't know that, in a place like the Two Henrys, nobody got to talk quietly that way, other than L'il Henry, who wasn't like the tough guys in any movie I'd ever seen.

Laurits grinned, nodding slightly. 'Listen,' he said. 'We're just minding our own business here, having a quiet drink on a Saturday night, as is the time-honoured custom.' My heart lifted. He was going to play smart. Leave it to Henry. I was wrong, of course. 'We don't want no trouble, mister,' he said, the way the snivelling weak guy always says it in old Westerns. 'So why don't you just go on home, download some porn and find the love that you so desperately need?'

Now the blow-in was angry. 'What did you say to me?' He looked to see where his buddy was, in case he needed backup.

Laurits stood up and turned to face him. He spoke slowly, not concealing his contempt. I always wondered why he did these things. Was he brave, or just pig-headed? I would have preferred neither. 'You need me to explain?' he said. 'Okay. Buy a six-pack. Take it home. Find the love you need on the Internet.'

The dark-haired guy lunged. Laurits sidestepped, then slammed his forearm down, hammer-blow style. Then, as the first guy fell, he turned to look for the shorter one, but it was too late for that. L'il Henry was there already – and now I knew why he had waited. He'd wanted to see what Laurits would do, because he wasn't sure if this smart-mouthed college-boy type was just a smart-mouthed college boy or a cousin-in-waiting. Because he liked Laurits, he really did. He liked the way Laurits didn't change his game when he walked in the door. The way he was always Laurits, even when it would have been smarter to be somebody else for a while. But what he'd been waiting for was restraint. Trust. Right then, he thought Laurits didn't have enough trust, after all the space he'd been allowed. Right then, L'il Henry was wondering if Laurits only trusted Laurits, which would have been a dangerous road to take.

Boys and their games. Either I could never understand them or I understood them only too well.

That night, L'il Henry hadn't thrown Laurits out right away. He'd waited till he was sure the blow-ins were long gone, then he'd come over to where we were sitting at the bar. We hadn't ordered more drinks. We were waiting for Henry's dispensation. Laurits knew that he'd broken one of the house rules – there were fights at the Two Henrys all the time, but never with anybody outside the group and they always got taken outside – and he ought to have known better. When there was stranger trouble, L'il Henry liked to deal with it himself, in his own way. Which was usually minimal, because this boyish boy turned into someone very frightening in the wink of an eye. Usually, all he had to do was stand in close and watch the problem fade away. That was fine with him, he had nothing to prove, and it meant that the place didn't get any more than the usual run-of-the-mill attention from law enforcement. Or rather, from the *Federales*, as both Henrys called any officer of the law. Nobody knew why, it was some kind of private joke.

Finally, when he was ready, L'il Henry came to where we were and stood close to Laurits, almost leaning against his shoulder. He spoke quietly. 'I'm not about to throw you out,' he'd said. 'But you should probably go. Have one on the house before you leave, then blow.' He studied Laurits' face to see what was being understood. It was obvious that he regretted this. Maybe he even felt a little responsible. 'Have another drink, then don't come back for a while. Clear?'

Laurits nodded. Anybody else would have apologised, or tried to win something back, but he didn't. 'Clear,' he said.

L'il Henry nodded. 'Okay, then,' he said. 'You keep out of trouble now.'

Now, here we were, testing the water. Only L'il Henry wasn't there – and though it was a Saturday night, it was very quiet. Really quiet. Even some of the cousins hadn't showed – which meant we stood out all the more as we walked in. Big Henry was behind the bar. He shot Laurits a warning look that I didn't know was serious or not, then he stepped over to serve us.

'You're lucky,' he said. 'L'il Henry ain't in tonight. I'm not sure how happy he'd be to see you here.'

Laurits nodded. Not quite penitent, but sober. 'I know Henry knows I didn't mean him any disrespect,' he said. 'He knows who I am.'

Henry grimaced. 'That's the problem,' he said. 'It don't matter whether he knows *you* or not. It's whether you know *him* that matters.' He let out a big breath, then looked us up and down as if he couldn't quite make out what species we were – his way of changing the subject. 'Okay,' he said, finally. 'What's your poison?'

By the time we got to the second drink – I was on what Big Henry insisted on calling sarsaparilla – Laurits' mood had changed. I guess he felt he was back in the fold. After all, Big Henry wouldn't have served him if he didn't know L'il Henry was ready to forgive. Still, I couldn't help thinking he had some other business on his mind, something he didn't want me to know. That bothered me, but this wasn't the time to talk about it. I just wanted to get through the evening and back to the apartment, preferably sober, at a reasonable time. A few more drinks, then Laurits could go home happy, knowing that he'd been forgiven. Accepted again. I had no idea why it was so important to him and I didn't care to try and work it out.

Big Henry hadn't done with us yet, though. My first order of lemonade had surprised him – 'Aw, man,' he said, 'I just *know* we got some of that sarsaparilla somewhere around here' – but by the second time, he was really curious.

250

'Well, now,' he said. 'What's this I'm thinking?' He looked at me, then at Laurits, and grinned. 'You kids got something you want to share with ol' Henry?'

Laurits looked at him, puzzled. I didn't get it either, to begin with, the idea being so preposterous and all, but I figured out a second after. I laughed. 'Oh, no,' I said. 'We definitely don't got anything to share.'

Henry looked crestfallen, and shook his head. 'You sure, now?' he said. 'It's a long time since anybody in here has up and demanded sarsaparilla two whole times in a row.' He gave me a sweet, pretty much but not entirely avuncular smile; then, after a long moment, he turned to Laurits, who'd only just figured things out. 'Hey, Laurits,' he said. 'What is this I hear about you and Axel Crane?' His voice had hardened slightly. Not much, but enough.

Laurits looked startled. 'What do you mean?' he said.

Henry didn't look at him; instead, he poured himself another beer and let his eye drift around the room, the way he always did, just to be sure nothing was brewing. Henry didn't allow drugs on the premises – deals, like fights, were to be taken outside – and he insisted, as he'd once said in my hearing, that that any female dumb enough to frequent the Two Henrys in the first place was to be treated with the utmost respect because, like the Indians that once lived around these parts, he believed crazy people were holy. 'Well, now,' he said. 'A little bird told me you had dealings with Axel.' Now he looked, straight into Laurits' eyes. 'Or did I get that wrong?'

Laurits shrugged. 'I met the guy,' he said. 'He told me he was interested in cinema.'

Big Henry guffawed. He did that often. People still guffawed at the Two Henrys. 'I'm sure he is,' he said.

Laurits didn't guffaw. He didn't guffaw and he didn't say anything. I could see he felt caught out, like a base runner trapped between second and third on a misjudged steal.

Henry's voice was quiet now. 'Listen,' he said. 'You do what you think you can get away with. But don't fool yourself, Professor.' Laurits winced. *Professor* had been the Henrys' handle for him when he'd first started coming to the place. Gradually, it had been dropped, which Laurits had taken as a sign of at least partial acceptance. Now it was back, and Laurits had to be wondering if it had ever really gone away. 'This ain't no chess game out here. And Axel Crane is most definitely *not* interested in cinema.'

For a moment, Laurits looked crumpled. He'd had his head down, staring into his drink, not wanting to look Henry in the face. Now that the sermon was over, however, he picked up his glass and emptied it. He looked at Henry. 'Well,' he said, 'you know what Oscar Wilde said about chess, don't you?' He set the glass down carefully on the counter.

Henry didn't say a word, but I could see he was curious. Not because he cared for one second about anything Oscar Wilde did or didn't say. Finally, when Laurits didn't elaborate, he reached out and picked up the empty glass. 'Same again?' he said.

After that, Laurits' mood shifted. He wasn't depressed, though; it was more that a kind of dry hysteria had crept over his mind, a feverish desire to make a night of it, no matter what. I wanted to go, but I knew we wouldn't be leaving till that fever burned out. I knew I should just ride along, weather it out, and mostly I tried to do just that, but I couldn't help remembering what Big Henry had said earlier. 'It don't matter whether he knows *you* or not. It's whether you know *him* that matters.' It had got me thinking about a line from an old Butch Hancock song, *You're just a wave, babe, you're not the water* – or something along those lines. Laurits hadn't got round to learning that – and I suspected that the Henrys had some kind of tacit project going, maybe, to teach him before it got too late. The look on Big Henry's face, as he poured that next shot of Jack D, had got me worrying that too late wasn't too far away. Still, I held my tongue until the crowd *really* thinned out, when we were getting ready to leave. It was only after we'd said, or waved, our goodbyes, and were heading out into the night, that I brought it up, casually, no big deal, just conversation as we made our way along the dirt path that led from the Two Henrys to the paved road. 'Who is Axel Crane?' I said.

'It's nothing.' Laurits had had plenty to drink, but now that we were out in the air, he seemed just as sober as I was. 'Henry's just got the wrong end of the stick.'

'It must be *something*,' I said.

'He's just a guy. I thought he wanted to put some money into a project I was working on. But he didn't come through.'

I couldn't see his face in the dark, but I knew he was lying. He was a bad liar – and then, all of a sudden, it hit me. 'Wait,' I said. 'I remember now.'

'No, you don't,' Laurits said, a note of strained patience in his voice. 'You've never met him.'

'He was that guy in the pickup, wasn't he?' I said. 'At the slaughterhouse. The guy in the red pickup.'

Laurits sighed, but he didn't say anything.

'So who is he?'

'Nobody,' he said. There was a note of resignation in his voice. 'Just a friend.'

'A *friend*?'

253

'An acquaintance.'

We had reached the road now. It was still dark, though there were some scattered lights through the trees. Not much, but enough to see our way. Occasionally a passing car or the headlights of some biker heading out from the Two Henrys illumined the way, the black asphalt road straight and wide between the looming trees. Most of the time, I liked this walk. It marked the end of a night I didn't usually enjoy and I was glad of the cool air, the stillness, the glimmer of lights in kitchens and yards where other people, strangers with their own lives, their own narratives, were sitting up late, drinking bourbon, drinking coffee, making conversation or watching TV in some blue-lit room, alone or in couples, the children upstairs, the unanswered questions continuing unanswered, whatever they were hoping for, or dreading, still far enough away for them to carry on as usual.

Dad used to say, *Be careful what you fear*, but I wasn't aware of any specific thing at that moment, when the black pickup came up behind us and slowed, the lights singling us out and lingering, so Laurits turned around to see who it was. I imagine he thought it was somebody from the bar, maybe come to offer us a ride, but while I didn't look back, not at first, I knew, without knowing why, that it was nobody from the Two Henrys. By now the pickup had slowed to a complete stop and it just sat there, the lights on us, somebody behind them watching. I turned around. Be careful what you fear, he used to say – the implication being that, if you fear something enough, your fear makes it real and there's already enough trouble out there, in the big world, trouble you can't even imagine. Now, trouble was coming, I didn't need to imagine anything. There was no right or wrong thing to do, it was too late for that, but when Laurits turned and started walking toward the vehicle, I felt sure that was a mistake. Before he'd got ten paces, two men – men I didn't think I'd seen before – jumped out of the pickup, one from the passenger side, one from the back, which meant, of course, that there was at least one more. The driver, whose face I couldn't see.

When I saw the men running toward Laurits, I didn't think, I just ran at them, no thought in my head, no plan, just fear. I could have run in the other direction – I think, now, that I should have, because maybe, then, I could have got help, or got help sooner – and I could have stopped to think, for a moment at least. Long enough to get the licence plate, or put together some kind of mental image of the men. They were tall, I remembered later, one had a carefully manicured goatee and short, maybe black or dark-brown hair, the other had a lighter complexion, the body of somebody who worked out seriously but, in a town like Scarsville, that could be anybody. I could have done any number of things, but there was something at the back of my mind, something that had been there for a long time, it seemed, that made me want to hurt somebody, no matter how lightly, before whatever was about to happen happened.

But it happened, fast. So fast that I couldn't do a thing. Or maybe I did – maybe I distracted the dark-haired guy just long enough for Laurits to get the first strike, feinting with his right hand while his left came around in a hammer punch, though by then I could only see him out of the corner of my vision, and a moment after the dark-haired guy was slapping me away, slapping me right off my feet, like he was swatting away a fly. I felt like nothing, then, a body without mass, without gravity, it was almost as if I were floating. Then I came down hard, yards from where the others were, everything slowed in my head, my arms and knees jarring on the ground, a ringing in my ears, a long, slow sinking in my entire body before I felt the blood spurting from my nose. Strangely, that seemed to help me focus. It was a real, physical fact, unlike the fog in my head, the cold chalky feeling in my knees and shoulders. It was blood, my blood, and it was real. Wet on my face and then on my hands. Warm. It probably took longer than I thought it did, but at the time it seemed to me that I got up right away. Or almost right away. By that time, though, the pickup was backing up the road, away from the town and too far into the darkness for me to see the plate. Slowly, with all the time in the world, it did a wide U-turn, the driver turning slightly to look at me – or was he just looking at the road – though not for long enough for me to notice anything special about him. Then, accelerating rapidly, the pickup sped away, back in the direction from which it had come.

I looked at Laurits. He was on the ground, struggling to get to his feet, blood all over his hands, blood on his face, blood on his shirt – too much blood, I thought, until I realised. At some point, maybe when he was fighting with the light-haired man, he had been stabbed. He had surprised them – they were expecting an easy mark and one of them had panicked. Or had they meant to stab him all along? Was that their main intent? Was it what they had been told to do? Told by whom? By this man Crane? What had Laurits done that called for such a punishment?

'Stay there,' I said. I looked for where he was hurt, but I couldn't find it at first for the blood. I checked his neck, his chest, his stomach, and I couldn't find it. Then I did, blood bubbling through my fingers from a gash at the back of his lower abdomen. 'Be still,' I said, as he struggled to rise again. I cast about for something to staunch the flow of blood, but there was nothing, so I pulled off my shirt, balled it up, and

256

pressed it as hard as I could against the wound. 'Stay here,' I said. 'Can you hold this?' I looked at his hands, clawing at the ground by his side. I felt completely helpless.

Finally, he raised one hand and pressed it to the shirt. His head moved slightly, a movement I took for a nod, and I felt more hopeful. If the knife had cut a major artery, he would be close to death by now, surely. I remembered this from *Death in the Afternoon*, how the gored matadors would bleed out before they could even be carried from the arena, and I felt less frightened. They had hurt him badly, but he was going to make it. He was conscious; he had enough strength to hold the makeshift bandage himself. That was good. Now, all I had to do was get help. I never took my cellphone with me on these nights out and Laurits didn't even own one. I did a quick calculation. I figured we were closer to the town than we were to Henrys – and anyway, neither of the Henrys would have thanked me for bringing this problem into their house – so I picked out a light and headed for it.

By the time I got back, Laurits was sitting upright against a big rock, just a few feet from where I had left him. It seemed lighter now, though it was nowhere near dawn. I wondered where the emergency people were. I had knocked at one house but, even though it was lit inside, a lamp burning on a kitchen table, another somewhere deeper in the house, nobody had answered. At the second house, a woman had come to the door, opened it a fraction, checked to see if I was alone, then opened it a little more.

'My friend's been hurt,' I said. 'Can I use your phone?'

The woman looked me up and down. I had forgotten that I'd taken off my shirt to staunch Laurits' wound, and was now standing on her doorstep in a camisole that had once been white, but was now streaked with blood and dirt. 'Well,' she said. 'I don't know that you need to come in.' She looked beyond me into the dark. 'What happened to your friend?'

'It was a hit-and-run,' I said. I knew I had to lie. She'd close the door right in my face if she heard the word *stabbed*. 'He's badly hurt. Please.'

The woman frowned. 'Where is he?' she said. I could see, in the half-light, that she had just applied some kind of skin treatment to her face, one of those avocado and tea-tree, or persimmon and date-oil products that people only ever thought to buy when their skin was beyond preserving. 'Is he all alone out there?'

I nodded. If she knew Laurits was alone, she would be more likely to help. 'He's bleeding,' I said.

She looked me up and down again, then she nodded. 'You just tell me where your friend is located,' she said. 'I'll call 911 right away.'

'But—'

She shook her head. 'I can't let you in, darlin',' she said, her voice dropping to a whisper. 'My brother Wes is here right now. And you really don't want to meet Wes. Especially not looking like that.' She leaned forward conspiratorially, so her head was almost outside the door. 'He's very *excitable*,' she said. Then she stepped back, 'Don't you worry now,' she said. 'Tell me where you all are located and I'll call 911 right away. You just go tend to your friend.'

Now I was beginning to wonder if she had just been bluffing. Maybe there wasn't even a Wes, though I'm not sure about that. She'd had a look in her eye, a mix of apprehension and pride, like you see in certain types of pit-bull owners, and I really didn't want to test her story. But now, maybe fifteen minutes after I left her to make the call, nobody was here.

258

Just Laurits, still clutching my shirt to his side, a bemused look on his face, like he couldn't quite remember what had happened. But then, maybe he didn't remember. He'd been pretty drunk when we left Henrys. It hadn't been obvious – it never was – but he'd been drunk all right. Now, as I crouched next to him, checking to see if the bleeding had stopped, he looked up.

'Hey, there,' he said. At that moment, he didn't seem too bad. Maybe a little drowsy, but he didn't look like he was dying. Just a drunk guy who'd had a knock and was sitting things out for a while.

'Hey,' I said.

'You're back already,' he said.

'Yeah. I'm back. Help is coming soon.'

He nodded. 'Okay,' he said. There was a long pause and I could almost hear him thinking. 'Hey,' he said again.

'Hey,' I said.

'Maybe you should get out of here,' he said. 'In case those guys come back.'

I shook my head. 'They'll be long gone by now,' I said.

He nodded again. He seemed to have been reduced to a very limited repertoire of communicative gestures: nods, slight flutters of his free hand, simple words like 'hey' and 'okay'. In fact we both had. This situation was too real for us, and we didn't know how to be there, together, with the quiet of the woods all around us, and the smell of blood, and the night. 'Okay,' he said. 'I just . . .'

I knew what he wanted to say before he said it. He didn't know how to say it, but I knew what it was. He wanted to be alone. All that *Ashes and Diamonds* Zbigniew Cybulski stuff was going round in his head, Anthony Perkins laughing contemptuously at the end of *The Trial*. If he was dying, he'd rather be alone. If he wasn't, he'd see me later. Nothing about this was in any way insensitive or upsetting, to his mind. After all, he was the one who had been stabbed. 'Okay,' I said. 'You sit tight. I'll stand over there and look out for them.'

He nodded yet again, an odd slightly mechanical movement. 'Thanks,' he said. Then, just as I was about to stand up, he touched my hand. 'It's all right,' he said. I didn't say anything. Then he spoke again, but I didn't quite hear and I didn't work it out exactly until later.

By now, I wasn't quite sure who *them* was, but I left him and walked over to the far side of the road, so I could look back toward town and see the ambulance, or the police car, or whatever was supposed to be coming. I waited a long time – or maybe not. Maybe it just seemed like a long time. Still, by the time the ambulance did arrive, Laurits was unconscious. I had gone back over to where he was sitting to find him slumped over on the ground, my shirt lying useless by his side. I didn't know if he was dead, or just dying, but the blood lay in a wide dark pool all around his body and he was lying very still, stiff-looking, like he had been frozen or cast in plaster. There was no colour. That is what I remember most, the absence of colour. His skin, his hair, even his clothes seemed to have been drained. His face was grey and damp-looking, like wet ash after a fire. Everything around him was black, from his blood I guess, but there was nothing else. Just black and grey. Like one of those old photographs Weegee used to take, sitting all night by the radio for something like this to happen to someone, car wrecks and murders, all the unlucky ones whose lives had ended by the side of a road or on a backstreet some-where, their faces emptied and expressionless, their overcoats heavy with their own blood.

The paramedics, or whatever they were, took over as soon as they descended from their vehicle. There were two of them, a man and a woman, and it seemed like the woman was in charge, or maybe she had to be the one who led when they were dealing with a woman. 'Are you the individual who made the call?' she asked.

I shook my head.

She looked annoyed. 'Who made the call, Miss?' she asked.

'I don't know,' I said. 'My friend was attacked, and I ran down to the nearest house to—'

'So you did not make the call?'

I shook my head.

'Are you the gentleman's wife?'

I nodded. 'I'm his . . .'

She looked at me and registered something. That I was in shock, maybe. Was I in shock? I didn't know, but her voice softened. 'All right,' she said. 'Wait here. We're going to look after your friend. Right?'

I nodded. All this time the man had been working on Laurits, but I didn't know what he was doing. Checking for signs of life, I suppose, or maybe he was making sure the bleeding had stopped. The woman went over and crouched down. They exchanged some words. I couldn't hear what they were saying, but I sensed, just from the tone of their voices, that it was bad. But then, I knew that already. I had seen for myself how grey he was. How colourless and empty he looked. Was that what death was like? I don't know if the thought occurred to me then, or later, but it stayed in my mind for days, along with the last words he had said to me – words that were only now becoming clear in my mind. What had he said? At first I'd assumed it was some kind of reassurance, or maybe he had been trying to shrug things off with a joke.

Then again, it could have been some kind of apology – an apology that, later, when I found out why all this had happened, I seriously hope that I'd have refused to accept. Probably not, though. There had never been enough of me to refuse Laurits anything – and besides, he'd never asked very much. Maybe that was the problem.

But it wasn't a reassurance, and it wasn't a joke. It wasn't exactly an apology, either, but it was as close as he probably could have come. Laurits would have said that it was just an observation. A statement of fact.

It's not personal. That was what he'd said, or something like it. Maybe he'd intended more but that was all that came out. *It's not personal.*

I watched as the man and the woman stood up, almost in unison, and turned back toward the ambulance. I knew he was dead, just from their faces. 'Oh, Laurits,' I said, in a whisper, not caring that they might hear me. After all, I was in shock. I could say anything I liked. Still, I kept my voice to a whisper because, as somebody used to say in one of Dad's old stories, the dead can only hear you when you whisper. 'I know it wasn't personal,' I said. I found myself smiling suddenly. The female paramedic saw, and she came over to me and took my arm very gently, which came as a surprise, because I'd thought she didn't like me. I'd thought she didn't like either of us, because we got ourselves hurt out in the woods and died while she and her partner were trying to find us, probably because Wes' sister had given them bad directions, and because I hadn't insisted on making the call myself. But she didn't dislike us, she was just tired at the end of a long shift, and she wanted to go home and take a shower and sleep till the next shift began. She was probably married to a cop, or a fireman, and they never saw each other because they were always out on the street, or on some back road somewhere, cleaning up somebody else's blood or putting out a fire, all the while trying not to let it mess with their heads. The woman looked at me. 'I know you're not all right,' she said. 'I'm not asking you that.' She studied my face. 'I just want to know if you understand what's happening right now.'

I nodded. I might have been smiling, still, which probably didn't help. But then, she would have seen all kinds of reactions, in her job. She would have seen crazed smiles, heard screams and mad laughter, seen grown men curled up like babies in landfills, like Zbigniew Cybulski at the end of *Ashes and Diamonds*. I nodded again, hoping my face looked right to her. Appropriate. At the same time, I was thinking how Laurits was right. *Ashes and Diamonds* probably was the best film ever made. I looked back at what I knew was just a body now. It was still a fact that nobody had said Laurits was dead, but the lack of any hurry was all the evidence my mind needed. The man was behind me, talking on a radio. The woman wanted me to go with her, but I stood my ground for just a moment. I looked at Laurits.

'You didn't have to tell me that,' I said, as softly as I could. Not that it mattered. I smiled, then, but only to prevent myself from crying. 'I know it wasn't personal,' I said. 'But then again, it never was.'

JUST LIKE TOM THUMB'S BLUES

What's cooler than jazz?
   Country.
   You cannot be serious.
   Sub-country covers of old punk songs.
   As if.
   Barry Manilow.
For much of the time, I just closed my eyes and listened
to the voices. They weren't as bad as the visuals, I guess. I
had known these people ever since that first night when
I walked into Sidetracks and met Laurits, though none of
them were close, and some of them, I didn't even know their
names. They weren't my friends, but that's what happens
when somebody dies. You become part of a group you probably never would have chosen, united in something, though
what that something might be is another question. Not
mourning. Not grief. It's just that there's an event that has
to be marked and you mark it with whoever turns up. Still,
I didn't want to be there, with these people. I was pretty
sure I'd never see any of them again – not by choice, anyhow.
They were part of the furniture of Laurits' life and it was
typical of his perversity that he would surround himself with
rejects and crazies. There was Slim, whose extensive wardrobe
of rock-concert T-shirts was apparently inexhaustible (tonight

he was wearing a Grateful Dead Europe 1972 shirt, which was pretty faded, though it surely couldn't have been an original). On either side of him, the Roberts twins, both of whom claimed to be Slim's girlfriend, were matching each other in vodka shots. All the usual crowd, old hands and newish faces, anybody who had known Laurits and had survived his verbal attacks and harangues was there. But it was a sad crew and it seemed to me that none of these people had really known him. He was only three days gone, and somebody was already doing his Barry Manilow shtick, but they didn't know what a fake he was, and they didn't know how real he wanted to be. Like, real, as in honest, in a world where honesty might have meant something. But then he would have laughed at that too. I caught the waitress' eye and signalled for another Jack.

I didn't realise who she was until she brought the drink. She had cut her hair differently and was wearing heavy, goth-style make-up; that, along with the grotesque uniform that all the female Sidetracks servers had to wear – short black minidress, with a white bow tie and frilly white apron – had transformed her so much I barely recognised her, even when she put the drink in front of me and smiled. 'Ruth?'

She nodded, happy to see me and, at the same time, a little embarrassed by the circumstances. I hadn't seen her for months and, for the first time, I understood how thoroughly Laurits had taken over my life. Ruth hadn't cared for him and his friends. The night he and I met, I hadn't even found her to say goodbye. 'How are you holding up?' she said. 'I heard what happened.'

I nodded. I was hoping to seem grave, I suppose, but what had happened three days before still wasn't real to me. 'I'm fine,' I said. 'Well, till the Jack Daniel's runs out.'

'We've got plenty,' she said. She smiled again and touched my arm gently. There was a hint, in the gesture, not only of moral support, but of forgiveness too.

I smiled. I was glad it was her, but I felt lonely too. You have to know things are bad, when the only person you know or like in a place is the waitress.

Couples. They were the worst. Boys sitting with proprietorial arms draped around their girlfriends, just loose enough to look casual. Like, she's mine but hey, it's no big deal. Worth something, but definitely replaceable. Some girl stroking her boyfriend's back in long, slow caressing movements. Laurits wouldn't have gone along with any of that. The contact, the proximity, the faintly simian display. We never even touched outside the apartment.

The police had questioned me for hours about the attack, but they wouldn't let me see Laurits. They kept asking if I knew the men in the pickup and when I told them no, they wrote that down, but they didn't seem to believe me, and they came back to that subject several times. Did I know the men? Had I seen that car before? Had I ever seen Laurits with any of the men, maybe individually? Had Laurits been involved with any criminal activity that I was aware of? As if he would have told me if he had been. As if I would have told them. They kept asking the same questions – the men in the car, money, drugs, criminal activities – round and round and round, and I didn't know what to do, I only knew what I had seen in movies, but then, in the movies, the person being questioned was usually guilty. After a while I wondered if maybe I was supposed to ask for a lawyer, but then I remembered how, on TV, asking for a lawyer was always read as a sign of guilt.

I asked about Laurits, about where they had taken him, but they wouldn't tell me anything. They wouldn't even confirm that he was dead, though I knew he was. He'd gotten his wish and died alone out there, under a wide sky full of stars. I admit, I was angry now, when I thought about him sending me away, but in the end I understood. We weren't that close, really. He preferred the world in abstract to people and I had always known that. That was probably the reason I stayed with him so long.

It wasn't until they were a couple of hours into questioning that they asked about Axel Crane. I told them I'd never heard of him.

Now, three days later, the Sidetracks crew were having a wake for 'an absent friend', as Slim had put it, only for a girl called Julie to come in with some remark about how he was just as absent before he died, which was true in some ways, even though he was always talking, always arguing with somebody about something. Usually something trivial, though. Nothing had been serious. I had always known that too, but Julie's outburst made me notice her for the first time – she'd always been there, quietly watching from the edge of the main action and, now that I thought of it, her eyes had always been on Laurits. I should have guessed, of course, that she had a thing for him, but it wasn't till one of the others said in passing that Laurits and Julie had been an item a couple years back that I put it all together.

We were having a wake – without the Finnegan, as Schuyler put it – because there was no funeral to attend. When they were satisfied they had all they needed, the police released Laurits' body to his mother, who flew in from Jersey the night after he died to claim him. She didn't make contact with any of us. She only dealt with the authorities. I couldn't imagine any of us figured in his occasional calls home, least of all me.

Best ever cover of anything?

Nobody said anything.

Best ever song?

'Just Like Tom Thumb's Blues'.

It was starting to bother me, the way they were all playing Laurits, throwing out trivia questions, trying to get one of those endless, meandering and utterly pointless conversations going the way he always did, but nobody here was as bored, or as contemptuous of himself with others as Laurits had been. They had come to hold a wake, but now they were just stealing his shtick, and they couldn't even do that right. I caught Ruth's eye and made the sign for another JD. I felt sad, all of a sudden. Not for Laurits, but for Ruth and me. For the conversations we'd had about Emily Dickinson and Marianne Moore. For how we could have been friends.

Rules for the drunk and fearful. First, always pretend you know exactly what you are doing. It doesn't matter how obvious it is that you are clueless, keep going. Pretend to the others, but also pretend to yourself. If you believe, they will. Tell yourself that. You have been doing this for years. Become indignant if anybody suggests otherwise.

The night ran on. I didn't even remember leaving Sidetracks, or where I went next, or with whom. I remember, later, seeing a sign through a window somewhere, a crimson neon light through streams of rain, and I wondered, for a moment, how you would go about painting that. After that, I have zero recall.

Nada.

Blackness.

Nothing.

JENNIFER'S ROOM

It is possible that, back then, my principal area of expertise was waking in a strange room, then working out how I got there, tracing time backward through the blackouts and elisions to what I last remembered, or almost remembered. Usually, this was little more than an image, a blurry snapshot and, sometimes, even that was a phantom of my own imagination. A face in the half-light, a voice asking me some dumb question, a moonlit backstreet seen from a moving window, the feel of someone holding me up, or letting me slide into place somewhere. The last bar. The last drink. The last time I knew the people I was with. The troubling closeness of unknown bodies, touched with the possibility of sex or violence. A woman laughing, who might be me. A woman crying. All I ever needed was a strand or two of evidence that might lead me, in my mind's eye, to the unknown location where I had just woken up – a couch in a basement, a child's room that hadn't been used since the heyday of Wayne Gretzky or Reggie Jackson, a stained mattress on a bruised wood floor.

Laurits told me a story once about how he had woken up in a hotel room, convinced he had severely injured or killed a man he had met the previous night, and he had laughed when I asked him what happened.

'I don't know what happened,' he said. 'That's what I'm trying to tell you.'

'But didn't you try to find out?' We were at home, in the apartment, after a long night that had ended, for once, with us both waking up, still half drunk, in his antique bedroom.

He laughed. 'Why would I do that? There was blood on my shirt. I had scratch marks and bruises on my arms.' He shook his head. 'Oh, no.' he said. 'I'm not that curious.'

'So what did you do?'

'What do you think? I showered, changed my clothes and got the hell out of there.'

'But—'

'But what?' He laughed. 'But what if somebody saw me? What if there were witnesses? Maybe there were. But I certainly wasn't going to wait around to find out.'

'What I mean is—'

'What you mean is, why isn't there more of a story? Why isn't this like a movie? Why isn't there closure?'

'Screw you.'

He laughed. 'Americans,' he said. 'You'll do anything for a good storyline. Or not even a good one – just something with an ending. What is it with you people? What is it with your addiction to obvious conclusions?'

I laughed back, but at the same time, I didn't want to be part of his game. I wanted him not to have told me anything, and he knew that. He had known it before he told me. *That* was why he had told me. 'What are you talking about, "you people"?' I said. 'Don't give me that Estonia crap. You're just as American as I am.'

He seemed put out by that, but he might have been pretending. We lay silent for a moment, waiting. Then he got up and started putting on his clothes from the night before.

'So where was this?' I asked.

'Ohio.' He double-stepped into his jeans.

'Where in Ohio?'

'I'm not giving out any more details,' he said.

'Why?' I laughed. 'Do you think I'm going to turn you in?'

'Stranger things, Kate,' he said, pulling on his T-shirt. 'Stranger things.'

'You're unbelievable,' I said.

'Thank you.' He sat down on the edge of the bed and slipped on the absurd loafers he had found in a thrift store. Over bare feet.

'What are you doing anyway?' I said. 'Why are you getting dressed?'

He snorted. 'We need stuff,' he said. 'I'm going to the store.' He jumped up and headed for the door. He always had too much energy the morning after. I could just see him, checking out of that hotel, getting rid of the previous night's clothes on the way to the bus station, or wherever he had gone next, ditching it all item by item on one street after another, unrepentant, giddy with the irony – he might have done something, something real, he might have killed, and now he couldn't remember what happened. It would have been so very *existential* for him at that moment, like something out of Camus, or Zbigniew Cybulski staggering across a field at the end of *Ashes and Diamonds*.

I called after him, but he was too quick. I wanted to say that it was six in the morning, that it was Sunday, that the stores in our part of town were all closed. Something he knew anyway. But then, I knew that he would keep walking till he found some place that was open, some tiny convenience store on a backstreet somewhere, or a Russian grocery, full of stuff that had long passed its display date, a man who looked like Rod Steiger watching him from behind the cashier's desk, one hand on the cash register, the other on his wartime service revolver.

I had woken up in various states from blissed out to near dead in all kinds of places, but this one took the cake. This one was beautiful, a high-ceilinged, old-fashioned bedroom like something out of an old movie – Judy Garland's room in *Meet Me in St Louis*, say – and at first I had no idea where this was, because it was just *too* beautiful. Too perfect, too clean, too still. So perfect, so still, it almost frightened me. It was the kind of large bedroom you didn't see any more, with a table at the centre and an old-style, possibly antique cheval mirror off to the side. One entire wall was lined with books. There was even a stove and a door that led, as I later discovered, to a small, but bright en-suite bathroom with a shower and expensive-looking natural stone tiles. The one detail that I found most striking, however, was what I took to be a Native American mask, hanging on the wall opposite the bed, so whoever slept there would see it every time they woke. It was powder blue and blood red, with thin remnants of gold around the eyes, the face human, the mouth beaklike, the eyes huge, ringed round with stark white pigment, like some night bird from a mescaline vision. It was beautiful and disturbing at the same time – and it was this clue, this mask, that made me realise that I was in Jean's house. I was sure of it, even before I got up and crossed the room to look out at the garden. The country-style drapes were lightly printed with a leaf-and-bird motif that my father might have designed years before. I peeked out, but I didn't open the drapes for fear of being seen, though by whom I couldn't have said. Maybe Christina

Vogel would be there, hiding amongst the trees, spying. I drew back from the window, turned around and saw myself in the cheval mirror. I was wearing a clean white shirt that I'd never seen before, over the baby-blue boy shorts I remembered putting on – when? Two days ago? Three? I didn't know how long I had been asleep, or how long, before that, I had been drunk. I couldn't remember anything. I looked up at the mask: it stared back at me, feral, uncompromising, like some rebuke from the spirit world for all my failures. My disgrace. The word came to me from nowhere – it wasn't a word I would have used, normally – and for a moment, I felt like I had been transformed into someone else. Then I heard a sound that could have been someone on the stairs, but was just as likely one of those noises an old house keeps in its repertoire of sighs and creaks and shuffles, so I slipped back into the wide, white bed and pretended to sleep for a few seconds before I did sleep, falling so suddenly into dreamless oblivion that I thought hours had passed when I woke again, about forty minutes later.

I never did find out how Jean Culver came to rescue me that night. Did she follow me, or had she come across me in the street on one of her night walks, delirious, covered with vomit and blood, too drunk and high to know who she was? Had she dragged me back to the house to clean me up and cradle my lost, demented soul in this beautiful room – a room, I discovered later, that was more than just a guest room, a room that was, in fact, a holy of holies, the one room in her house that she never usually entered, the room she had set aside years ago for Jennifer, should she ever return and need a place to stay – or a place to hide. If she had been following me, I wouldn't have been surprised. It wouldn't surprise me either if she was good at following people, staying hidden in plain sight, a spy like her brother, skilled in concealment, close to invisible when she needed to be. I never found out, because I never asked, just as I never asked why she had brought me to this particular room, when there were others in the house – several, in fact – where she could have dumped me to sleep off my disgrace. I didn't ask that question because I was afraid of the answer, an answer she wouldn't have to give me in so many words, because I would know, from whatever lie she did tell, what the real truth was. I didn't want to ask, or be lied to, or have confirmed the suspicion that came to me, when I woke again, a suspicion that grew into an elaborate narrative in a matter of seconds. In that story, Jean wanted me to stay with her, to live in this room forever, not as myself, but as a replacement for the niece she had lost. At that moment, I didn't want to go back to my own life and I certainly didn't have the strength to return to the apartment – not yet, not yet. The very idea of going back there, to Laurits' things, to the lingering scent and the thick, blinding memory of him – *that* was what had driven me out into the cold, dark night, drunk out of my mind, to be lost forever or rescued from disgrace, it hadn't mattered. I knew that – and I knew that, for now, I had nowhere else to go. But I also knew that it would take too much grace, too elegant a spirit to live in that room, amidst the ghosts and echoes, like a refugee from the lit world, the moon on my bed when I sat up at night, reading the books on these shelves one by one, slowly and carefully, sounding out the words in some futile attempt to understand who or what I had become.

Jean waited a long time before she came to see me. It was hours before I sensed her again on the stairs, hours in which

I drifted in and out of sleep, sometimes not at all sure of which was which. She knocked twice, very softly; then, after a slight pause, she let herself in. By then, it would have been close to evening and I was wide awake, lying flat on my back with my arms by my side, thoughtless, strangely silenced, aware only of the smooth, clean sheets and a sweet, dark scent, like mock-orange blossom, only heavier. Jean came and stood at the foot of the bed, where I could see her. I tried to sit up, but I couldn't.

'How are you?' she said.

I tried to say something, but I couldn't. My head felt heavy as a bell and empty at the same time.

'Well,' she said, 'it will take time. No need to hurry. You can stay here as long as you want.'

I tried for, and managed, a nod, a single, almost imperceptible movement of my head that I hoped she would interpret correctly.

She smiled grimly. 'You could have died out there,' she said. 'You know that, don't you?'

I didn't. I had no memory of anything that had happened after I left Sidetracks. Finally, with real effort, I managed to speak. 'I don't remember,' I said.

She studied my face, then she nodded, a kind of benign resignation in her eyes. 'Better you don't,' she said. She stood watching me a moment longer, a moment in which I thought that she wasn't sure I was telling the truth – that I did remember something, and I was hiding it from her, out of shame, or self-disgust. Disgrace. Though if I was hiding something from her, I was also hiding it from myself – and it came to me, then, that I really *was* hiding something, some half-memory that I didn't dare to drag into the light. Something had happened – and Jean had witnessed it, whatever it was.

Suddenly, I was struck with a terrible sense of foreboding. *You could have died out there.* What had she seen? What horror had she rescued me from?

'What happened?' I said. My voice sounded faraway and strained. 'What did you see?'

She shook her head. 'It's over now,' she said. 'And you need to rest. Are you hungry?'

'Yes,' I said, surprising myself. I hadn't thought about it before, but now I really was hungry – which was a good sign, I knew, because normally, after I'd been out drinking for days, I couldn't even think about food.

'I'll make you some soup,' she said. 'You stay there. Rest.'

Over the next several days, I spent most of the time in bed. Jean brought me soups, thin slices of home-made bread, no cake. I think she enjoyed having someone to look after. She was certainly good at it. She knew I'd mostly want to be left alone, and I don't suppose that would have been any hardship for her, but she was good at guessing other things, too. On the third day, she brought me some fine soap, milk white but tinged with that same orange-blossom scent I'd smelled earlier, and a huge bathrobe that would have been too long even for her. It looked new. 'You can use the shower here,' she said. 'Or the bathroom, which is two doors down the hallway on the left. You choose.'

'Thank you.'

'I was wondering if you wanted music. I have an old Walkman I bought on a whim, and some halfway decent headphones. I've never really used them. I couldn't get used to having those things on my head.' She gave me an odd look, curious, almost shy, and I realised that this was the first time she had really looked me in the face since she'd rescued me from whatever it was that could have killed me out there. 'You said you liked to listen to music.'

I managed a smile. 'That would be great, thanks,' I said. 'I'm sorry to have put you to all this—'

She raised her hand and shook her head for me to stop talking. 'Let's not have that kind of talk,' she said. 'Whatever we are, we are not those people.'

'Okay.'

She nodded. 'Okay,' she said. 'So what do you like?'

'What do I—'

'Music,' she said.

'Oh.' I thought for a moment. I didn't have one specific thing. I listened to everything. Scarlatti. Bach. Keith Jarrett. Pere Ubu. 'I like most music,' I said.

She smiled. 'That's a little indiscriminate,' she said. 'Still, I'll bring you a few things and you can tell me if anything is to your taste.' She laid the bathrobe on the bed, then lingered, knowing that she was lingering. 'Did you ever play an instrument? In school, say?'

It might have seemed an odd question, under the circumstances, but I saw right away what she was doing. For most people, even if they never played very well, the memory of playing music as a child is usually a pleasant one – and even though the ruse was completely transparent, it also worked. 'I had a clarinet for a while,' I said. 'My dad gave it to me.'

'Clarinet?'

'Yes,' I said. 'He used to play and he taught me what he could remember. I gave it up at some point, I can't even remember when. I've been thinking of taking it up again, as a matter of fact.'

'Well,' she said. 'Maybe you can.' She retreated to the door and made ready to leave. 'Have a long, relaxing shower,' she said. 'Take your time.'

It took longer, this time, to feel well again. True to her word, Jean didn't rush me. At one point, she asked if I needed anything from the apartment, but I told her I couldn't face it. She had already been in touch with Laurits' friend, Antoine, who owned the Blue Barn Antiques store and was now my landlord, more or less. Though, of course, he wasn't my landlord, because his arrangement had been with Laurits. Still, he knew what had happened and he had told Jean there was no problem, the rent was actually paid up for three months and, after that, I could decide what I wanted to do. I could continue to stay in the apartment on the same, rather generous terms that he had agreed with Laurits if I liked. For old friends' sake. I didn't know what I wanted to do, but I did know that I could never live in that apartment again, even if I could afford it.

Jean had guessed as much. 'Listen,' she said. 'Why don't I get the car out and fetch your things. You can stay here until you know what you want to do next. School doesn't start again till – when?'

'The end of the month,' I said. 'Late September.'

'So. You have a couple of weeks to think it through,' she said. 'You know you are welcome here. And by now I hope you know that I would be deeply offended if you didn't let me help in whatever way I can.'

When I remember that time now, I wonder what would have happened if Jean had not intervened. Perhaps she was right and I would have died. Almost certainly, I would have dropped out of school for the second time. So it is no exaggeration to say that I owe her my life. But what is really striking, when I look back, is how simply it all took place. I got up, first for a few hours each day, and began helping around the house. Jean talked to Antoine and he helped her bring my few things over from the apartment. When the new semester opened, I decided to try to continue at school and people were kind, sometimes painfully so, till I thought I couldn't bear it, but with Jean's help I did, and by the time the first leaves were falling, I was living a fairly normal existence. My teachers and classmates had begun to let me get by on my own – and it was interesting how I began to find a new sense of direction, a new confidence in what I was doing. Laurits was no longer there. It was as if a lamp had been lit and his shadow had been erased. I started sketching out a short film about a girl whose family move away without telling her. Because she has nowhere to live any more, she takes up residence in a wood because she loves birds. Based on a story I had read in a magazine, I had her decorate the wood with doll heads and pieces of glass and crockery she dug out of the earth. In the last scene, she turned into a bird.

Between classes, I did things around the house, or Jean and I went out on what she insisted on calling excursions. I noticed these excursions were more often by car than before, and she was happy to let me drive. I also noticed that she wasn't chopping as much wood as she used to do. I reasoned that she had too much piled up already, but I had already guessed the truth. She was ill. There was a darkness to her face in the mornings, suggesting that she hadn't slept well, and her energy levels were generally lower. She talked less and, quite often, I would find her in the kitchen, staring out the window at her woodland domain. This loss of energy, this dimming, happened so quickly – it seems, now, that it all took place in less than a month – that I was shocked at the sudden fact that I might lose her soon. I had agreed to stay in the house until I was well; now, I didn't want to leave in case she needed me. One night, when she had turned in early, I sat in the kitchen drinking verbena tea with honey and considered, for the first time, the proposition that, if I were to leave, she would not be able to carry on alone for much longer. It was such a terrible thought that I couldn't help myself and I broke down and began crying like a baby. The idea of her dying left me desolate. I hadn't experienced this moment with Dad – he had kept his illness secret to the end and now, suddenly, I was angry with him for that, even as I cried inconsolably – though silently, so Jean would not hear – in the gold lamplight of her kitchen.

LAURITS' FILM

The invitation came in early November. The School of Art was to hold an evening celebrating Laurits' work, including a showing of his last, unfinished film, and they wanted me to come. I would not be expected to do anything – there would be no valedictory speech, no eulogies. In fact, there would be no words at all. Just Laurits' work, from his earliest film to his most recent. I showed the letter to Jean. 'What do you think?' I said.

'I don't know,' she said. 'Do you want to go?'

'I think I do.'

'Think you do, or think you ought?'

'Both.'

'If you want to go, really, then go,' she said. 'But you have no obligation to anybody. You have no obligations, at this time, to anyone but yourself.' She laid her hand on my arm. Her eyes were bright. 'Do you know why I told you all those stories?' she said.

I nodded. 'It was a trick,' I said. 'You thought that it was a way to keep me from drinking.'

'That's true. But that wasn't all.' She lifted her hand and sat back. 'I told you all those stories and you listened. You didn't question anything, even though you had no way of knowing whether I was just spinning you a bunch of yarns out the back of my head.'

I thought for a moment – or I pretended to. I had asked myself that question, early on, not long after we'd first met, but I'd always known she wasn't lying. 'I knew it was true,' I said. 'All of it. And your trick worked – or it would have done, if Laurits hadn't been . . .' I faltered, then, but not through emotion. I didn't know what I felt about Laurits now. That question was on hold. I needed more strength, and more quiet, to think it through.

'It wasn't a trick,' she said. 'Or maybe it was, partly, but that was just – I don't know . . . A side benefit. What really mattered was that I needed to tell somebody about these things. Seventy years, all those people . . .' She paused for a moment, looking for the right word. 'I needed a custodian,' she said. 'I needed to pass all this on, while there was still time.'

'And you did.'

'Almost.'

'What does that mean? Almost?'

'It means I did lie,' she said. 'Just once.'

'Ah.'

'So you know?'

I didn't know what to say. I had guessed something was missing in her account of Lee's disappearance, but now, suddenly, I didn't want her to tell the whole story, not just for her sake, but also for mine. I hadn't wanted to hear what she had called the tragic part, because she had made it seem inevitable. 'You mentioned a brush with the Reaper,' I said. 'It was early on. Jeremy called, after you had some kind of surgery.'

'You promised not to take notes,' she said.

'I have a good memory.'

'So you knew,' she said. She was serious, but her face had brightened and there was a new energy to her now, even though she was the one who had chosen to lie about that one story – whatever the story was. 'But you didn't say.'

'It was for you to decide.'

She smiled. Then she stood up and went out into the hall. When she came back, she was wearing a waist-length plaid coat and leather gloves that I had never seen before. 'All right,' she said. 'You go. I'll drive you.'

'Thank you,' I said. I knew, now, that I could never argue with her about her health again.

'Then, when it's done, you'll find me waiting outside,' she said. 'It's a fine evening. It will be good to get out for a while.'

I didn't go into the Art School cinema till the very last minute. I didn't mind people seeing me there, but I didn't want anybody to know where I was sitting. There was a delay, however, so the first film didn't start for another ten minutes. As I sat waiting, I remembered Laurits talking about his many journeys, about how, for him, being in a place didn't matter that much. How what mattered was the flight itself. What mattered, what gave his life texture and substance was an entire history of what he described as remarkable flights: descending toward Buenos Aires in the early morning, the Plata shining in the clear light; crossing Australia when the booking person insisted he have a window seat because it was going to be one of those days, hours of open land, the Northern Territories stretching for miles below him, seemingly endless and always changing. Flying from Newark to Nova Scotia in deep winter, the earth shining as the plane descended to meet it; crossing the Danish flow country in half-light; flying from St Louis to Detroit in stormy weather, the terrified girl in the next seat grabbing his arm as the plane dropped suddenly, as if it would fall to earth that very moment. The exhilaration of that sudden fall, the excitement of heavy turbulence. The feeling he'd had of coming home, flying into Tallinn late on a summer's evening, sun going down, the curve of the earth rimmed with soft wet gold and citrus hues before it deepened to thick blues and mauves, the green of the island clenched in darkness below, then the shoreline picked out in faint silver and the lights of the city precise and delicate in the blackness of sudden night. And as I waited, with Laurits' descriptions of places I had never seen running through my mind, I sensed people looking at me from across the hall, sympathisers, the curious, people who had resented Laurits' freak success. I couldn't help thinking that it said a great deal about their world, if Laurits' modest achievements were worthy of resentment, but I didn't feel angry, or defensive, or nervous. I just wanted to see the films one last time – and then forget them.

They showed four films in all. The first, with its fleeting landscapes and the spiral staircase, was followed by a very short piece in which Laurits had filmed a variety of shadows in motion or in stillness: the dark, unmoving shadows of a line of trees on lush grass in late-afternoon sun; shadows of people crossing a bridge in a big city; high expressionist shadows sampled from classic films like *Nosferatu* and *The Cabinet of Dr Caligari*. Whenever I tried to describe a Laurits film, to myself or to somebody who had never seen them, it all sounded so minimalist, but it wasn't like that at all. The films were deeply emotional, full of suppressed passions. The third film was a case in point. Fifteen minutes long, it showed nothing but rain falling on a patch of grass and weeds, intercut with a child's hands – the child itself was not shown – practising scales at a piano. This film was called *Waldszenen*. It sounds dull, but it was beautiful. When, at the end, the child executes an utterly perfect run of A-minor scales, followed by a series of arpeggios, there is a kind of joy in the release, the joy of suddenly finding competence in something you thought you would never be able to do.

Finally, the last film flickered on to the screen. For the first few frames, I thought it was going to be bad. The same crude images I had seen earlier, first of the matador taunting the bull with his cape, then the woman with the glasses, lying spreadeagled on the bed, the shot fuzzier than I remembered. I hadn't known there was any more to it than that. I hadn't seen Laurits do any other work, besides this basic collage, and I thought it would be embarrassing, trite, an ugly remnant that finally exposed him for the fraud he had always been. After all, hadn't he always been a fraud? A self-confessed fraud, in fact, who couldn't even bring himself to lay claim to the films he made as artworks. I thought this film – he had titled it *A Piercing Comfort*, a phrase I knew immediately from Emily Dickinson's poem, 'I measure every Grief I meet' – would be a disaster, people would laugh or get bored, or they would feel insulted and realise that this was Laurits' primary skill, this ability to insult, to degrade. Then, after about thirty seconds, everything changed. The screen still moved between the porn film and the bullfight, but now it moved swiftly from one to the other, so it was like watching some kind of subliminal thing, a secret message insinuated into the banal images, until finally, after three minutes or so, I became aware of something else, another set of images mixed in with the first two. It was still a long moment before I realised what I was seeing.

It was the old slaughterhouse. Nobody was visible, the camera simply moved from one tableau of hooks and chains to another, from sinister machinery with leather restraints hanging loose to shallow troughs and drainage ducts – one

285

was labelled WATER, the other BLOOD. It was matter-of-fact, plain: a blank wall, a stone floor covered with rubble, the hosepipes I had seen hanging from a rack, what looked like some kind of stun gun, which I hadn't seen. The whole thing played out in silence, except for the sound of footsteps, off-camera, pacing up and down just a few feet away, a sound that exaggerated the hollowness and vastness of the place. Even when a bird flared up into the shot, it made no sound. The camera finally came to rest – stopped, utterly, in fact – on a half-open door, through which I could just make out a cascade of heavy chains, amidst shadows – and that was when the voice-over began. That troubled me too, it seemed so gauche to have a voice-over, but it was redeemed by the uncertainty of its tone, by a slight slurring of the speech, as if the actress saying the words was stoned or drunk.

Which, of course, she was. For it was me speaking, me on some wine-darkened night that I couldn't remember now, reciting Emily's poem, one of the hundreds I had memorised through my sad adolescence, getting them fixed in my mind, sometimes, before I really understood what was being said.

A piercing Comfort it affords
In passing Calvary –

There was a slight pause. I didn't remember this, I certainly didn't remember ever being recorded. Had it happened in the apartment, or elsewhere? There was no background noise, just a voice, in a room, audibly recollecting the words from whatever haze it was in.

To note the fashions – of the Cross –
And how they're mostly worn –
Still fascinated to presume
That Some – are like my own –

It was on that last measure of the poem that everything shifted again – though only for a moment, so that, afterward, the audience couldn't be sure of what it had seen: a real animal's throat, spurting blood? Some kind of fakery? All that remained, when the screen darkened, was the sense of something visceral, something horrific.

I had thought, when the screen darkened, that this was the end. It would have been like Laurits, to end it like that. The contrast between that lonely drunken voice reciting poetry and the real cross, the real Golgotha of casual slaughter. But the screen lightened again on a suburban road that looked familiar to me, a suburban road with trees and lawns and picket fences. Pleasant Valley houses with drapes at the windows and flags hanging over the front doors. The camera tracked slowly along the street for a minute or so, then it caught a flight of birds – cardinals, like the ones that used to live in the woods around Stonybrook – and followed them quickly, till it came to rest on the figure of a woman, standing under a tree. It was a bright summer's day, in a kindly neighbourhood with green lawns and flowers and birds, but the woman was weeping, sobbing uncontrollably, in fact, and the woman was me. Very slowly, almost reluctantly, the camera zoomed in on her face – my face – as if it wanted to ask her why she was so unhappy, as if the camera, not whoever was operating it – I don't know how best to express this, but somehow the film made it clear that it was the camera and not its operator that was concerned for this woman's suffering. Then, when it was very near, like some Pasolini close-up, the camera stopped and stayed fixed for just long enough that anybody watching would feel they were intruding and want to turn away. It was then that the screen dissolved, not into darkness, but into a brilliant white light, like the light you see in a TV movie where somebody dies on a gurney on the way to the ER and goes into the afterlife. The light was silent, still – and then, through the light, a voice, not mine, not drunken or high, but soft, not much more than a whisper, repeating that last line. *That Some – are like my own . . .*

The screen went to black, the lights came up – and I knew, before I saw, that people were looking at me, wondering what part I had played in the making of the film, assuming, I guessed, that I had been acting in that scene under the tree, just as I had been acting when I said the poem, pretend-drunk, fake-stoned. As I grew accustomed to the light, I saw that many of them, of the people nearest me at least, were annoyed, as if they thought that they had been duped, that they had been lied to, and that I was part of the lie. That was all I saw at first, that anger – but then a woman in the row directly in front of me, a woman I didn't know, laid her hand on my arm and told me it was beautiful. She was smiling, but there was a damp light to her eyes and I knew that she had been moved and, when she let go of my arm, another woman, someone I did know, though I couldn't remember where I had met her, touched my wrist very lightly and set her mouth as if she didn't trust herself to speak. All she could do was shake her head slightly and gaze at me – and I could see they both meant well, but that was when I knew I had to get away, not from the anger, but from the sympathy and the – admiration, was it? But for what? For the film? For the part those women assumed I had played in its execution?

I nodded at the women, then I started for the aisle, people standing up and drawing back to let me through. Someone called out, someone who knew my name, but I didn't recognise the voice and I didn't look back. I made it to the door then I hurried out and into the cold, clear air, breathing it in, letting its iciness in my throat cancel out the memory of summer's heat. I wanted to stand still then, to stand still and gulp down great lungfuls of winter air, but almost as soon as I got clear of the building, I sensed movement behind me, movement, then voices and I hurried away again, crossing the pool of yellowish light outside Webster Hall where Jean, true to her word, was waiting in the car at the exact spot where she had dropped me.

KAY STARR

Jean did well, hiding how ill she was. Maybe I was too caught up in my own memories to notice it sooner, but now, as I got into the routine of school and home, reading, working on projects, having meals and Saturday-afternoon tea parties in the kitchen, I began to see that she was getting worse. I tracked back to the day when Christina Vogel had been waiting for me, and it didn't take a degree in logic to figure out that, whatever she had, it had started about then. Or no – there had been times before that, when she got tired, or seemed dark around the eyes. I'd never seen serious illness up close, but it was clear to me that this was serious now. Jean was putting up a brave front but when I noticed that she hadn't been out chopping wood at all for several days I began to worry. There was no point asking her about it, I knew that. I also knew that, if she knew where Jennifer was – and I felt certain that she did – she wouldn't tell me. Yet it upset me to think of her dying without seeing her niece. At the time, I believed that Jennifer was all the family she had, and surely she too had the right to say goodbye to the woman who had risked jail for her.

The idea of the letter came by chance. I had wakened early, and I was sitting in bed, reading a book. Times like that felt like a gift: the house silent around me, no need to be anywhere, a new book off the shelves in Jennifer's room that had nothing to do with schoolwork. I'd had glimmerings before that any problem I'd had with drinking and drugs had to do with time. Now I was sure. If you need to recover from anything, having time, being slow, is the best therapy. Because getting high is nothing more than an attempt to stop time. To be still. To be.

I was thinking all this when I looked up and saw the mask on the wall opposite the bed – and for the first time it struck me how out of place it was in that room. So why was it there? Hadn't Jean said that Jennifer loved making masks, when she was young? And hadn't she said that she'd bought a piece of her artwork, on that road trip when she thought she was being followed? Maybe this mask really was something the grown-up Jennifer had made. Of course, she could have made it years before she went into hiding, but that didn't seem likely. The mask looked too new, and it struck me as very sophisticated for a young girl, even if she had been as brilliant as her doting aunt made out. Right now, I'm making this sound logical, a process of stepwise deduction, but it wasn't to begin with. Something just hit me, so I dragged a chair over to where the mask was and, very carefully, I lifted it from the picture hook where it was hanging. It smelled of varnish and dust in my hands, especially when I turned it round and peered into the dark interior behind the baked face. Into where the soul, or the mind, or the psyche would have been, had it been a living creature. That was when I saw the label – a tiny silver label with black printed letters, spelling out a trade name – Wishram Arts – and an address in Oregon. I allowed myself a moment's doubt – there was no evidence at all that Wishram Arts had anything to do with Jennifer – but it didn't last. I *knew*, just as Jean had known when she found the mask, that she had finally found the way back to Jennifer – only to have the whole thing unravel, just a few minutes later. In my heart, I just knew that I'd guessed right. I also knew that Jean would never have agreed to what I was about to do next, but I had no choice. Because I knew that I couldn't have lived with myself, afterward, if I didn't try.

I kept the letter simple, and concise as a telegram – JEAN ILL, PLEASE COME, YOU KNOW WHERE – and I sent it that afternoon to John Banister, c/o Wishram Arts. It was a long shot, a Hail Mary throw, and I didn't know what would happen. Either the letter would find its way to Jennifer and she would come, or she wouldn't. If she chose not to visit, Jean didn't have to know. If she needed help, at the end, I would be there to look after her. It seemed just, at that moment, that having saved me, she would now have a companion, and a helper, for whatever it was that lay ahead.

Time passed slowly and I didn't think to ask myself if I was happy, as the winter drew in slowly, and Jean and I lived our simple life together in her house. If someone had described that life to me a year earlier, I would have imagined it as dull and lonely; now, I could have said that I was glad enough to be sober and fitter than I had been in years, but I really was happy, too. Contented. Jean did her best to conceal her illness and, most days, I managed not to think too much about it. We kept the house warm and the kitchen well stocked – I hadn't known what a pleasure it was to go shopping, but then, I wasn't used to seeking out small wholefood suppliers and specialist groceries, and I wasn't used to lugging home fresh seasonal vegetables from the farmers' market. Because Jean was a vegetarian, I became one too, by default, but I didn't mind losing out on meat, when there was so much else to enjoy.

We ate fish sometimes. I did more of the cooking as time went by and I learned new dishes from Jean's old handwritten recipe books. It was a good life. I didn't want it to end, ever.

One day, early in December, I came home from school a little early. I was walking homeward about halfway along Audubon Road, when the first snowflakes fell, wavering uncertainly on the grey air, like something that wants to come into being, but can't quite make it happen. That sense of the snow being almost there lasted until I got to the house, it was only when I closed the gate behind me that one big, powdery flake brushed my hand – and then it began in earnest, thick flakes darkening the air as I hurried to get inside. In the kitchen, Jean was listening to the radio. She smiled at me when I came in. 'You're back early,' she said. 'And you brought the snow.'

'I did.'

She took a knife from the rack and began chopping carrots. 'There's something special about the first day of real snow,' she said. 'It's a special season, that time between apple fall and first snow, and its ending ought to be marked. The last apple of the fall. The first snow of the year. You have to make an occasion of these things.'

'How?'

'You'll see,' she said. 'Go and do whatever you need to do and I'll make some tea. Then we'll prepare a feast for tomorrow's celebration.'

By the time I got out of my coat and boots and headed back to the kitchen, the first snow of the year had already begun to settle, on the sills to begin with and, then, in layers across the windowpanes, veiling us in so the kitchen had the enclosed, separate atmosphere of a theatre set, the lamps a little warmer and more golden, like the lamps in the old *Woman's Home Companion* illustrations and *New Yorker*

Christmas covers from the 1940s that Dad had collected over the years, some framed on the walls of his studio, the rest in drawers, carefully laid between sheets of plain newsprint. Jean was moving about the room, gathering together the ingredients for our recipe. Finally, when it was all ready, she moved over to the corner by the pantry door and switched on the radio. 'We need some music,' she said.

She gave me an odd, conspiratorial look, as if having music while we baked might be some act of unnecessary self-indulgence – and maybe it had been, once, in the house where she had grown up, learning the skills that, though they had been chores in that house, she had transformed into perfect and private things. The radio flickered on; it looked ancient, with its glass-plate facade inscribed with the names of long-lost stations and its dusty gold light shining through, but it worked and, after a moment, a woman's voice emerged through a lush string arrangement, a voice that seemed to belong, not just to another time, but also to another place. Another world.

'Ah,' she said. 'I love this one.' She stood still, her head to one side, listening. 'Kay Starr,' she said. 'That woman had a beautiful voice.'

I listened. The woman from another world was singing about loneliness, about walking alone after midnight, staring at the people passing by and knowing that it wasn't the proper thing to do, but unable to help herself because maybe, just maybe, her lover might be there, somewhere amongst the crowd. I cannot remember the words now, not exactly, but somehow they fit my sense of who Jean was, or who she had been, when the song was in vogue, so it was as if she was the one who was singing, and I felt sorry for the woman she had been, alone after Lee went away – but I also felt proud of her, and I felt her pride in herself.

The music sounded vaguely familiar, though I'd never heard of Kay Starr, and I was puzzling about where I might have heard it, while Jean listened, not altogether gone from this kitchen, or from me, but halfway to a world where she had once belonged. Or had she? I had no idea, even now, what any of that might have meant for her – belonging, or love, or happiness or even, for that matter, the sweet, transfigured sadness in the lyrics of this pop standard.

> *I something something in the moonlight*
> *Along the crowded avenue*

– no, that wasn't it. And now, even though I know they were banal, the formulaic sentiments of a million such songs, I wish I could remember the words, just once.

Jean was still halfway lost in a dream when the next song came on, 'Maybe You'll Be There' fading straight into another 1950s classic, the same lush string arrangement cueing in the voice Kay Starr again, from the sound of it – and I knew this one, but for a moment I didn't know from where. Then, I realised. It had been in my father's highly eclectic record collection, amongst the bebop and cool jazz and medieval music and Indian ragas, a golden oldie from when he himself couldn't have been much more than a boy. It sounded different now, though, slower, almost stately, the voice deeper, more melancholic. Without thinking, I walked over to where Jean was standing, not at all sure what I was doing until I heard my own voice, hushed by the music, but clear and innocent, I knew, of what my friend would have called impropriety.

'Miss Culver,' I said. 'May I have the honour?'

She smiled, but I think she was about to wave me away until she noticed something, in my face, or the tone of my voice, or maybe just something about the moment that changed her mind. She stood up, her face quietly solemn, all of a sudden. 'Do you know how to dance to *this*?' she said.

I nodded. 'My father taught me,' I said, which was only half true. He had taught me to dance, a little, but he'd never made much of a success of it and I had almost forgotten those bizarre lessons in the niceties of another era, one to which neither of us had belonged. Why he had wanted me to learn, I don't know – maybe he had visions of me being embarrassed by some obscure lack at the school prom – but he had taken it seriously, for a while at least.

It had started just after my mother left. Dad would put on some old record from before his time, a 1940s or 1950s song that he must have heard on the radio in his parents' house, something his mother might have sung along to while she worked in the kitchen. 'Blue Moon'. 'Stormy Weather'. 'The Man I Love' – and this song we were listening to now, in Jean Culver's kitchen, a song whose title I couldn't remember. He didn't just choose them at random, he had favourites and, though they weren't his usual taste, his affection for those songs was clear. Maybe it was because they had just enough jazz in them, maybe they contained memories, or some imagined romance that, as a child, he had concocted from hints and images and scraps of conversation. Old movies. Fantasy. What did it matter? All that mattered was to love somebody, at a certain time, in a certain place. He would put on one of those old songs and then he would take me by the hand, carefully manoeuvre us into a starting position and move me around the room and out into the hall, his face solemn, his body guiding us both through the moves as if from somewhere else, from one remove, as it were, so it seemed like we were animated by remote control. I tried to stay with him, to keep my head up – he always told me this, as we began: *Keep your head up, pretend there's a string running from the ceiling and down through your body, holding you upright* – but I could never stop myself from looking down. Even if I managed it for a while, I always ended up at some point where I lost faith and looked down at my feet, like St Peter trying to walk on the water, all fine for a few moments and then, suddenly, everything a muddle, panic setting in, the two of us faltering to an awkward standstill. Sometimes he would try to avert the catastrophe before it happened – *Head up, head up* – but that only made us both laugh and we would have to break off and begin again anyway. I never knew why he thought he should be teaching me to dance. Maybe he thought it would be good for us to do this together, to take my mind off my mother. Something special that suited our being two, and not three, but the truth is, I would have preferred it if he'd taken me fishing, or hiking in the woods. I would have preferred it if we had just sat around listening to Charles Lloyd or Miles Davis, for that matter. Something *he* liked. Something he wanted to share.

We had only taken a few steps when Jean stopped, my hand still in hers. She treated me to one of her ironic smiles. 'Perhaps it would be better if you let me lead,' she said.

I looked at her, puzzled. I thought she had been leading.

Something in my face made her laugh; a moment after, she lifted her head, straightened her back. 'Don't worry. I've had lots of practice.'

I am not sure – the kitchen was warm now, the windows fogged – but I may have blushed at that. But I couldn't deny the common sense of the proposition. 'All right,' I said.

We continued – and though I noticed no change, things improved immediately. 'You have to keep your back straight,' Jean said. 'Head up. Don't look down. That's all there is to it.'

I nodded. 'I know,' I said.

She laughed softly. 'Your *head* knows,' she said. 'But your body is still wondering what it's doing here.' She craned her neck back and gave me a mocking look, but I could see that, behind the ironic facade, she was happy. Then the song stopped and we stood apart slightly, made awkward again by the interruption. The DJ was saying something, but I didn't hear what it was. Then another song began, a song I didn't know. It wasn't the kind either of us would have been inclined to dance to and it felt, in that moment, that something had broken, albeit very gently. Jean fixed me with her pale grey eyes and smiled. 'Thank you, Miss Lambert,' she said. 'Now. Let's make some pies.'

For the next hour, we set to making fried apple pies, filling the kitchen with warmth and the sweet smell of warm oil and cinnamon. The radio was mostly background now, though every now and then Jean would lift her head to listen, remembering something that had happened before I was born. It turned out that the making of fried apple pie was, on the face of it, a fairly straightforward process, but there were subtleties to be considered in the quantities and textures – for twelve ounces of fruit, Jean said, there should be just over half, though by no means a whole teaspoonful of cinnamon; the apples should be cooked until tender, before they were wrapped in the pastry for frying, but everyone had a different idea of what tender meant. The main consideration, however, was in the size of the pastry triangles and the length of time they were fried. Still, I thought I had got the hang of it by the time we finished the first batch, and she must have thought so too, because that was when she left me to my own devices. With all the care and attention I'd devoted to the art of pie-making, I hadn't noticed that a cloud had come over her face, a grey veil that, when she turned to me in the light of the kitchen lamps, looked like dust around her eyes and mouth.

'I'm sorry, Kate,' she said. 'I have to go lie down for a while.'

'Are you okay?'

'It's nothing,' she said. 'I've just . . . Well, I've been up and down lately. I'm an old woman, you know.' She ventured a reassuring smile; in that light, it only made her look more frail. 'I'll be tip-top in the morning. We'll have a fine day of it.'

'What about the pies?'

'Oh, you can finish this, if you like.' She studied my face as if she was looking for – and I had the impression that she was finding – something new there, some subtle quality that hadn't been there before. She patted my arm. 'You know what to do. Besides, every pie should have its own character. Individual.' She patted my arm again, as if she was checking to see if I was real, or maybe just really there, then she made her way slowly to the door. She was hiding something, that was clear. Something had stolen up on her suddenly, and now she was doing all she could to keep me from worrying. In the doorway, she turned, smiled again. She was hiding something, but she wasn't being brave: what she was concealing didn't matter to her, and she didn't want it to matter too much to me. 'I'll see you tomorrow,' she said. 'Our first day of real snow.'

I nodded. 'Sleep well,' I said.

She nodded too, then, as she turned to go, she said something else, but I didn't quite catch what it was and it was not till some moments after the door closed that I worked it out. 'We'll celebrate.' That was what she had said. 'We'll celebrate.' For minutes I stood where I was, as if something had caught me unawares, something astonishing, then I went back to work in the kitchen, peeling a new batch of apples and setting them in the saucepan to simmer, as if this was something I had been doing all my life.

I was about to put out all the lamps and go to bed when I realised that somebody was outside in the yard. I went to the door and opened it a matter of inches, no more, and looked out. The snow had stopped, and it was perfectly still, like a scene from a Christmas card. At first I had thought that the intruder had to be Christina and I had a worrying vision of her standing out there in the snow in her First Holy Communion dress. Then I saw a tall, dark figure in the clear area between the house and the woods – a man of maybe fifty or so, in a long winter coat and a black fedora, looking up at the lit window where Jean must have fallen asleep with the lamp on. She did that, sometimes. She told me how she had always read a book for an hour or so before she fell asleep, but now she couldn't get past three or four paragraphs before she nodded off. She didn't sleep for long, though. I knew that. I would hear her moving about in the small hours, slipping down to the kitchen to make valerian tea, or moving around her room, doing who knew what.

I opened the door wider and the man stepped forward. 'Can I help you with something?' I said. I could see that this man was no danger to me, or to Jean – when I saw him first, I had a vision of some stubborn old FBI man from the past, still trying to get to Jennifer through Jean – but this man was clearly no government agent. He was well dressed, and seemed clean-cut, but there was a light in his face, a brightness in the eyes, that suggested someone else altogether.

He gave a wry smile at the formality. 'I hope so,' he said. 'My name is Simon Culver. I've come to see my aunt.'

'Excuse me?'

He stepped closer and took off his hat. He was very handsome, his eyes a deep blue, his nose aquiline, and there was a hint of permanent amusement about his mouth. A thin scar ran through one eyebrow. 'My name is Simon Culver—'

'It can't be,' I said. 'She told me—'

'She told you I was dead,' he said. 'Well, she's not to blame for that. I asked her to tell everyone I was dead.'

'She didn't say you were dead,' I said. 'Not in so many words. She said you – vanished completely.'

He nodded. 'And so I did.' He put his hat back on. 'It's cold out here and it looks like it might snow again. Do you mind if I come in?'

I stepped aside. 'Come in,' I said; then I added, without meaning to, the words Jean would have spoken, had she been present. 'Welcome home,' I said. 'I'll make some tea.'

RAIN ON A FOREIGN ROOF

The next morning, I overslept. When I finally came downstairs, just before nine, Jean and Simon were eating breakfast in the kitchen, casual as you please, as if this was an entirely usual occurrence. The room smelled of coffee and buttered toast, a faint blue at the windows from the snow. Jean got up slowly – I wondered if Simon could tell how frail she had become – but I made her sit down again, and poured myself some coffee.

'So you've met our new ghost,' I said.

Jean pretended to wince. 'I'm sorry,' she said. 'He made me promise.'

'Apology accepted,' I said. 'More toast anybody?'

'Yes, please,' Simon said. He looked tired. I'd put him in the spare room, at the back of the house, not wanting to disturb Jean, but it didn't look as if he'd slept much. Maybe the owls had kept him awake.

'Did you sleep at all?'

He shook his head. 'Not too well,' he said. 'I'm not used to a soft bed. And the barred owls kept me awake.'

I laughed.

'What is it?' he said. 'Did I say something funny?' He looked at Jean and, for the first time, I could see a family resemblance.

Jean shook her head. 'You'll get used to her in time,' she said.

What seems strange, now, looking back over the weeks that followed, was how very quickly I got used to Simon. I guess that was natural, as Jean got weaker and had to spend more time in bed, but we seemed to get used to each other's company very quickly and, as we did, he began to fill in some of the gaps in Jean's narratives. And that in itself is surprising, because he wasn't a storyteller, like Jean. Quite the opposite. Sure, he talked about things he had seen, just as he talked about books and art and horses, but he didn't tell stories. Even his Vietnam story, when it came, wasn't really a story. In truth, it was more of an account. A report of things observed. I think Simon Culver had heard too many glib and misleading stories about things he had seen with his own eyes, to tell any of his own. Too many movies and bad books about the hell and the camaraderie of war, too many glamorous accounts of being 'on the road', too many tragic-but-cathartic endings that were always, apparently, based on a true story, though whose true story that might have been was never really clear. And yet, at the same time, we talked pretty much every day. He had come to see Jean but, because of her illness, we were obliged to spend a good deal of time together and it's surprising how easy that felt. I guess I fell for him a little over those few weeks, though he was old enough to be my father. But that wasn't why I felt so comfortable in his company. It was something else, something to do with whatever he did when he wasn't with me, or sitting by Jean's bed. The things he did in the early morning, out in the woods by himself. The thoughts he had, or maybe the absence of thoughts. The stillness he obtained. Once, I saw him out there, in the half-light, talking to Christina Vogel – and I wasn't quite sure of what I was watching, but the girl was so different, so changed. So – natural. I had no reason to think he had met her before, but she acted around him the way she might have done with a trusted companion. Or another creature half-animal, like her. A horse, maybe. Or a deer. Then again, maybe, like me, she had fallen for him a little too.

Nevertheless, as curious as I was about him, as much as I would have liked to know what was in his mind, I never asked Simon to tell me anything. I don't even know why we got into his story, one grey afternoon when Jean was asleep upstairs, lost in a dream of this life, or some premonition of the next. Maybe it was because I had been telling him about what Jean had told me, or some of it at least, and maybe it was because he felt bad for turning up that first night as a ghost.

'I didn't mean to scare you,' he said.

'You didn't,' I said. 'I just assumed you were an impostor.'

He laughed. 'I told Jean to tell people I was dead, because I wanted to disappear. I *needed* to disappear. I was an army deserter. I had good reasons for not being alive.'

'But didn't they have an amnesty on Vietnam?' I said.

'Well, Jimmy Carter put out an amnesty for draft evaders,' he said. 'But that didn't cover regular army deserters. The government still takes a dim view of soldiers who go AWOL.'

'But it was so long ago,' I said.

'Not that long,' he said. 'And I had another reason for not wanting to go back. Though I'm not sure you'd want to hear *that* story.'

'I've heard all the others.'

'Did she tell you about the massacre that my dad witnessed in France?'

'Yes – wait! What do you mean by *witnessed*?'

304

He considered for a moment. 'She told you the official version,' he said. 'The one where he and the Resistance fighters he was tagging along with went in afterward, right?'

'Yes.'

'Well, that *is* the official version,' he said. 'The one the army finally accepted in his report, after he'd rewritten that report three times. What they didn't want to know was that he, and five members of the French Resistance, had observed the massacre, or the final stage at least, directly.'

'Directly?'

'He saw it,' Simon said. 'He saw people being killed. They all saw it, but what could they do? They were outnumbered by around eight to one. More, probably. Not that he ever forgave himself. I think he would have gone in there alone, if the others hadn't stopped him. But the army didn't want to hear about that. It would have been bad for morale and the French would have been pissed as hell when they found out there was a story going around about five French Resistance fighters who stood by while French civilians were slaughtered.'

'How do you know this?'

'He told me. He wanted to stop me going to Vietnam and he thought . . . He did everything he could to get me out of going and I hated him for it. I should have thanked him.' He took out a packet of cigarettes. 'It's all right,' he said. 'I'm not going to smoke it. Sometimes I just need to hold one in my hand.'

'You can smoke if you like,' I said. 'We could go outside.'

'It's fine,' he said. 'Officially I've given up. Addict no more. Now it's just psychological.'

'You don't have to tell it if you don't want to,' I said.

He nodded. 'I know,' he said. He took an imaginary pull on the cigarette, then he began his story.

'I sometimes think, in some dark room at the back of their minds, that the higher-ups were grateful for My Lai. Not that it happened, but for how things turned out. I know a few other incidents got reported later, but at the time it was almost perfect, an example of temporary group insanity under a weak leader, a classic case of the unfortunate but wholly exceptional events that can happen in war. The exception, you see, that proves the rule. That's a harsh judgment, I guess, but there was an upside to My Lai and it was this invention of the exceptional case, the freak series of events, the rogue lieutenant, the few-bad-apples story. It wasn't supposed to happen, and usually it didn't. Only it did. It happened far more often than anybody would admit, because we were at war.

Mordlust. Do you know what *Mordlust* is? It's a specific term, a technical term. You could say bloodlust, but that sounds too ordinary – sometimes you have to import a word from another language to give it the necessary gravitas.

'My Lai wasn't an exception. We know more now, but we still don't know the half of it, and we never will. Even if we did, even if every single incident was catalogued, described in detail, the names and atrocities fully recorded – even if we had all of that, it wouldn't change anything. All of those events would be explicable. There would be extenuating circumstances. Temporary insanity, under extreme pressure – and I know how extreme that pressure is. I know that terror – but then, terror is complicated. It isn't just fear. It's participatory. I saw friends die in the most degrading and painful situations. Worse, I heard them die, and I couldn't do anything to help. That makes you angry, that fills you with rage, and when you combine extreme rage and terror, you have a perfect recipe for *Mordlust.* In the fury of a moment, anything can happen. Under certain unbearable circumstances, anything can seem, if not forgivable, then at least understandable. It's even understandable that this inclination to *Mordlust* that all of us have to some degree or other, is encouraged and fortified every day in basic training. Every day. All those chants about sex and killing, how to kill is a pleasure, how your weapon isn't just your best friend, it's also . . . Well, you know how it goes. That's understandable too, in a way, because when they drop you into a war zone, you had better be ready to kill, or else you die. I was trained to think – to *know* – that if I faltered for one moment, if I hesitated for a split second, then I, or worse, my comrades, could die screaming. And here's something the news reports and the documentaries don't tell you. What they won't acknowledge is that, if you take any of those bad apples who, in exceptional circumstances, committed such terrible, cowardly acts in Vietnam, or any other theatre of war, if you took any one of them and scratched the surface, ninety-nine times out of a hundred you would find a soldier who would do anything not to leave a fellow soldier behind. So – you see the problem. It's not the bad apples who are responsible. They are just instruments. It's the system. It's war itself.

'That was what finally broke through to me. That was why I left. I wasn't drafted, I signed up, I *believed* – and I deserted *because* I believed. I walked away, knowing what I was doing, knowing the shame I would be inflicting on my father, not because of the massacre I'd witnessed, and taken part in, not because I'd been fighting an unjust war – I didn't really know or care about the politics then. No. I walked away because our side wasn't fighting honourably. It was an unjust war, I'm sure of that now, but what mattered to me was that it was dishonourable. On our side. What mattered to me, the reason I walked away, defeated, was that I had more respect for the enemy than I had for us. I loved my fellow soldiers, I would have done anything to save them from the horrors they faced – and not just the horror, but also the boredom, the shame. But even though I could have continued to bear the horror, I could not endure the shame. I was ashamed. We had the best-equipped, most powerful military in the world and we ran that war like a bookkeeping exercise. Body counts. Statistics. That war, and pretty much every war we have waged since, was run by accountants. Actuaries. Project managers in fatigues.'

He stopped talking suddenly, and looked me in the face. I realised that, for a while there, he had forgotten who he was talking to. He shook his head. 'I'm sorry,' he said. 'I didn't want to give you a lecture.'

'No,' I said. 'Don't be sorry. I really don't know much about any of this.' I smiled. 'When I first met Jean, she was shocked how little I knew.'

He shook his head again. 'No,' he said. 'She wasn't shocked, not really. That's how she plays things. There's a touch of the schoolmarm about Aunt Jean.'

I laughed. 'I'll say.'

'She knows how the system works,' he said. 'My sister taught her well. There's a whole cartload of the schoolmarm in Jennifer.'

He frowned then, remembering why he was here. Why he was, and his sister was not – and I had a sudden memory of something Jean had said: how, once, she had told me that, even though they didn't spend much time together, growing up, even though they had very little in common, Simon always stood up for his sister, defending her against all criticism, as if she were some kind of saint – but that wasn't because he thought highly of her. On the contrary, in fact. As Jean saw it, Simon was awed by Jennifer's intelligence, and yet, at the same time, he didn't see that kind of intelligence as an asset. To him, it was a burden she had to bear. A burden – and a limitation. It got in the way of living life to the full, like the heavy braces children used to have to wear back when people still got polio.

'You have to understand that she can't help it,' he said. 'She's fallen in love with the idea of invisibility – or no, she's fallen in love with this person she has become, this self she invented so she could live alone all this time. It's not just the predictable fear of being caught that prevents her from going anywhere, though I sometimes think she believes that something she's done will put her in prison for the rest of her life, if the FBI ever catch up with her. Which is crazy, just pure paranoia. And maybe that's just an excuse to stay where she is. As she is. I don't know. When I ask her about it, she says that surfacing isn't an option. If she were to surface, that would be to accept that something is over and, as far as she is concerned, it isn't over. It's just not as visible, for now, but it hasn't ended. She quotes Che – silence is argument carried on by other means . . . She quotes Abbie Hoffman, how he would say that the time would come when we all have new names and new faces. I don't remember . . . I was never part of all that. I didn't join. Not that I completely disagreed, I just didn't like . . . I didn't agree with their methods. And anyway . . . I couldn't.'

'You couldn't what?'

'Join,' he said. He seemed troubled by this idea, as if it were a new one. 'I couldn't join.'

'So what happened to Jennifer?' I said. 'After she left.'

'She didn't leave. She was abandoned. And that was how she got her new life. It was a last gift from the 60s underground.' He laughed. 'She was hanging around one day in some Midwestern town, waiting for a call to say where she was meant to go next. You have to remember, by that time, people had nothing outside the group. Money, resources, false papers – whatever they needed to stay hidden, it came from the movement, one way or another. So when she found herself alone, after three weeks of waiting – she was staying in a motel, walking over to a public telephone outside a gas station every day at 3 p.m. and waiting for a call that never came – she had nowhere to go, almost no money, no friends, no identity she could trust. She was scared to go home. I think Jean wired her money at some point around then, but even that felt too risky. So she got a job. And gradually, she became somebody else, though of course that wasn't the end of it. It was, if anything, a new beginning. She's been that person ever since. Someone with a different history from the one anybody else has for her. A history she invented. A history that makes her what she is now. A history that she can't risk losing. So I can tell you, when your letter came, she was pretty mad—'

'I'm sorry,' I said, and I was. 'I just thought—'

'Oh, don't be sorry. She understands. But even when you understand, that doesn't stop you being mad.' He smiled sadly. 'And she wanted to come. Or one part of her did. But she couldn't. And she knew Jean would understand.'

'How could she know that?'

'Because Jean tracked her down once,' he said. 'Jennifer didn't find out till later – and she figured out what had happened, how Jean turned around and drove away.'

'So how did it come about that you are here in her place?' I said.

He shook his head. 'It was an accident, really. I just happened to be there – nearby, anyhow.' He studied my face.

I must have seemed so young to him. So unready for the world he knew. 'Where I live, the casualty rate is unusually high. You lose people, one way or another. I had just lost someone and Jennifer took me in when I had nowhere else to go. She knew it wasn't permanent, and she knew I wouldn't do anything stupid. Besides, she trusts me, because I'm invisible, too, in my way. It's easy to get lost in America, and that's fine by me.' There was a sound, a low murmur from upstairs, and he paused a moment to listen. Then, as it fell quiet again, he resumed his account. 'Jennifer has been underground for so long, she'll do anything, lose anything, give anything not to get caught. Not because she's afraid of prison so much – well, she probably is, but what she really can't stand is the idea that *they* would be able to chalk up a win, finally.'

'They?'

He smiled wryly. 'The FBI, the cops, the system. They failed so miserably to catch anybody for all those years. That's a matter of pride for her. They cheated and they lied and still they failed.' He sat quietly, suddenly still. It made him look younger. He could have been sitting out in the forest somewhere, by a campfire, alone, during those first weeks when he was drifting from place to place, drifting away from the war, and his father and everyone he could never go back to.

'And you?'

'What about me?'

'You didn't join,' I said. 'But you did leave. You refused to go on with—'

'I didn't have a choice,' he said. 'All I'd ever wanted to do was serve my country, like Dad, then come home and do a regular job. Something to do with horses, maybe. But you can't go to a war and then come back – or not in that way, anyhow.' He considered a long time, staring away from me out into the garden, then he shook his head. 'I don't want to say the name of the place,' he said. 'I don't know why. I have a kind of superstition about that. Anyway, they even got the names wrong in the official report. The report that recorded the number of enemy dead. The body count. We suffered no casualties that day, presumably because the people we attacked were all unarmed civilians. But that's not the point either. Two days earlier, a boy from Fairfax was killed by a booby trap. That hit me hard. It hit everybody hard. So when we went into that village, and we were told that warnings had been dropped there, the day before, we decided it was safe to assume that everyone who was a non-combatant would have left already. When they tell you they have leafleted a village, it's clear what has to be done. You kill anybody who hasn't left. If you don't, then they will kill you.

'That boy from Virginia. We'd talked a while, a couple of days before he died. It was like some scene in an old movie, he even showed me a photograph, only it wasn't the usual picture of his girl. It was his sister, a girl who would have been pretty, if it wasn't for the harelip. He told me one of the reasons he'd signed up was her. He wanted to make her proud, do you see? It's all corny. It's all stuff you've seen before. But then, a booby trap blows a boy to pieces and that's something you can see a hundred times and you'll never get used to it. You can't show that on a movie screen either. It's too unreal.

'So, going in, we were fired up. Something should have clicked, early on, when there was no return fire. But it didn't. The people in that village were women, children, a few old men. Babies. We shot babies. One guy was using an old man for target practice. He took aim at the man's head, from about ten feet away, and he missed. Guys were laughing at him. He got five steps closer and shot again, and he missed. I remember how it got to me, then. It was like a dream. I don't think any of us knew what was happening. Everybody was laughing now, so the failed marksman walked right up to the old man – he was frozen, terrified, completely uncomprehending – and he shot him point-blank in the head. I turned away. Up ahead, I could hear somebody screaming. It was a woman's voice, so I knew it was one of them. She was calling out the same word over and over again: a name, maybe, the name of a child, or her husband, or her father. I don't know. It sounded like a name. It wasn't a word I knew from the little Vietnamese I had managed to pick up along the way, but what struck me was, if that had been one of our people, they would have been doing the same thing. They would be calling out the name of someone they loved, just like she was. It could have been a boy calling for his mother, or his girlfriend, it might have been an older man calling for his wife, or his child, but it was all the same in the end. I didn't know what I was doing now. I was just doing what I was trained to do. I walked to where the voice was coming from, and I found the woman She would have been thirty, maybe thirty-five. She was very thin, her face was spattered with mud – and I could see that she was in horrible pain. When she saw me, her voice went quiet, but she didn't stop talking altogether, she was still saying that one word. I didn't know what to do. I could tell she was going to die, but then, everyone in that village was going to die. The only question was how. Somewhere off to my right I heard more screams – they had found a girl and it looked like . . .' He gave me a brief, desperate look. 'I don't know why that always seemed so much worse to me,' he said. 'The rapes, I mean. I hated that.' He considered for a moment. 'There were more shots. The screaming stopped, then some-body else screamed somewhere to my left. I looked at the woman one last time and she saw what I was going to do, but she wasn't afraid. She just said the word again and I shot her, twice. The first shot would have finished it, though. When I walked away I tried to tell myself that it had been a mercy, but that idea didn't last more than a minute. After that, I just felt numb. We killed forty-six people that day. For statistical purposes, all were considered enemy combatants.

'After the woman, I walked about the village in a daze. Or not dazed so much as wide open, neutral, everything just there, almost abstract. The people had been preparing a meal when my unit arrived, making the most of not very much, whatever they had to hand – fruit, rice, green leaves, root vegetables. It was a poor village, I guess. The food was simple, it would have taken skill and care to make it appealing. Not just bulk to fill the belly, but a real meal. Something to take pleasure in, to gather round and – but maybe that was the pleasure for them. Gathering round. Making the best of what they had together. Families. Friends. I was ashamed, then, thinking how little I knew about these people. I knew a few words of their language, pidgin really, but I didn't know anything else, except how to kill them. This was what I was thinking as I walked about that scene of devastation, how simple the food was, and how I didn't even know the names for these basic items. The word for rice, say. Someone had shot three pigs that had got out of their pen; here and there, baskets of food and produce had been toppled and trampled into the mud. Why did we do that? We always spoiled the food. We shot the livestock. I didn't know why we did that and I didn't even know for sure that it was true, but it seemed we did that all the time, out there. I would see good food spilled into the dirt and trampled down. Cooking vessels smashed. I seemed to remember that happening often – and as I was walking around the village, I thought I knew what it meant. Why it happened. It wasn't deliberate, it just happened, but it was a way of erasing the event, a way of imagining that this place had never really existed and there would be nothing to be ashamed of later. We didn't ask, why this village, why these people, because they didn't really exist. If their world could be erased so casually, how could they have been substantial and real, like us?

'There were no consequences for what happened. If there had been, I would have been as guilty as anyone. Still, I knew I couldn't go back. I was exhausted. I wasn't suffering from some syndrome or post-traumatic disorder, or whatever they're calling it these days. I was just exhausted. Finished. Beat. Maybe that's a syndrome in itself, when you get to the point where exhaustion is so total, it feels like the beginning of some new condition, a purge, say, of everything that had accumulated over however many years, so the last traces of fear, or pride, or desire, all the ordinary emotions are stripped away, leaving nothing behind but an empty frame, a cat's cradle for the wind to blow through out on some trail in Khánh Hòa, or a back road in Kansas, or wherever you happen to be when the change happens. And maybe where you are decides what happens. If you're Saul on the road to Damascus, maybe you see God, if you're somewhere else maybe you find some hidden talent you never knew you had. Somewhere else, you find some hidden vice. What I found wasn't much to talk about – no God, for sure, and no hidden talents or vices, just a kind of empty space that, when I felt it opening around me, I just had to step into it and walk away. I wasn't walking away from the war, I was walking away from everything I had ever trusted. My father's world. A world of hard work and honour and faith. A world of my country right or wrong. All the old clichés, which weren't clichés then. Not to me, at least. I had always believed. Till I went to Vietnam I believed that my father was right, and my country was right, and even if they both did things that were questionable, I loved them and I trusted that they were acting in the context of some bigger picture that I couldn't see.

'So I got out. It wasn't easy to desert from Vietnam, but I made it. I got some fake R&R papers, and disappeared. It took me three months to get back to the US, but I never once doubted that I was doing the right thing. The only question I had was – why go back? I didn't want to go home to Virginia. That was the one thing I knew for sure. Besides, I couldn't have gone there, anyway. It would be like going straight to the brig.

'No – what I wanted to do was what I needed to do. I had to keep moving. *Moving*. I wanted to wake up on a Sunday morning in a strange town and stand at the window looking out at snow-covered streets and people I didn't know going to church. I wanted the mystery of a black car stopped by a country crossing. I didn't want to run away, I wasn't trying to escape. Or at least, I didn't think of it like that. It was more like I was trying to opt out of one state in order to arrive at another place. The trouble was, I couldn't find that place. In fact, I couldn't find anything but road. Leaves, and more leaves, a flicker of light off to the west and suddenly everything is different. Transformed. Which is not to say that the road is romantic. It's not Jack Kerouac. It's not Woody Guthrie. It's sleeping in railroad stations at night, because you missed the last train and the next one out is at O-six-ten. It's the drunk at the back of the bus who smells of tobacco and beer. The boy on his way to work, in his watch cap and some old hunting jacket his father doesn't want any more. It's the

Sunday crowd coming home from a day of church, all the painfully obese women who think that somebody's going to cure them of appetite. It's the boy with the withered hand gazing out into the grey of a fall night, not because there's anything out there, but because he can't bear to look at the other passengers, to see himself, still not healed, through their eyes. Because if he sees that, then he'll lose his faith in Jesus, and faith is all he has. And, over the last while, it's the pretty girl in the station café, the way she pours the coffee, the way she smiles at me exactly the same way as she'd smile at a nine-year-old, because I'm not twenty, or thirty-five. Because I am safe. I never thought of being old enough to be safe. It wasn't my intention.

'The other thing about the road is that it doesn't lead anywhere. It took me a while to see it clear, but from the start, no matter how far I travelled, it was always elsewhere that I truly loved. Elsewhere, with the scent of home drifting away through the pines and that last stretch of grassland running for miles in a dewslick of water and stars. A big moon over an empty parking lot. Icy stars over the roofs and what's left of the grasslands. Blown snow muddling the road and a few horses standing off by themselves, in a dark that might just go on forever. Elsewhere. You find it from time to time, and then it's gone. You can even find it here, in the suburbs. The absence of something, a silence at the edge of the yard where something is waiting for you to go back inside. You're safe inside, but out in the night, you're in their territory and there isn't a map or a field guide that can help you. When you catch a glimpse of elsewhere, no matter how brief it is, you could be forgiven for thinking that happiness and time are the same thing.'

*   *   *

When it came, Jean's descent was very quick. I guess I should be grateful, that she didn't suffer for as long as she might have done – the doctor had told us that some cases lasted for months, others for a few weeks, so we should have been grateful for that mercy. But there was no time to think about that. Meanwhile, I had a major assignment to complete, and Jean knew about it, so there was no chance of my asking for an extension. I could have told them my grandmother was dying. But I didn't. I kept going to school, and helping out when I got home. Simon did the rest. He kept the place clean, he cooked, he made sure Jean had everything she needed. In the afternoons, he would read to her. Poetry, mostly. Simon might have been a drifter all his life, but he proved to be an excellent nurse. He kept Jean in bed, even though she was always trying to be up and about, he kept her engaged in long and sometimes desultory conversations about nothing, he made sure she took the medicines that her doctor had prescribed. Whenever I could, I stayed home and took a turn in the sick room, so Simon could head out, away from everything, in search of elsewhere. There was one story that had still to be told, and I was waiting for Jean to bring it up, but she didn't say much at all, she just lay still, while I read to her, or talked about my work. Finally, she spoke up and I knew, from her tone, that she wanted to tell me one last story. The story of what really happened with Lee.

She talked slowly, with a brief pause every few words, so it seemed she was working something out as she was speaking, working it out slowly and carefully, with no particular hurry, but with a real concern to get things right. Or maybe, I thought, it was more a fear of being wrong in some unexpected way.

'I remember,' she said, 'when I was little, and I had that moment, you know, that moment all children have, when you realise that everyone dies . . .' She smiled and I noticed how discoloured her teeth had become – not yellow, but a smoky, almost golden grey, like old vellum, or the pieces of whalebone and tusk carved with ships and women's faces in some town museum – and she saw that I had noticed, but it didn't bother her. Nothing bothered her. She was an old woman who had lived well in spite of the hurt that had been visited on her, and she was – happy, I think. Happy, or if not happy as such, then accepting. Quiet. Self-sufficient. 'Everybody dies,' she said, and she seemed contented with that thought too, like it was a gift, or a blessing that she'd been promised, or had promised herself, long ago. 'Mother, father, brother . . . Lover. We all have that moment,' she said. 'It's not out of the ordinary . . . but for me, at that age, what was out of the ordinary, was that I didn't feel, sorry, I didn't feel the, inevitable, childish grief, for my mother or father, or even for . . .' Her voice trailed off and she glanced out the window. 'No,' she said, looking back at me suddenly, as if she had heard the question that was forming in my mind. 'The one I grieved for, the only one, was Lee. Because she was, always, so alive. You see? It seemed worse to me that she had to die. For the others, for my mother and, in a different way, for my father, it didn't seem like such, a loss, but *she* . . .

'I look back now, and I see it all clearly. It was like one of those tests they give you in school. You know the answer, it's there in your head, but you can't say it, because everyone who has ever been in charge says that this answer can't be right. So you think again, and the clock goes on ticking, and before you know it, the test is over. And you haven't written a thing. And it was the right answer.'

'What was?'

'Happiness,' she said. 'You have to take it where you can, no matter what. It was hard, afterward, to be reconciled to the fact that the only thing that came between us, really, was that we had different notions of happiness. It was hard and it felt as if she was still there. That she persisted in this world even when I knew . . .'

'What happened?' I said.

'She . . . I . . .' She gave me a confused look. 'There was an accident,' she said. 'In the car.'

'An accident?'

'Yes. It was an accident.'

'Who was there?' I said. 'Who was driving?'

'It was me,' she said. 'We were trying to get away. You see, I found her again and that man . . . John Cameron. He hurt her. He hurt her badly. So we were trying to get away and then . . .'

She was becoming agitated now, and I realised I had let things go too far. I put my hand on her arm. 'It's all right,' I said. 'Everything is fine. Rest now.'

She had been trying to sit up, her whole body straining to lift herself, Now, in a matter of seconds, she fell back and lay utterly still. I thought, for a few short seconds, that she was going to die. Then the faintest of smiles flickered across her face. She was looking at me, but she wasn't seeing me, she was staring at something from long ago, though I had no way of knowing what it was.

The next morning, early, I went into her room and found the bed empty. I called Simon and we threw on coats and boots and hurried out into the cold. It was still dark, with just a hint of grey beyond the trees. Luckily, it had snowed during the night, and we managed to pick up Jean's trail and follow it along Audubon Road to where we found her, wrapped in her old coat and what looked like several scarves. She had been walking and had just recently stopped, but whether from fatigue or because some new thought had arrested her mid-flight, it was impossible to tell. She was very pale, her skin like wax, though it was like the wax of a candle that is still lit, a faint, almost rose-coloured glow, just visible, somewhere within.

'It could have been different,' she said, as we came up on either side of her. Simon stepped forward and took her arm. If he hadn't, I think she would have fallen into the snow and what mattered most at that moment was that she should not fall. I took hold of her other arm as gently as I could. She swayed slightly, but she kept her feet. She looked into Simon's face. 'It could have been different,' she said again. 'You know that, don't you?'

Simon nodded. 'I know it,' he said.

Jean turned slightly to look at me. There were tears in her eyes. It might have been the cold and nothing else. It probably was. Still, it seemed to me that she had come to the end of the journey she had begun an hour earlier, when she had walked out of the house and into the snow. There was no telling where she had come to, but I had to believe that, in her mind, we were on the corner of Ashland and Vine. Maybe she read that thought in my face, because she smiled then, just slightly, an encouraging, brave smile – not for herself, but for me. So I would know she understood. Then she leaned into Simon a little more and he shifted to take her weight, the way a father takes the weight of a child when she is tired of walking, takes the weight, not upon, but *into* himself. Jean's eyes closed, not out of fatigue alone, and certainly not because she was giving in to something – least of all death – but because she had seen what she needed to see and what remained of her story had to happen in darkness and stillness, somewhere at the back of her head.

'Let's get you back to the house,' Simon said. He wasn't really talking to Jean, though; he was addressing me. It was an invitation to help him get her home, but it was also an acknowledgment that I was there, with them, party to their kinship, an honorary member of this family. I took Jean's arm – it felt thin and brittle – and together we led her back along Audubon Road, but she wasn't really there now. She had slipped away, or aside, into that place in her memory where all the people she had lost in her life were still visible, like shadows on a wall, faint patterns of what were now little more than phantoms, and unrecognisable unless you already knew what you were seeing.

It took some time to reach the house. As soon as we got her into bed, I called the doctor. He came immediately, but there was nothing more to be done. That night, at exactly eight o'clock, she whispered something that I couldn't make out, though I was sitting just three feet away, keeping vigil. A moment later, she let out a long, low breath, as if she had just heard something she hadn't heard before, something with which she thoroughly agreed.

On the morning of the funeral, I went out to look around. I thought I'd heard something, early that morning, and I had been thinking about Christina and if she was out of the cold. I had visions of her, I guess, wandering around in the snowy woods in her First Holy Communion dress, but I didn't see her, and there were no human footprints in the snow, other than my own. I wondered if Christina knew Jean was dead. She had always seemed attuned in some way to that old woman, as if there was some unwritten kinship between them.

As I turned to go back in, a green delivery van pulled up at the gate and a man got out.

'Are you Kate Lambert?'

'Yes.'

The man smiled. 'Delivery for you,' he said. He reached inside the passenger side of the van and took out a box. 'Careful,' she said. 'It's fragile. And it's heavier than it looks.'

The funeral was as close to what Jean would have wanted as we could make it. Simple, no fuss, a handful of friends, nothing religious. Annette came, along with a few of the servers, and a couple of customers from Sacred Grounds. Some other people were there, but I didn't know who they were. Simon had decided to keep it as simple as possible. No eulogy. I read a poem – Emily Dickinson, of course – and Simon spoke a few lines from Ted Berrigan's 'A Good Land':

> my land a good land
> its highways go to many good places where
> many good people were found; a home land,
>   whose song comes up
> from the throat of a hummingbird & it ends
> where the sun goes to across the skies of blue.
> I live there with you.

Afterward, people didn't quite know who to shake hands with or offer condolences to, and we hadn't planned any kind of reception, so they drifted away in twos and threes, leaving Simon and me to walk back alone together. Annette came to me and kissed me on the cheek. She was crying. 'You were a good friend to her,' she said. 'Having you around made her very happy.'

I nodded. 'She loved you,' I said.

Annette blushed slightly. 'I'm glad we met,' she said, then turned and walked away, so I didn't know which of us she was talking about.

Then Simon and I were alone. He took my arm, and we walked slowly back to the cemetery gate, where the car was waiting. 'Jennifer will never come out of her bolthole,' he said. 'It's not her fault. She's just scared of what the world might do to her.'

'I know.'

'And I'm not cut out for Audubon Road,' he said. 'I need to be—'

'Elsewhere,' I said.

He laughed. 'Wherever that might be.'

'Maybe it's here,' I said.

'I don't know. But what I wanted to say was, I don't want the house and Jennifer obviously doesn't want it. You are happy here, I think, and I don't see why—'

I felt a sudden rush of panic. I didn't want Simon to go, not yet. I needed to talk to him more. I needed to ask him something, only I didn't know, yet, what it was. 'Maybe it's time to forget about elsewhere,' I said. 'Maybe it's time to think about home.'

'I have,' he said. 'I've been thinking about home for thirty years. It's just that I'm not ready for it.' He stopped and looked into my face. I was struck again by how beautiful he was. 'But I know it's there,' he said. 'And when I'm ready – well, who knows? In the meantime, why don't you look after the old place? For now, at least?'

We stood like that for a long time, then we walked the rest of the way to the funeral car in silence. Our driver, a thickset younger man with a buzz cut, had been reading a book, but he put it away as we approached. The snow was beginning to fall again. Simon opened the car door for me, and I got in. On the passenger seat, laid flat down, was a brand-new paperback copy of *Selected Poems*, by Emily Dickinson.

A GOOD LAND

Today it snowed again. It came thick and fast at first, then it slowed, large, blue flakes drifting slightly as they fell through the cottonwoods. Out here, it feels like the snow is personal, that even as it falls up and down Audubon Road, even as it falls in the middle of town, on the churches and the bars and the lit windows of Sacred Grounds, it is different here, fuller and more generous, part of an older country. I've been living in Jean's house for a month now, and all that time, it has snowed off and on, so it feels like a gift, or a confirmation – and maybe it's only a form of superstition that makes me think this, but I tell myself every day that I can't say how much longer I will be able to stay here. Simon could come back at any time and rightfully claim this house as his own, or he could sell it, not because he wanted to, but out of necessity. On the other hand, it might just be that I like to remind myself that my time here is not fixed, that this is a matter of grace, rather than logic or law. It might just be that, on days like this, I like to wonder how much longer I can enjoy this strange tenancy. For as long as it lasts, I want never to take one moment for granted. I remember what Emily Dickinson said, how the mere sense of living is joy enough – and I linger, every day, on the moment when I wake at first light in my new, calm body and go downstairs to start up the first of the day's coffee. Now, while it is percolating, I stand at the window, looking out at the backyard. Although the snow is deep today, I know it won't be here long: soon the serviceberry that Jean planted against the side wall will come into flower, the first sign of real springtime, green buds will open on the trees in her hidden woods – she had known all along that Christina was living there, off and on, but she had pretended not to notice, so as not to frighten her away. It was as if the girl was just another of the animals that came through, like the deer, or the various birds. I stand at the window in the pyjamas Jean gave me, surprised, still, by the gift of a new body, a new prototype of myself that Jean had known was there all along, cleansed, slender, vein perfect, my reflection in the glass as much a part of this garden as the serviceberry and the cottonwoods, as native to this patch of ground as the deer and the cardinals.

The day after Simon left, I fetched in some more of the apples that Jean and I had stored to make a fresh batch of pies. It was a clear, white morning, the snow tracked with prints, tree shadows sharp and dark against the wall of the woodshed. I stopped a moment, to breathe in the cold and clear my head. Now, even though the snow was pitted with deer and bird tracks at the edge of the woods and all across the yard, I sensed an emptiness, a quiet all about me, from right where I stood to the end of the drive and out as far as the other houses all along Audubon Road, and I knew that I was utterly alone. It was a good feeling, a feeling of being blessed, somehow, a sense at the back of it all that I had learned some new skill, or some new art form. That was what Jean would have said. Anything could be an art, in itself, everything depended on how well it was done – and I was learning mine just by being there. What that art was, I couldn't have said, but it amounted to more than noticing each mark in the snow and recognising its pattern, and it amounted to more than sensing that nobody was near without having to look. If I could have described it, I would have said it was the art of knowing what I was in the landscape. What place I had in the field of being around me, if that is something that can be said. Not who I was, but *what*: a body, a system of in-breath and out-breath, a creature capable of making those sounds and movements it needs to make and nothing more. When I had first come outside, I had imagined Christina Vogel standing in the white space under the trees, her pale face striped with shadows. In fact, I had almost wished her there, but I knew right away that she was gone for good now. I told myself that it didn't matter, that her only link with this house, or with this patch of ground, had been Jean Culver. Still, I missed her a little, on Jean's behalf, and I hoped she was in a good place.

It was strange, to begin with, having the use of everything in Jean Culver's house. To be able to go anywhere and linger over things that she had accumulated over a lifetime, all the cans and jars and packets she had put up in the larder, the jars of leaves that might be herbs or home-made teas, decades-old products that she had never gotten around to throwing away, residues of blue powder or sticky, greenish resin in the bottom of an ancient coffee can, the one jar of crusted oil and spider dust on a shelf in the cellar. Who knew what any of this was for? Their uses had been forgotten long ago, like the old tools I found crammed into a drawer in the kitchen, tools for punching holes in who knew what, tools for working leather, or hot glass – I had no idea, but everything I found I wanted to learn about, to make use of. I wanted to live in this house as fully as I could, because I didn't know how long I would be staying, and it mattered that my occupancy should not be idle.

My main project, though, was the clarinet. I had been mystified by the package that arrived on the morning of Jean's funeral, though I should have known it was from her. For one thing, nobody else knew that I was living in her house. I didn't open the parcel until afterward, when we had got home and Simon was making coffee in the kitchen – and that was when I cried, properly, for the first time, standing in the hallway where I had left Jean's gift in my hurry to get ready for the service. I didn't break down, I just stood very still, tears rolling down my face, staring at a Buffet Crampon R13 Bb African Blackwood clarinet, an instrument I hadn't even dared to dream about when I was playing with my father, ten years earlier.

Maybe he heard something – the rustle of paper, or some involuntary sound I had made on opening the box – but at that moment Simon came into the hall and stood looking at me. 'How are you doing?' he said.

I nodded. 'I'm fine,' I said. 'It's just . . . Jean sent me a gift, but it didn't get here till this morning.'

I lost it, then. All at once, the full weight of grief overwhelmed me. Grief for Jean. Grief for Lee, whose story I would never know in full. Grief for Laurits. Grief for Dad, who hadn't wanted to tell me he was dying so I could enjoy my first semester of school. It was pouring out of me now, everything I had contained so carefully, with drink and drugs and self-deception. All the stupid games I had played with Laurits, who must have been in trouble with Axel Crane long before that night at Henrys. He'd needed money, he said. I hadn't even registered what was going on.

Simon put one arm around my shoulder. 'It's all right,' he said. 'Let it go.'

I nodded, but I was sobbing now.

'It's a beautiful instrument,' he said.

'It's too good for me,' I said. 'It's a professional—'

'Shh, shh.' He pulled me to him, so that we were standing side by side, gazing at the clarinet. 'She chose it for a reason,' he said. 'She wanted to give you something, a gift that was also a responsibility, something you would have to care for.' He kissed the side of my head, the way Dad used to do, then let me go, gently. 'Coffee's in the kitchen,' he said. 'And I found some cookies. Later, I'll cook for you. Something *special*. Did Jean ever tell you what a great cook I am?'

He wasn't joking. I had thought he was, but it turned out that he really *was* a great cook – and, because that night was going to be our last, he made it into a special occasion. No alcohol, of course. Jean would have warned him about that. No meat, either.

'So – you're a vegetarian too?' I said, as he served up large, steaming bowls of bean stew and a bright winter salad.

He grinned. 'I eat wild meat,' he said. 'Fish, too. But I don't eat plastic chicken in plastic wrappers . . .'

I remembered what Jean had said about the industrial-agricultural complex. 'Ah,' I said. 'So it was you.'

He passed me a plate of freshly baked bread. It was a deep brown colour, moist and still warm from the oven. 'It was me what?' he said.

I laughed. 'Never mind,' I said. 'It was just something she said . . .' It came to me again that Jean Culver was dead, and I couldn't go on for a moment.

Simon didn't speak. He watched as I struggled to control my grief, then he began to eat, spearing pieces of butternut squash on his fork and chewing thoughtfully. I had already sensed that he was one of those people who could stay quiet for hours, just eating, or reading, or staring out a window. Like Jean, he lived by a different clock from other people, but he was quieter in himself than she had been, and the difference, I guessed all at once, as I watched him eat and waited till my own emotions had settled – the difference was that he didn't have any stories. I don't know how I knew that, but I was sure of it. Nothing that had ever happened had turned into a story for him. Moments were moments. Days were days. Nothing bound them together. Everything was essence. I had wondered, more often than I cared to admit, what it might be like to live like that.

He looked at me. 'So,' he said, 'did Jean tell you about the accident?'

His words took me by surprise, coming out of the blue like that, and I didn't know what to say. 'Well,' I said, 'I guess she tried.'

'So she didn't tell you,' he said.

I shook my head. 'Not – everything.'

He nodded. 'She wanted to,' he said. 'But I guess she couldn't live through it all again. She waited too long.'

'She told me there was a crash,' I said.

'There was a crash,' Simon said. 'But wait. She gave me something. I think she wanted you to have it.' He stood up. 'Excuse me a moment,' he said. 'I'll be right back. Eat some stew.'

I was puzzled. I had guessed that he would know about the stories. I had guessed that Jean would have said something to him about how we'd met, and what she had been doing since then, exchanging stories for sober days, like some latter-day Scheherazade. Maybe she had explained what she hadn't really said in so many words to me – that, yes, she had told me those stories so I would have the excuse I needed to quit drinking, but also because I was, for her, a vessel. A repository. A listener who might help make sense of all that had happened in her life, and to the people she had loved. Why she had chosen me was the one thing I still didn't understand, of course. Maybe the simple fact was that she'd had no choice. That I was all she could find.

Simon returned, holding what looked like a newspaper clipping. It was old, somewhat yellowed: a brief news story with a faded photograph – that much I could see. He handed it to me. 'Read this,' he said.

I took the paper. It wasn't a big story, a piece from a local newspaper, one of those fleeting accounts that suggests more than it tells, where the reader ends up asking what really happened. Alongside the minimal narrative – a local businessman and his wife killed in a freak traffic accident, another woman seriously injured – there were two photographs. The first was of a man – John Cameron, I assumed – who stared out of the depths of the picture with an air of utter self-regard. Below that, with a caption that read, simply, CRITICALLY ILL, was a head-and-shoulders image of Jean as a young woman, her hair longer than I was used to seeing it, her eyes bright and knowing.

'Lee called her in the middle of the night,' Simon said. 'She needed help. It seems her husband wasn't quite the flawed but essentially decent man he'd seemed when she married him. Of course, Jean went straight over there – and it appears that Lee was in a pretty bad way when she arrived. Cameron had beaten her coldly and systematically – they didn't report that, of course, because Cameron had important friends. Besides, her body was so badly damaged in the crash that nobody could have proved . . . Anyway, when Lee called, Cameron was supposed to be on his way to a business meeting in St Louis, but he turned back when he was halfway there. Nobody knows why. Maybe he suspected something – maybe he just forgot his briefcase – but when he got to the house, Lee and Jean were driving away. Jean had wanted to take her to a hospital, but Lee begged her not to.' He reached out his hand and I passed the clipping back to him. 'Cameron went crazy when he saw what was happening. He tried to intercept them; then, when it looked like they were getting away, he just rammed his car into Jean's and both vehicles came off the road. Cameron and Lee died instantly. Jean was in hospital for months. Her injuries were so bad, they had to teach her how to walk all over again. She didn't tell the police what really happened. She said she couldn't remember much about that day's events, but it just seemed like some terrible, insane accident . . . Which it was, in one way. But look. Here's what I wanted to show you.' He handed me the clipping again. 'Look at the picture. Who does she look like, in this photograph?'

I studied the image. Jean's mouth was set hard – she clearly didn't sit well for portraits – but her eyes were bright. There was something in the way she looked back at the camera, at whoever was taking this picture, that didn't *look* so much as *feel* familiar. I handed the clipping back to Simon. 'I don't know,' I said. 'Who does she look like?'

He shook his head. 'You don't see it?'

'No.'

Simon laughed. 'I guess it's not surprising,' he said. 'People don't see themselves . . .' He held the clipping up so I could take a proper look. 'She looks like you,' he said. 'Or let's say you look like her, back then. That's why . . .' He broke off. 'We should eat,' he said, as if he was deciding that he had already said too much. 'The stew will be getting cold.'

'It's already cold,' I said. 'That's why – what?'

He looked at me. 'That's what she saw in you, when you first met,' he said. 'She didn't know it herself, not to begin with. It was only later that she realised.'

'What?'

'That you were the one who could save her,' he said.

'That's crazy,' I said. 'If anything, she saved me.'

He shook his head. 'Maybe you saved each other,' he said. 'She gave you a place that felt like home. And you gave her a second chance.'

'For what?' I said. I wished Jean was there to tell him he was wrong, that he had assumed something that wasn't true.

'I don't know,' he said. 'Forgiveness? Atonement? Does it matter what we call it?'

'I don't understand,' I said. 'What did she have to atone for?'

He didn't say anything. He just looked at the picture of his aunt, fading into newsprint that had itself been fading for almost fifty years. After a moment, he looked back to me. 'Jean tried to save Lee and through no fault of her own she only succeeded in getting her killed. And she never forgave herself for that.' He studied my face. He was looking at something I still couldn't see, finding her likeness in me, even though it wasn't really there. But then, maybe Jean *had* found that likeness too, whether consciously or not. Maybe that was why she had saved me. It was her second chance at saving herself. 'Maybe it doesn't make sense, not in the usual way,' he said. 'Maybe atonement never does. It defies ordinary logic.

But we all have to atone for something. It's most of what we're good for, people like us. Beyond that, it really doesn't matter what we call it.' He smiled. 'Sit down,' he said. 'I'll warm up some more stew and we can start over.'

The next morning, he was gone. No note, no lingering farewell. That evening was our goodbye. Which was fine by me. Not everything needs to be said. And some things are better unspoken.

Since he left, I have practised on the clarinet every day, and though I make only middling progress – it's a long time since I played, and I've forgotten so much of what I learned – I will never give up. I take it out at exactly two in the afternoon, and I practise for an hour. No more, no less. Like the house, this gift must be honoured. Anyone could have walked to the end of Audubon Road, late morning on a hot summer's day, birds calling in the strips of garden between the houses, almost nobody home and the streets quiet, no traffic, no mowers or children's games, no bleat of radio through a kitchen window. Anyone could have stumbled into Jean's web of stories and remembrances that last summer before the millennium. It just so happened that it was me. Anyone could have walked this far, to a house that doesn't even appear on the map and, if they had, I wonder how long it would take them to figure out, at some level, that history is not the sum of what matters here. That it's not a single, or even manifold, narrative that makes reality. What matters is the fabric of time and place, all the events that ever happened leading equally to a meeting that did not happen by chance, morning heat and bird calls and a conversation between two women who, in their different ways, needed to say aloud the stories they had kept *sub voce* for so long – ordinary stories, no doubt, of lost love and grief and, more than anything, of things not done or said, but stories that are no less a part of the fabric for that.

Later, when the pies were done, I went out and walked to the far end of Audubon Road. I was wearing Jean's old coat and a scarf I had found in the hall. I'd never seen it before, but it still smelled of Jean, a mix of wood resin and soap and some herb or spice – cinnamon, maybe – that immediately made me think of her. The sun was out, and it was warmer than it had been for weeks, and I walked slowly, taking in the whiteness, knowing it would not last much longer. Then, after I had been walking for a little while, maybe fifteen minutes, I noticed that everything had stopped. The woods, the road, the houses were utterly still, but it wasn't just a stillness, it was as if time had stopped, the way time stops on a movie set, when the camera is switched off. There were no birds, no people, even the wind was gone – and yet there was a feel, not of stopped time so much as eternity, an intimation of something not unlike the Pentecosts I imagined as a child in school, a sense that, at any moment, a cold blue flame could come shivering out of the air to fill me with unlooked-for knowledge. I stopped walking and turned around. I don't know what I expected to see, but there was nothing there, other than my own footprints, a blue trail of the marks I had made, leading back the way I had come. I don't know why that should have seemed magical to me, but it did. *I* was the one who had made those marks. *I* was present on this winter's day. It was a childish notion, perhaps, but I realised, then, that I had forgotten that presence in the world for too long a time and the only reason I had recovered it was because one old woman, for no reason that I can think of, other than native grace, decided to make me a gift. It suddenly seemed a beautiful thought, that I owed my life to her.

*　　*　　*

I woke up and lay still, listening. There had been a sound I was hearing in my sleep, a sound enough like music to waken me, only now that I was conscious, I didn't know what I was listening for. At first, all I could hear was the sound of melting ice dripping off the eaves and then I realised what it was I had been listening to in the dream. It was this. Nothing more. The sound of thaw. A kind of music. An end, and a beginning. Here, and elsewhere.

ACKNOWLEDGEMENTS

I would like to express my deepest gratitude to the Eccles Centre for American Studies at the British Library, where I was a Writer in Residence in 2013. The generosity of the Eccles Centre, both in terms of financial assistance and the kind support and advice of the research staff, greatly enriched the gradual development of this novel. My particular thanks to Professor Philip Davies, for his immense kindness, patience and encouragement through what was, at times, a fraught period.

I would also like to give thanks to the Deutscher Akademischer Austauschdienst (DAAD) for their immense generosity and support during and after my fellowship in Berlin. This book could not have been completed without that support.

At an early stage of the writing of this book, I wrote to several people, asking for advice on historical matters. One of these was the American radical organiser, author and prisoner, David Gilbert, whose kindness, patience and example made me ask serious questions about what this novel was really about. My sincere thanks to him, as well as my heartfelt admiration.

Huge thanks to Carne and Karmen Ross, who continue the real struggle daily, and to Patrick Deer and his students at NYU, all of whom did me that rare honour of active listening, when this book was still just a notion.

Finally, a note on Yonas Sax, the man who gave the secret of the A-Bomb to the Soviets. This character is very loosely based on Theodore (Ted) Hall, who was a kind friend to me for many years. I greatly miss his supreme integrity, his kindness and his rigorous intelligence.

penguin.co.uk/vintage